THE DAMNATION OF PYTHOS

THE NAVIGATOR SAID little, contenting himself with brief assertions in support of the astropath. Filling the view from the oculus was Pythos, the innermost planet of the Pandorax System.

'This world is the source of the anomalous warp effect?' Atticus asked.

'The source lies on it,' Erephren corrected.

Atticus contemplated the planet. 'Could such a thing be natural?'

'I cannot conceive of how it could be. Why do you ask, captain?'

'There is no civilisation here.' The *Veritas Ferrum* was in orbit above the terminator. The nightside of the planet was utterly dark. There were no lights of cities below. The dayside revealed blue oceans and green landmasses.

Galba was looking at a garden world. He thought about all the planets he had fought on over the centuries of the Great Crusade. They had all borne the disfigurements brought by intelligent life. What turned below was pristine. It did not know the machine, and its order and strength. He knew what all that green meant: organic life in full riot, undisciplined, chaotic. His lip curled in disgust.

'I cannot explain what you are seeing, captain,' Erephren said. 'But what we seek is there. I know this as surely as I breathe.'

THE HORUS HERESY®

Many of these titles are also available as abridged and unabridged audiobooks.
Order the full range of Horus Heresy novels and audiobooks from
blacklibrary.com

Download the full range of Horus Heresy audio dramas from
blacklibrary.com

Also available

THE HORUS HERESY®

David Annandale

THE DAMNATION OF PYTHOS

Thinning the veil

BLACK LIBRARY

For Margaux, with memories of Paris in the snow.

A BLACK LIBRARY PUBLICATION

Hardback edition first published in Great Britain in 2014.
This edition published in 2014.
Black Library,
Games Workshop Ltd.,
Willow Road,
Nottingham, NG7 2WS, UK.

10 9 8 7 6 5 4 3 2 1

Cover illustrations by Neil Roberts.

A CIP record for this book is available from the British Library.

UK ISBN: 978 1 84970 751 0
US ISBN: 978 1 84970 752 7

See Black Library on the internet at

blacklibrary.com

Find out more about Games Workshop
and the world of Warhammer 40,000 at

games-workshop.com

Printed and bound by CPI Group (UK) Ltd, Croydon, CR0 4YY

THE HORUS HERESY®

It is a time of legend.

The galaxy is in flames. The Emperor's glorious vision for humanity is in ruins. His favoured son, Horus, has turned from his father's light and embraced Chaos.

His armies, the mighty and redoubtable Space Marines, are locked in a brutal civil war. Once, these ultimate warriors fought side by side as brothers, protecting the galaxy and bringing mankind back into the Emperor's light.
Now they are divided.

Some remain loyal to the Emperor, whilst others have sided with the Warmaster. Pre-eminent amongst them, the leaders of their thousands-strong Legions are the primarchs. Magnificent, superhuman beings, they are the crowning achievement of the Emperor's genetic science. Thrust into battle against one another, victory is uncertain for either side.

Worlds are burning. At Isstvan V, Horus dealt a vicious blow and three loyal Legions were all but destroyed. War was begun, a conflict that will engulf all mankind in fire. Treachery and betrayal have usurped honour and nobility. Assassins lurk in every shadow. Armies are gathering.
All must choose a side or die.

Horus musters his armada, Terra itself the object of his wrath. Seated upon the Golden Throne, the Emperor waits for his wayward son to return. But his true enemy is Chaos, a primordial force that seeks to enslave mankind to its capricious whims.

The screams of the innocent, the pleas of the righteous resound to the cruel laughter of Dark Gods. Suffering and damnation await all should the Emperor fail and the war be lost.

The age of knowledge and enlightenment has ended.
The Age of Darkness has begun.

~ DRAMATIS PERSONAE ~

The X Legion, 'Iron Hands'

DURUN ATTICUS	Captain, 111th Clan-Company, commander of the *Veritas Ferrum*
AULUS	Sergeant, 111th Clan-Company, acting Master of Auspex of the *Veritas Ferrum*
ANTON GALBA	Sergeant, 111th Clan-Company
CREVTHER	Sergeant, 111th Clan-Company
DARRAS	Sergeant, 111th Clan-Company
LACERTUS	Sergeant, 111th Clan-Company
CAMNUS	Techmarine, 111th Clan-Company
VEKTUS	Apothecary, 111th Clan-Company
ACHAICUS	Battle-brother, 111th Clan-Company
CATIGERNUS	Battle-brother, 111th Clan-Company
ECDURUS	Battle-brother, 111th Clan-Company
ENNIUS	Battle-brother, 111th Clan-Company
EUTROPIUS	Battle-brother, 111th Clan-Company
VENERABLE ATRAX	Contemptor Dreadnought, 111th Clan-Company
KHALYBUS	Captain
SABINUS	Captain

PLIENUS   Captain

RHYDIA EREPHREN   Mistress of Astropaths
BHALIF STRASSNY   Navigator
JERUNE KANSHELL   Legion serf
AGNES TANAURA   Legion serf
GEORG PAERT   Legion serf

The XVIII Legion, 'Salamanders'
KHI'DEM   Sergeant, 139th Company

The XIX Legion, 'Raven Guard'
INACHUS PTERO   Veteran
JUDEX   Battle-brother

The III Legion, 'Emperor's Children'
KLEOS   Captain, Master of the *Callidora*
CURVAL   Ancient

Colonists of Pythos
TSI REKH   High Priest
SKE VRIS   Priestess-novitiate

The Adeptus Terra
EMIL JEDDAH   Astropath
MEHYA VOGT   Scribe
HELMAR GALEEN   Administrator

PROLOGUE

The flesh of mercy. The blood of hope. The splintered bones of joy. It would have this feast. It would have the taste in its mouth. Its jaws would chew through gristle. Its claws would feel the sensual, despairing rip of opening wounds. It would revel in all these dark glories, and soon. It knew this.

It had faith.

And what did it mean, for a being such as itself, to have faith? What did it mean for a timeless entity to be in the service of patrons? There was so much opportunity to ponder these questions in the flow of melting time and churning space that was the realm of the gods. So much opportunity to explore their shapes, to tangle in their contradictions, to savour in their perversities.

Too much opportunity.

Because there was always the impatience, the need, the hunger. They were never answered, never satisfied. How could they be? They were the very matter of this maelstrom, the sinew of the monster's existence. But though the passions were all-consuming, they left room for the questions and speculations, because these were the fuel for the beast's needs. They were the whetstones for the blade of its intent.

But what did it mean that it had faith? How could the concept have meaning, here where meaning itself was tortured to death, and where the murderous existence of the gods was not a question of belief? The answer was simple in expression, a complex and exquisite agony in its full manifestation.

To have faith was to trust in the promise of the revel. To believe that the time of feeding was drawing near.

The feast would begin on this planet. The barriers to the universe of matter and flesh were thin here, and growing ragged. The entity pushed against them, eagerness and frustration twinning and entwining, becoming a growl. And this growl coiled through the warp to sink into the minds of those keen enough to hear it, bringing them nightmares, bringing them madness. The barriers held, but only just.

The thing's consciousness seeped out. It moved over the face of the waters, where unthinkable leviathans hunted, and it saw that this world was good. It reached the land, where nature was given over to a carnival of predation, and this, too, it saw was good. It saw a world that knew nothing but fangs, a world where life itself existed only to build death's great kingdom. It experienced something very like joy. It laughed, and this laugh skittered across the galaxy, through the dreams of the sensitive, and those who began screaming would never stop.

Its mind ranged over the serpent world. It travelled jungles of endless night. It soared over mountain ranges as barren of hope as the light from dead stars. It learned the threats that lived here. It learned the promises that killed here. It saw that there was no difference between the two. It bore witness to a planet that was, in its monstrosity, the worthy image of the warp itself.

The thing amused itself for a day and a night with the concept of home.

Then it grew restless. To look was not enough. To have the material world, the canvas for the artist of pain, so close, yet still out of the reach of claws, was maddening. Where was the promised feast? The planet writhed in the grip of its own horror. It was existence as carnivore, as predator. But the entity was not a guest at the table. It could do nothing but watch. What was more, the planet was a wasted paradise. Where was the sentient life? Without intelligence, there could be no true innocence, no true victims. Without victims, there was no true horror. The world was a massive, unrealised potential. Though the entity had faith, and though it was a loyal servant, it was also impatient. It made to withdraw its mind from the planet.

But it could not.

It struggled briefly, but the powers it served told it no. They held it in place, and understanding dawned. It had been drawn here by something more than a promise. It brushed once more against the frayed veil. It read the currents of the warp, and again it laughed, and again it snarled. It found the necessary patience. The planet was but a stage. No actors strutted upon it yet, but they would not be long in coming. The beast would wait behind the curtain, and its moment would come. It whispered its praise.

All around it came answering whispers, its fellows here to do its bidding, here to worship, here to join in the revel. The moment was coming for all of them. The moment when they would at last be free to spread their slavering truth over the breadth of a shrieking galaxy. They pressed forward, straining to taste the flesh of the real. The whispers built upon one another, desire feeding desire until the immaterium echoed with raging hunger.

The beast called for silence. It sensed something momentous was transpiring. It looked away from the planet. It was like staring up from the depths of a well, for this world had become a prison, the gravitational force of destiny holding the beast here so that it might fulfil a role. It strained the limits of its perceptions of the material world. At the very edge of its knowledge and awareness, there was movement, like a fly touching the outermost strands of a web.

The promise had been kept. The stars were right.

Someone was coming.

PART ONE

THE PROMISED LAND

ONE

Scarred
Role models
Cells

'SCARS ARE A thing of the flesh,' Durun Atticus had once said. 'They are the mark of a weak material that tears easily and is repaired imperfectly. If the flesh is scarred, it should be excised, and replaced with a more perfect substance.'

Did he still think so? Anton Galba wondered.

The captain had made this speech, Galba remembered, in the aftermath of the Diasporex campaign, during those last days of illusion, when the shadow of treachery was already falling over the Imperium, but the Iron Hands still believed that when they fought at the side of the Emperor's Children, they were amongst brothers. There had been many wounds taken in that battle. The *Fist of Iron* had suffered the worst of the damage, but the strike cruiser *Veritas Ferrum* had been far from unscathed. An energy weapon salvo had struck the bridge. Critical systems had continued to function, but Atticus, unwavering on the command throne, had been badly burned.

The vessel had been repaired. Atticus had been, also. He had

returned, it had seemed, not from the apothecarion, but from the
forge. There were no scars on him. And very little flesh. That was
when he had made the speech. Galba, who bore plenty of scars
on a face that was still mostly flesh, understood that Atticus was
speaking in metaphorical terms, indulging in the hyperbole that
was one of the rewards of victory. The *Fist of Iron* also carried its
brands from the battle, but they would be expunged in due course.
So Atticus had maintained.

So they had all thought.

And then had come the Callinedes campaign. And the betrayal.
The crippling of the fleet. The X Legion's darkest moment.

So they had all thought.

But Callinedes had been nothing more than a prologue. Its name
had been supplanted in the pantheon of infamy. Who could brood
over Callinedes IV when there was Isstvan V?

Isstvan. The word was a hiss and a blade to the spine. It was a
toxic sibilance that would never die. It was a wound that would
fester until the galaxy's last stars flickered out.

It was a scar. Not a surface one that marked what had been healed.
It was a deep one, the site of pain that would never be soothed, of
rage that would never be quenched. *Is this weakness?* Galba asked
the memory-Atticus. *How can we excise this torn flesh? The wound
reaches to our souls.* He glanced back and up at his captain.

Atticus stood before the command throne, at the front of the lectern,
arms folded. He was motionless, his eyes fixed on the forward oculus. His face bore no expression. It had not since the Carollis System
and the battle with the Diasporex. Atticus's augmetic reconstruction
had replaced most of his skull. Of all of the 111th Company's warriors, he was the one who had come closest to a complete conversion
to the machine. Inside the captain's metal shell, Galba knew, blood
still flowed and hearts still beat. But the exterior was the same dark
grey as the Legion's armour. The profile was human, but almost

without features. Atticus was more iron sculpture than living being now: unyielding, without mercy, without warmth.

But not without passion. As still as the captain was, Galba could sense his rage, and not just because he felt the same fury smouldering in his veins. Atticus's left eye was organic. Galba did not know why he had kept it. Having lost or replaced so much of the weakling flesh, why keep any trace of it? He had not asked. But that last remnant of the human was all the more expressive for being isolated. It glared at the void, rarely blinking, barely moving. It was rage itself. Galba had seen Atticus in full, molten wrath. But in this moment, the rage was frozen, colder than the void it reflected. It was a rage that went as deep as the wound, and it answered Galba's question. There was only one way to heal the X Legion: by exterminating the traitors. Every single one.

Galba faced forwards again. His left hand, bionic, was still, impassive, but the fingers of his right curled in frustration. That which would heal the Iron Hands was beyond reach. No amount of discipline or skill in warfare could change that fact. Isstvan had seen to that. Horus had smashed them, as he had the Salamanders and the Raven Guard. They were shadows now, all of them. *We are ghosts,* Galba thought. *We thirst for vengeance, but we have no substance.*

He was not being defeatist. He was not being disloyal. He was being truthful. Only fragments remained of the three loyalist Legions that had been on Isstvan. They were scattered. Their forces were small. The *Veritas Ferrum*'s escape from the Isstvan System was miraculous. To still have an operational strike cruiser was no small thing. But in another sense, it was very insignificant. The *Veritas* was one ship. What could it do against fleets?

Something, Atticus had promised. We will do something.

'Captain,' Auspex Master Aulus called. 'Navigator Strassny reports we have reached our destination. Mistress Erephren asks that we proceed no further.'

'Very well,' Atticus answered. 'We hold.'

A rocky mass the size of a mountain passed before the oculus. The *Veritas*'s position was just outside the Pandorax System. The outer edge of the system was marked by an asteroid belt of unusual density. As the planetoid tumbled away into the night, Galba could see another far to port, a moving patch of grey in the reflected light of Pandorax. The *Veritas*'s sensors were picking up dozens of targets in the near vicinity, all of them massive enough to wreck the cruiser in the event of a collision.

These were not the remnants of an accretion disc. They were not chunks of ice and dust. They were rock and metal. There had once been something else here, Galba deduced. Something huge.

Something grand?

The thought was involuntary, a product of his mood. He realised that it was important he hold on tightly to his anger. It was keeping him from despair. He shoved away dark meditations about destroyed magnificence. But there was still the question of the asteroid belt. He *was* looking at wreckage. Something had been here, and it had been destroyed.

By what?

To starboard was the dirty brown orb of the planet Gaea. Its orbit was deeply eccentric, at a steep angle to the ecliptic. It crossed the orbit of Kylix, the next planet in, and, over the course of its year, briefly passed beyond the asteroid belt. At this time, it was still within the belt. Its surface was pockmarked by overlapping craters, its thin atmosphere filled with dust from the latest impact. The possibility of a planetary collision crossed Galba's mind. But no, Gaea could pass for a large moon. Perhaps it had even been one, spinning off on its bizarre path after the destruction of its parent.

There had been a cataclysm here, but its nature was unknown. So was what had been lost. Despite himself, Galba felt the temptation to see omens in the wreckage-strewn doorway to Pandorax.

He fought it back. The impulse was dangerously close to superstition, and such an indulgence was a betrayal of what he stood for. There had been more than enough betrayals of late. *Do you want to see a lesson here?* he asked himself. *Then learn this one: what was here has been shattered, but it is still dangerous.*

'Any word from our brothers?' Atticus asked.

'The astropathic choir reports none as yet,' Aulus answered.

The door to the bridge opened. Two warriors entered, neither of them Iron Hands. The armour of one was the dark green of the Salamanders. Khi'dem, a sergeant. The other wore the solemn black and white of the Raven Guard. He was the veteran, Inachus Ptero. At their arrival, the atmosphere on the bridge changed. To the rage, frustration and sorrow was added a thread of resentment.

Atticus turned his head. The movement was so cold, it was as if he had trained a bolter on the two Space Marines. 'What is it?' he snapped.

The onyx features of Khi'dem seemed to darken further. 'The very question we were going to ask you, captain,' he said. 'We would like to know what your purpose here is.'

Atticus waited a few seconds before answering, and that beat was concentrated anger. 'Your rank does not grant you leave to question me, *sergeant.*'

'I speak for the Eighteenth Legion as it exists on this vessel,' Khi'dem answered, calm but firm, 'as does Veteran Ptero for the Nineteenth Legion. We are therefore owed the courtesy of being informed about the prosecution of the war.'

'*Legions?*' Atticus spat. The sound of emotion being expressed by his bionic larynx was an eerie one. The larynx was capable of variations of intonation and volume, and it sounded not unlike Atticus had when his voice had been entirely his own. Now, though, there was a hint of the uncanny, as though Atticus were mimicking himself and not quite succeeding. 'Legions,' he repeated. 'Combined, your numbers are not much more than a dozen. Those are–'

'Captain,' Galba said, preferring the risk of interrupting Atticus to that of his commander speaking words that could never be withdrawn, 'with your permission.'

'Yes, sergeant?' There was no pause before Atticus's response, but there was a shade less venom, as if he were half-willing to be stopped.

'Perhaps I can address our brothers' questions.'

Atticus favoured him with a long look. 'Elsewhere,' he said, his voice soft with anger barely and provisionally contained.

Galba nodded. To Khi'dem and Ptero he said, 'Will you walk with me?' To his relief, they did without saying anything further.

Galba led the way from the bridge, through corridors of iron and granite, back towards the barracks, where there was so much space. Too much space.

Ptero said, 'Are you trying to store us away?'

He shook his head. 'I am trying to keep the peace.'

'So I noticed,' Khi'dem said. 'You interrupted your captain. What was he about to say?'

'I am not privy to his thoughts.'

'I can guess,' Ptero put in. 'Those are not Legions. Those are ruins.'

Galba winced at the truth. 'As are we,' he said. And they were. The Iron Hands numbered in the hundreds on the *Veritas* instead of the thousands. They were a shadow of their former strength.

'Your honesty does you honour,' said Ptero. 'But we would still like our answers.'

Galba bit back his own exasperation. 'You will have them once there are answers to give.'

'There is no campaign plan?'

'We are here to learn it.'

Ptero sighed. 'Would it have done your captain an insurmountable injury to tell us that much?'

Galba thought about what he had to say next. There was no easy way of doing it. No diplomatic way, either, though if he was honest with himself, he was not that interested in pursuing one. It was enough that he had moved the discussion away from the bridge. There was much less likelihood of irrevocable violence occurring away from the command throne. 'Captain Atticus,' he said, 'is not inclined to share operational information.'

'With anyone? Or simply with us?'

There was no escaping this moment. 'With you.'

'Why?' the Salamander asked.

'Because of Isstvan Five.' They wanted to know? Good. He would tell them. He would tell them of his own anger. He stopped walking and faced them.

'What about it?' Khi'dem asked. 'We all suffered our tragedies there.'

'Because you turned your backs on our primarch.'

'Ferrus Manus led a charge into madness,' Khi'dem answered. 'We might as well say that he abandoned us.'

'He had Horus in full retreat. He could have ended the war there and then.'

Khi'dem was shaking his head slowly. 'He ran into a trap. We were all caught in it. He just plunged further into its maw and made the rout that much worse.'

'Together, the three Legions would have been strong enough,' Galba insisted.

'If Manus had stayed,' Ptero said, his voice not angry but sad and surprisingly gentle, 'do you think we could have taken back the dropsite from four armies fresh to the battlefield?'

Galba wanted to answer in the affirmative. He wanted to insist that victory would have been possible.

'Three Legions, but against *eight*,' Khi'dem said before Galba could answer. 'With the three caught between hammer and anvil. There was never another possible outcome. The only dishonour lies with the act of treachery.'

Khi'dem's logic was rigorous. But it was not enough. The anger that was souring Galba's blood, the anger that he shared with every warrior of the Iron Hands, was as large as the tragedy engulfing the Imperium. It was too deep, too complex to be soothed by a simple recitation of reality. The facts that Khi'dem presented only made things worse. The rage ran up against maddening impotence, built up, and lashed out at ever more targets. Galba knew Khi'dem was right. The Raven Guard and the Salamanders had been badly bloodied by the first phases of the fighting. Their tactics had been sound in seeking the reinforcements at the dropsite. But Ferrus Manus had smashed hard into Horus's forces. Torture came from the thought that with the additional force of two further Legions, perhaps the blow would have been massive enough to crack open the Warmaster's plan. And beyond tactics, beyond strategy, there was the principle: the Iron Hands had called out to their brother Legions, and been denied. In the wake of defeat and the loss of their primarch, how could they not see that abandonment as another form of betrayal?

There was only one thing that kept Galba from lashing out at the warriors before him. It was the recognition of the other facet of the anger: self-loathing. The Iron Hands had failed, and for this they could never forgive themselves. They had faced the most crucial test in the history of their Legion, and they had been found wanting. Excise the weakness? Galba wanted to consign his failed flesh to oblivion, replace it with the machinic infallible, and crush the skull of every traitor in his fists. He was conscious of this wish, though, and of its futility, and of its origin. He knew that he was seeing the world through the filter of his self-directed anger. So he did not trust his impulses. He forced himself to wait a beat before any response. He forced himself to *think*.

But what of Atticus? What of the warrior who had no flesh left to condemn? He felt the anger in all its forms. Of that, Galba was certain. But was Atticus aware of its toxicity? Was he conscious of its shaping nature? The sergeant did not know.

He knew this: as brutalised as the Iron Hands had been on Isstvan V, even fewer Salamanders and Raven Guard had survived. And he knew that if the hope of victory was to survive, it would not be through reaching for the throats of other loyalists. It was possible that the fatal mistakes had been made long before the engagement. His blood chilled when he thought of how the fleet of the X Legion had been divided, the faster ships leaving the *Veritas Ferrum* and others behind in the race to the Isstvan System. And maybe even that decision had not made the difference. Maybe there had been too many forces arrayed against the Emperor's faithful. There was talk among the astropaths about agencies other than the traitors at work. So many possibilities, so many errors and coincidences and treacheries becoming the drip, drip, drip of bloody fate.

All that was past. For the future, he knew one more thing: the loyalists, however few they were, must work together.

If he could ensure even that small ember of hope, then he would fan it.

He sighed, exchanging a look with Ptero and Khi'dem. He managed to summon a wry grimace. It was the closest he could come to a smile.

'What are we doing?' Ptero asked quietly. The veteran was not talking about strategy.

Galba shook his head in sorrowful agreement. 'I will keep you briefed,' he said. 'In return, will you do me this favour? Approach me rather than my captain.'

Were positions reversed, he thought he might well consider the request a gigantic insult. But Khi'dem nodded in understanding. 'I can see that would be for the best.'

'Thank you.' He started back to the bridge.

Ptero caught his arm. 'The Iron Hands are not alone,' he said. 'Don't make the mistake of fighting as if you were.'

JERUNE KANSHELL HAD just finished cleaning Galba's arming chamber when he heard the heavy steps of the sergeant approaching. He grabbed his bucket and cloths, hurried out, and stood to one side of the entrance, eyes trained on the floor.

Galba paused in the doorway. 'A fine job as always, Jerune,' he said. 'Thank you.'

'Thank you, lord,' the serf answered. Galba's acknowledgement was not unusual. It was what he said every time he returned and Kanshell happened to still be present. Even so, Kanshell felt a rush of pride, less for his work itself than for having been spoken to by his master. His duties here were simple. He was not to touch anything of real importance: armour, weapons, trophies, oaths of moment. It fell to him to clean the armour rack, to mop up the spills of oil from Galba's own cleaning sessions. They were tasks a servitor could perform. But a servitor could not understand the honour that came with this duty. He did.

Galba drummed a pensive rhythm against the doorway with his fingers. 'Jerune,' he said.

Startled by this departure from the norm, Kanshell raised his head. Galba was looking down at him. The sergeant had a metal lower jaw. He was bald, and war had burned and slashed his face until it was a mass of scored, hardened tissue. It was the forbidding face of a being slowly moving further and further away from the human, yet it was not unkind.

'My lord?' Kanshell asked.

'I know that the serf quarters took serious damage during the battle. How are the conditions?'

'We are making good progress with the repairs, lord.'

'That isn't what I asked.'

Kanshell swallowed hard as his throat closed in shame. He should know better than to dissemble before a warrior of the Legiones Astartes. He had spoken from an excess of pride. He wanted the god before him to know that even the humblest inhabitants of the *Veritas* were fighting the good fight. He wanted to say, *We're doing our part*, but could not bring himself to utter words so presumptuous. But he did speak the truth. 'The conditions are hard,' he admitted. 'But we fight on.'

Galba nodded. 'I see,' he said. 'Thank you for telling me.' His upper lip flattened out, and Kanshell realised that was how the sergeant now smiled. 'And thank you for fighting on.'

Kanshell bowed, his pride now as overwhelming as his shame had been a moment before. He must be glowing, he thought. Surely his skin was shining with the light of renewed purpose and determination granted to him by those simple words from Galba. And indeed, as he made his way back down the decks, it seemed to him that his path was more brightly lit than it had been earlier. He knew the impression was an illusion, but it was a helpful illusion. It gave him strength.

He needed it when he reached the serf quarters.

The humans who cleaned the ship, prepared the food and performed all the miscellaneous tasks too complex, too unpredictable or too varied for servitors, lived on one of the lowest decks of the *Veritas Ferrum*. There were thousands of them, and their home was something more than barracks, but less than a community. Before the nightmare of Isstvan V, this had been a space of regimental order. A vast, vaulted hall ran the length of the ship's spine. From it, access to all the other decks was a direct, simple matter, though far from being quick, given the thousands of metres of foot-travel required. The hall was wide enough to support any degree of serf traffic. Over the course of the Great Crusade, because it was the one space where all could be present, it had gradually taken on the qualities of market, feasting hall and meeting place. However, those aspects always gave way before discipline and the efficient movement of personnel, and so there was always a steady, unimpeded flow of serfs cutting through every gathering, meal or trading bazaar. Running off the great hall, on either side, were the living quarters: primarily dormitoria, each sleeping one hundred, but there were also modest private quarters for the more valuable menials.

The culture of Medusa was single-minded in its obsession with strength and condemnation of weakness. The Iron Hands had taken the animating spirit of their home planet to its furthest conclusion, despising the weakness of the flesh to the point that to be human at all seemed a regrettable flaw. Anything that did not contribute to the forging of perfect strength was a pointless distraction. Ferrus Manus had resented the imposition of remembrancers on his 52nd Expeditionary Fleet, and those irritating, unnecessary civilians had been left behind in the Callinedes System as the Iron Hands had rushed to confront Horus. Kanshell had been glad to see the back of them. As humble as his work was, it had a purpose in the great work that was the Iron Hands' machine of war. But those other citizens of the Imperium who believed the Iron Hands to be without art, or a sense of aesthetics, were wrong. Art must have a clear, forceful purpose, that was all. Kanshell had heard whispers of the marvellous weapons Manus had possessed aboard the *Fist of Iron*. He believed the stories. The idea of the strongest, deadliest instruments also being the most beautifully wrought was utterly *right*. It was in line with everything that life on Medusa had taught him about the brutal ways of the universe. Strength of will could be given a physical shape, one that could be used to bring the savage universe to heel.

The idea of Manus's weapons was also in keeping with the art on the walls of the *Veritas Ferrum*. And, unlike her sister vessel, the *Ferrum*, there was art here. Kanshell had been surrounded by majesty for every moment of his existence on the strike cruiser. To move through the great access hall was to pass between relief sculptures of giants. The heroic figures were rendered in simple, bold lines. There was not a single superfluous detail, but there was nothing crude about the representations, either. They were direct. They were colossal. They were inspiring. They struggled and won against mythic beasts that symbolised the unforgiving volcanoes and ice of Medusa. They showed the way to strength. Weakness was foreign to them, and they were the spirit that even the lowest serf was duty-bound to embody.

But this was all memory now. This was all as Kanshell's world had been before Isstvan V. This was before the terrible shattering. The *Veritas Ferrum* had been badly damaged in the void war. The shields had gone down on the port flank, towards the stern. Fire had swept through that end of the serf quarters until an entire sector of the ship had been sealed and vented. There had been further torpedo strikes, catastrophic hits to port again just prior to the leap into the empyrean. The greatest wound had been to the upper decks, killing over a hundred legionaries. Even so, there had been further destruction at this level. More collapsing bulkheads, more fire, and then, when the tear in the ship's flank had become deep enough, more of the terrible absence and cold that quenched fire, ended struggles, and purged the corridors of life.

At least the Geller field had held. At least the voyage through the warp had not bled the ship even more.

The hull had been repaired, but in the interior of the *Veritas*, entire decks were still strewn with wreckage. Some regions had become entirely inaccessible. Kanshell was glad that there were no wounded in those areas, no desperate survivors waiting for rescues that would never arrive. He had no reason to venture down the blocked paths, so he did not have to think about them. But there were plenty of scars in the serf quarters. Plenty of reminders of failure and defeat.

The stern end of the great hall was still sealed. The serfs whose duties took them to that end of the ship had to travel a maze of byways to reach their posts. Elsewhere in the hall, fire had scorched the walls, defacing the art. Some of the dormitoria chambers had been destroyed, and the lines of the hall had been ruined by buckled and torn metal. The floor was rippled, uneven. Kanshell had to leap over half a dozen fissures as he made his way to the midships region of the hall.

The space was still a thoroughfare, the servants of the Iron Hands still making their way at all hours from one end of the ship to the other, but its character had changed. The transformation was more than simply physical. The spirit of its inhabitants had been altered. The people of Medusa were no strangers to hardship and death. Those were the perpetual facts of existence on that planet. But the coming of Ferrus Manus had been the dawn of something new for the clans of Medusa: hope. It was not a weakling's hope that a better, easier future lay just over the horizon. It was hope that took the form of belief in the strength to carve out that future. The Iron Hands were the realisation of that hope. Their victories were triumphs, not just in the Emperor's name, but for Medusa itself.

Now Manus was gone. The X Legion was gutted. The *Veritas Ferrum* journeyed on, but no one knew to where. Though it was not the serfs' place to know their destination, Kanshell had heard some whispers that the legionaries did not know their goal either. The whispers were few, and the whisperers were terrified, not angry, and more than a little ashamed to be entertaining such thoughts. No amount of guilt changed the fact that the thoughts had been spoken and now had their own life. Kanshell would not believe the whispers. But having heard them, he could not escape the question.

Kanshell slowed as he approached the centre of the hall. Straight ahead, there was a gathering of a few dozen people. They stood close together, forming a tight circle, their faces towards its centre, their heads bowed. The duty-bound serfs flowed by on either side of the group, like a stream around a stone. Every few moments, one passer-by or another stopped for a moment to join in the communion. Others glanced at the circle with undisguised contempt. Georg Paert, a wall of a man who worked in the enginarium, snorted as he walked past. He grinned at Kanshell when he drew near. 'Don't let them put you off your appetite,' he said.

'I'll do my best,' Kanshell muttered, but Paert had already moved on.

The group was between Kanshell and the mess tables. He thought about hanging back until the meeting was finished, but he was famished, and he was due on a repair detail in a few minutes. He began to move across the width of the hall, cutting across the traffic to make a wide arc around the group. He had only taken a few steps when he heard his name called out. He grimaced and turned around. Agnes Tanaura had moved away from the cluster and was gesturing him over. Kanshell sighed. Might as well get this done. Better meet with her now, when he had a good reason to make this short, then to have her corner him later when he came off his shift.

He joined her at the line-up to the mess service. Heated rations were distributed by a dispensary in the middle of the hall. It was surrounded by long, high iron tables. There were no benches. People ate quickly while standing, then moved on.

'I saw you watching us, Jerune,' Tanaura said.

'You saw me *seeing* you. There's a difference.'

'Just like there's a difference between looking at something from the outside, and being part of it.'

Kanshell suppressed a groan. Tanaura was hardly being subtle. She was watching him intently, as she always did. Even the most casual conversation with Tanaura felt like an interrogation. Her eyes were a translucent grey, the same shade as her short hair. They shone with a predatory care. She was one of the older serfs on the *Veritas Ferrum*. Kanshell was not sure of her precise age. The life was a hard one, and used up the body quickly. Kanshell had friends he had grown up with, but they had drawn duties of such rigour that they looked more like his parents than his peers. Tanaura came by her leathered skin honestly. As far as Kanshell and anyone of his acquaintance knew, she had always been here. She had taken on the role of collective mother, whether her uncountable foster children welcomed her attentions or not.

'Agnes,' Kanshell said, 'we've already had this conversation.'

She clasped his upper arm. 'And we'll keep having it. You need it, even if you don't think so.'

He gently removed her hand. 'What I need now is some food, and then I need to be about my duties.'

'Yes, there is much work to do. There is so much to rebuild. Not all of it can be forged by tools and hands. Our strength needs to be rebuilt, too.'

Kanshell grunted. His temper was slipping. After his encounter with Galba, he had little patience for Tanaura, and he felt strong enough to confront her. He took his tray of food: a slab of processed protein and a square of compressed vegetable matter. The basic necessities to keep the human mechanism viable and contributing, in its turn, to the X Legion's war machine. Kanshell moved to a table and put his tray down with a clatter. He began to tear the rations into strips. 'Do you see what I'm doing?' he said. He chewed and swallowed. 'I'm rebuilding my strength.' He met Tanaura's gaze and, pleased with his fortitude, refused to blink first. 'My true, valuable strength. Turning to superstition is a weakness.'

'You're so wrong. Realising that we have limits, and that we have weaknesses, takes courage. It takes strength. We have to accept that we must turn to the Father of Mankind for his aid. The Lectitio Divinitatus teaches us–'

'To go against the very teachings of the Emperor, even as it purports to worship him. The logic is ridiculous, and it is forbidden.'

'You don't understand. The Emperor's denial of His divinity is a test. It reminds us to reject all false gods. But when we have done so, casting down all the idols who claim to be divine, the one true god remains. We have to see through the paradox he has given us. When you reach the other side, there is such comfort.'

'I am not looking for comfort,' Kanshell spat. 'None of us should. That is unworthy of who we are.'

'You really don't understand. If I could show you the strength needed to commit to faith, you would see how wrong you are.'

Kanshell finished eating. 'That isn't about to happen, is it?'

'It could.' From a pocket in her worn tunic, Tanaura produced a worn book. She placed it against Kanshell's chest. 'Please read this.'

Kanshell shoved the book away as if burned. 'Where did you get that?'

'I've had it for years. It was given to me by a serf of the Word Bearers.'

'Who betrayed us at Isstvan! What are you *thinking*?'

'I think it is a tragedy that those who first knew the truth have turned away from it. And I think it would be another tragedy if we did too.'

Kanshell shook his head. 'No. I won't have anything to do with this cult, and I want you to leave me alone.' He glanced back at the circle of worshippers. They were still deep in prayer. 'Don't you realise the risk you're taking, carrying on like this out in the open?'

'The truth should not be kept to the shadows.'

'And if any of the legionaries sees this? If Captain Atticus finds out?' Tanaura was in charge of the upkeep of Atticus's quarters. Kanshell could not understand why she would jeopardise such an honour. The only reason he could think of why nothing had been done about the growing cult was that the Iron Hands had far more pressing matters to concern themselves with than the off-duty activities of the serfs.

'We aren't interfering with necessary work. We don't speak to any-one who doesn't want to listen.'

Kanshell gave a short bark of laughter. 'What do you call this, then?'

That intense gaze, a mix of ecstatic revelation and a determination of steel. 'Because I can see your need, Jerune. You want to listen.'

He backed away from her, shaking his head. 'You could not be more wrong. Now please, leave me alone.'

'Think about what I've said.'

'I will not,' he shot over his shoulder as he marched away.

HE MADE HIS way toward the stern. A massive, closed bulkhead sealed off the damage beyond from the rest of the ship. There, Kanshell received his assignment and worked his way into the twisted, fractured corridors to join other serfs and repair servitors in the slow process of restoring rationality, order and mechanical precision to the interior of the *Veritas*. His group worked to clear a corridor of tangled metal. The passageway had run in a straight line, but now it resembled a fractured bone. There was a sharp cleavage in the floor, with the section running to port now raised half a metre above the rest. There was no way to bring the halves of the corridor back into alignment, but the disfigurement could be alleviated with a ramp.

The work was cramped and stifling. Kanshell had new cuts and burns within minutes. He welcomed the strain. He welcomed the pain. It seared away Tanaura's superstitious fancies. More impor-tantly, it put her insinuations about him to the torch. She was wrong about him. He did not deny that he needed to draw strength from somewhere outside himself. He knew he had limits, and he knew these dark days had pushed him to them. But he would draw his strength from the object lessons of the legionaries of the Iron Hands.

He vowed unswerving loyalty to the Emperor *and* to his teachings. One implied the other. It was that simple. Everything he needed to know about strength, he could see for himself in the ceramite-clad giants he served. He had no need for a grubby octavo that sought to undermine everything the Imperium and the Great Crusade had brought about.

And for just a few moments, cocooned in the sweat-box darkness lit only by the painful glare of soldering tools, he was able to hide from the knowledge of what had happened to the Great Crusade, and what was happening to the Imperium.

Then the floor collapsed. Its remaining strength had been a lie. With snaps and shrieks of tortured metal, several metres of decking fell into the lower depths of the vessel. Most of the work detail plunged with it. Kanshell felt the terrifying jerk and give beneath his feet and threw himself backwards. He caught a jagged corner of torn wall with his left hand. His feet scrabbled for purchase and he was suddenly holding almost his full weight with one hand. The metal cut a deep gash into his palm. Blood slicked his fingers. His grip began to slip. He flailed with his right hand, grasping air. His flesh tingled as the chasm before him drew nearer.

Then his heel caught a ridge in the decking. He steadied, and found a hanging pipe on his right. He took a careful step back onto level floor. There was no give, no creak of treacherous metal. He collapsed on all fours, gasping for breath, and crawled away from the hole. In the light of guttering flames and sparking cables, he stared at the hungry darkness, made dizzy by the act of chance that had spared him. His ears were filled with the echoes of settling wreckage, but there were no screams of the injured.

The silence of the dead was deafening.

✠ ✠ ✠

THE HOLOLITHIC GHOSTS of his three brothers were fragile. They kept dissolving into jagged flickers, their words disappearing into static. Several times, Atticus had to ask the other three captains to repeat themselves. And given how often he had to do the same for them, his transmission was no better than his reception. There was little of the illusion of presence in the lithocast chamber. As sentences fragmented and faces lost definition, what Atticus felt instead was the reminder of absence. The candle-flame brittleness of the hololiths was the health of his Legion, what was left of its strength.

The *Veritas Ferrum*'s lithocast system was humble compared to those on the flagships of the Legions. It was also more private. Rather than being integrated into the bridge, it occupied a chamber next to Atticus's quarters. The lithocast plate was in the centre of the space, surrounded by three-metre-high panels that acted as sound baffles. The lithocast operators' stations occupied the periphery of the chamber. Atticus's isolation during the lithocasts was not a matter of secrecy, but of efficiency. The panels were there to keep sound out, allowing the captain to turn his undivided attention to his distant visitors.

The operation of the system was energy intensive. It was not used lightly. The conferences that took place through its agency were always on matters of great import. In the past, they had almost always been initiated by Ferrus Manus himself.

In the past. Atticus suppressed that thought, because behind it lurked a worse one that he refused to countenance: *Never again.*

'What are your auspex scans showing?' Khalybus asked.

'They aren't *showing* anything unusual. We are experiencing the expected erratic behaviour this close to the Maelstrom, and it has been growing worse as we enter the Pandorax System. But they can't pinpoint a source of interference themselves.'

'But something else can,' Sabinus deduced.

Atticus nodded. 'The mistress of our astropathic choir thinks she can find it.'

Sabinus grunted. *'Not your Navigator?'*

'I grant this is odd. But no. Though Mistress Erephren is working with Navigator Strassny to translate what she is reading from the empyrean into actual coordinates.'

'What is she experiencing?' Plienus asked. It took him three attempts before Atticus could make out what he was saying.

'She says her perception is reaching a clarity and range she has never known before.'

'I am surprised,' Plienus responded. *'My choirs are finding your messages harder and harder to transcribe.'*

The other two captains were nodding in agreement.

'That appears to be the other facet of the phenomenon,' Atticus said. 'The more clearly the choirs receive, the more difficult it is for them to send.'

Khalybus said something that was lost in a scraping whine of interference. When the sound cleared for a moment, he said, *'Where does this lead, brother? To total awareness and absolute silence?'*

'How can I know? Perhaps.'

'Are you sure of the wisdom of your course?'

'Am I sure of the end result of this venture? Of course not. Am I sure of its necessity? Without a doubt.' Atticus paused for a moment. 'Brothers, our reality is hard, and we must face truths just as unforgiving. We cannot prosecute this war in our traditional manner, and we cannot reach Terra.' What he did not add, but they all understood, was that they would not make for Terra even if they could. They would return as a smashed Legion, one to be absorbed, its culture forgotten, into the others. There had been too many humiliations already. There was no reason to willingly submit to this final one. 'We have agreed,' he continued, 'to fight the enemy using what means we have to the fullest. We have no fleet. But we still have ships, and this region favours the individual predator. There remains the question of tracking the prey.'

'You think you have found a way of doing so?' Plienus asked.

'I see the *possibility* of a great deal of useful intelligence.'

Sabinus was not convinced. *'That is supposition.'*

'One that I believe is worth acting on.'

All three ghosts dissolved into a flashing phantasmagoria. Sound became a wailing electronic wind. In the midst of the storm, Atticus had a momentary impression of something distinct emerging from the static. It was as if a new voice scraped past his ear, whispering syllables both concrete and incomprehensible. As he tried to listen more intently, the storm passed, and his brothers stood before him again.

'...you realise?' Sabinus was saying. When Atticus asked him to repeat himself, he said, *'I was asking if you are fully aware of what the loss of a single ship now means to the Legion.'*

'Of course I do. Just as I know the vital necessity of any tactical advantage.'

'There is little point in arguing,' Khalybus put in. *'Captain Atticus is correct about the realities we face. Whatever any of us thinks of the wisdom of his strategy, it is his decision to make. By rank and by necessity, we will each be fighting our own war.'*

There was a pause. It was a silence without static. Atticus felt a new weight pressing down on him, as he knew it was on his brothers. It was not the responsibility of command. It was something akin to isolation, only much more powerful, much more profound. It was loss. The Iron Hands fought on, but the X Legion was no more. The collective body of which Atticus had been a part for centuries had been dismembered. Atticus refused to believe in the death of Ferrus Manus. Such a monstrous impossibility could not be, not in any universe, no matter how insane. Did iron yet bend in the breeze? No? Then Manus was not dead. Some truths were that simple. They had to be, if there were to be such a thing as truth at all.

But Manus was not here. He was lost to his sons, and the great war machine he had forged had been smashed to a few scattered components.

As if speaking Atticus's thoughts, Sabinus said, '*The body of our Legion is gone.*' Of the four, Sabinus was the least transformed. His was the voice that could still express the depths of grief and anger for them all. '*And our blood is adulterated.*' The *Veritas Ferrum* was not alone in carrying surviving Salamanders and Raven Guard. The other captains also had to look upon the allies who had failed their Legion.

Atticus held up a hand. He made it into a fist. It was unarmoured, but it could still punch through steel. Sabinus was correct – the collective being of the Legion was shattered, but he could rely on his own force, and that of the legionaries under his command, to crush the skulls of traitors to dust.

'No,' he said, and he revelled in the inhuman, fleshless rasp of his own voice. 'We are its body yet. If we can no longer strike with a hammer blow, we shall erode our enemies like a cancer. We are in their domain. They will think themselves safe here, but they are mistaken. We are too small to find, but we are here. We will harry them, and bleed them, and if they should be lucky enough to destroy one of us, what then? Will that affect the operations of the rest? No. One blow destroyed the greater part of our forces. It will take more blows than the enemy can count to kill the rest. We have a strength, brothers. We have but to recognise it.'

They talked for a few more minutes after that. Atticus heard about the operations that the other captains planned, and how they hoped to track their targets. He listened. He committed the information to memory. But he knew how little that knowledge mattered. The *Veritas Ferrum* was on her own.

The lithocast ended. The ghosts vanished. Yet for a moment, the isolation vanished too. Atticus was seized by the certainty that if he spun around, he would see something else standing with him on the lithocast plate. He quelled the urge to turn and walked forwards off the plate. The sense of a presence evaporated, as he had known it would. No matter how much of the weak flesh he sacrificed to the Apothecary's knife, his mind remained human, and subject to its perversities and compulsions to deceive itself. The key was to recognise this vulnerability, and to counter it with the empirical rationality taught by his primarch and his Emperor.

But when he returned to the bridge, and stood in the command lectern, and gave orders that the *Veritas Ferrum* cross the boundary of the asteroid belt and venture into the Pandorax System, one more thing happened. It was brief, so brief it should have been instantly dismissed. And he did dismiss it. It was faint, so faint he should have been able to ignore it. And he did ignore it.

What he dismissed, what he ignored, was an irrational phantom. It was as trivial as a hair in front of an eye.

It was as precise as a claw caressing the cerebral cortex.

It was a welcome.

TWO

Mistress of the song
Age of wonders
A verdant land

FEAR WAS THE normal condition when touching the current of the warp. It was also the necessary one. Rhydia Erephren held it close to her being. She made it her constant companion. It was the friend she could count on. She had even trained herself to respond with terror should the fear ever diminish, because that would be the sign she was dropping her guard and in greatest danger.

Erephren believed in the secular universe promulgated by the Emperor. She celebrated the toppling of all gods. The extirpation of the irrational from the human race was a glorious quest, and she believed in its necessity with all of her strength and all of her yearning. Despite her bedrock loyalty to the precepts of the Imperium, or perhaps because of it, she also experienced awe, and knew it in the form of sacred horror. That was the power of the warp. It was everything the Imperium stood against, yet it was the precondition to the spread of the Emperor's light. It was the impossible given a non-existent reality. It was the denial of place that was also the supreme means of travel. It seduced in order to destroy.

On this day, the warp was seductive as she had never experienced it before, and it was growing more persuasive by the second. It beckoned her with clarity, dropping one veil after another, filling her head with knowledge of the near systems, and promising more. It hinted that omniscience was just over the horizon. It would be hers, if she and the *Veritas* would come a bit nearer to a certain spot in the Pandorax System. *Come to Pythos*, it murmured. It promised so many sights to parade for her behind her blind eyes, so many secrets to whisper. As she stood at her pulpit in the chancel, leading the astropathic choir, the growing clarity became a kind of ecstasy. A brilliant dawn was flooding the night of the warp. Turning to find the sun was not difficult. It would have been impossible for her to do otherwise. The challenge came in not losing herself. It would have been easy to let her consciousness drown in the light of knowing.

Discipline held her back. Discipline, fealty and will. She was an astropath of the Iron Hands, and she had a war to wage.

'THIS IS A rare sight,' Darras said under his breath as the bridge doors opened.

Galba glanced at the other Tactical squad sergeant, trying to read his tone. That was never easy with Darras. The legionary was forever deadpan. He did not have a bionic voice box like Atticus. He just spoke without expression, machine-like in his soul. His face, Galba had long thought, was that of a corpse, as if it were a flesh mask hanging off a metal skull. He was, like all the other legionaries aboard the *Veritas Ferrum*, from the Ungavarr clan of northern Medusa. But Darras was more visibly a product of the glaciers than his brothers. He was beyond pale. His skin was sallow, his hair sparse. Were he a non-genhanced human, he would have seemed sickly. But his thick, corded neck and the bunched muscle of his pate said otherwise. He was the death of his enemies, and he looked the part.

He was also the death of the polite lie and the meaningless turn of phrase. For unfortunate emissaries from the Administratum of Terra who crossed his path, he was the death of diplomacy. In the past, Galba had laughed at their discomfiture when Darras had punctured their unctuous patter. On this day, though, given the balancing act in which he was engaging, he was nervous about his friend's mood.

'What do you mean?' he asked.

To Galba's relief, Darras nodded at the doorway. Rhydia Erephren and Bhalif Strassny had arrived on the bridge together. It was unusual to see either of them away from chancel or out of the nutrient tank while the *Veritas Ferrum* was on active duty. The two of them present at the same time was unheard of.

Atticus was standing before the primary oculus. 'Mistress Erephren, Navigator Strassny,' he said. 'Please join me.'

The two humans crossed the floor of the bridge. Galba was surprised to see Erephren walk ahead of Strassny, unguided, her step sure. In her left hand, she carried the two-metre-high staff of her office. The haft was of a wood so dark it was black. It was topped with an ornate, bronze astrolabe. Her right hand wielded a cane of silvered steel, its head the Imperial aquila. Its tip was sharp enough that she could have used the cane as a sword. The rhythm as she tapped the decking before her was so subtle, it seemed impossible to Galba that she was using it to find her way. Strassny, two paces behind her, was slumped, and looked like he needed a cane more than she did.

They were both Terran-raised. Strassny was born there, a member of one of the second-tier Houses of the Navis Nobilite. His long hair, pulled back and braided in the helix fashion of his family, was both lank and so fine that stray strands floated around his head like smoke. His features were as fragile as thin porcelain. He was the result of centuries of House Strassny's intermarriage. The blood that made him a superb Navigator also made him so weak a physical specimen, it took a conscious effort on Galba's part not to regard him with untempered revulsion.

Erephren was a different case. She had been brought to Terra in a Black Ship while still an infant. No one, herself included, knew the planet of her birth. Her robes bore no family markings, but were rich in the awards of service. A bronze receiving plaque, engraved with the emblem of the Astra Telepathica, was embedded in the top of her bald skull. The soul-binding ritual had robbed her of her sight, and altered her eyes in a manner that Galba had never encountered in any other astropath. He had seen many whose eyes had become clouded, some so milky it was as if they had turned into pearls. But hers were utterly transparent. They were immaculate, crystalline orbs with nothing inside. Viewed face-on, they were invisible; Erephren's eyelids the open doorways to sunken hollows of tissue and darkness. Blasted by constant exposure to the warp, she appeared to be in her late-seventies, almost twice her real age. Though he was centuries older than she was, Galba found it impossible not to see her as a venerable figure. She had paid for every message received and transmitted with a piece of her life. Strassny's weakness had been his from birth. Erephren's infirmity had been acquired in the performance of duty. There was honour in that.

Yet Erephren carried herself as if there were no infirmity. Her posture was pitilessly straight, her stride sure, and her robes the black-and-grey scheme of the Legion she served. She was regal. She deserved Galba's respect, but she also commanded it.

'An unusual day,' Galba said to Darras, agreeing with his first assessment.

'For you especially,' Darras said.

Galba kept his face neutral. 'Yes,' he said. So Darras had been digging at him after all. He had reached the bridge only a few moments before Erephren and Strassny, and he had not come alone. Khi'dem and Ptero had accompanied him. They now stood at the rear of the bridge, near the entrance. They were out of the way, but they stood with arms folded, their body language asserting their right to be there.

'Shouldn't you be keeping your new friends company?' Darras asked.

'I've come to relieve you.' Darras had been manning his station, monitoring the scrolling hololiths that tracked the vessel's health.

'No need. I believe your services as diplomat are still required.'

'You do me an injustice.' Galba managed to keep his voice steady, doing his best to refuse Darras's bait. *Diplomat* was a term of immense derision among the Iron Hands.

'Do I? Then enlighten me, brother. What is it, exactly, that you are doing?'

Galba almost said, *Trying to keep the peace.* He caught himself. 'A lack of unity will not help our war effort,' he said.

Darras snorted. 'I will not fight alongside them.'

'Then you're a fool,' Galba snapped. 'You speak as if there were a choice.'

'There is always a choice.'

'No, there is not, unless you see failure as a choice. I do not. Our situation is what it is, brother, and if you think we can dispense with allies, then you are refusing to see clearly.'

Darras paused, then nodded, once, in bitter acceptance. 'These are cursed days,' he muttered, venom dripping from each clipped syllable.

'They are.'

'The captain doesn't seem to be objecting to the presence of our guests.'

'He knew I was bringing them.'

Darras opened his mouth slightly. It was what passed for a laugh with him. 'How did you manage that?'

'I said much the same things to him as I did to you. I told him that we must not turn from reality.'

'You didn't.'

It was Galba's turn to laugh. He was glad for the familiarity of banter. 'Not in so many words, perhaps. I did say "reality" at one point. I remember that because it seemed to strike a chord.'

Darras raised an eyebrow. 'You detected facial expressions in the captain?'

'No. But after I used the word, he agreed to my request.'

'Then we are in for a day of wonders.'

Galba turned with him to watch Atticus speak to Erephren and Strassny. The Navigator said little, contenting himself with brief assertions in support of the astropath. Filling the view from the oculus was Pythos, the innermost planet of the Pandorax System.

'This world is the source of the anomalous warp effect?' Atticus asked.

'The source lies on it,' Erephren corrected.

Atticus contemplated the planet. 'Could such a thing be natural?'

'I cannot conceive of how it could be. Why do you ask, captain?'

'There is no civilisation here.' The *Veritas Ferrum* was in orbit above the terminator. The nightside of the planet was utterly dark. There were no lights of cities below. The dayside revealed blue oceans and green landmasses.

Galba was looking at a garden world. He thought about all the planets he had fought on over the centuries of the Great Crusade. They had all borne the disfigurements brought by intelligent life. What turned below was pristine. It did not know the machine, and its order and strength. He knew what all that green meant: organic life in full riot, undisciplined, chaotic. His lip curled in disgust.

'I cannot explain what you are seeing, captain,' Erephren said. 'But what we seek is there. I know this as surely as I breathe.'

Atticus did not move. He had so completely given his physical self to the reign of metal that his stillness was absolute. He stood as a statue, an inanimate *thing* that would spring to terrifying life if confronted. He faced the sight in the oculus as if it were an opponent. Iron challenged the garden. 'Can you pinpoint the location more precisely?'

'I believe I can. The closer we come, the more intensely I experience its effects. If we pass over it, I am convinced that I will know we have done so.'

'Then, with your guidance, that is what we shall do.'

The *Veritas Ferrum* began a slow orbit of Pythos, level with the equator, moving with the rotation. Strassny left the bridge, returning to his tank. Erephren remained at the fore, standing beside Atticus, facing the oculus as if she could see the object of her scrutiny. She called out directions with the certainty of someone who could see something, and see it more clearly with every passing second.

The closer the strike cruiser came to the source of the phenomenon she was experiencing, the more it seemed to Galba that she was losing herself. The reserve that had always been her armour crumbled. Her voice grew louder, more ferocious. When the search began, she had simply spoken quietly to Atticus to tell him in which directions the ship should go. But now she gestured with staff and cane as if conducting an invisible orchestra the size of the planet. A rhythm entered her movements. They became hypnotic. Galba had trouble looking away. Her voice changed, too. The furious power was still there, but she was not shouting anymore. She was chanting. Galba was seized by the impression that she held the entire ship in her will, moving its millions of tonnes as she moved her cane. He tried to shake the illusion away, but it was persistent. It clung with the tenacity of something that was perilously close to the truth.

And then, '*There*,' she gasped. '*There, there, there.*'

'Full stop!' Atticus ordered.

'*There.*' Erephren pointed with her cane with such ferocity and precision that surely it was impossible that she was still blind. She was motionless for several seconds, as still as the legionary at her side.

Something immense passed through the bridge. The thinnest of barriers blocked a whisper. There were terrible words that wanted to make themselves heard.

The moment passed. Galba blinked, disturbed that he had allowed himself such an excess of imagination. Erephren lowered her cane and slumped, using the staff now to support herself. She breathed heavily, and there was a rattle in her chest. Then she straightened, once again cladding herself in the armour of her reserve. She shivered once, and then she was calm.

'Are you well, Mistress Erephren?' Atticus asked.

'I am now, captain. Thank you.' But there was a new strain in her voice. 'I must tell you, though, that this is a place of incredible temptation for the likes of me.'

'What kind of temptation?'

'Every kind.'

Atticus made no comment, and turned back to the oculus. Galba frowned. Erephren's choice of words was disturbing. There was something of the superstitious about them.

Atticus said, 'Is it possible to pinpoint the location more precisely?'

'Take me to the surface.'

Atticus made a gesture of surprise. 'An astropath in the field?'

'I will serve in whatever manner is necessary. This is necessary.'

The captain nodded. 'Master of the Auspex,' he called. 'I want a deep scan of the region below us. Whatever is affecting the warp, it has a location, so it must have a physical manifestation. We may be close enough to find something now.' To Erephren, he said, 'We may have other means.'

The astropath pursed her lips, doubt on her face.

'Commencing scan,' Aulus confirmed.

Several minutes elapsed. The company on the bridge stood by, the only sound the murmuring of cogitators. The spectacle of the Iron Hands waiting was a vista of stillness. Men who had been turned into engines of war paused, inert, until the signal for action would unleash them.

'All returns negative,' Aulus reported. 'Auspex banks find nothing–' He stopped. 'One moment. There is an irregularity in this area.' At his command, a large-scale hololith of Pythos was projected to the centre of the bridge. A point in the northern hemisphere, on the east coast of the continent visible from the oculus, began to flash.

'Still too wide an area,' Atticus said. 'Narrow it down.'

'Captain.' Erephren's tone was a warning.

Aulus leaned closer to his screens. 'There is something,' he said. 'Let me focus the beam to this–'

The lights of the bridge went down. The Pythos hololith vanished. Darras grunted. Galba glanced down, and saw that his readouts had gone dead.

The auspex bank exploded. The framework launched itself at Aulus in a torn ecstasy of metal. A fireball engulfed him, and it was the colour of incandescent flesh. Kaleidoscopic lightning crackled up the walls. Its infection ran down the spine of the vault, jolted open the door and shot down the corridor, spreading an electric howl to the rest of the ship. The *Veritas Ferrum* shook. The tremor came from the core, a deep, powerful thrum that almost threw Galba off his feet. It was the jerk of the already wounded vessel being stabbed with an assassin's blade.

Galba and Darras raced to Aulus's post. Atticus was there first, reaching the stricken legionary just as the fireball dissipated. Flames quivered along the perimeter of the explosion. They did not crackle. Instead, they made a noise that sounded to Galba like sighs. A choir of thousands pressed against a weakening wall with desire and hatred and laughter. And then the flames died, taking with them the sighs and Galba's belief in what he had heard.

The deck steadied. The bridge's lumen-strips brightened again. Smoke coiled through the space, filling Galba's nostrils with the smell of burned graves. Aulus was lying motionless. The savage angles of the auspex frame had plunged through his armour in half a dozen places. It looked as if a metal talon had seized him. One claw had gone all the way through his throat, impaling him to the deck. Another had punched the bridge of his nose out the back of his skull.

Atticus wrenched the twisted framework away from the body. Darras began to say, 'The Apothecary–'

Atticus cut him off. 'There is nothing to recover.'

He was right, Galba saw. The wounds had destroyed Aulus's progenoid glands. There would be no preserving his genetic legacy for the future of the Iron Hands. The shape of the ruined auspex bothered Galba. The talon declared that Aulus had not been the victim of an accident. He had been attacked.

The idea was ludicrous. Galba knew he should not be entertaining it. He was doing an injustice to his fallen brother to engage in irrational fantasies about his demise. Once again, he pushed the impossible away.

He refused to think about how often he was having to keep such ideas at bay.

'What is the status of the ship?' Atticus asked.

Galba ran back to his post. With a stuttering flicker, the hololithic display came back to life. He surveyed the readings. 'No further damage,' he reported. His words rang false in his ears. There were no fires burning anywhere beyond the bridge. The integrity of the hull had not been compromised. All life support systems were functioning. Shields were up. The auspex was destroyed, and a battle-brother was dead. Otherwise, the ship was unharmed. Only Galba knew this was not true. This was not a matter of irrational intuition. He had witnessed destructive energy arrive and pass through the vessel. It could not have passed without effect. He did not believe that it had. He could feel a difference in the *Veritas*, even in the deck beneath his feet. The ship had lost something essential, and it had acquired a new, distressing quality: brittleness.

Galba willed his impressions to be false. But when he looked up, and saw the expression on Erephren's face, he knew, with a sinking in his gut, that they were true.

THE VERITAS FERRUM moved into a low geosynchronous orbit over Pythos. The ship had been hit. An enemy on Pythos had drawn first blood. And so the strike cruiser unleashed war into the skies of the planet. Retaliation descended to the surface on the wings of Thunderhawks. With the *Veritas* strategically blind until its Mechanicum adepts could repair the auspex system, Atticus had to rely on pict-captures of the surface. They showed no clear sign of the anomaly, but they did offer a few landing zones in the area Aulus had designated before his death.

Three gunships took part in the planetfall. Two of them, *Unbending* and *Iron Flame*, carried Erephren and sixty Iron Hands for a reconnaissance in force. The third was *Hammerblow*, and it was a Salamander craft. It was one of the two recovered, at terrible cost, from the low orbit of Isstvan V before the savaged *Veritas* had made its escape from the hopeless void war. *Hammerblow* and *Cindara* had been among the very few ships of any kind to survive the massacre on the planet's surface. Khi'dem's Salamanders had managed to gather a few Raven Guard during their fighting retreat to the gunships, along with some Iron Hands who had been too badly wounded during the initial phase of the battle to advance with their primarch into the jaws of Horus's trap.

Seated in *Unbending*, Darras glanced out the viewing block at *Hammerblow* as it flew level with them. 'Well,' he said to Galba, 'will they fight with us to the end, do you think?'

Galba shrugged. 'If you think I find this conversation invigorating, you are mistaken.'

Atticus emerged from the cockpit and opened the side hatch of the Thunderhawk. Wind whipped through the troop compartment. Galba freed himself from his grav-harness and joined the captain. He looked down at the landscape rushing past below. They were flying over a solid canopy of jungle. The wind was thick, hot, a blast of steam. Galba's neuroglottis parsed a cornucopia of scents and tastes. The sensory flood was dizzying. Pollens from a thousand different species fought with the stench of a loam that must have been metres deep with rotting organic matter. And there was blood. Hidden beneath the green was crimson, streams of crimson, an ocean of crimson. The taste of the blood was a corrupted amasec.

There were too many flavours, too many beings. None of it was human. *Unbending* was flying above a primordial field of combat. Galba thought about the difference between his home world and what he was rushing towards here. Life was violence on both planets. But on Medusa, life had to struggle simply to exist. Medusa was a world that rejected the organic. It was a test, and only the strongest forms found a purchase on its surface. Pythos, though, was monstrous in its all-encompassing welcome. Life had exploded here. Life piled on life. The only shortage was space, and that was enough to ignite a war of all against all.

Medusa forged unity and steadfastness. Galba was not surprised that no civilisation awaited the Iron Hands on Pythos. There was, he was sure, no order possible in this place of orgiastic growth.

Ahead, not far from the western edge of the target zone, the land rose, and a rocky promontory broke free of the canopy. Atticus pointed. 'We land there.'

The peak of the promontory was bare and level, about half a kilometre on a side. To the north, west and south, it ended in steep cliffs. To the east, the slope was a gradual descent back to the floor of the jungle. The tree line was about ten metres down from the peak. The Thunderhawks circled the area once, then landed. The assault ramps slammed down, and the legionaries marched onto the surface of Pythos. They spread outwards from the gunships, forming a ceramite barrier to the east.

Galba had been tasked with ensuring the safety of Rhydia Erephren. The members of his squad surrounded her, and they measured their pace. He was surprised by how quickly she moved in completely unknown territory. She stood still for a moment after she walked away from *Unbending*. She frowned as if listening. Galba saw a vein in her forehead pulse rapidly, the one sign of the strain she was experiencing. Then she turned and made for the eastern line. Her stride was almost as assured as on the *Veritas*.

Atticus was waiting. 'Well, Mistress Erephren?' he asked.

'The anomaly is already powerful here, captain, but this is not yet the source. I can feel the current of its presence, though, much more sharply defined. It lies in that direction.' She pointed east.

'Very well,' Atticus said. 'We shall burn our way through the jungle if necessary. I will take point. Mistress, you will remain in the rear lines under the protection of Sergeant Galba. Should we deviate from the correct path, inform us immediately.'

'As you say, captain.'

The Iron Hands plunged into the jungle. The Salamanders and Raven Guard followed behind, the true rearguard even though Atticus barely acknowledged their presence. Within a hundred metres, the legionaries were deep into a green night. The sky vanished behind the unbroken shield of intertwining branches. The occulobes of the Space Marines compensated for the dim light, and the legionaries marched on as if in broad day. The air grew thicker yet, and Galba wondered how long Erephren would be able to function. Already he could hear a liquid rattle in her breathing, but she did not slow.

The trees were gigantic, rising thirty metres or more. Galba saw a few leafed varieties, but most were conifers with needles like curved claws. Almost as common were growths that turned out not to be trees at all, but immense ferns. Vines twisted from trunk to trunk, their stems thick as cables, the blades of their leaves so sharply angular, Galba found himself thinking of razor wire designed for Dreadnoughts. The lower trunks and jungle floor were covered by carpets of moss. It was so deep and wrinkled that it camouflaged roots, and on several occasions Galba was about to warn Erephren of a hazard at her feet, but she stepped over the obstacle each time.

'You are sure-footed,' he told her.

'Thank you.'

'How do you sense your surroundings?'

'You misunderstand my abilities, sergeant. I do not have an image of what is before me, except what my imagination reconstructs after the fact. I am making use of the knowledge that flows to me from the immaterium. I receive the messages sent by my brothers and sisters of the Astra Telepathica, and I have grown accustomed to retrieving other information as well, such as what movements I should make. I do not know why I must move to the right,' and she did, avoiding the trunk that stood in her way. 'Perhaps I am sensing the eddies in the warp caused by the physical realm, and this is my new sight. I do know that listening to these promptings serves me well.'

'Clearly,' said Galba. He thought for a moment. 'What happened on the bridge...' he began.

Erephren gave her head a solemn shake. 'I know no more than you.'

'But you tried to warn Captain Atticus.'

'The barrier to the empyrean is very thin here. The forces at work are very powerful. I felt a surge, but why was it caused by Sergeant Aulus's scan? And why did it take the form that it did? I have no answers.'

'I am not just concerned with why it took that form,' Galba said. 'I want to understand what that form *was*. I've never witnessed the like.'

'The warp defies understanding, sergeant. That is its nature. I do not believe we need to look any more deeply than that.'

She made her last sentence very emphatic. It was on the tip of Galba's tongue to ask if the truth was that she did not *want* to believe in the need to look more closely. He stopped himself. He could see the strain in her face. The astropath was always linked to the warp. Her consciousness was always divided, her self shaped by two inimical conceptions of existence. He could not begin to understand the risks she ran every second after eternal second. If there were paths that she recoiled from treading, he would respect her wishes.

Then Erephren spoke again, startling Galba with her confiding tone. 'I have a great admiration for the tenets of this Legion, sergeant,' she said. 'I am not a native of your world. I serve the Iron Hands, but I do not flatter myself that I am of your number. But you should know how important what you represent is for me.' She tapped her leg once with her cane. 'This body is weak. It is a barely adequate vehicle. That is the cost of my gift and my service. I pay it gladly, and seek my strength elsewhere, where I need it most, in my will and my sense of identity.' She paused as she negotiated a root almost as high as her knee. 'The Iron Hands are without compromise. You do not tolerate weakness. You expunge it from yourselves and from others. This rigour means you must make hard choices, and engage in harsh actions.'

'Harsh?' He was taken aback. Was she questioning the honour of his Legion? The Iron Hands had never acted with anything less than justice on their side. Any punishment meted out was deserved.

'You misunderstand me. The word is a term of praise. The galaxy is a harsh place, and must be answered in kind. You are that answer. There have been several occasions, sergeant, during our Great Crusade, when duty has required that you cull the entire human populations of non-compliant worlds.'

'That is so. Sometimes the xenos taint is too great, the resistance to reason too entrenched.'

'Do you know what I hear during those purges? Do you realise that those deaths are marked in the warp as they are in the materium?'

'No.' He had not known.

'You cannot imagine the horror,' she said. 'But I can stand it, because I know you enforce the Emperor's will, and if you have the strength to do the hard thing, then it is my duty to find the strength to bear witness to it. You despise the flesh, and become iron. I tell myself that I must do the same. You are models, sergeant, for the mortals who serve you and follow you. We are not as powerful, nor as resilient. But we can aspire to be better than we are, because *you* are better than we are.'

She paused again, and was silent for so long that Galba began to think she had said her piece. But then she spoke, and he could hear each word chosen with care. 'This is a difficult time. The Iron Hands are…'

'We have suffered a defeat, mistress,' Galba said. 'Do not disguise the truth.'

'But you are not *defeated*. And you must not be.'

'It seems to me that you wish to turn away from something you fear would have the best of us. Closing one's eyes to the enemy is not a defence, and it does not speak well of your faith in us.'

'I do not think that is what I am doing. I believe I am acting for the sake of reason and light. What happened on the bridge was an eruption of the irrational. To investigate its depths invites the sleep of reason. One does not engage in a dialogue with insanity, just as one does not accept a tainted people into the Imperium's embrace. What is called for is quarantine. And then excision. Do you understand?'

'I think I do,' he said. 'But are you sure this fine reasoning isn't being shaped by your fear?'

'No,' she answered very quietly. 'I am not sure.'

The jungle became more and more dense the further the legionaries descended the slope. They hacked through the choking vegetation with chainswords. Sometimes, all trace of a path was swallowed up, and a new trail was created with the flamers. Vines and moss burned where touched directly by the promethium, but the humidity was so high that the fires died out within seconds. Galba chafed against the slow progress. He resented any march whose momentum bled away, but one where the only enemy was the landscape was galling. The rest of the reconnaissance force snaked away before him, black-and-steeldust-grey vanishing into the emerald gloom. It was impossible to see more than a dozen metres ahead through the undergrowth. The moss became even thicker. It was so yielding, and went down so far, it was like tramping over deep snow. Galba was startled when one leg sank almost to the knee. His boot rested on a thick root. It felt disconcertingly like standing on a muscle. He hauled himself out of the depression and found firmer ground.

His vox-bead crackled. *'Clearing ahead,'* Atticus reported. *'Auspex indicates multiple large contacts.'*

Galba and his squad moved forwards with Erephren. Atticus was waiting for them where the path opened into the clearing. The other legionaries had spread out to either side, forming once more the defensive wall they had established at the landing site. 'What is our course?' he asked Erephren.

'Straight ahead.'

'That is what I thought.'

The clearing was a rough circle about a kilometre in diameter. A small stream ran through the centre, crossing the path of the advance. Gathered not far from it was a large group of quadruped

saurians. Galba guessed their numbers at a hundred. They stood
about three metres high at the shoulder, and were about twice that
in length. Their tails stopped just short of the ground, and ended
in twin bony hooks. Rows of forward-curving spikes covered their
backs. Their legs were thick, massive trunks, evolved to support
weight, not run. Their heads were down, turned away from the
Space Marines.

'A species of grox, do you think?' Galba asked.

'They appear to be grazing.' Khi'dem and his pariahs had arrived.

'Grazing on what?' Ptero pointed out. The ground had been trampled into hard clay.

Under the stink of the massive animals, Galba caught the other
stench. 'There's blood there,' he said. 'Lots of it.'

'Rid my sight of them,' Atticus ordered.

Even as he spoke, the animals caught the scent of the intruders.
They turned from the carcasses they had been devouring. Their
heads were massive, boxy, with enormous jaws like power claws.
They roared, revealing teeth so jagged and narrow, they seemed
to be the weapons of a torturer instead of the tools of a predator.

'They should be herbivores,' Ptero said, and Galba thought he
heard awe in the Raven Guard's voice.

Galba raised his bolter and took aim. 'What do you mean?'

'The shape of their bodies, their heads. How can they be effective
predators? They must be too slow.'

The herd charged. The earth shook. 'They seem to be managing,'
Galba said, and opened fire.

The line of Iron Hands unleashed a continuous barrage of bolter
fire into the saurians. The mass-reactive rounds punched into the
hide of the beasts and blew out chunks of flesh and bone. Roars
became shrieks of agonised rage. The leading monsters collapsed
with the thunder of granite. Galba slammed half a dozen shots into
the forelegs of his target. The saurian's joints exploded, severing

the limbs in two. The animal smashed to the ground, rolling and howling. Two others lost interest in the Space Marines and set upon their fallen kin. They tore open its exposed belly with claws and teeth. Within moments, they were covered in fratricidal gore. Their victim was gutted, flaps of skin like fallen sails on either side

of its torso. It was still alive, its stumps twitching, hind legs flailing. It was a keening, writhing mass of butchered meat.

A dozen saurians downed. Half again as many fighting over their corpses. And still the avalanche with teeth came on, its momentum unchecked.

Unblinking, the Space Marines kept firing. More of the predators fell, the shorter range making the wounds even more catastrophic. The clearing became a giant's abattoir. The stench of blood filled Galba's nostrils. It was hot, clammy and suffocating, a sweat-slicked fist. It was also the smell of falling enemies, the first kills the legionaries of the *Veritas Ferrum* had claimed since Isstvan V. A low, vibrating rumble came to Galba's ears over the shattering roar of the saurian assault, and it was a moment before he realised he was hearing his own growls. They were the expression of his fury at betrayal, and they were the primitive satisfaction that came with the release of slaughter. Each recoil of his bolter was another blow struck at the humiliation that had been visited upon the X Legion.

The saurians fell, and fell, and fell. Their numbers were cut in half in the time it took them to close with the Iron Hands. They were still an avalanche. And now they hit.

'Flank and crush!' Atticus commanded in the final seconds before impact. The legionaries parted to the left and right, armoured might sprinting up the sides of the herd, and turning to catch the animals in a crossfire. They moved with speed and precision. They were the individual gears of a terrible mechanism, jaws of ceramite and steel that would rend all the flesh that passed between them.

But the saurians were fast, too. The leading beast scooped its head down and snatched one of Darras's men up in its maw. It bit down, and ceramite cracked like bone. Galba heard the cry of the legionary over the company vox-channel. It was a howl of outrage like those of the beasts, dragged from a perfect killer. The saurian bit harder. This time the snapping was bone. The lower half of the Space Marine fell to the ground. The reptile raised its head and choked the legionary's head and upper torso down its gullet.

Atticus had not been close enough to aid the fallen man, but he was the first to reach his killer. Still pouring fire into the rampaging beasts, Galba watched, out of the corner of his eye, as the Iron Hands captain leapt at the saurian. He had mag-locked his bolter and was wielding his chainaxe with both hands. Atticus said nothing as he attacked. He swung the axe at the animal's throat. His movements had a mechanical perfection and grace. The weapon was massive, but in his hands, it seemed to have the weight and speed of a rapier. Its snarling head chewed through the monster's hide. Machine and animal shrieked, one in high gear, the other grasped by death's pain. A waterfall of vitae burst from the saurian's neck, slicking Atticus from head to toe. The animal's head lolled, half-severed. The body remained standing for a full five seconds after it had died. Then it fell over.

The Iron Hands pressed in, constricting the herd between walls of fire. The mortification they wrought on the flesh at last took its toll. The landscape turned into a panorama of bleeding meat and splintered bone. Their charge broken, the saurians circled in confusion and pain, lashing out at each other as well as the Space Marines.

One lunged clear of the pack, bulk and momentum propelling it through Galba's bolter-rounds. Galba shoved Erephren further back. Blood pouring from craters in its body, the saurian smashed into him, knocking him onto his back. A massive paw pressed against his chest and crushed him into the clay. His bolter landed a hand's width away. It might as well have been the next continent over.

Erephren could have reached down for it, but she did not know it was there, and she took more steps back from the slavering roars.

The saurian's rasping, foetid breath washed over Galba. The jaws opened wide, a cave coming to engulf his head. He lashed out with his fist, striking the beast's lower jaw, shattering it, sending shards of teeth into its palate. The saurian shrieked and staggered to the side. Galba rolled away, snatched his bolter and came up firing. The reptile's head exploded.

After that, combat ended, replaced by simple butcher's work as the last of the saurians were cut down. Then it was done, the final *krump* of the bolters muffled by the surrounding jungle. The ground was slick with blood. The clay had turned to dark, clotted muck. This was no longer a clearing. It was a swamp. Galba rejoined Erephren, and the ground made sucking noises as they made their way over to where the legionaries were mustering.

Ptero was standing over one of the more intact carcasses, his helmet angled down as he stared at the creature. 'It's dead,' Galba said. 'I shouldn't let it trouble you any further.'

'But you must admit this is all wrong,' the Raven Guard insisted. 'These animals are built like herbivores. You can see that, can't you?'

'Yes, but they aren't herbivores, and there's an end to the matter.'

'I disagree, brother. We would be wrong to dismiss this aberration as insignificant, when this is what we must fight.'

'And what do you call this aberration, then?' Darras called. He was standing a few metres closer to the upslope side of the clearing. He, too, was staring downwards, but not at a carcass.

'What is it?' Galba asked.

'Look at the blood.'

Galba did. There were currents in the puddles. The blood was draining away.

It was flowing *uphill*.

'Captain,' Galba voxed, 'there is something drawing the–'

An earth tremor cut him off. It was shallow but widespread. It was like the movement of muscle beneath skin. Galba flashed on what he had stepped on in the deep moss. He grabbed Erephren by the arm. 'Quickly,' he hissed, and he began to run. He already knew that what was coming could not be fought. Ahead of them, the other squads were already moving at forced march speed out of the clearing.

The ground erupted. For a moment, Galba thought tentacles were bursting from the clay. Then he saw that they were roots. Thick as his arm, dozens of metres long, they tangled like a net, and reached out like talons. Clods of earth rained back down as the root system twisted and flexed, blind serpents seeking prey. A tendril struck one of Khi'dem's Salamanders. It coiled around his arm. The roots whipped to the legionary's location. In moments, he was cocooned and immobilised. He fell. Khi'dem and another of the Salamanders tore at the roots, but more came faster.

Galba hesitated. The rest of the Salamanders were rushing to help, but he was closer. He cursed, then left Erephren with the rest of his squad. 'Keep her safe,' he said to Vektus, his Apothecary, and ran back.

Khi'dem's other squadmate was caught now, too. A root looped around Khi'dem's gauntlet, but he yanked and tore the tendril, then sidestepped the others that came hunting for him.

Galba revved his chainsword and turned its teeth against the roots enveloping the first victim. As he did, Atticus's voice crackled over the vox-channel. *'Leave them.'*

'Brother-captain?'

'Now.'

He hesitated, the first of the monstrous roots just beginning to part beneath his blade. And then the entire spiral around the Salamander contracted with a jerk. The movement was so violent that Galba stumbled back a step. Blood, under immense pressure, spurted from between the coils of the roots. It was as if a fist had crushed an egg. A second later, as the other Salamanders reached his position, the other cocoon underwent the same traumatic constriction. More blood, an aggressive spray, and nothing more than a brief grunt of terminal pain from the legionary as a force of unimaginable pressure smashed ceramite to bits and a body to pulp. The root system twitched and thrummed. It was feeding, and Galba had the ghastly impression of satisfaction radiating from the vegetation.

And then the thing being fed by the roots invaded. It rushed in from the upslope tree line. First there was green flesh racing along the roots, but this was only a harbinger. Behind it came a green wave, a writhing tide three metres high. It was the moss, Galba saw, swollen with blood and frenzied with the thirst for more. It was growing, spreading like a plague, but with the speed and relentless advance of a storm surge. It was also moving, dragged forwards by the tangling, swelling roots.

It was hunger given being. It wanted the world.

THREE

Six seconds
Unnatural selection
The call in the wild

FEWER THAN FIVE seconds had elapsed since Atticus's order. Galba's delay was already unforgivable. It might yet be fatal. There was nothing to shoot here, nothing to stab, nothing to fight. Perhaps the moss could burn, and two of the Salamanders were bringing flamers to bear. But the ravening moss was a wall as wide as the clearing. It would take a heavy flamer mounted on a Land Raider to stop it.

'Leave it!' Galba yelled.

Another second passed. He saw the frustrated rage in Khi'dem's posture. The idea of flight from so mindless a foe, and with the death of battle-brothers unavenged, was obscene. But any other action was insane.

'Retreat, brothers,' Khi'dem voxed, and every toxic syllable was choked with bitterness.

They ran, and Galba shared the Salamanders' fury. They were Legiones Astartes, and retreat was unthinkable, but they ran, and behind them, an emerald storm raged. The wave grew higher yet.

A shadow filled the clearing. It stretched over the jungle ahead. The sound was more terrible than all the predator roars that had preceded it. It was the sibilant, monster exhalation, a *hhhhsssssssiiiiih-hhhhhhhh* of a hurricane-tossed forest, but there was no wind. The air moved, though. There was the breath of a monster, a displacement caused by the march of the jungle floor itself. Immensity *heaved*, and there was eagerness – a blind, mindless, but all-consuming desire, and it reached forwards to smash all flesh and smother all hope. It was called by blood, and it had come, unquenchable, in answer.

The ground rippled beneath Galba's feet as he left the clearing. He pounded down the slope, hoping the trees would slow the tide of moss, but wondering how large the growth truly was, and whether they were all merely running into its enveloping embrace. The vox chatter coming from the rest of the forces was a chorus of over-lapping urgency, but there were no calls of casualties or struggle.

'*Your position, Sergeant Galba?*' came Atticus again, the bionic voice as cold and precise as ever, but its rasp somehow encoding a sharp edge of rage.

'Approaching rapidly, captain. Can you see what is behind us?'

'*Enough of it. We will continue moving at speed. Catch up.*'

They kept running. The way forward was made easier by the passage of the others. Brush was trampled, vines and low-hanging branches chopped away. There was moss here, but it was dormant. The million tiny deaths that were the constant reality of a jungle were not enough to rouse it into frenzy. And now Galba heard the green wave crash into the trees. It was the sound of a massive surf and heavy rock, soft with bodies, strong with serpents. He pictured the moss flowing between the gigantic trunks, the tide turning into a thirsting stream. The hissing, rustling and snapping pursued. But the tremors in the ground diminished. They were putting distance between themselves and the hunger. Its blood-fuelled run was slowing.

Then came the fall once more into quiescence. There could be no true silence in the jungle. There was the perpetual whine of insects. Galba had seen no birds yet, but he could hear the distant snarls and shrieks of hunters and prey. There was the rustle of the unseen. But when the pursuit ceased, the calm that descended was as oppressive as lead.

The hunger subsided back into the earth, unsatisfied. The knowledge of its existence spread over the land. Everywhere Galba looked now, he saw the potential for its re-emergence. He thought with regret of the lethality of Medusa. He longed for the purity of its cold indifference. Pythos was unclean. It was anything but indifferent. It was desire at its most naked and inchoate. Such obscenity of the organic deserved but one thing: flame.

He rejoined the other squads at the bottom of the slope. Underbrush and moss had been burned away. There was nothing but ash between the trees here, a space in the jungle carved on the Iron Hands' terms. There was a chance now to regroup.

Atticus was waiting at the end of the path. Galba wondered again how absolute stillness could be so expressive. As they approached, the captain pivoted on one foot, as if he were the steel door of a fortress gate opening. He was, Galba thought, formidable enough to be one. He was a colossus of war, a being no more to be moved by thoughts of mercy than a Fellblade tank. Those who passed him did so only on his sufferance. Knowing what was coming, Galba slowed down, letting the Salamanders go first. Khi'dem nodded briefly to the Iron Hands' commander. Atticus made no response. Galba drew abreast with him and stopped. He opened a private vox-channel. 'Captain,' he said.

'Sergeant.' No *brother*. And then silence. At least, Galba thought, he had responded on the same channel. Whatever was about to transpire, it would be between them alone.

The silence continued. Galba found himself counting the seconds.

He began to see a painful meaning in their number.

'Six seconds,' Atticus said. 'That is a noticeable period of time, is it not?'

'Yes, it is.'

'When I issue an order, I do not simply expect immediate compliance. I *demand* it.'

'Yes, my lord.'

'Is there anything I have said that is less than clear? Less than precise? Open to *interpretation*?'

The last word was especially damning. Interpretation and all the other luxuries of artistic contemplation were the domain of the Emperor's Children. What had been the subject of playful banter and fraternal jests had, since the Callinedes betrayal, become a symptom of corruption. Interpretation and lies were the same thing. That which had more than one unarguable meaning had clearly been created with deception at its heart.

'No, brother-captain,' Galba replied. 'You are being very clear.'

Atticus turned to go. 'I do not have the time or resources to waste on disciplinary action,' he said. 'But do not fail me again.' The tenor of the mechanical voice was clear. Galba was not being given a second chance. He was being given an ultimatum.

'I shall not.'

Atticus looked back at him. 'I am not in the habit of explaining my orders.'

Galba was taken aback. 'Nor should you be, my lord.'

'I shall, however, seek clarity from *you* on one point. You believe, do you not, that I commanded you to abandon the Salamanders to their fate. You believe that I was motivated by spite, rather than strategy.'

'No, brother-captain.' He was shaking his head, horrified. 'I believe nothing of the kind.'

'Then why did you hesitate?'

He should have had an answer. He should have had a reason. He should not have met the question with ghastly silence. Galba felt a void gape in his chest, an abyss in which might lurk the most pernicious doubt, and into which he was refusing to gaze. Yet Atticus was forcing him up to its edge. The awful seconds ticked away once more, and Galba had no answer to give. Instead, his captain's toxic questions bred others, just as poisonous.

Galba looked at the legionary that stood before him, at the being who had exterminated his flesh to the point that there was very little to distinguish the armour from the form beneath it. He thought about that one human eye that still gazed from the metal skull, and it seemed to him, in this moment, that Atticus's remaining concessions to humanity were nothing more than expressions of scorn. Worming its way out of the dark was a deep question, never articulated before, but expressed perhaps in the moderation of his own bionic enhancements. If the full rejection of the flesh was the goal, why had Ferrus Manus never completed that journey? The primarch's silver-metal arms had been the limit of his metamorphosis. What did it mean that Atticus had gone so much further?

Six seconds. Galba blinked. He rejected the absurdity of this train of thought. If he continued to follow it, he would be brought to doubt the most fundamental tenets of the Iron Hands. And he did not doubt them. If anything, the disgusting, chaotic explosion of the organic he had just witnessed only reinforced the sane and ordered virtues of the machine. As rationality returned to him, he felt his answer come to him. It was a simple admission of shame.

But before he could express it, Atticus spoke again. 'Did you accomplish anything in your delay? Was a single warrior, of whatever Legion, saved?'

'No, my lord.'

'What purpose was served by anyone remaining on that field for another six seconds?'

'None.'

'And what would have been the result if Mistress Erephren had come to harm as a result of your choices?'

'Disaster.' He did not try to exculpate himself with the sorry excuse that he had confided her safety to the care of a subordinate. He sought no forgiveness for his past actions. He would seek redemption in his future ones.

Atticus nodded with the smooth up-and-down motion of a turret. 'None,' he repeated. 'I feel no great warmth for our brothers from the other Legions, Galba. But I act for the Emperor. *Always*. And what I command is what I believe will bring us victory. *Always*. Am I clear?'

'Yes, brother-captain.'

'Good. Then let us see what Mistress Erephren can tell us next about our quest through this obscenity.'

The astropath was standing with Vektus. 'Our thanks, brother,' Atticus said.

'My duty, brother-captain,' Vektus said, pleased, and withdrew.

Galba was grateful for Atticus's implication that Vektus had been acting under orders flowing down a unified chain of command. The humane gesture in the captain's choice of words surprised him, and his surprise shamed him. He hurled his doubts back into the pit, and declared it sealed.

Erephren's posture was as rigid as ever, but strain had etched deeper furrows into her brow. A narrow trickle of blood fell from her left eye. 'We are close,' she said. Her voice was flat. It was not weak, but it was diminished, as though her presence were an illusion, and she was calling to them from a great distance.

'The warp is taking you from us,' Atticus said.

'It is attempting to,' she agreed. 'But it will not succeed. Have no fear, captain.' She smiled, looking like an ancient icon of death. 'But then, you don't, do you?'

'I have full confidence in your strength, mistress,' Atticus replied, the embodiment of metal addressing the triumph of determination over the flesh. 'Show us the way.'

She pointed, and Atticus led the way forwards. Due east still, deeper into the jungle. The ground was level. There were no features to distinguish this direction from any other. The trees, even more dense than on the slope, surrounded the Iron Hands in a green prison.

'*Brother Galba,*' Khi'dem voxed. '*I know the help you tried to give us came at a cost.*'

Galba did not answer. He was not interested. The field of blood and green was behind him.

'*I would have you know,*' Khi'dem continued, '*that though your orders were correct, your actions were, too.*' Then he clicked off, sparing the Iron Hands legionary the need to respond.

Galba wanted to deny Khi'dem's assertion. He wanted to regard what he had done as a lingering weakness of the flesh, one that he must, in time, shed with all the others.

But he did not.

'I'M SORRY WE were not close enough to help,' Ptero said.

He and Khi'dem were marching together. Their two squads followed behind. Ptero held no official rank over his fellows. But he was a veteran, and in the chaos of Isstvan, his greater experience had made the difference in saving even a few of his battle-brothers. Unit cohesion demanded leadership, and the survivors had deferred to him. Khi'dem wondered if the weight of Ptero's new responsibility dragged at his shoulder in the same way as his own rank did. To be a sergeant of such a reduced squad was a constant reminder of failure.

He shook his head. 'No help was possible,' he told Ptero. 'We should have retreated more quickly, but…' He moved his hand in a gesture of tired frustration.

'No one saw that coming, brother.'

'That moss, perhaps not, but you sensed something was wrong. Those beasts disturbed you.'

'They did,' the Raven Guard agreed. 'Those animals made no sense. Everything about them, from their herding instinct to their build, announced them as plant-eaters.'

'Apart from the fact that they were not.'

'Exactly. Our experience of this planet's life is still limited, but have you noticed the pattern?'

Khi'dem saw where he was heading. 'Everything is carnivorous.'

'Even the plants.'

'That should not be sustainable.' He thought about the punishing geological cycles on Nocturne, and of how tenuous life's grip was on his home world. Nocturne boasted many dangerous species, but there was also a balance between predator and prey. Without it, Nocturne would have no ecosystem at all.

'It's worse than that,' Ptero said. His helmet turned to face Khi'dem. 'How did this come to be?'

The implication was obvious. 'Not through natural processes.'

'No.'

'You think we might have a sentient enemy on Pythos?'

Ptero had returned his gaze to the jungle. Khi'dem could almost see the wheels turning in the tactician's mind as he scanned for threats. 'I do not know,' Ptero said. 'Our information is suggestive enough for concern, but too incomplete to be of use. The Iron Hands found no sign of a civilisation, or even of its ruins, so that is encouraging. But it is not conclusive.'

The land began to rise again. The slope was far more gentle than the descent from the promontory had been. It was consistent, though. The elevation increased step by step. The line of Space Marines detoured around a massive fern, its trunk thick as a flagship's cannon. Its enormous fronds hung low over their heads.

They moved back and forth, their blades passing over each other, creating shifting, interlocking patterns. They were the hands of a mesmerist, summoning the gaze, luring the mind. Ptero slashed at them with his lightning claws.

'Dangerous?' Khi'dem asked, watching green shreds flutter to the ground.

'Perhaps,' Ptero answered. He gave the trunk a parting gouge as they passed.

'You are frustrated, brother.'

'I am.'

'You doubt the wisdom of this mission?'

Ptero's sigh was a crackle of static over the vox. 'I hope it succeeds. The potential for valuable intelligence is great, and given the loss we have suffered, we have very few credible means of striking back open to us.'

'But?'

'I am troubled by what we are fighting here. The hostility of this planet is something more than feral. There is an enemy here, but I do not know how to fight it.'

'Neither do I.' The combat philosophies of the Salamanders and the Raven Guard were poles apart. Neither the unbreakable line nor the lightning strike would serve here, though. When the land itself was hostile, there was no ground to hold, and no terrain to exploit.

As the land continued its slow rise, the jungle unveiled variations in its character. The legionaries passed through areas where the trees had been toppled. Some had been uprooted. The trunks of many others had been snapped in two, or had their top halves sheared away. Khi'dem saw a cluster of conifers that looked as if they had been flattened into splinters, and at least one tree suspended by the branches of others a good ten metres off the ground, as if it had flown there. The clouds were dark, angry bruises visible through the ragged wound in the canopy.

The slope levelled off. The terrain was flat for several hundred metres, then began a descent as gradual as the ascent had been. They had been moving, Khi'dem realised, over a low plateau, its features rounded by erosion and accumulated vegetation. They had descended, he judged, about two-thirds of the way back towards the jungle floor when Atticus spoke on the open vox-channel. '*Mistress Erephren says we are very close*,' he said.

And Ptero paused, head cocked, and said, 'We are being hunted.'

GALBA COULD SEE the sky again. He could also hear the pound of surf. They were less than a kilometre from the coast. The trees ahead were dead. Their branches tangled with each other, creating a web of talons. Light filtered down from above, broken into harsh fragments, like stained glass in a cathedral of predation. The trunks were more spread out here, and there was no underbrush. The ground was covered in desiccated vegetable matter, so brittle it turned to dust under the tread of the legionaries. But then, about fifty metres ahead, there was a cluster of trees that had grown together so closely, they formed a wall. They were dead, too. They were the skeletons of giants, pressing in against each other to hide the secret that had killed them.

Erephren had been walking faster during the last few minutes. Her face was etched by canyons of exhaustion. Her skin, already a bleached, unhealthy pale, had turned the grey of crumbling bones. But she moved as if hauled forward by a terrible gravitational force. When Galba spoke to her, her answers were brief, distracted. It seemed to him that her consciousness had already reached their destination, and now her body was hurrying to catch up.

There was a strip of open ground just before the tree cluster. Atticus ordered a stop at its border. Galba had to restrain Erephren from charging across.

'It's there,' she gasped, pointing and reaching. The empty orbs of her eyes were fixed on the trees. 'I have to be there.'

'You will,' said Atticus. 'Once I know what those trees conceal.' He turned to Camnus, the Techmarine. 'Auspex?'

'Nothing organic, brother-captain. Nothing sensible, either.'

Then Galba was hearing from Ptero. '*Sir,*' the sergeant said. '*We have an attack approaching from the rear lines. Multiple large contacts, moving to surround.*'

'Confirmed!' said Camnus. 'Closing in from downslope as well.'

Atticus cursed. 'Darras, take those trees down. The rest of us, testudo formation.' He pointed at Erephren. 'You will be in the centre, and you will find the strength to resist the call, or you will be of no use to this Legion.' He stood in front of her as he spoke, between her and her goal. Galba knew that Erephren could see neither Atticus nor the trees, but she reacted as if she could. Her near-madness diminished, the drive forwards breaking like surf against the immovable thing of war before her.

'So ordered,' she responded.

Darras charged forwards with a demolitions team. While they set explosive charges, the other squads came together in a tight box. They were shoulder to shoulder, guns facing out on all sides. There was no space between them. They were a mass of ceramite, a moving fortress, every bolter a turret to cut down any foe that dared approach. There was a moment of tension, brief but real, over the role of the Salamanders. Khi'dem made no request of Atticus. Even so, with a curt nod, the captain of the Iron Hands indicated they should join the formation. The Raven Guard preferred speed and flexibility, and remained a group apart, moving in parallel with the main force.

In the few seconds that had passed since the warning had been given, the approaching enemy had come close enough to be heard. Snarls echoed in the green darkness. Branches snapped before the passage of heavy bodies. The formation began its advance across the open area to the cluster.

'Darras,' Atticus said. 'Status?'

'At your command.'

'Do it.'

A series of explosions blew apart the bases of the trunks. The trees wavered, then, with deafening cracks, pulled away from each other's embrace and fell. They came down like the hatches of an immense drop pod. From his position on the right flank, Galba watched their descent, not worried that they would fall on the formation. Darras was a master of the physics of demolition. The ground shuddered with the impact of the huge trunks on either side of the legionaries.

The trees had concealed a column of black stone. The colour was deep as obsidian, but there was no sheen, no reflection. It seemed to absorb light, spreading a halo of shadows. It was twisted, curving away from the vertical as it reared up like a striking serpent. Its peak was split into three hook shapes, like an open talon. Its surface was cracked and lined, and it seemed to Galba that there was a pattern there to see. But his gaze kept slipping away. He could not focus on a single spot on the column. At first glance, he had assumed the structure was artificial, but there was also a suggestion of *flow* to the rock, as if it had erupted molten from the earth and cooled into this shape. His gut told him that somehow both possibilities were wrong and correct.

The Iron Hands were only a few metres from the column when the hunters arrived. They emerged from the jungle on all sides. They hesitated for a moment, sniffing the air and staring at their prey, choosing the angle of their attack.

'Brother Ptero,' Galba voxed, 'I hope you don't object to the biology of these beasts.'

'*No,*' Ptero replied. '*Those are flesh-eaters. Without a doubt.*'

They were bipedal saurians, perhaps eight metres tall. For creatures that size, their build was surprisingly lithe. Their forearms were long, and ended in five-fingered hands whose thumbs were blade-shaped claws the size of chainswords. Their necks were long and sinuous, accounting for almost a third of their height. Their jaws, filled with gladius-sized teeth, hung open as they panted. They looked like they were smiling.

Galba counted twenty that were visible. He could hear more in the jungle behind the front lines. The individual merged into a single collective growl that resonated in Galba's chest. It was a carnivorous song, a choir of animal hate and eagerness. The saurians began to advance.

'Fire,' Atticus said. His rasp over the vox was just as predatory.

For the first few seconds, the transhuman hunters controlled the field. Their weapons tore the leading saurians apart, blasting heads, severing limbs and necks, shooting torsos to pieces. Then, with lethal agility, the reptiles retaliated. They could leap. The second line exploded from the tree cover, vaulting over the twitching carcasses of their fallen. Galba's shots were suddenly too low as a creature soared two metres above the ground, coming straight for him. It landed just in front of him, smashing into the ground with such force that the tremor almost knocked him from his feet.

The beast slashed at him with thumb-blades. He parried with his bolter. The saurian arched its neck over his defences and clamped its jaws over his head. He heard teeth shatter against ceramite, but he also felt others dig into his gorget, stabbing for his throat. He fired blind. The impact from the shells tore the monster away, knocking it back a step. Roaring pain and rage, its ribs visible through the holes in its torso, it lunged at him straight on. He crouched, firing up through the saurian's jaws, and blew out the top of its skull.

As he straightened, a glancing blow to his left made him stumble. Another reptile had landed full on the brother at his side. The beast was crushing the legionary, tonnes of bone and flesh smashing his armour open like an eggshell. Galba stitched fire up the beast's flank and through its neck. Its frenzy refused to let it die. Before it fell, it raked its claws through the body of its victim, ripping him open.

Other Iron Hands were slaughtered by the saurians, and the formation contracted, an ever-tighter fist. The warriors adjusted their fire. No longer taken by surprise by the agile leaping of the monsters, they killed more of them at a distance. Yet the saurians kept coming. The blood in the air was calling the hunting packs, and the numbers were growing.

The formation reached the column. 'Mistress Erephren,' Atticus said. 'Do what you must. Brothers, conserve your ammunition. Our journey is only half done.'

Galba switched to his chainsword. The battle turned into a melee. The saurians crowded in, fighting and clawing at each other for a chance at the prey. The Iron Hands were surrounded by a wall of hide and fangs and claws. Galba's chainsword whined, the blade biting through muscle and bone with every swing. It was impossible to miss, but the attacks were almost as hard to avoid. The blows rained down with massive animal fury.

The column was at his back now. He was no psyker, but he felt something emanating from the stone and seeping into his consciousness. It was vibration, it was heat, it was insinuation. For a moment, he thought he heard laughter, but then a drooling maw was filling his sight, and there was only roaring in his ears, and he answered with his own roars of war and of blade.

Over the vox came Erephren's gasp. Both hands on his chainsword, reptilian blood cascading over him, Galba kept his gaze forward, surviving second by second. But he knew that the astropath had touched the column. He felt her shock as a jagged cut in the uncanny presence of the stone. He heard grunts of surprise over the vox, and knew that the moment had resonated over the entire formation.

'Mistress Erephren?' Atticus said, the strain of combat coming through even his mechanical tones.

'*Yes, captain.*' Erephren's strain was different in kind and degree. Galba was astonished that she could speak at all. Her voice was brittle as ancient paper, faint as the shadow of hope, its mere existence an act of extraordinary will. '*We can go,*' she croaked. '*We* must *go.*'

'Bolters,' Atticus ordered. 'Fire at will.'

Galba brought the chainsword down in a lethal arc, gutting the saurian before him. He mag-locked the chainsword to his side and pulled up his bolter in a single fluid motion. He pulled the trigger at the same moment as his battle-brothers. The blast of point-blank mass-reactive shells hit the saurians like an artillery barrage. The animals screamed, the sound high and gurgling, and cut short. Carcasses blown wide open, they were propelled backwards into their oncoming kin.

'*Punch through,*' said Atticus.

The formation turned into a wedge. With the captain at the front, the Iron Hands and Salamanders broke the line of predators, a blunt arrowhead tearing through the barrier of raging flesh. The Raven Guard had been harrying the rear of the saurian packs, undermining their siege of the larger formation. Now they concentrated their attacks on the reptiles attacking from upslope. The saurians were caught between the two groups of legionaries, and the attack faltered. The wedge picked up speed. The weapons fire was continuous, and at last the numbers of saurians began to drop. No more packs were joining the hunt, and the survivors began to hang back.

By the time the legionaries reached the top of the plateau, the reptiles had given up the pursuit. They contented themselves with the corpses that surrounded the column. Galba could hear them snarl and squabble over the spoils. He knew there were many of their own kind for the reptiles to feast upon. He tried not to think about the other bodies left behind. But then he heard Vektus's low, steady cursing. The Apothecary was two men up from Galba's position.

'Not a one,' Vektus was saying. 'Not a solitary one recovered.' He was furious.

Galba winced. More losses the Iron Hands could not afford. More gene-seed gone forever, and so the future of the Legion impoverished by just that much. More brothers denied the most basic dignity in death.

And now he could not stop thinking about what was being devoured in the shadow of the column.

FOUR

Foothold
Nothing to fear
Synaesthesia

THE BASE WAS established at the landing site. It could only be approached by land from the east, but Atticus still ordered walls constructed along the entire perimeter of the promontory's level peak. Modular fortifications and housing were brought down by lighter from the *Veritas Ferrum*, along with the construction teams of Legion serfs. Reinforcements came too. By nightfall, a fortress had risen on Pythos. It was an iron riposte to the planet's savagery. If the jungle had tried to scour the Iron Hands from Pythos's surface, it had failed. They would be here for as long as they chose to be.

Erephren was aware of the stronghold coming into being around her. Though she could not see it, she felt its weight. She was responsible for the coming of the walls, the command post, the dormitorium, the supply depot and more. The base was, in no small measure, her creation. It was her quest that had driven the legionaries through the jungle, and that had exacted a heavy toll. It was her decision to have the base constructed here, rather than at the site of the column, and she was grateful to have been able to make that choice.

'Are you certain?' Atticus had asked her when they had returned to the landing site. 'We will take the land around the column, if you need that level of proximity.'

'Captain,' she had replied, 'that terrain is indefensible.' She was still horrified by the thought of the lives necessary to seize and hold that low-lying section of the jungle. She was terrified by the prospect of remaining that close to the column.

'There is no terrain that cannot be taken,' Atticus had said. 'If that is what is required, that is what we shall do.'

'No, the initial contact was enough, captain. This degree of proximity will suffice. I can do what must be done from here.'

Inside the command block, there was a small, windowless room, barely large enough for her astropath's throne. Here she sat, and as the construction carried on outside, she opened her mind's eye to the column, a few thousand metres in the distance.

She had not told Atticus what she had experienced when she touched the column. In that instant, the warp had unfolded before her like a sudden blossom. Revelation upon revelation had poured into her consciousness, vistas of madness and immensities of the impossible cascading over each other. Just before she had pulled away, she had caught a glimpse of things just over the horizon of her knowledge. *A palace, a fortress, a maze and a garden.* The impressions were ludicrous, she knew. They were merely her interpretation of formlessness, her mind's need for patterns imposing them where none existed, like seeing shapes in the clouds. That was all they were. They could be nothing else. Yet her terror at the prospect of their unveiling had jolted her hand away from the column.

She did not like to think about what she had witnessed, but she had no choice. It was the singularity nestled at the centre of her mind, and all her thoughts now circled it. She could not escape its pull, but she feared the annihilation of her self if she gave in to its spiralling fascination. That fear, she hoped, along with the physical distance, would give her the strength she needed to read the unfolding of the warp without disappearing into it. And read it she must, because she had caught a glimpse of something else in those moments of contact.

She had seen a fleet.

Night fell on Pythos, and was its own sort of predator. The cloud cover was thick, not to be pierced by star or moon, and so the darkness was complete. It was a smothering obscurity. Jerune Kanshell found it hard to breathe. The too-rich scents of the jungle, carried on a humidity he could almost touch, wrapped themselves around his head and squeezed. It took a real effort not to gasp. If he began that futile struggle for cleaner air, he would not be able to stop. He had already seen several of the other serfs who had come down with him succumbing to hitching, desperate gulps. They found no relief, and he could see panic growing in their eyes. So he kept his breathing steady.

The dark had other weapons, too. The sounds of the jungle seemed to grow louder. Kanshell had not been able to see more than a few metres into the trees when he had arrived in the daylight hours. The walls had been completed before twilight. His duties did not take him to the ramparts, so he no longer saw anything of the jungle, and had not for several hours. But when the last of the light in the sky had faded, the calls and cries of the land had grown in intensity and frequency. He was sure of it. He listened with dread as the overlapping snarls of perpetual war had taken on an awful kinship to a choir. Pythos was singing, and its song was murder.

The serf dormitorium was a large, rectangular structure near the northern wall. His construction shift done, he walked across the compound, his shadow a jagged, angular thing in the harsh arc lighting. He slowed as he approached the doorway. Agnes Tanaura was sitting on the ground beside it. She was staring up into the void of the sky. There was nothing beatific in her face tonight. She seemed worried.

She looked down and saw him. She must have noticed his reluctant pace, because she said, 'I'm not going to preach to you tonight, Jerune. Not here.'

'Worried you'll be caught?' He was not in a teasing mood. But the weight of the night was oppressive, the cries of the jungle a snapping of jaws against his psyche. Taunting Tanaura was nothing more than bravado.

'No,' she answered, not rising to his bait. Either she saw through it, or she did not care. 'I need all my faith for myself tonight,' she said. 'I'm sorry.' She was genuinely ashamed.

'Don't be,' he said, feeling the flush of his own shame. 'Be strong,' he said, not sure why he did so, but answering a need for solidarity. Confused, nervous, he avoided looking at her as he entered the barracks. The interior was a single open space filled with rows of bunks stacked five high. Kanshell made his way between them, following the dim lumen-strips on the floor to his billet towards the rear. Most of the others were occupied. The dormitorium was quiet, and the silence made his skin crawl. There was no snoring. Every serf he passed was lying still, fully awake. The breathing he heard was shallow, hesitant. He was surrounded by people who were watchful, waiting, straining to hear. The effort was contagious. When he climbed a ladder to his top bunk and lay down, he too began to listen.

He was listening for something he did not want to hear. He did not know what it would be. It was something beyond the growls of beasts. It was something that coiled behind the night. Reality was a membrane. It was too thin, and stretching thinner as it fought to contain what pressed against it.

He pressed his palms against his eyes. Where was he finding these ideas? They were nonsense. They were relics of a dark, superstitious age. They had no place in the enlightened Imperium. Tanaura and her cronies could preach what they wanted about divinity, but he knew the Imperial Truth, and so he also knew what it had to say about these irrational terrors.

'That's enough,' he whispered, barely loud enough to hear his own words. 'Enough, enough, enough.' The words were brittle. They crumbled like charred paper, flaking into ash. When they were gone, the false silence in the dark slithered closer. He held himself rigid, tendons popping with the effort of denial. He tried to whisper again. He tried to say, 'There is nothing there.' The words died before he could speak them. What if they prevented him from hearing what he feared to hear? What if he did not know it was upon him?

On all sides were row upon row of men and women lying just as still, just as terrified as he was. Anticipation was turning into madness. Within minutes of lying down, Kanshell was no longer trying to talk himself out of his fear. He was consumed by it. And still he heard nothing and saw nothing.

Nothing to hear. Nothing to see. Nothing to fear. Nothing, nothing, nothing. But the nothing was fragile. It would take little to shatter it. And when that happened, what would come? His imagination ran riot at the thought. It could not conjure an answer, so it subjected him to an avalanche of shapeless terrors, malformed deaths and creeping, dreadful intangibility. He was suffocating. His hands curled into claws. He wanted to rip the air so he could breathe again. His chest began to hitch with silent gasps. His mouth opened wide. The scream was silent. Sound was forbidden, because of what it might conceal. And still there was nothing.

Until, like insects at the edge of his vision, there was something.

DARRAS SAW KHI'DEM heading towards the rampart. He moved forwards to intercept. 'Are you looking for something, son of Vulkan?' he asked. He congratulated himself on keeping his tone polite, but firm. He had not given in to his instinct to open with hostilities. He walked a few steps ahead of the other Space Marine and then stopped, facing him.

Khi'dem did not force the issue. He stopped too. 'I was going to walk along the wall,' he said.

'You think we might have been negligent in our defences?'

'Not at all.'

'Then I don't see why this tour of yours would be necessary.'

'Are you forbidding me access?' Khi'dem asked.

Darras was impressed in spite of himself. The Salamander had every right to be in a blind rage, but he was calm. The question sounded more like an honest enquiry than a challenge. 'No,' he said. 'But I am suggesting you go elsewhere.'

'Why?'

'Our captain is up there. So is Brother-Sergeant Galba.'

'I see.'

'Do you? Do you understand the harm you do Galba in our captain's eyes whenever you are seen in the sergeant's presence?'

'Ah,' said Khi'dem. 'I think I do now. Thank you for speaking to me, Sergeant Darras. I will do as you suggest.'

Darras waited while Khi'dem walked away. *Go on*, he thought. *Make yourself useful and stay out of our way*. He could see the logic behind Galba's peacemaking efforts, but he saw nothing to be gained by them. There could be no relying on the Salamanders and the Raven Guard. Galba was giving in to an indulgence if he thought otherwise, one that could hurt his own reliability in the field.

Darras hoped he could make him see sense.

THE NIGHT TASTED wrong.

Galba stood on the eastern rampart of the base, watching the jungle. He had stood there for half an hour, trying to identify what was bothering him. It was more than the darkness that cloaked Pythos's carnivores. He realised what it was just as he became aware of a looming presence to his right. He turned to see his captain striding his way. Atticus was the rational embodied. What was not genhanced was bionic. His existence was the triumph of science. Illogical thought broke apart as he walked. Atticus demanded discipline of reason as well as strategy, and he would have both.

Even so, the night tasted wrong.

'Brother-sergeant,' Atticus greeted him.

'Captain.'

'You are watching for something. What is it?'

Galba chose his words carefully, and doing so was duty, not evasion. He would never dissemble from the captain. But nor would he be imprecise, and he was wrestling with a frustrating vagueness. 'I am not sure,' he said. 'There is a taste in the air that I cannot identify.'

'We are in a jungle, Sergeant Galba. Given the sheer abundance of life, some confusion of scents and tastes would hardly be surprising, even with our senses.'

He had not mentioned scents. 'You are experiencing something similar, captain?'

'Nothing I would not expect.' Atticus spoke without hesitation, as if this was something he had already debated on his own.

Galba hesitated, then decided he could not accept this explanation too readily. 'There is blood in the air,' he said.

'Of course there is. We have seen the feral nature of this planet.'

'But there is something underneath that taste,' Galba insisted, 'and I have never encountered it before.'

Atticus was silent for a moment. Then he said, 'Describe it.'

'I wish I could.' He closed his eyes and took a deep breath of the foetid night. He concentrated on the work of his neuroglottis as it analysed the odours at a near-molecular level. 'The taste makes no sense,' he said. 'It doesn't taste like anything.' He stopped. That was wrong. What was there beneath, *beyond* the blood, yet linked to it, *did* have a taste. It tasted of...

He staggered. He broke through the sensory camouflage and plunged into an abyss of impossibility. 'It tastes of shadow,' he gasped, and the shadows filled his throat. He coughed, trying to expel them. But they were known to him now, and he could not shed the knowledge.

'Brother-sergeant?' Atticus asked.

Galba could barely hear him. 'I smell whispers,' he said. He did not know if he had spoken aloud. The shadows and whispers were the whole world. They were a synaesthetic hell. Gagging on the wet, clinging smoke of the shadows, he could not see what cast them or discern their shape. Because he did not hear the whispers, he could not understand them. He sensed the contours of words, and the malevolent stench of a language that must never be understood by anything sane. Meaning hovered just outside his awareness. It had a shape, a shape that sounded like the laughter of prey and the scream of a star.

Atticus caught him by the arm as his knees began to buckle. A strange noise buzzed and echoed around him. It seemed to be coming from the captain himself. It kept repeating. After an age, Galba realised that it was his name he was hearing. He grabbed on to that handhold of rationality and used it to climb back to steady, logical ground. Reality became solid once more. His senses righted themselves. He straightened.

'I don't understand what has happened,' he said. 'I am not a psyker.' He disliked his defensive tone.

Atticus's remaining organic eye fixed him with a purposeful glare. 'Remember where we are,' he said. 'The barrier between reality and the warp is thin here. We cannot be surprised by effects caused by intrusions of the empyrean. It would be strange if we did not experience some kind of hallucination.'

'This was more than a hallucination. The whispers–'

Atticus cut him off. 'They were not whispers. That is how you interpreted what you experienced. I heard nothing.'

Because you chose not to listen, Galba thought. Then he pushed the thought away. Atticus was right. He was reacting as if he had never heard of the Imperial Truth. There had been no whispers. There had been no shadows under his tongue. Most importantly, there had been no brush with a malign intelligence. 'Neither did I,' he said, agreeing with the captain and finding that what he said was true. He had *heard* nothing.

Then someone started screaming.

FOR A MOMENT, Kanshell thought the screams were his own. His mouth was still wide open. He had his hands pressed against his ears, his eyes shut tight against the moving dark. But still he could sense the rustling flow of a million insects. He could feel the breath of lipless mouths shaping words of obscenity. So of course there was screaming.

But it was not his. His throat was locked tight by the terror of the almost-seen. He felt the visitation pass over him. It was no more substantial than a thought. Perhaps that was all it was. But an idea could be dangerous. It was thoughts and nothing more that had reduced him to paralysis. The thought ran a claw down his flesh. It scraped his heart with ice. And it was not his thought. It was not the thought of any human, yet it had come from something that knew the fears of men and women, knew their every shape and nuance and flavour, knew them as if it were forged of those very fears.

Kanshell's breath wheezed out of his taut throat with a tiny, high-pitched whine. The idea hovered over him for a moment, and then it moved on. He did not know where it had gone, only that it was no longer trying to tempt him to open his eyes and let the madness take hold.

But someone was looking, because someone was screaming. Someone had looked upon the thing that did not exist, except as a concept, and that had been enough. The voice was male. It was hitting registers more animal than human. The man shrieked without stopping for breath. Then Kanshell heard running feet.

The thought faded. With it went the fear. In its place came a shame that was almost welcome. He lowered his hands and opened his eyes. There was nothing lurking by the ceiling. The dormitorium was as it had been earlier, only now there was stirring in the bunks. The screaming bounced off the walls, tearing at Kanshell with its pain and horror. His shame forced him into action. He jumped down from his billet, landed awkwardly, and stumbled down the aisle. The screams were coming from the mess hall attached to the dormitorium. He ran for the doorway, racing ahead of the shame. His terror of nothing had put a lie to his faith in the Imperial Truth, and he would redeem himself by bringing comfort and reason to the tormented man.

As he reached the entrance to the mess hall, the quality of the screams changed. They became ragged. A terrible wet retching choked them off for a moment, and then they started up again, at a higher pitch. It sounded to Kanshell as if there were two voices now, the screams entwining in a choral helix of despair.

He burst though the plasteel door. Georg Paert stood in the centre of the hall with his back to Kanshell. He was alone. His shoulders were shaking. His arms were up, elbows out, as if his hands were at his face. Both screams were coming from him.

Kanshell made his way between the metal tables towards the enginarium serf. 'Georg?' he said, trying to keep his own voice steady and calm, yet loud enough for Paert to hear over his shrieks. As he drew near, he saw that Paert was standing in a spreading pool of blood. 'Georg?' he said again. Calm and purpose were deserting him. The terror was returning.

Paert turned around. Kanshell recoiled. The other serf had torn his own throat apart. Flesh and muscle hung like tattered curtains. Blood soaked Paert's tunic and hands. His mouth hung open, but no sound would ever come from it again.

Yet still there was screaming, still the two voices came from one man, and now the screams formed contrapuntal syllables: *MAAAAAAAA, DAAAAAAIIIL*. They created a single word, and the word was blood, and it was madness, and it was despair. And it was a prayer.

Paert fell to his knees, his life gushing from his body. He raised his hands to his eyes and plunged his fingers into them. He dug deeply and pulled, as if wrenching choice meat from a carcass. His hands full of jellied ruin, he collapsed.

Kanshell stepped backwards, his vision still filled with the worst horror, which had not been Paert's suicide. The worst horror latched on to his reason like a cancer.

He heard the tread of ceramite boots behind him, and he turned to see Galba and Atticus. The gods of reason had arrived too late. There would be no reassurance for him now. The awe he had always felt in their presence was drowned by the worst horror. He stared at the Iron Hands, and he gave words to the worst horror.

'His eyes,' he croaked. 'His eyes were screaming.'

FIVE

The prize
Hamartia
Perfection

'WE KNEW THERE would be hallucinations,' Atticus told his assembled officers. They were standing in the command module of the base. The chamber was a sparse one, reduced to the bare tactical. A vox system occupied one wall, and in the centre of the room was a circular hololith table. That was all. Atticus stood before the table. He had Rhydia Erephren at his side. The hololith projector was powered up, but Atticus had not turned the display on yet. He was disposing of a distraction first.

'We knew what would come,' Atticus went on, 'and it came. This system and this planet are dangerous for the weak-minded.'

'He means you,' Darras whispered to Galba. They were positioned near the module's outer wall.

Galba did not answer. He thought of the ruined corpse, and of the look of surpassing terror on Kanshell's face. It was a wonder that his serf was still sane.

'These are the risks and costs of this mission,' Atticus said. 'Pythos is hostile to flesh and to reason. These are the simple facts of this terrain. Its wildlife is dangerous, and the warp is close to the surface.'

'Did we lose many serfs?' Vektus asked.

'One dead,' Atticus told the Apothecary. 'Four others are demented, their prognosis uncertain. The one who died was unaccompanied when the suicidal fit came upon him. One of his fellows reached him too late. I have therefore issued a standing order forbidding any serf to be alone, for no matter how brief a period. Solitude is fertile ground for madness.'

Galba frowned. Atticus's response smacked of expediency rather than conviction. It was true that the dead serf had had some time alone. But Kanshell's account, to the extent that it was coherent, suggested that the victim had been in the dormitorium, far from alone, when reason had deserted him. Galba's senses still carried the traces of his own experience. He knew that Atticus's explanation for what had struck him was correct. There was no room, in the galaxy of the Emperor's singular vision, for any other possibility. He knew this. But he *felt* the contrary, and this irrational instinct troubled him. It had no place in a legionary of the Iron Hands. But it was powerful enough to assail him with questions he could not answer.

'There have been sacrifices,' said Atticus. 'There will be more. They will not be in vain.' He turned to the astropath. 'Enlighten us, Mistress Erephren.'

'I have been tracking a fleet,' she said. 'The ships belong to the Emperor's Children.'

The sound of hatred could be dead silence. Galba discovered that now. His doubts evaporated. He shared in the rage. Its purity burned away weakness. It forged unforgiving metal.

'Go on,' said Atticus. There was more than hate in those two syllables. There was eagerness. The captain of the *Veritas Ferrum* had prey in his crushing grasp.

'A smaller squadron has detached itself from the main group.

There are three ships. Their destination is here in the Demeter Sector. The Hamartia System.'

'Tell them the names of the ships,' Atticus said.

'The two escorts are the *Infinite Sublime* and the *Golden Mean*.
There is also a battle-barge, the *Callidora*.'

Galba's eyes widened. Beside him, Darras was a study in aston-
ishment. It was impossible that Erephren should know such
detailed information. Yet she spoke with unwavering authority.
And the *Callidora*... Now he truly understood the fire in Atticus's
organic eye. The *Veritas Ferrum* had followed the battle-barge on
joint missions between the III and X Legion. It was a ship all present knew well. It had once lit the void with the jewelled glow
of brotherhood.

It had fired upon them in the void war over Isstvan V.

'Do you know when they'll reach their destination?' Darras asked.

'I do.'

'We will be there first,' said Atticus.

'Captain,' Galba spoke up. 'My faith in the *Veritas Ferrum* is
unwavering. But it is wounded. It would be outnumbered...'

'And what madness would possess us to assault a battle-barge?'
Atticus finished for him.

'I would not have said madness.' Though he might have thought
it, and hoped to be proven wrong. He watched the captain closely.
Galba would have sworn the expressionless face was smiling.

'Brother-sergeant Galba is right to voice his doubts,' Atticus
announced to the assembled legionaries. 'Without the knowledge
Mistress Erephren has acquired, what I propose would be worse
than insanity. It would be criminal. But we know the enemy. We
know his disposition. We know where he will be and when. He
knows nothing of us. And he shall remain ignorant, until he feels
our blade in his hearts.'

✠ ✠ ✠

THE HAMARTIA SYSTEM was made for ambushes. Its only inhabited planet, and its innermost, was Tydeus. The forge world was a small, dense furnace of a place. Hab-domed manufactorae covered its surface like fungi. Beyond Tydeus was nothing but a series of gas giants. The largest, Polynices, was also the furthest from the star, and its gravitational force had a long reach. The outer bodies of the crowded scattered disc suffered under its tyranny. Orbits were wildly eccentric. Planetoids and chunks of frozen volatiles were in constant collision. The zone was a disordered web of shifting trajectories. For helmsmen and navigators, it was a foul place.

It was also the location of Hamartia's Mandeville point.

This was where ships travelling the empyrean would transition into the system. The point was a difficult one to negotiate. Many inexperienced pilots, and more than one veteran, had exited the warp only to drive their vessels into a chunk of ice the size of a city. No such accident could befall a ship of the Legiones Astartes, but even their crews had to proceed with caution. Their focus would be on the known natural hazards of the system. They would not, Atticus had said, be expecting, or be ready for, an attack. Not here, so deep within their own lines.

On the bridge of the *Veritas Ferrum*, Atticus stood in the command pulpit and revealed to his legionaries the mechanics of the coming war. Opaque shielding covered the forward oculus, shutting out the toxic sight of the empyrean as the strike cruiser travelled its currents, making for Hamartia. The warp was in storm. Turbulence and navigational anomalies were to be expected this close to the Maelstrom, but the degree of violence was unprecedented. There was also the disturbing news about the Astronomican. Locating it was difficult. Navigating by it was impossible. But Bhalif Strassny had found an alternative, and was guiding the *Veritas Ferrum* with assurance. The anomaly on Pythos was so strong, it was as powerful a beacon for the Demeter Sector as the Astronomican was for the galaxy.

The implications were dark. Atticus ignored them. Their contemplation would not help him with the mission.

Atticus touched the control panel before him, and the oculus acted as a giant screen, projecting the schematics of the *Callidora*, the *Infinite Sublime* and the *Golden Mean*. Camnus had retrieved the information from the massive databanks of the *Veritas*'s cogitators. The Iron Hands' prey appeared before them with every secret exposed. Camnus and his fellow Techmarines had analysed the schematics, and their work now displayed something more vital than secrets: weaknesses.

'There is where we will strike them,' Atticus said. 'The escorts must be eliminated in the opening moments of the operation. When we remove them from the battlefield, the *Callidora* will be ours.' He spoke in certainties. He had no doubts about this engagement. He did not pretend to himself that he was approaching it with dispassion. Though his tone was measured, there was a searing heat in his chest, and it had a name: *vengeance*. He wanted to find himself knee-deep in the blood of the Emperor's Children. Beneath his boots, he would hear the crunch of the skulls of those aesthetes. There would be nothing but fury in the war he was bringing to the traitors. But he had gone over the plan of attack with a cold, unforgiving eye for flaws. He exacted the same discipline from himself as he did from the men under his command.

He knew no plan was perfect.

He knew his primarch had gone down to defeat while consumed by the need for vengeance above all things.

He also knew that he would succeed. The data that Erephren had given him was so detailed, so precise, that only the worst fool could fail with it in hand. And this, too, Atticus knew: he was no fool.

He changed the display to a map of the region around Hamartia's Mandeville point. 'And this,' he said, 'is *how* we shall strike them.'

He could already taste the blood.

✠ ✠ ✠

THE EMPEROR'S CHILDREN squadron translated out of the warp a
full twenty-four hours after the *Veritas Ferrum* had reached the same
Mandeville point. There was no delay between the arrival of the
traitor forces and the launching of the Iron Hands' strike. With a
shriek of cancerous colours, a bleeding emanation from the immaterium where there had been only the void, there were three ships.
The sudden presence of their enormous masses triggered the minefield that had been waiting for them. The trap was primitive in its
simplicity. The usual configuration of a minefield was designed to
interdict a wide area with the risk of a lethal collision, the mines
a lurking possibility. But Atticus knew where his enemy would be.
His mines were not a barrier. They were his closing fist. The passive auspex of each mine reacted to the ships and the explosives
flew towards the monuments of iron and steel that had arrived in
their midst. They descended on the ships like swarms of terrible
insects. Their stings lit the void with dozens of flashes. Fireballs
rippled along the lengths of hulls.

The *Infinite Sublime* was hit by a cluster of mines amidships. Blast
built upon blast. The void shields collapsed, their energy sparking
over the ship like jagged aurora. The blows continued, punching
through the starboard plating, reaching into the core of the ship,
snapping its spine. The *Infinite Sublime*'s ammunition depots felt
the kiss of flame and erupted. The ship broke in half. It hung there
for a moment, its shape bisected but still distinct, the pride of its
spires and the challenge of its prow untouched, as if the memory
of centuries of victories would knit the vessel back together. Then
it was swallowed by its death, a raging, squalling newborn sun
bursting from the heart of its engines. Burning plasma bathed the
eternal night of Hamartia's cold frontier. It washed over the rest
of the squadron.

Flame followed the pressure wave, overwhelming the reeling
defences of the *Golden Mean*. The other escort ship had begun a

turn as soon as the mines had struck. It had been hit by almost as many as the *Infinite Sublime*, but they were less concentrated, spreading their wounds like a plague of boils over the full length of the ship's body. When the death cry of the *Infinite Sublime* hit it, the *Golden Mean* shuddered, and its engine flare died. Its turn continued, the movement clumsy and slow, the stagger of a wounded animal.

The stagger took it broadside before the sights of the waiting *Veritas Ferrum*. The strike cruiser announced its presence. Its lance turrets and batteries opened up. Energy beams shot across the void. They annihilated the *Golden Mean*'s weakening void shields. They cut the ship open, slicing through its plating. Then the shells arrived, delivering devastating blows of high explosives. The barrage was continuous. It was a judgement late in coming, an answer for the humiliation of Isstvan.

Hell came to the corridors of the escort. A wall of purging flame raced down their lengths, consuming legionary, helot and servitor. All were reduced to ash. The *Golden Mean* never returned fire. An iron fist smashed it into submission, into silence, into oblivion. Its death was not an exultation of fire. It was a fall to ruin. Within minutes, the only light on the ship was from the dying flames. A battered hulk sank into eternal night. It shed wreckage as it drifted off in a slow, tumbling spin, just another dead chunk of flotsam entering its wandering orbit around distant Hamartia.

That left the *Callidora*. The battle-barge was a leviathan. It was so covered in weaponry it resembled a spined creature of the oceans. But it was also a brilliant, crystalline city. It was a violet jewel, malevolent, illuminating the void with an arrogance of light. It was a celebration of excess. Its superabundance of guns was matched by a baroque profusion of ornamentation. The line between weapon and art was erased. Statues reached out to embrace the stars with arms that were cannons. Lances were incorporated into non-representational sculptures that resembled frozen explosions, or embodied the concepts of ecstasy, of extremity, of sensation.

The mines struck the *Callidora* too. The battle-barge rode out the attack. Its titanic silhouette shrugged off the damage. Four times larger than its escorts, twice the size of the *Veritas Ferrum*, it would not be humbled by such petty means. The Iron Hands vessel bombarded it, but that would not be enough, either. The *Callidora* could be hurt, but it could not be killed by the weaponry available to the *Veritas*. Not before its own retaliatory fire reduced the strike cruiser to scrap.

Atticus did not expect the mines or lance fire to kill his prey. He did not expect the battle-barge to be crippled. He did not even hope for a serious blow. He planned on a moment of blindness, of distraction. There was one way the forces of the weaker, smaller, battered *Veritas Ferrum* could kill the *Callidora*.

Decapitation.

At the moment of the squadron's translation, the *Veritas* launched another barrage. This one travelled more slowly. It was still some distance from its target as the death of the *Infinite Sublime* broke over the *Callidora*. It approached from the starboard side of the bow, in the lee of the battle-barge as the great ship was rocked by the incinerating wave. On the port side, the bristling spines were sheared away by the blast. Energy surged over the hull. The jewel flashed a greater brilliance, then flickered, menaced by eclipse. Its void shields did not die, but they faltered, creating the opening for Atticus's strike.

The swarm of projectiles closed with the *Callidora*. They were boarding torpedoes. Dozens. They crossed the void like metal sharks. They were the dark, blunt, direct violence against the shining, exuberant glory of the Emperor's Children. They were Atticus's message to the traitors who had once been the Iron Hands' closest brothers. They were justice, and they were vengeance, but they were also a lesson. He was about to repay humiliation with humiliation, and do so with interest. The traitors had triumphed on Isstvan V through the agency of surprise and vastly greater numbers. Atticus would show them the fatal truth that was the Iron Hands' way of war. It had none of the ostentation practiced by the Emperor's Children. It was not a display, but it was no less precise, no less finely crafted an art.

The *Callidora*'s long-distance ordnance roared in answer to the *Veritas Ferrum*. The strike cruiser began to take damage, but it was already in retreat. It maintained its attack, drawing the rage of the *Callidora*. The battle-barge pursued, bringing it closer to the rain of boarding torpedoes.

Bringing it within range of another move in Atticus's lesson.

The orbits of the scattered disc objects were a study in lethal chance and unpredictable intersections. Travel from the Mandeville point was dangerous for any ship until reaching the frontier cleared of debris by the immense gravity of Polynices. There were too many bodies, too many trajectories that might change through random collisions. There was always the risk of catastrophe.

Sometimes, risk could be turned into a certainty.

Wandering though the battlefield was a chunk of ice the size of a mountain. Of irregular shape, and several thousand metres wide, it was large enough to be a threat to ships, but it was also highly visible, even in this dark quarter, shining a dull blue-white in the cold light of the sun. Its journey was also angling it away from the void war. The *Callidora* passed it on the starboard side in pursuit of the *Veritas Ferrum*.

Aboard one of the leading torpedoes, Atticus looked through the forward viewing block. He saw the blinding amethyst of the *Callidora* put the dim pearl of the debris to shame. He thought, *Now*.

As if obeying the order, the fusion charges planted on the ice chunk went off. Searing light flashed. The explosion broke the body in half. One piece went spinning off into the black. The other was propelled towards the *Callidora*. The frozen fist was a third of the ship's size. The battle-barge's engines flared with the urgency of its manoeuvre. The bow lifted as the vessel tried to climb out of the threat's path. The starboard weapons were brought to bear, stabbing at the oncoming mountain with lance and cannon and torpedo. The ferocity of the bombardment punched craters into the ice and boiled the surface. Debris and vapour streamed off it in a tail. A ship would have been destroyed, its crew incinerated. But there was no crew, and this was a solid mass. Its course was unalterable. The *Callidora* did nothing except turn it into a comet.

The comet struck the bow. The hit was not direct, and the ship was strong. Even so, the ice crumpled the forward plating like parchment. It crushed the prow, obliterating the golden-winged emblem. Weapons systems vomited arced plasma auroras as they died. The explosions engulfed a thousand metres of the ship's length. A hundred spires disintegrated. For a few moments, the battle-barge resembled a torch, driving into its own flame. The *Callidora* went into a forced spin. The surge from the engines only pushed it further out of control. The lights flickered. For the length of a full revolution, the glittering arrogance of the Emperor's Children went dark.

The boarding torpedoes were on final approach. Atticus watched the *Callidora*'s slow tumble. The ship was so huge, its helplessness seemed impossible. It was like seeing a continent knocked adrift. He drank in the view of his enemy turned briefly into dead metal framed by the glow of its pain. One full turn, bereft of all power and control. Then the power returned. The void was lit once more by the *Callidora*'s pride. The ship arrested its spin. It came around to its pursuit heading. It was wounded. It was still trembling with secondary explosions. It was also angry, and it was seeking the target of its fury.

The torpedoes passed over the shattered, smouldering bow. They flew over the length of the battle-barge. Below them was a jewelled city of towers, an artist's tools of destruction. Ahead was the command island, a massive, crowned structure built up over the stern. And now, only now, the veil was lifted from the eyes of the Emperor's Children, and they realised the true threat. Turrets changed orientation. Cannons trained their fire on the boarding torpedoes. Some were hit. Atticus saw fireballs he knew to be the pyres of legionaries. But he did not see many. The attack ripped through a paltry defensive net.

In the last seconds before impact, Atticus spoke over the vox to all the torpedoes. 'The Emperor's Children worship perfection. Let them behold our gift to them, brothers. We are bringing these traitors the perfection of war.'

SIX

Philosophy in the abattoir
Decapitation
Creon

THE BOARDING TORPEDOES hit the command island and bored their way into it. They were multiple stab wounds, gladius jabs into the throat of the *Callidora*. Atticus's decapitation strategy called for the torpedoes to strike the upper quadrant of the structure in what amounted to a cluster. They would overwhelm the defences by hitting the Emperor's Children with too many attack vectors. And they would be close enough to each other that the squads could link up quickly. Atticus was not interested in the seizing of the enginarium or the hangars. He wanted the bridge. The goals of the mission were simplicity itself, which was its own form of perfection: kill everyone, destroy everything.

Galba's torpedo chewed its way through the *Callidora*'s plate one level below most of the others. Its hatch hissed open and, past the drill head heated almost to incandescence by the violence it had inflicted, the Iron Hands poured out. With them were Khi'dem and Ptero. Atticus had bent this far to allow the Salamanders and Raven Guard a measure of restored honour. But no further: only one representative of each Legion had been granted passage to the field of vengeance.

The space that Galba led the way through was a gallery. It was lit with the same amethyst glow as the exterior of the ship. Now that he was surrounded by the light, it seemed to him that the hue was less that of a precious stone, and more that of a bruise. The marble of the decking was carpeted, and the material felt strange beneath Galba's feet. There was something wrong with the texture.

The gallery ran to port. It was twenty metres wide and over a thousand long. It was designed to hold visitors by the hundreds, that the wonders on display should be seen by as many eyes as possible. Two massive bronze doors, four times the height of a Space Marine, stood at the far end. The squad moved towards them, passing beneath banners hanging from the ceiling and tapestries draped on the walls. Focused on the doors, alert for incoming threats, Galba gave the art only the smallest splinter of his attention. He registered its presence, nothing more. The Emperor's Children's mania for painting, sculpture, music, theatre and literature did not interest him. In the days of brotherhood with the III Legion – how long ago? Weeks? An eternity? – Galba had spent some time aboard the vessels of Fulgrim's legionaries. He had always found the opulence suffocating. Everywhere he had looked, there had been some masterpiece calling for his attention. It had been too much, a clamouring of sensations that was a threat to the clarity of thought. It was on those occasions that he had come closest to understanding Atticus's systematic stripping away of all that made him human. There was a purity to the machinic. It was a bracing tonic against the indulgence of the Emperor's Children.

In those days, Galba had thought of the difference as little more than an aesthetic parting of the ways. Now he felt an instinctive distaste for the art around him, and he refused it notice.

But the carpet still felt wrong.

'Brother-sergeant,' Vektus said. 'Do you see what the traitors have wrought?'

So he looked. He saw. He had supposed the banners to be commemorations of battlefield triumphs. They were emblems of a kind, but there were no flags, coats of arms or symbols of any kind that he recognised. Runes proliferated, their shapes and angles alien to him, their meaning beyond comprehension, yet squirming just beneath the thin ice of reason and denial. Two configurations kept repeating. One resembled a group of spears crossing to form an eight-pointed star. The other resembled a pendulum crowned by sickle blades. It made Galba grimace in distaste. He could not put aside the sensation that the symbol was *smiling* at him, and doing so with the most obscene eagerness. It was an abstraction of perversity, and all flesh that fell beneath the curve of its grin was soiled. Galba was seized by the wish to purge all that he still possessed of the organic. Only then would he be rid of the taint that tried to creep deeper into his being.

He ripped his gaze away from the banners. Still moving forwards, he took in the truth of the rest of the art. The Iron Hands were running down a gallery devoted to corruption, delirium, torture and the most exquisite artistry. The tapestries were narratives of butchery rendered as the luxury of the senses. Figures that might once have had a relation to the human sank fingers into the organs of their victims, and into their own. They devoured living skulls. They bathed in blood as though it were love itself. Worse than what the tapestries portrayed was what they were. They were silk and skin interwoven. They were the very crimes they celebrated. They were hundreds of victims turned into the illustrations of their own deaths.

And now Galba understood why the carpet felt wrong. It was a kindred atrocity to the tapestries. Flesh, muscle, sinew and tendons had been turned, by a hand as gifted as it was monstrous, into textile. The pile was deep. What should have felt like tanned leather had been rendered, thanks to the addition of hair, so fine that it had the soft give of cotton, yet it retained the wet-silk smoothness of tissue. Its pattern was abstract, its shades and flows suggesting music that was the origin of all screams. It was the work of many hands, and Galba had no doubt that the owners of those hands had been, one by one, incorporated into their work. Their bodies had become the ultimate signature. These artists would be forever present with their masterpiece.

Surely the dead could not feel pain. So why did it seem, as the Iron Hands thundered along the length of the gallery, that the carpet writhed? It was the material, Galba told himself. It was the terrible genius of the craftsmanship. Any other explanation was impossible, a sign of reason being contaminated by fantasy. He would give the traitors and their ship no such victory.

Instead, he brought annihilation. He and his brothers would end this violence with another: the cleansing, pure violence of the machine. His bionic arm felt like a bulwark against a plague of insanity. His bolter was more than an extension of his body. It was the lodestone of his journey, pulling him towards becoming the most perfect weapon of war.

For his Emperor, for his primarch, his every act on board this ship would be the promise of that perfection. A clean perfection, untouched by the insanity of the flesh around him. A perfection that would destroy the illusion worshipped by the Emperor's Children.

'What happened to this Legion?' Vektus wondered.

'Nothing compared to what we are about to do to it,' Galba answered.

'We cannot ignore this,' Khi'dem put in. 'I have never seen such madness. There is more than simple treachery at work.'

'There is nothing simple about treachery,' Galba snapped. 'And there is no greater crime.'

'What I mean,' Khi'dem said, 'is that there are terrible implications in what we are seeing. Your brother is right to ask what happened. Something did. We turn from that question at our peril.'

'Once we have killed them all, there will be all the time you would like for questions,' Galba said. His answer rang hollow and insufficient in his ears.

They were now only a few hundred metres from the bronze doors. The relief work was coming into focus. Even from this distance, it was clear that it was composed of bodies that had been covered in molten metal. From the other side of the doors came the sounds of battle: the deep drumming of bolter fire, the bone-sawing shriek and growl of chainblades, and the cries of rage of clashing legionaries. Rising above the white noise of shouts came a louder, hectoring voice, though its words were still indistinct. Then the volume of the roar rose like a cresting wave, and the doors opened with a deafening boom. The Emperor's Children rushed through the doorway. They were here to repel the transgressors of their domain.

They ran headlong into Galba's welcome.

The sergeant was at the head of the arrowhead rush. The gallery was wide enough for the entire squad to spread out, giving every battle-brother a clear field of fire. They opened up with their bolters before the doors had finished opening. The Emperor's Children charged. They were not wearing helmets; whether through arrogance or surprise, Galba neither knew nor cared. The skulls of the front-rank warriors exploded like overripe fruit when hit by the mass-reactive shells. The legionaries who followed on had their own weapons up. They returned fire, breaking the momentum of the Iron Hands' advance.

'Evade,' Galba voxed. 'But keep closing.' There was no cover. The only way to avoid a slaughter was to reach with the enemy and smash him in close quarters.

The wedge lost its clean symmetry as the legionaries began to zigzag at random. They ran forwards still, jerking left and right to deny the enemy a clean shot. They fired to suppress. There was no way of targeting with any precision in these conditions. But the spray of rounds was still deadly. Galba saw another enemy choke as his throat disappeared.

The Iron Hands' fire bought them a few precious seconds and several more metres. They were that much closer to the foe when the return fire began in earnest. But the Emperor's Children seemed just as eager for the violence of melee. They did not stop to aim. They charged, and their voices were raised in shouts of delight as much as they were in howls of rage.

The two forces closed with each other, and Galba could see the faces of the traitors more clearly. The transformation his former brothers had undergone was at least as disturbing as the art they now celebrated. They had attacked their own flesh. Galba saw runes made of wounds. He saw scalps turned into flaps, pulled away from skulls by metal armatures. Spikes, barbed wire, twisted bits of sculpture and other painful detritus of a depraved imagination disfigured the legionaries. They were laughing at their own pain.

Rushing towards Galba was a grim mockery of his own Legion's fusion with the inorganic. Where the Iron Hands replaced the weak flesh with the strength of metal, the Emperor's Children used each to ruin the other. The Iron Hands sought purity. These creatures were lost in a hellish revel. There was no reason here. There was only sensation, more and more and more sensation. To resort to these mutilations, to exult in agony, could only mean a hunger that could never be appeased. The Emperor's Children now worshipped sensation, and its absolute condition tormented them by remaining just out of reach.

These thoughts flickered through Galba's mind as he stormed towards the killing. They were not conscious reflections. They were instinctive, recoiling knowledge, an atavistic response that the appearance of the Emperor's Children summoned from depths that an earlier, benighted time would have called his soul. To the rage of betrayal was added disgust. Honour demanded the slaughter of the traitors. Something less rational needed all trace of them expunged.

For a few more seconds, bolter fire criss-crossed the space between the two forces. Legionaries on either side staggered. Galba saw two more of the Emperor's Children fall to head-shots. All of his own brothers were still at his side, the fist of vengeance unbroken. Then the warriors of the two Legions met. They were two waves smashing into each other. The gallery resounded with thunder built of armour against armour, blade against blade, fist against bone, and the throat-tearing roars of giants at war.

In the last moment before the collision, Galba mag-locked his bolter to his thigh and took up his chainsword. He swung it over his head with both hands, bringing it down with all the momentum of his charge. The nearest of Fulgrim's sons tried to counter the attack. Too caught up in the ecstasy of the rush to battle, he had not yet switched to a melee weapon. His bolter was a poor defence against the force of Galba's blow. The teeth of the chain whined as the sword swatted the barrel aside. The *chunk* of the blade digging into the skull of the traitor was wet, grinding, satisfying. Galba drew his first blood of the war. The debt had been owed him since the Callinedes betrayal. At last he could strike with his own hands in the name of his fallen primarch.

He saw his enemy's eyes widen in agony. But they also shone with excitement at the extremity of the experience as Galba sawed the legionary's head in two. Then the eyes dulled with death, and that was all that truly mattered. Galba yanked his chainsword free of the corpse and parried a strike by the Space Marine who leapt over his fallen comrade's body, swinging his own revving blade for Galba's throat. Galba ducked low and barrelled into the traitor, knocking him off balance. Galba followed up with the chainsword against the foe's cuirass, cutting deep.

Iron Hands and Emperor's Children tore at each other. Galba was submerged in a maelstrom of clashing ceramite and gouting blood. His consciousness shrank to the scale of mere seconds. He knew nothing except the need of each moment. He moved forwards step by step, kill by kill. His armour was gouged by dozens of blows, but he shrugged them off and struck home again and again. He pulverised faces to slurry. He hacked his way through armour and reinforced ribcages to black, beating hearts, and he silenced them.

A new noise grew in volume, cutting through the thunder, demanding his attention. It was a voice, amplified by vox-caster to deafening levels. The voice was that of a machine. There was nothing human in its rigid, unchanging inflection, yet it was preaching, and its words conveyed a ghastly passion.

'There are no limits,' it declared. 'Live the truth of the senses. Their reach must be infinite. Extend your own grasp, brothers. Plunge it deep into the perverse. All sensation is the fuel of perfection. The more extreme the sensation, the closer we come to perfection. The more debased the act, the greater the sensation. What is the command? That everything is permitted? No! Everything is *compulsory*!' The volume spiked on the last word. 'What the pallid would forbid, we must embrace to the end. Live the words of the prophet Saad! The only good is excess! The only true knowledge lies in sensation!' The voice launched into a litany of obscenities. It seemed to be reaching for the greatest atrocity that could be committed by words alone. It drew closer, and so did a steady, hammering beat of a great weight slamming against the deck. When he heard the *boom, boom, boom* closing in, Galba realised what was coming.

A Dreadnought.

Galba had been confused by the voice's preaching. There was a hunger in the words, an extolling of the flesh in all the worst contortions that he would never have imagined a Dreadnought uttering. The voice went on and on, urging itself to ever deeper abysses of depravity. With his physical self all but annihilated, the Dreadnought had only language and thought as the means by which he could join his brothers' frenzy, and so he ranted as if he might articulate the ultimate perfection of violation, and so find the supreme, transcendent experience.

The press of Emperor's Children suddenly diminished. Their ranks parted. Galba knew better than to press forwards. Ahead, the doorway was filled by a colossal shape. The Dreadnought had arrived. He advanced with words to damage the mind. For the flesh, he had many more tools. There was the weight of his tread, the grasp of his claw and the final illumination of his twin lascannons. The Ancient moved down the gallery towards the Iron Hands, never pausing in his black gospel. Gold filigree had spread over the violet of his armour like a disease. Its arabesques threatened meaning. They twisted into shapes whose trailing ends seemed to move with the pulsing of veins.

Even with the new, grotesque ornamentation, Galba recognised the figure. Ancient Curval. He had once been a philosopher of the war, one who spoke of perfection and loss in equal measure. Now his vox-casters greeted the Iron Hands with grating, monotone hunger. He had become a walking altar, an icon of demented worship. 'I seek the boon of your extremity,' he said, and fired.

The crush of the melee had pushed the Iron Hands close together again. They all saw the danger as soon as it appeared, and threw themselves to either side. The squad escaped extinction by lascannon barrage, but on the command display of Galba's helmet lenses, the runes of three brothers flashed red and vanished.

Flanked by his fellow legionaries, Curval marched forwards. He strafed the gallery left to right to left with a steady fire. The foul tapestries and carpet vanished, seared to ash. Galba dropped and rolled, the barrage passing just over him, charring the top of his power pack. Another battle-brother was incinerated.

They did not have the numbers or the weapons to fight Curval head-on. Galba had to remove him from the battlefield. From his belt clip, he grabbed a melta charge and hurled it at the Dreadnought's feet. 'Drop him,' he voxed.

The squad responded before he had finished his order. The warriors of his command had seen what he was doing, and understood. They were all the lethal components of a single engine of war. Four more grenades landed before Curval within a second of Galba's. The Dreadnought slowed, trying to arrest his next step. He paused with one foot suspended in the air. Shutters dropped before Galba's eyes as the grenades went off. The flare was a light so bright it made everything vanish for an instant. The heat was so intense, it made the deck vanish forever. Stone and steel turned molten, and a gap two metres wide opened in front of Curval.

The Dreadnought fought gravity and momentum. He lost. His foot came down over nothing. He pitched forwards and vanished, dropping twenty metres to the deck below. He landed with the crash of a meteor. His howl of rage had the same flat tone as his sermon. A handful of the Emperor's Children fell with him.

'*The flesh is weak!*' Galba roared as he rose to his feet and charged. The battle-cry of the Iron Hands was a riposte to the debased ecstasies of the foe. Galba's squad raced forwards to either side of the hole. Curval was firing wildly upwards, blasting further chunks out of the deck. As they passed the gap, Ptero dropped another melta charge. In the hissing blast that followed, Curval's raging cut off with an electronic squeal. His firing became even more erratic, the lashing out of a wounded beast.

The Emperor's Children tried to regroup. Their lines were broken, and they could not maintain a defensive position with the random destruction slashing upward through the gallery from their tormented Ancient. The Iron Hands had speed with them. It became force. They reforged the wedge on the other side of the gap and rammed their way through the ragged defence of the traitors. Galba tore into the foe. Warriors fell before him. Corrupt as they had become, they were still Legiones Astartes in form and strength. But Galba's arm struck with the might of justice, of vengeance. The purity of the machine devastated the monstrosity of the flesh.

Battered, reduced, defiant, his squad punched through and emerged from the gallery. Beyond it was a wide space, a radial node for half a dozen other major arterial passages through the battle-barge. At the centre was a wide spiral staircase. There was more marble here, veined with the purple of the Emperor's Children. It made Galba think of rotten, aristocratic blood showing through pale skin. Legionaries battled up and down its upper half. The *Callidora*'s defenders were attempting to reach the next level to repel the invaders gathered there.

Galba led his warriors up, taking the steps three at a time. With their brothers above, they trapped the Emperor's Children in a vice. The staircase was wide enough for two legionaries to stand abreast. Galba stopped a few steps away from the enemy. He and Vektus crouched out of the line of fire of the warriors behind them. Their bolters hammered the enemy with concentrated hell.

The vice closed.

MOST OF THE boarding torpedoes had drilled into the deck immediately beneath the bridge. Galba's squad was one of the last to join up with the gathered force. By then, the demolition charges had been set. As the siege of the bridge began, the explosives went off. Corridors and stairwells collapsed, sealing off the top decks, buying time for the Iron Hands. For the moment, they had the numerical superiority. Throughout the ship, there were many hundreds more of the Emperor's Children. But if the reinforcements' access could be blocked, even temporarily, the numbers would become irrelevant.

After the blasts, the boarding torpedo that had carried Galba and his brothers was inaccessible. So were three others. Those numbers, too, the Iron Hands knew, were irrelevant. The grinding truth of war was its power to cull. Many legionaries had already been lost. There would be more than enough room in the torpedoes that were still reachable.

While two squads remained to guard the exit point, the door to the bridge was breached. Galba joined in the push to the interior. There was no time for anything except a great storm of an assault. As the Emperor's Children had rushed the gallery, so the Iron Hands took the bridge. Theirs was the greater fury, and they attacked with the largest part of their forces.

The vital heart of the *Callidora* was well defended. The Emperor's Children fought hard. They fought with skill. They fought with desperation, knowing what defeat here would mean. And their struggle was futile. Atticus had come to kill their ship. They could not stop him. Nothing could. He was an engine of fate.

As Galba fought, emptying his bolter clip into the traitors before him, he saw Atticus take the upper level of the bridge. The captain moved with lethal economy. He swung his chainaxe with a grace that should have been foreign to the weapon. In Atticus's hands, the blade was not the messy butcher's tool of the World Eaters. The master of the *Veritas Ferrum* carved the air as if he were conducting an orchestra. Swing and blow flowed into one another. Chain snarling, the weapon never paused. Even when it was cutting through armour and bone, it did not seem to stutter in its graceful arc from kill to kill. It was an extension of the machine-warrior who wielded it, as much a part of his arm as his hands. And though there was the perfection of art in its death-dealing, there was not a single superfluous movement. There was no display. There was the murderous regularity of a piston. Atticus destroyed in the name of his primarch. He fought as iron, and flesh was in eclipse.

The captain of the *Callidora* met Atticus at the pulpit. Galba's peripheral vision caught flashes of the duel. The captain was named Kleos. The noble warrior of refined tastes now had, draped over his armour, robes of human silk. His face was an intricate cross-hatching of burns and deep cuts held open so they would not heal. He attacked Atticus with a charnabal sabre. The weapon was art transmuted into pure, press-folded steel. In Kleos's hands, it could almost draw blood from the air. The captain struck with such speed, the blade was invisible.

Atticus did not block it. It sliced through the seam of his armour beneath his left arm. Kleos paused for a moment before the lack of blood. His blow had been for a being of flesh, but this foe was metal and war. Atticus turned into the cut, forcing the blade deeper, trapping the sabre against his ribcage. Kleos tried to tug the sword free. Atticus brought the chainaxe down on his skull.

The slaughter on the bridge lasted less than five minutes. The Iron Hands fell upon the Emperor's Children like a moving wall and crushed them. When the last of the traitors fell, there was a moment of silence. Galba let himself savour the humiliation of the enemy. Then the next phase of the execution began. Atticus mounted to the command pulpit. With a snarl, he smashed its ornamentation. 'Get me the coordinates,' he ordered.

While Techmarine Camnus took the helm, Galba consulted the vox. 'A message has been sent,' he reported.

'A cry for help, no doubt,' said Atticus. 'Has there been a response?'

'Yes.'

'Then we will not tarry. Brother Camnus?'

'It will be visible in a moment, captain.'

Galba looked out through the forward oculus. The debris of the scattered disc floated past, the larger chunks of ice a faint grey in the void, the closer pieces picking up the violet glow of the *Callidora*.

'There,' Camnus said.

In the centre of the oculus, there was a sphere of concentrated darkness.

'Good.' The single syllable was the toll of a bell.

Camnus needed no further orders. Galba watched the ball of night begin to grow closer. He was seeing one of the few rocky planetoids of the scattered disc. It was large enough to have a name: Creon. Barely a thousand kilometres in diameter, it was an airless world of eternal night. It was a tomb. And it awaited its charge.

The deck vibrated as the *Callidora*'s engines surged.

'Full ahead,' Camnus announced. 'Coordinates locked.'

'Good.' Atticus said again. 'Now, brothers, put an end to this obscene vessel.'

They turned their weapons on the consoles, screens, cogitators and controls of the ship. In seconds, the bridge was in ruins. The *Callidora*'s fate was unalterable.

'Do you feel that, brothers?' Atticus asked as he descended from the shattered pulpit. 'There is a stillness beneath the vibration of the engines. It is death. This ship is already dead, and our enemy knows it.'

There was nothing the Emperor's Children could do to prevent what was coming. But they tried. Atticus led his legionaries back to the boarding torpedoes, and as they passed the interdicted tunnels, they could hear the frantic sounds of the traitors trying to break through. The first of the torpedoes drew into sight, its drill projecting through the hull and deep into the accessway, when the warriors of the *Callidora* resorted to desperate measures.

The breacher charge was powerful. It vaporised the metal blocking one of the primary arteries leading to the bridge. It was directly behind the Iron Hands. It was as if a solar flare filled the accessway.

A heat beyond flame incinerated the rearguard. They fell to the twisted deck, their armour changed into blackened, molten sarcophagi. Galba was near the front of the line, and he was still thrown against the inner wall by the force of the blast. His auto-senses lenses lit up with warning runes. He kept moving, but he could feel his armour's actuators catch and hesitate, breaking the cadence of his run. He heard Vektus cursing. They were having to abandon still more bodies of their brothers, their progenoid glands unrecovered.

The roar of the explosion faded. Now came the sound of boots. An army was in pursuit.

The instinct to stop and fight was strong. Then Atticus spoke over the vox. 'There is no need to confront the enemy,' he said. 'The traitors have already lost. They are already dead. Humiliate them by leaving here alive.'

The Iron Hands obeyed, and they ran. They were racing with their own victory, Galba now realised. The doomed masses of the Emperor's Children were in futile pursuit, still unaware of the executioner's blade descending upon them.

The warriors of the X Legion boarded the torpedoes. Engines pulled the vehicles out of the flesh of the *Callidora*. They left gaping holes behind. Atmosphere rushed into the void, the gale carrying traitors with it until bulkheads sealed. The hull breaches were neutralised. The lives of those aboard were preserved for another minute.

But not much more.

ATTICUS WATCHED THE battle-barge as the boarding torpedoes moved away. The departure was slow. The torpedoes' propulsion systems were not designed for speed. They served to manoeuvre the vessels to a recovery point, and little more. The torpedoes could not perform evasive action, and they were vulnerable to the *Callidora*'s armaments. Their presence was no secret now. The *Callidora* had hundreds of cannons, turrets and missile launchers. Most of its crew was still alive. The damage to the ship was minimal. The Emperor's Children could have vaporised the torpedoes, erasing the blemish from the perfection of the void.

But for the first moments of the retreat from the *Callidora*, the Iron Hands still had the benefit of surprise. They had sown disorder on the ship. The enemy was scrambling to catch up. And when the surprise was no longer a factor, the Iron Hands were no longer of interest to the Emperor's Children.

Creon was.

The *Callidora* approached the planetoid, bringing light to its darkness. Its course was direct, and it would not be changed. Every weapon on the battle-barge fired at Creon. Bombardment cannons pummelled the crust with magma bombs. That was an act of defiance, a defacing of an uncaring enemy whose trajectory would not be changed even by so devastating a weapon. Every turret, torpedo bay and lance was also unleashed. These were acts of desperation. They could add nothing to the blows of the cannons.

Then the Emperor's Children launched cyclonic torpedoes, and this was an act of madness. *What were they dreaming?* Atticus wondered. Did they imagine the planetoid vaporising before them, with the *Callidora* sailing safely through a cloud of debris? Had the traitors really fallen that far into utter dementia?

What they thought did not matter, he decided. In this moment, the only action that mattered was his own. Everything now happening was a consequence of his will, and there was nothing that could alter its edict. The *Callidora* poured destruction upon Creon, and all it was doing was stoking the fires of its destined hell.

The *Callidora*'s bow was trained on the centre of the planetoid. Creon's surface turned molten under the fury of the bombardment. The epicentre of destruction glowed white, a terrible eye opening in the rock.

The incandescence spread wider. It became a maelstrom of flowing stone hundreds of kilometres in diameter. The planetoid convulsed. The dead world of cold and darkness screamed, illuminated by pain. After billions of years of quiescence, Creon underwent a tectonic awakening. Fountains of lava shot up to celebrate the arrival of the *Callidora*. The ship did not slow, and its course did not falter. It flew on the strength of Atticus's will into the heart of the fire. Its bow plunged into brilliance.

The *Callidora* was still accelerating when it hit Creon. It vanished from Atticus's sight, an arrogant violet tear swallowed by the inferno. Moments later, the cores of the plasma drives were breached. The flash filled the void with day. The shock wave raced around Creon, and it killed the planetoid. It split in two. The halves tumbled away from each other and the rage of destruction, falling back into frozen night.

'Perfection,' Atticus muttered.

SEVEN

The spirit of the age
The abandoned hall
Journey's solitude

'WE HAVE PLENTY of mines left,' Darras said.

'And they have plenty of ships,' Galba countered.

Atticus stood above them in the command pulpit of the *Veritas Ferrum*. The clean, impersonal lines of the bridge were soothing after the ornate perversities of the *Callidora*. Erephren, called away once again from the rest of the astropathic choir, was just behind him.

'Mistress?' Atticus asked.

Erephren shook her head. 'I'm sorry, captain. The clarity of my sight is a product of my proximity to the anomaly. I can tell you the size of the fleet that I saw before our journey here. As to how many of those ships are on their way here...' She raised her left hand, palm up, knowledge flying away from her grasp. 'I cannot say.'

'But something is coming.'

'Disturbances in the warp suggest as much.'

'How much time do we have?'

'That too, I cannot say.'

'Brother-captain,' Galba and Darras began together.

Atticus held up a hand. 'You are both correct,' he told his sergeants. The icy metal face looked at Darras. 'Do not think I am unmindful of our strategic advantages here. I know that this victory has only sharpened our thirst for revenge. But we have our limits. Though we do not like to admit this truth, if it were not so, we would have triumphed on Isstvan Five. We will quit the field.' He leaned forwards. 'I make you a promise, brother-sergeant,' he said. His voice box struggled to convey his tone. His voice rasped over the bridge. It sounded to Galba like the angry hiss of a great, electronic serpent. Its promise of doom filled him with joy. 'We will learn more on Pythos. We will strike again. And again. We will awaken the Emperor's Children to the idea of fear. We will teach them to have nightmares.' He swivelled his head to look at Galba. 'You are correct, sergeant. We must choose our battles. And I choose to leave the foe one more gift before we depart. One more lesson.'

THE VERITAS FERRUM did not have unlimited supplies. Her stores had not been replenished since before the Callinedes pacification. The Iron Hands might find raw materials on Pythos, but eventually the ship's manufacturing plants would no longer be able to churn out ordnance. Unless the tide of fortune changed, the time would come when the *Veritas* would no longer be able to wage war.

That time had not yet come. And mines were plentiful.

The *Veritas Ferrum* crossed and recrossed the close neighbourhood of the Mandeville point. It left a trail of mines behind it. Its route was a gradual weaving as helmsman Eutropius guided the ship past the scattered disc debris. Not all of the dead bodies were ice and rock now. There were small traces of the *Infinite Sublime*, larger ones of the *Golden Mean*. They were the tears of defeat, Galba thought.

The strike cruiser passed a number of larger bodies. Some were big enough to damage a vessel. Others could smash a capital ship to dust. Galba glanced back and forth between the oculus and the captain. Atticus watched the major debris go by. The only sign of his hunger was a slight shifting of his grip on the pulpit.

Darras picked up on it, too. 'Captain,' he began.

'I know, brother-sergeant. I know. I'll thank you not to tempt me. There is no time.'

The trap with the mined ice chunk had worked before because the *Veritas Ferrum* had been there to control the moment of detonation and use the body as a missile. Its continued presence now was tactical madness. The Iron Hands would have to rely on chance to inflict harm on the arriving fleet. They could help chance along with the mines, but they had no alchemy that could transmute the chance into a certainty. The randomness was an offence to the Legion's philosophy of war. The promise of the machine was the promise of the reproducible, the understandable, the unbending. It was the promise of control.

But they were a different Legion now. Their control of the battlefield was doomed to be a transitory thing. Strike and fade, strike and fade. Was that, Galba wondered, to be the new piston movement of the Iron Fists' war machine?

If it kept them in the fight, and it hurt the enemy, then he could accept it, he decided. The limits of the strategy were the evidence of his Legion's great wound. But he could adapt. He glanced again at Atticus. The captain had returned to his preternatural stillness. The iron statue was impossible to read. How was he adapting to this reality? Was he? Again he wondered whether Atticus had shed too much of the human.

That he should think along these lines rattled Galba. The flesh is weak: that was a foundational tenet of the Iron Hands. Once more, he thought of how little Ferrus Manus had changed. Perhaps it was Galba's own limited journey to the purity of the machine that lay at the root of these doubts. Perhaps doubt was inherent to the flesh itself.

But perhaps so was adaptability.

He wanted to hurt the Emperor's Children as much as any legionary aboard the ship. He looked forward to the next time their craven blood slicked his armour. He also believed that foolish risks would bring an end to vengeance. Perhaps the mine-laying was a managed risk. He just was not sure how much the hope of accomplishing something was real, and how much the action was a flare of anger. How many ships could they kill this way? How many future actions of real worth were they risking by tarrying here?

'You disapprove, Sergeant Galba,' Atticus said.

Galba turned and looked up. 'It is not my place to question your orders, captain.'

'And yet you do. I can see it in the way you are standing. Your displeasure is obvious.'

'I apologise, my lord. I mean no disrespect.'

'I am acting on a balance of probabilities,' Atticus told him.

'You do not need to justify–'

Atticus raised a finger, silencing him. 'We are more likely to cause injury than we are to be injured. Is that not so?'

Galba nodded. He was not sure that it was, but he could not prove the contrary.

'This is an act of reason, sergeant. Everything we do in this new war will have an element of desperate risk that is unpleasantly novel to us. We have always been strong. We still are. What we are no longer is an overwhelming force. We are assassins. We are saboteurs. We must think like them.'

Then we should have melted away. Galba said nothing. He tried to shift his stance to something more neutral, but he did not know what that would be. Atticus watched him a few seconds longer. There was a cold glint in his unblinking human eye.

Unwelcome revelation crept up on Galba: that glint was the light of Atticus's rage. The fury had been kindled over Callinedes IV. It had been stoked to a holocaust in the Isstvan System. Perhaps Atticus believed he had damped it to a controlled, imperious anger. But his eye betrayed him as Galba's body language had. Atticus had not mastered his rage. It had mastered him. It did more than distort his thoughts: it shaped his reason. It determined his existence.

Atticus had, over time, removed all but the most vestigial traces of humanity from his being. He was a weapon, only a weapon, and a weapon directed by the master passion of rage.

It occurred to Galba that Atticus might agree with this judgement. He might even take a certain pride in it, should the rage grant the pride room enough to exist. He would consider himself a gun, aimed at the heart of the enemy.

But bombs were weapons too.

Galba felt sick. He wanted to look away. He wanted to deny his insight. He wanted to scrape the human from his own identity, the human that was responding to its near-total lack in the massive warrior looming above. What good was this epiphany? None. Yet it filled his consciousness. He had no choice but to accept it, just as he had to accept how pointless it was. There was nothing to be done.

He had his own share of Atticus's rage.

The captain straightened, returning his attention to the oculus. Galba faced forwards again. He looked at his battle-brothers. He saw the rage in all of them. It was a freezing passion. It took hope, compassion, the dream of a just galaxy, and even the desire for such a thing. It made them brittle, fragile. It turned them into the thinnest of ice, then shattered them. Galba's gaze settled on Darras. There was more of the human in his face. It revealed more of what the immobile impassivity of Atticus's features concealed. It showed the rage-fashioned hunger.

The destruction of the *Callidora* had done nothing to appease that hunger. It had given the Iron Hands their first taste of revenge. It was a sensation as new to the Legion as defeat. Born of that defeat, the hunger was as ineradicable as the anger, the shame, the hatred. It was more than a symptom. It was more than a developing character trait. Galba knew what it was, and he wished he did not. He wished to be wrong. He wished that he was still capable of wanting something more than the brutal deaths of the betrayers of the Imperium.

He could not. He was not wrong.

This thing that permeated the air of the bridge, and threaded through his hearts and bones, and thrummed in the decks and walls of the ship, this rage, it was the new spirit of the Legion. *This*, Galba thought, *is who we are now.* He was human enough to feel regret. He was distant enough from the human condition to know the feeling would pass.

When two hundred mines had been sown in the night of Hamartia, Atticus declared the mission complete. 'Take us down the safe channel,' he told Eutropius. 'Get us up to speed for the translation.'

'So ordered,' said the helmsman.

The *Veritas Ferrum* accelerated. The warp engines powered up. When the urgent signal came from the astropathic choir, Galba was not surprised. Neither, he suspected, was Atticus.

No one was.

'*Captain,*' Erephren's voice emerged from the primary vox-caster in the centre of the bridge. '*There is a massive displacement in the warp. It is very near.*'

'Thank you,' Atticus said. 'Navigator, we are in your hands. As interesting an experiment as a mid-translation collision would be, I would prefer not to subject my ship to it.'

'*Understood, captain,*' Strassny broadcast. He was floating in his tank of nutrients, deprived of all sensory input, in a blister at the peak of the strike cruiser's command island. The black plasteel dome that covered him was shaped like an echo of his psychic eye. So long attuned to the Astronomican, that eye would be seeking the anchor of the Pythos anomaly. Right now, its quest was an entry into the nexus of the Mandeville point that was not about to disgorge an enemy fleet.

Eutropius responded to the coordinates relayed by Strassny. The *Veritas Ferrum* picked up speed, leaving the minefield at its stern.

'Wait for my word,' Atticus said. The hololithic screens on either side of the command pulpit displayed the void on the ship's flanks. 'Sergeant Darras, I want to know the moment you receive sign of the enemy's presence.'

'Understood, captain.' Darras did not look up from the repaired auspex bank.

I think we'll all know, Galba mused.

He was right. The flesh of the void tore open not far to port of the bow. Nightmare unlight flashed from the rent. Colours that were sounds and ideas that were blood poured out. Behind them came the ships. The translation was endless. Vessel after vessel entered the system. The violet of the Emperor's Children spread in all directions, a miasma of excess, as though the ships were forming their own diseased sun.

'Go,' said Atticus.

The deck vibrated with the familiar rumble of the warp drive energies building to the critical point. The jump tocsins sounded. The forward elements of the fleet began to turn in the direction of the Iron Hands, but they would travel many lengths yet before they could complete the turn and engage in pursuit. By then, they would be in the minefield.

'I regret that we cannot linger to see the fruits of our labour,' Atticus said. Then a second wound opened, reality's agony filling the span of the oculus, and the *Veritas Ferrum* plunged into the empyrean.

✠ ✠ ✠

'THE QUESTION,' INACHUS Ptero said, 'is not whether the Emperor's Children have followed us. Of course they have. The question is whether they will be able to keep tracking us.'

Khi'dem grunted. They were walking the length of a reviewing hall. It had been built to hold thousands: the full complement of the company along with any visiting squads from other Legions. It had not been used since Callinedes. Khi'dem doubted it ever would be again. The *Veritas Ferrum* had lost too much of its complement – first all of its veterans and senior officers to Ferrus Manus as he raced off with the elite of every company to the confrontation with Horus, then to catastrophic damage and the venting of entire sections of the ship during the battle in the Isstvan System. Any gathering in this space would be dwarfed by the vastness and rendered solemn by the echoes of absence. According to the ship's horologs, it had only been a few weeks since the disaster of Isstvan V, but the hall already had the staleness of disuse. The steel chandeliers descending from the vaulted ceiling were extinguished. The only light was from parallel lumen-strips forming a wide alley down the length of the marble floor. The banners of triumphs hung in shadows. Soon after their arrival on the *Veritas*, the two legionaries had found that they and the rest of the handful of their surviving battle-brothers could walk and converse here at their leisure. Khi'dem had not seen a single one of the Iron Hands set foot in the hall.

'Sergeant Galba tells me that the Navigator has plotted a convoluted route through the immaterium,' Khi'dem told the Raven Guard. His voice bounced around the walls, the sound hollow. 'Unless the enemy is also using the anomaly as a guide, which seems unlikely, we should lose them.'

Ptero thought about this for a moment, then said, 'The tactic seems sound.'

'Agreed. But that is not the only question, is it?'

'No. We remained in-system too long, and without good reason.'

'*We* did not,' Khi'dem corrected. '*They* chose to do so. You and I are barely tolerated passengers.'

Ptero uttered a short, bitter laugh. 'Do you think our participation on this raid was intended as a favour or an insult?'

'Both, I suspect. It would depend on the moment you asked Captain Atticus.'

'You don't believe he knows his own mind.'

Khi'dem deliberated for a dozen strides before answering. 'I'm not sure what I believe on that count,' he said.

'Nor do I,' Ptero said softly. He continued, 'Regardless of the success in evading pursuit, I am troubled by the decision to lay the mines. *That* tactic was unsound. Atticus is right about the strategic advantage of Pythos. He risked losing something of paramount importance in order to engage in the trivial.'

'His need for revenge is strong. It is for all of the Iron Hands.'

'Ours isn't?' Ptero demanded. Even in the dim light, Khi'dem could see his face turning red. 'Have we not lost as much as they have?'

Khi'dem remained calm. 'I did not mean that,' he said.

They reached one end of the hall and turned around. They moved down the centre of the floor, the walls so distant that they seemed insubstantial.

Ptero mastered his temper. 'Forgive me, brother,' he said. 'You are not the source of my frustration.'

Khi'dem waved off the apology. 'Your anger reassures me,' he said. 'It tells me that your worries are mine.'

'And they are?'

'That the Iron Hands have changed at a fundamental level. The death of their primarch has done something dangerous to them.' He allowed himself a sorrowful smile. 'Perhaps we flatter ourselves that we would not have made the same reckless decision. I don't think we would have.'

'Their anger is becoming toxic.'

'Yes. To them.'

'And to us?' Ptero asked.

'Our fates are slaved to theirs,' Khi'dem said.

'They are,' Ptero agreed. They walked in silence for a short while. In the centre of the hall, where they were most isolated by gloom and space, the Raven Guard spoke again. 'So the true question is what we should do.'

'I would welcome your thoughts.'

Ptero laughed again, with no more humour than the last time. 'And I yours. Our options are quite limited, it seems to me. The decisions that will govern this campaign are not ours to make, but we are subject to them. And we can hardly depose Captain Atticus.'

Khi'dem gave Ptero a cold stare. 'I know you are joking, brother. But I will not have even the idea of treachery discussed in my presence.'

Ptero sighed. He closed his eyes and pinched the bridge of his nose. For a moment, Khi'dem saw his own exhaustion reflected in the Raven Guard. 'I'm sorry,' Ptero said. 'I spoke without thinking. I was wrong.' He looked up. 'We are living in strange times, though, brother. We have witnessed the impossible. We have been its victims, in no small part because what happened on Isstvan Five was, until that very moment, *unimaginable*.' He lowered his voice to a whisper. 'We cannot afford to view *anything* as impossible. We must imagine everything, including the worst. Especially the worst.'

Khi'dem raised his eyes to the ceiling. The gloom was almost physical. It clung to the banners, obscuring the victories, casting them into a meaningless past. They seemed to hang limply, made heavy by the weight of tragedy. He found himself thinking of the monstrous gallery on the *Callidora*. It had been the perversion of the Emperor's Children made physical. This space, he realised, was just as metonymic of the damage to the Iron Hands' psyche. Something dire had happened to the X Legion, something that went far beyond a military defeat, beyond grief, beyond loss. He knew those emotions. He lived with them. They had been the painful bedrock of his existence since the massacre. Not knowing the fate of Vulkan had him trapped in an eternal pendulum swing between hope and mourning.

What was happening to the Iron Hands was wholly other. It was a *change*. It was also, he worried, permanent.

He faced Ptero again. 'Well?' he said. 'Where does that leave us?'

'We watch. Closely.'

'Do you think Atticus's strategy is madness?'

'Do you?'

Khi'dem shook his head. 'It is risky, certainly. I do not agree with all of his decisions.' He shrugged. 'But it is not mad.'

'Not yet.'

'Not yet. So it falls to us to try to be the voice of sanity?'

'I fear so.'

Now Khi'dem laughed. It was either that or despair. 'And who will hear our voices?'

'Sergeant Galba for one, I think.'

'He may well be the only one.'

'Better than none.'

Khi'dem sighed. He had not trained for this kind of war. He knew senior officers who had an instinct for the political. He had never possessed it. War was war, though. Whatever mission lay before him, he would not shy from it. 'Atticus might not listen, but he will hear me,' he said. 'I will see to it that he has no choice.'

Ptero nodded. 'We are agreed, then.'

They started walking again, heading for the great archway of the hall's entrance. Still fifty metres from the doors, Khi'dem came to a sudden halt. He felt breathless, a sensation he had not experienced since his elevation to the Legiones Astartes.

'Brother?' Ptero asked. 'What is it?'

The feeling passed. His skin prickled in its wake. 'Nothing,' he said. 'It's nothing.' It could not be anything. The Imperial Truth forbade any other possibility.

There was no such thing as a premonition.

THE VERITAS FERRUM followed a route that twisted through the empyrean. The ship raced down currents of dementia, shifting from one tributary to another, never staying with one flow for long. There was no reason to its movements. In the realm where directions had no meaning, the strike cruiser fled as if panicked and lost.

It was neither. The beacon on Pythos called it back. The anomaly was insistent. It would not tolerate an escape. For Bhalif Strassny, it was as clear a marker as the Astronomican had ever been. But rather than a lighthouse beam, it was present to his psychic eye like a scratch on a retina. He saw through the warp to the anomaly, much as he would the Emperor's beam. But this was no illumination. It was a stable, jagged slash in the warp. As the endless death of the real and cauldron roil of thought washed over his consciousness, the Navigator experienced one concept after another clinging briefly to the manifestation of the anomaly before being swept away. At one moment he was seeing a *trace*, and then a *crack*, and then a *fracture*. Once, and only once – and for this he was grateful – he saw it as a *door*. Its meaning was in perpetual flux, for meaning was forbidden by the warp. Its presence, though, was steady, and grew ever stronger.

Rhydia Erephren also knew its growing strength. She experienced it as the returning clarity of her dark sight. She and her choir braced themselves as best they could as the warp unfolded its nature before them. It seemed to her that her vision was growing sharper, and reaching father, than on the ship's first approach to the Pandorax System. Something like the whisper of serpent

tongues caressed her mind. It insinuated the possibility of perfect clarity. It threatened absolute vision. She shuddered. She
accepted the knowledge as she sank deeper and deeper into the
razored river. She worked on her defences so that she would not
drown, so she would not bleed. The duty of mission granted her
breath. She spoke to her charges, reassuring as she could, imposing discipline as necessary. In this way she held together a group
of fragile, tormented humans. Not all of them were able to grasp
the strength she offered. One man died of heart seizure. After the
gasps of agony, his final sigh sounded like thanks. Just before the
Veritas reached Pandorax, a second man started screaming. He
could not stop.

It was necessary to have him shot.

IN THE SERF quarters, Agnes Tanaura sensed this journey through
the warp was different. Everyone did. Tanaura had been glad that
her duties to the captain meant that she had left Pythos behind.
She would have preferred never to return. There was a word for
that planet, a word that officially had no place in the Imperium,
because it was meaningless. The word was *unholy*. She was not afraid
of using the word. She knew that it had a great deal of meaning.
Accepting the divinity of the Emperor meant acknowledging the
existence of dark forces. The reality of a god implied the reality
of His enemies. If the sacred existed, then there had to be words
to describe that which was utterly removed from the light of the
Emperor. *Unholy* was a good word. A strong word. It was not just
an epithet. It was a warning.

She had heard the warning on Pythos. She wished the demigods
she served had heard it, too.

She had always found the journeys through the warp troubling.
No matter how deep in the ship she was, no matter how thoroughly
shielded from the madness of the immaterium, she felt its tendrils.

Even when there were no storms, there was a latent charge to the ship's atmosphere.

This time was different. The tendrils reached deeper. They were stronger. She believed something had followed them from Pythos. That, or they had picked up a taint on that world. She knew something was wrong. The voices of the serfs in the great hall were subdued. People spoke quietly, as though they were listening for something. Or they were afraid something would hear them.

Tanaura wanted to hide. She wanted to find a small, safe corner in which to curl up and clutch her faith close. She also knew that her duty lay elsewhere. So she walked into the centre of the hall. She held the *Lectitio Divinitatus* in her right hand. She spread her arms, lifted her head, and smiled. 'I have words of hope,' she said. 'I have words of courage.'

People gathered to hear.

FLOATING AND TWISTING in his tank, Strassny called out his guidance. Helmsman Eutropius received the directions, and steered the ship as the Navigator desired. Eutropius could not read the warp. He was suspicious of any being who could. It was a domain that made a mockery of the Emperor's reason. Linked by mechadendrites to the magnificent machinic existence that was the *Veritas Ferrum*, he resented the absurdity of the warp, even as he relished the triumph over irrationality represented by the Geller field. Even though the ways of the empyrean were a resented mystery, he could tell that Strassny was taking them down a route bereft of any logical pattern. It was the most labyrinthine journey he had ever taken through the warp. He understood its tactical necessity. He mistrusted the fact that Strassny maintained that they were not lost. He knew the Navigator was not lying. It was the truth itself that he did not like. It had implications that were best ignored. If only they could be.

And in the command pulpit, Atticus stood motionless. He
appeared impassive. He was not. He was impatient to reach Pythos.
He wanted the knowledge Erephren would find for him, so he
could strike again. Frustration gnawed at him, too. He burned
to know what damage his minefield had caused the Emperor's
Children. He needed it to have been considerable. He needed confirmation of the validity of his strategy.

He could, at will, sense the condition of any component of his
bionic frame. In this moment, through no choice of his own, he
was conscious of his human eye and its island of flesh. He could
have replaced the eye years ago, and completed his journey to the
machine. He had not. He had not felt worthy. The body, he believed,
should not outstrip the mind. He kept his last vestige of the flesh
to remind himself of its weakness, a weakness that was more than
physical. He felt that weakness now. The flesh sat against his skull,
itself now mostly metal, like a chink in his power armour.

No, he thought. *Like a cancer.* That was what the flesh was. It was
a cancer that ate at the pure strength of the machine. It introduced
doubt through the toxins of the emotions. He did not resent his
rage. That was the necessary passion, the only just reaction to the
supreme crime of treachery. It was the servant of war. Yet it could
cloud judgement, too. He had seen its corrosive work on the World
Eaters. That was a Legion whose betrayal, in retrospect, seemed
inevitable. Its anger was a madness.

Was his? Was he harming his company by indulging in his wrath?

He was not. They had struck. They had drawn blood. They had
done real harm to the Emperor's Children. The loss of the *Callidora* alone would sit heavily. And now the *Veritas Ferrum* was free
to strike again. This was all the proof he needed that he was right
to follow the rage. If he had his will, his consciousness would be
reduced to fury and calculation. The fury would fuel the drive to
war. The calculation would produce the tactics to prosecute it.

The stubborn humanity of the flesh would not respond to his will. It tainted the rage with grief and reflexive mistrust. He resented even the awareness that there were members of other Legions aboard. He felt that the Iron Hands could count on no one but themselves. Those who had not betrayed Ferrus Manus had failed him. Those were simple facts. Universal suspicion was the logical, reasoned response. Or so his instincts would have him believe. Yet under the same rules of logic, he could not find anything to condemn in the comportment of the Salamanders and Raven Guard he had rescued. They had fought well on Pythos. And on the *Callidora*, so had the two he had allowed on the mission.

Contradictions. No distinguishing true reason from what he wished to believe. No way of purging the irrational from belief. And so another poison entered his system: doubt. His evaluation of the other legionaries was suspect. What else might be?

The look on Galba's face during the mine laying. The uncertain result. The close escape of the *Veritas*. The ship prolonging its stay in the immaterium in order to evade pursuit.

Where was his judgement now?

Eutropius interrupted his musing. 'Captain,' he said. 'Navigator Strassny informs me that we are about to translate back to real space.'

'Thank you, helmsman.' There was the answer he sought. He had followed his anger to a limit his reason had set. The mines *had* been laid, and they *would* plague the fleet of the Emperor's Children. With that concentration of ships, damage was inevitable. The *Veritas* had escaped. It *had* returned to safe port.

He had been correct. His judgement was sound. So he was able to purge some of the wasteful doubts.

This was what he told himself.

The shields pulled back from the oculus as the ship returned to the physical plane. At the same moment, the tactical screens flashed red. Threat klaxons began to sound.

'Battle stations,' Atticus ordered, swallowing a curse.

There was a fleet in the Pandorax System. A large one.

PART TWO

TOOTH AND CLAW

EIGHT

Travellers
The price of innocence
Charity

THERE WERE OVER a hundred ships. Auspex readings were translated into a hololithic projection in the centre of the bridge. The image showed the vessels clustered so closely together, they resembled a swarm. Galba stared. The grouping made no sense. Then speed and tonnage data began to arrive. They puzzled him even more.

'Captain?' Eutropius asked.

'Bring us closer. I want a better look at these intruders.' Atticus sounded baffled. He had already had the klaxons silenced.

'So ordered,' the helmsman said. He sounded surprised.

'Do you intend to engage?' Galba asked.

'Those numbers are beyond us,' said Darras. Even his enthusiasm could not change the hundred-to-one odds.

'Perhaps not,' Atticus answered. 'Silent running,' he ordered, 'and there must be no fire except on my command. Am I clear? That is not a formation. It is a conglomeration. There is no order there. I see nothing tactical. The tonnage of these ships is eccentric. They are also moving slowly.'

The *Veritas Ferrum* moved in from the edge of the system. It closed effortlessly with the trailing ships. The readings became more detailed. Their nature was as varied as their individual masses. Though there were a few Imperial transports, there were no combat vessels of any kind. Most of the ships were civilian, ranging from small traders to ancient, lumbering colonisers. Very few were of recent construction. All of them were limping, patched creatures. Some of the energy blooms indicated engines very close to explosive failure. It was surprising some of the vessels had survived travelling any distance at all. None of them appeared warp-worthy.

'How did they make it this far?' Galba wondered.

'This far from where?' said Darras.

'From anywhere. They aren't from in-system. We know that much. If these are the ships that survived the journey, how many did they lose along the way? It would have taken them a long time to reach Pandorax from the nearest inhabited system.'

Atticus said, 'That does not interest me half as much as why they are here.'

Galba monitored the vox traffic between the ships. It provided few answers. The communications were primarily routine navigational messages. They showed a marked lack of discipline and form. The pilots were not military. They were not even professional. They had still not detected the *Veritas Ferrum*. As the fleet drew closer to Pythos, the transmissions became more excited. 'Their presence here is no accident,' Galba concluded.

'Neither is ours,' said Atticus.

'You believe they were drawn here too?'

'This system has precisely one feature capable of drawing attention beyond its boundaries.'

Galba looked over the details of the patchwork fleet again. He could not imagine this ragged group of civilians finding any use for the anomaly. 'What would they want with it?'

'That is not my concern.' The captain's tone was flat and dark. 'My concern is that they want it at all.'

Galba exchanged a look with Darras. The other sergeant seemed uneasy, but kept his silence. *I am not the captain's conscience,* Galba wanted to shout. Instead, he asked the question he wished had not occurred to him. 'We cannot attack them, surely?'

A terrible silence ensued. *We can't,* Galba repeated to himself. These travellers were clearly non-combatants. They had committed no crime. They were Imperial subjects. No strategic consideration could justify a massacre. No application of even the coldest arithmetic could wash away the moral taint that would fall upon the clan-company if it committed such a crime. *That is not who we are,* Galba thought. *That is not who we are.*

We must not become our enemy.

'No,' Atticus said at last. 'That is not who we are.'

Galba started. He had not spoken his thoughts aloud, had he? No. He released the breath he had been holding. He felt the first moment of peace he had experienced since the beginning of the war. With that one sentence, Atticus had reaffirmed that the honour of the X Legion still extended further than a battle-field victory.

'We follow,' Atticus ordered. 'We observe. For now, that is all.'

When the fleet reached Pythos, the largest ships anchored in geostationary orbit above the anomaly. The smaller ones began their descent to the surface. Lighters began to shuttle back and forth, transporting passengers from the ships incapable of making planetfall. There were accidents. The *Veritas*'s auspex banks picked up the heat signatures of explosions from those landings that ended in disaster. The individual tragedies did nothing to dampen the enthusiasm coming from the ever-more excited vox traffic. Galba heard the word 'home' become a refrain. He doubted that most of the ships making a landing would ever be able to leave again.

'They have come to stay,' he said.

Atticus made no reply.

THE THUNDERHAWK GUNSHIP *Iron Flame* left the base and flew low over the jungle. The tree canopy was as opaque from above as it was below. At first, there was little of the ground that Atticus and his sergeants could see from the air. Even so, there was still more open to their gaze than during the initial foray. During the construction of the base, flights of Thunderhawks and Storm Eagles dropped dozens of payloads of incendiary bombs along the route from the promontory to the column. The jungle was put to the torch. The way cleared, Vindicators finished the job. Their cannons blasted into bloody mist any saurians who ventured within range. The huge siege shields scraped the smouldering ground raw and flat. There was now a scar twenty metres wide leading to the anomaly. The stream had been bulldozed underground. The swamp was drying mud. The moss was ash.

Already, the jungle was gnawing at the edges of the route, seeking to reclaim its domain. It would be a matter of weeks, Galba thought, before the bombing would have to recommence. He wondered how long the Iron Hands' store of incendiary munitions would hold out.

The state of the ground route was not the concern of the legionaries in *Iron Flame*. They had come to see the fate of Pythos's new arrivals.

The civilians had landed over an area of several square kilometres, with the column at the rough centre. Black, oily smoke billowed skywards from numerous locations. These were the pyres of dead ships. Some had broken up at high altitudes, killed by failing heat shields and weakened hulls. Others had slammed into the ground like meteors. Still others had missed the land entirely, plunging past the dark cliffs and into the restless ocean. There were also those ships whose deaths could not be explained. Whether through human incompetence, structural inadequacy or both, they exploded as they were touching down. While *Iron Flame* was being prepped for the mission, Galba had watched the last of the orbital descents. He had listened to the engine roars punctuated by the periodic, stuttering thunder of destruction. He wondered how many lives had ended in those few minutes. Many hundreds, certainly. A loss of that number of mortals was insignificant on the battlefield. For an unopposed landing, it was obscene.

Still, for every crash, there were ten successful landings. At least, that was what Galba had guessed from what he could observe from the base. Now, as the gunship reached the landing region, he took in the volume of smoke and frowned. 'There are too many fires,' he said.

'What do you mean?' Atticus asked.

'There have not been this many crashes.' The sky over this region was changing from filthy grey to choking black.

'I see no intact ships at all,' said Sergeant Crevther.

'There.' Darras pointed. 'At two o'clock.'

The vessel was a mid-sized colony ship. Its design was ancient, far older than the Imperium. That it had left its home berth at all, never mind survived a crossing of the void and a landing on hostile terrain, was miraculous. The last of its passengers were streaming down its disembarkation ramps as *Iron Flame* hovered overhead. They gathered around the ship, clambering over the trees that the ship had flattened on its descent. The transport was so old, its original name had been eroded away. A new one, *Great Calling*, was crudely emblazoned on the stubby bow.

The ship shuddered like a struck bell. Fire billowed from the open bay doors. A cascade of explosions at the stern built to a massive fireball that engulfed the engines.

'They're dancing,' Atticus said. He was standing at the open hull door of the troop compartment. The wind roared at him. His feet wide apart, arms folded, he was as steady as if welded to the deck.

The crowd, thousands strong, was capering around the stricken ship as if it were a community bonfire.

'They're mad,' said Darras. 'If they breached the plasma cores...'

'They appear to know what they're doing,' Atticus said. 'Otherwise that would have happened to at least one of the ships, and this entire region would be gone. These demolitions are being carried out with care.'

'But why?' Sergeant Lacertus demanded.

'Because they don't ever plan to leave,' Galba said. 'They kept referring to Pythos as "home" in their transmissions. Now it is. They are making it impossible to leave.' He eyed the burning colony ship, and thought that it had remained true to its first purpose all the way to the end. These people were not just civilians. They were colonists.

'They want to stay here that badly?' asked Darras. 'Then they are ignorant, stupid or mad. All three, I suspect.'

'They can't be ignorant,' said Atticus. 'Not anymore.' He pointed.

The saurians had come. The call of abundant, easy prey had gone out to them on the breezes of Pythos, and they had answered. They were arriving in much larger packs than before, and there were many more species. They descended upon the colonists. They tore into them.

The dance ended. The celebrants struggled to defend themselves. They were carrying nothing. They had no firearms. They bunched together, and fought back with punches and kicks. Some of them had swords of some kind. The blades only enraged the animals they struck. The colonists' defence was a farce of the most tragic kind. The saurians feasted well.

'Circle around,' Atticus voxed Brother Catigernus, who was piloting *Iron Flame*.

The Thunderhawk flew from landing site to landing site. The same scene was repeated at every location. The ships were burning. The clearings created by their descent were filled with crowds defending themselves with poles, improvised clubs, and more of those swords. Now and then, Galba saw a flash of lasfire. He did not think there was more than one rifle for every hundred colonists.

Many people had congregated on the land cleared by the Iron Hands. More and more joined them, fleeing the steaming slaughter of the landing sites. Galba found it hard to gauge numbers. There were people in the tens of thousands, shoulder to shoulder in the space around the column and along the wide trail leading back toward the promontory. They were a giant herd. They were the tragic righting of the ecological imbalance that so troubled Ptero. Pythos finally had its herbivores, and the predators rejoiced. The front lines of the herd fought desperately, protecting those further back. Galba knew he was looking at acts of enormous heroism, but from above, all he saw was the ugliness of the deaths. The edges of the crowd turned into a swamp of bloody mud and mutilated bodies. More reptiles were arriving all the time. Pythos was unveiling the monstrous variety of its fauna.

The outcome of the struggle was preordained. It would take days, but in the end, the road to the column would be a lake of gore.

'Take us back,' Atticus told Catigernus.

'We aren't going to open fire?' Galba asked.

'At what?' Atticus snapped.

Galba did not answer. Atticus was right. The gunship was a blunt weapon. Its missiles and guns would kill more colonists than saurians. The reptile kills would be a drop in the ocean. The only result would be a speeding up of the inevitable.

'Do you hear that?' said Darras, expressing a mixture of disbelief, bafflement and contempt.

'I do.' From Atticus, there was only contempt.

Galba heard it now. Rising above the cries of the dying and the roars of the saurians, audible even over the roar of the Thunderhawk's engines, was the sound of joy. The crowd was singing. The people were a gigantic choir. They gave voice to a triumph. Even as their fellows were being devoured, they were celebrating their arrival. Galba could not make out the words, but the mood was unmistakeable. The tune soared, a crest of victory and strength. Whatever happened to them now, these people felt they had accomplished a great task.

To have travelled to this system in craft that looked rescued from the scrapyards, that was a feat. To have landed most of them was, too. But why such a struggle to reach this death world? Galba suspected he would never know. When the celebration was over, there would be no celebrants left to explain it.

'Idiots,' Atticus muttered, dismissing the song. He continued to watch, though, and did not look away from the struggling colonists until they were out of sight.

'They fight with spirit,' Galba offered.

'Their fight is pointless. They cannot win. They are too weak. They came here to die, and I will not admire that.'

Iron Flame returned to the base and the rest of the company. Khi'dem and his fellow Salamanders stood at the edge of the landing pad. They walked forwards as the Iron Hands disembarked from the starboard access hatch. Ptero and the Raven Guard were present, too. They advanced close enough to hear what was said, but remained in the background.

'What can you tell us, Captain Atticus?' Khi'dem asked. Tone and words were respectful, Galba noted. Even so, there was an expectation of confrontation in the air.

'The situation is as anyone would expect.' Atticus did not answer Khi'dem directly. His voice was raised. He was speaking to the ranks of his legionaries who lined the landed pad. 'These travellers are essentially unarmed. They will not last long against the saurians.'

'What do you plan to do?' Khi'dem was almost whispering now.

Atticus continued to address the wider assembly. 'Mistress Ere-phren is reading the immaterium once more. She will find us a target, and we shall strike again.'

'What do you plan to do about the people of the fleet?' Khi'dem insisted, as softly as before.

Atticus at last turned his cold gaze on the son of Vulkan. 'Do?' he asked. 'There is nothing to do.'

There was a pause. The warrriors behind Khi'dem stirred. He blinked a few times, but remained calm. 'I find that hard to believe.'

'And I find your confusion surprising. Within a few days at most, the situation will be resolved.'

'Resolved...' Khi'dem repeated. He was unable to keep the mount-ing horror from his voice.

'There will either be some survivors who have learned to fight back, or there will be none.'

'You do not believe the outcome to be any of our concern?'

'Why should I?' It was Atticus's turn to sound puzzled. 'Whatever happens, these colonists are not a threat to our position. They have destroyed their means of departure. If there are any survivors, it will be a simple matter to stop any communications they attempt to make with elements outside the system. Though I think that is highly improbable.'

'I was not thinking about this mission's integrity,' Khi'dem said.

'That is regrettable.' Atticus's voice was becoming almost as quiet as Khi'dem's. The more softly he spoke, the more anger hissed from his vocaliser.

'I was thinking,' Khi'dem continued, 'about our responsibility to the colonists.'

'We have none.'

'They are being slaughtered.'

'I am aware of that, *brother*. I have seen what is happening. You have not.'

'Then how can you stand by and do nothing?'

'They have made their decisions. They are celebrating their chosen path in song as we speak. We are Legiones Astartes. Our duty is to the defence of the Imperium. It is not the policing of mortal stupidity.'

'Nor is negligence taken to the point of murder.'

Silence descended. It was thick with potential violence. It smothered the sounds of the jungle. Atticus remained motionless. Galba checked his impulse to raise his bolter. A ripple spread through the Iron Hands. A word from Atticus, and the legionaries would avenge the honour of their captain.

He did not give the word. When he spoke, it was as if he were shaping the cold silence into words. 'Explain yourself, and do it well.'

The warning was given. Feeling sick, Galba braced for combat. *Withdraw your insult,* he willed Khi'dem. They must be spared the tragedy of bloodshed between loyalist Legions. *Withdraw. Withdraw.*

Khi'dem did not stand down. 'What are we, Captain Atticus, if we do not check the annihilation of a population of civilians? What are we defending? If the citizens of the Imperium count for nothing, then what is our purpose?'

'The Emperor created us to defeat the enemies of mankind. We are weapons, not nursemaids.'

Galba breathed a bit more easily. Atticus was debating Khi'dem. The moment of rage had passed. The sergeant was glad. Khi'dem's words were eating at his conscience.

'That *is* mankind dying out there,' Khi'dem cried, pointing in the direction of the butchery. 'Here, now, those animals *are* the enemy. To what principle are you being loyal, if not that?'

'They are nature,' Atticus replied. 'They are a test. If the colonists are strong, they will survive. These are the lessons of Medusa. Have you forgotten those of Nocturne?'

'No, I have not. The people of Nocturne do not abandon each other. Do the people of Medusa?' When Atticus was silent, Khi'dem pressed on. 'You say that these people have embraced their lot with song. Are they fighting back?'

Atticus's hesitation was not hostile this time. 'They are.'

'They are not suicidal, then. They are in the struggle to the end. Surely that is not dishonourable, even if, in your eyes, they are merely flesh. There are some battles that no amount of will or ability can win. You know this. We all know this, to our cost.'

Silence followed the reference to defeat. Khi'dem paused. Galba wondered if he had overplayed his hand. Galba found that he was hoping the Salamander would sway Atticus. He distrusted his reaction. It was felt rather than reasoned. Perhaps it was another result of his imperfect embrace of the machine. Its origin did not matter. It existed. He was stuck with his unwanted empathy.

Atticus turned his head away from Khi'dem. He looked in the direction the other had pointed. He seemed to be listening for the song.

No, Galba thought. *He isn't. You are.*

'There is also the colonists' utility to the mission,' Khi'dem said.

Atticus turned back to him. 'What utility? All I see is the waste of this company's time and energy in keeping them alive.'

'If you do that, think what it will mean. If they manage to make a home here, they will be bringing stability to this region. We do not know how long we will be on this planet. Would not some degree of pacification be useful?'

Atticus grunted. 'Perhaps. Perhaps not. I do not expect this to be a permanent base of operations.'

'No,' Khi'dem admitted. 'I hope it will not be.' He began to walk away. 'But you must do as you see fit. As must I.'

'Where are you going?'

'To help.'

Atticus's bionic larynx made a short burst of electronic noise. It could have been a growl as easily as a laugh. 'And you, Raven Guard,' he said to Ptero. 'You have been silent. Do you let the Salamanders do all your speaking for you?'

'We have said nothing because we were listening,' Ptero replied. 'You judge us, Atticus. You take our measure. As we do yours.' He and the rest of his reduced squad began following the Salamanders.

Atticus made the noise again. Galba knew now that it was both a growl and a laugh. 'You seek to shame us!' he called to the retreating legionaries. 'You think honour will not permit us to stand aside while you indulge your sentimentality?'

'They're right to think so, aren't they?' Galba ventured.

'Yes,' Atticus answered, the monotone cold again, the emotions unreachable, undetectable, 'they are.'

NINE

Salvation in iron
Ske Vris
Storms

THE BATTLES ON Pythos had been skirmishes before. They had not been real wars. The power imbalance on one side or the other had been too great. The saurians had outnumbered the reconnaissance force. The deforestation had been a mechanical exercise. After the airborne immolation, the few remaining saurians had been no threat to the tanks.

This time, the battle was real. It would be a true clash of forces. There was something almost joyous in that, Galba thought.

The initial stage was a lightning advance down the trail from the promontory. The Venerable Atrax, 111th Company's Contemptor Dreadnought, and two Vindicators, *Engine of Fury* and *Medusan Strength*, led the way, the infantry following behind at a run. There was little resistance. The reptiles on the path were blasted apart by the Dreadnought's twin-linked heavy bolters. Others, too slow to flee, were flattened, then scraped apart by the tanks. The Iron Hands reached the nearest portion of the crowd less than an hour after Khi'dem had carried the day.

The mechanised assault now was twin-pronged. While Atrax continued up the centre of the trail, the Vindicators moved to either side. The jungle barred the vehicles. It was home to shadows and teeth, and protected its mysteries. The tanks did not care. Each blast from their Demolisher cannons smashed trunks to splinters, toppling the giants, crushing whatever stalked beneath. The cannons were designed to batter down fortress walls. They devastated the jungle. As destructive as each shot was, the fire was also precise. Hitting a trunk at the wrong angle might bring the great tree down on the colonists. Overhead, *Iron Flame* flew in support, saturating the deeper areas of the jungle with incendiaries, strafing the larger concentrations of saurians with its battle cannon and the twin-linked heavy bolters of its sponsons.

Galba was near the front of the left-hand column. His sight down the path was blocked by the massive shape of *Engine of Fury*. His ears were full of engine growl and the slow doom beat of the cannons. Between each enormous pound of the drum, as its echoes shook the glowering sky, there came splintering crashes and animal screams. Pythos had come to fight, and it was being taught the foolishness of its action.

The din of reptile and artillery was so great, Galba could barely hear the colonists. The song was still there, though, still strong, its triumph untouched by the depredations of the saurians. And now the might of the Legiones Astartes struck the monsters of Pythos, giving truth to the hymn of victory.

The Vindicators drove between the colonists and the predators. More saurians went down under the massive treads. The cannons fired point-blank at the rampaging monsters, drenching the vegetation in red mist. In the wake of the tanks, the Iron Hands raked the jungle with bolter fire, pushing the reptiles further back, where many more fell under the withering attacks of the Thunderhawk.

The shock of the initial attack staggered the saurians. A gap opened between the mortals and the hunters. The Iron Hands rushed to fill it. As the advance moved further towards the anomaly, the legionaries formed a ceramite chain along the sides of the trail. Each Space Marine was a link, holding several metres on either side of him. They created an avenue of sanctuary.

Standing in the hatch of *Engine of Fury*, Atticus addressed the colonists. He vox-cast his commands on all speakers. When he spoke, he was the machine incarnate, as if *Iron Flame* and the Vindicators themselves had found their voice.

'Citizens of the Imperium! Your valour does you honour! But now is the hour of your salvation. Follow the route we have created for you. Down that path lies safety. Move now or die where you stand.'

As he riddled predators with bolter shells, still following the Vindicator, Galba nodded to himself. Atticus's words were mercy reinforced by discipline and steel. The Iron Hands had come to rescue these people. They would not coddle them. If the colonists wasted the opportunity with foolishness, then they truly were weak and deserved no consideration.

Galba realised he was having a mental debate with Khi'dem. He silenced the internal voices and focused on the killing.

The colonists began to move uphill. Atticus urged them on, and they began to run. They streamed between the legionaries. The Salamanders and Raven Guard ran at the head of the crowd, holding off the saurians that abandoned the packs and tried to follow the fleeing prey.

The mission was the largest planetary deployment of the *Veritas Ferrum*'s warriors since the Callinedes offensive. Galba glanced back at the unwavering line of legionaries. The 111th Clan-Company of the X Legion was a shadow of its former self. Yet still the company numbered its warriors in the hundreds. Still the fist of Atticus came down with the force of an asteroid strike. The Legion was injured, but the Legion fought on. The Legion was *here, now,* and its majesty of war was terrible to behold. Galba's chest swelled with pride. His hearts pumped with the need for combat.

'Now let this planet know our true measure!' Atticus called. 'Let it know that we have come! Let it know our wrath! And so let it know fear!'

The closer the front of the Iron Hands' advance came to the epicentre of the anomaly, the bigger the crowd grew, and the more ferociously the saurians attacked. As Galba drew near the rock column, the reptilian assault reached such a frenzy that it was as if the jungle had been replaced by a vortex of snapping jaws. Galba was fighting a solid wall of muscle, claws and teeth. Most of the animals were the bipeds that had attacked when the column had first been discovered. But the quadrupeds were here too, as were several other species. There were a few who stood out, hunting as individuals instead of in packs. These were monsters, ten metres tall and twenty metres long. They had long, powerful forelimbs, and a row of bony spikes running from their foreheads, down their spines, and along the length of their arms. They shouldered through their smaller kin, using the massive spikes on their elbows to stab rivals out of the way.

A quadruped charged at Galba, only to shriek and fall writhing to the ground when a spike as long as a chainsword jabbed into its eye. The massive killer made a wide sweep of its arm as it lunged for Galba. He ducked. A row of death passed over his head. The reach of the saurian was so great that the blow connected with the legionary behind Galba. The force of the hit shattered his breastplate. The spikes slammed home through his chest. The warrior gurgled as his lungs and hearts were punctured. The saurian lifted him, impaled, to its mouth. Blunt jaws with teeth the length of Galba's hand snapped down on the legionary's torso, severing it in two.

Shouting inarticulate curses, Galba stitched the creature with bolter shells from belly to neck. Blood slicked the saurian's torso. The animal roared, deep bass thunder mixed with an outraged shriek of agony. It lunged its head forwards. The forehead spike smashed into Galba's shoulder. Ceramite cracked. Muscle tore. He was thrown to the ground. The monster raised a clawed foot to crush him. He rolled to the side, firing again. The earth trembled as the saurian stamped. Then Galba's shots punched up through its lower jaw. The front half of the monster's head disappeared. Galba thought the shriek would tear the clouds from the sky. The saurian staggered, its claws grasping at the air where its jaws had been. Then it collapsed with a resonant crash.

Clambering over its body came more of the smaller bipeds. The monsters had been deprived of their easy, plentiful prey, and they were angry. They were coming to kill the Space Marines, to punish them for daring to invade their territory and thwart their desire. Their insensate fury was so focused, he could almost believe evil was possible in an animal.

The saurians were relentless. As before, their numbers seemed inexhaustible. But the Iron Hands had numbers now, too. And tanks. And a gunship. The incendiaries still fell. The Demolisher cannons boomed. The jungle was shredded and burned. Many reptiles died before they could reach the objects of their hatred. The others were brought down by endless, unwavering bolter fire. The Iron Hands were holding the line. They would do so until the mission was complete.

Or they ran out of munitions.

Galba dropped another saurian and checked his ammo clips. He had learned from his first experience here. They all had. They had brought plenty of rounds. But not an infinite supply. Galba had already used half of his. The battle could not go on indefinitely.

'Run!' Atticus commanded the colonists. He spoke even as his stream of fire decapitated two of the long-necked bipeds nearest him. 'We do not wait upon your pleasure. Run now and live. Wait, and you show yourselves unworthy of our efforts. Earn our help. If you do not, you will die.'

The colonists ran. Galba could feel the size of the crowd at his back diminishing. There was movement happening. They were clearing the thousands away from the column, moving them towards safety. The colonists were still singing. The sound, mixed with the snarling and the butchery and the barking of guns, was grotesque. Galba's admiration for these people evaporated. Their impermeable joy was insane. Were they stupid? Did they have no respect for the battle-brothers fighting and dying on their behalf?

Who are we saving? he wondered. He stepped back. Massive jaws snapped together a hair's breadth from the front of his helmet. He shot the quadruped through the eyes. *Are these people worth saving?*

He could guess what Khi'dem's answer would be. The Salamander would say that the act had its own value. It did not matter for whom it was done. If they were defenceless, if they needed help, then yes, they were worth saving.

To his right, a brace of quadrupeds descended on a legionary. He did not have time to switch from bolter to chainsword before they brought him down with sheer tonnage. They crushed his skull before *Engine of Fury* fired, blasting them from existence.

Another brother gone. The loyalist campaign weakened by just that much. In exchange for what? Was there anything these colonists offered in the war that had engulfed the Imperium? How many of their lives warranted one of the Iron Hands?

An inner voice that sounded like his captain's said, *All of them would be insufficient.*

Yet Atticus was there, fighting for the lives of the mortals with as much purpose and brutal grace as on the *Callidora*. He had come to agree with Khi'dem. Agree enough. Agree, at least, that protecting what it meant to be the X Legion was worth the losses.

Back at the base, Galba had been pleased by the decision. But now the song grated. The celebration sounded like mockery. He now preferred the honest savagery of the animals he fought. He channelled his anger through his bolter, into the flesh he destroyed. As he killed another behemoth, he thought of the pride he had felt to see the full might of the company unleashed.

To fight animals, said a bitter truth.

These people. Are they worth it?

Worthy or not, the colonists were herded up the slope. They were too numerous for all of them to take refuge within the base's walls. The wounded and the weak were protected there, along with the first to arrive. The others gathered on the plateau, their numbers spilling down the slope. But the position was defensible. The Vindicators took up stations below the mortals and pummelled the jungle. *Iron Flame* flew overwatch. More of the jungle was burned away, and it became possible to hold the upper reaches of the promontory with a relatively small contingent.

Evening fell, and the bombardment continued. The wildlife of Pythos refused to surrender its prize. Individual saurians, feral rage overwhelming self-preservation, attacked every few minutes. They were annihilated. And they kept coming, gradually eating away at the ammunition supplies.

STANDING NEXT TO the armoury, Kanshell watched Atticus speaking with a small group of colonists. They were standing on the landing pad, visible to all. They appeared to be of a warrior caste. They wore rudimentary armour. It was not quite patchwork. Kanshell could see, on the individuals nearby who wore it, evidence of metalwork in the designs of the shoulder guards. Some of the warriors, men and women, carried spears or swords with elaborate engravings. Perhaps there was an officer class, too. One of the party on the landing pad appeared to be a leader. He was power-fully built, and his armour was more ostentatious.

Kanshell wished that he were close enough to hear the conversa-tion. The crowd before him was too dense to push through. It was mostly made up of Pythos's new arrivals. There were some Legion serfs mixed in with them, though. Kanshell hoped someone he knew would be close enough to learn what was being decided.

'He is asking us to leave,' said a woman at Kanshell's right shoulder.

The serf twisted, startled.

The woman, like the other colonists, was very tall and wiry. Her hair was dark, unkempt and thick. Her features were flattened, almost simian, but her face was long, and there was an odd grace to her bearing, as if she were dancing while standing still. Her cloth-ing was hide and fur, the traces of the creatures still easy to see. A necklace of animal teeth hung around her neck. It was strange attire to see on someone who had just arrived in-system. The woman seemed like a primitive, Kanshell thought. She did not look like the member of a culture that could operate void ships. She bowed. The movement was liquid. 'My name is Ske Vris.'

'Jerune Kanshell.' He nodded in return. 'You were mad to come here,' he said. 'You should leave.'

The woman smiled. 'We cannot. Our ships are gone.' Her smile was beatific.

So the rumours that had raced through the compound were true. 'Why would you do such a thing?'

'We no longer had need of them.'

'But you see what the conditions on this planet are like! You can't mean to make this your home.'

'Home,' Ske Vris repeated. She closed her eyes as she said it again: '*Home.*' She was savouring the word. She opened her eyes. They shone with a profound joy. Kanshell felt a stab of envy. The woman standing before him had found her life's mission, and had answered its call. Kanshell had once thought that he was doing the same. But now uncertainty was his companion through disturbing days and sleepless nights. 'Where is your home?' Ske Vris asked.

Was it Medusa? No, not any longer. The planet of his birth was too distant a memory. 'The ship,' he answered. 'The *Veritas Ferrum*.' When he said the name, he startled himself by pronouncing the words as if he were praying.

'How would I convince you to abandon it?'

'You could not.' The idea was offensive.

'Precisely.'

'But you have never been here before,' Kanshell protested. Then he hesitated. 'Have you?' Could this be a lost people returning to its point of departure?

'No,' Ske Vris answered. 'None of my kind has ever set foot here.'

'Then how can this be home?'

'It was foretold.' The smile again. It bespoke a certainty so absolute, it would be more difficult to uproot than a mountain.

'Why did you not come here before now?'

'The time was not right. Now it is.'

'How do you know?'

'We could not begin our journey until we were forced to. War came to the world where we were living and brought an end to it. So we left, glad to be of the generation to see the prophecy fulfilled.'

Kanshell frowned. Ske Vris's language of prophecy and foretelling was light years from the orthodoxy of the Imperial Truth. It made him uncomfortable. Partly because he disapproved.

Partly because he wanted the woman's serenity.

He noticed now, scattered about the crowd, colonists wearing hooded robes. As people milled, they lowered their heads if they crossed paths with one of the robed. There was no doubt in Kanshell's mind: superstition had an active role in this culture. How isolated had this civilisation been? For how long? Had it never been made compliant?

Had the Iron Hands encountered one of humanity's forgotten tribes just as everything teetered on the brink of collapse?

'Where did you come from?' he asked.

'The world is lost now,' Ske Vris answered. 'So is its name. That is well. It was a false home. It did not test us.'

'You think that is what Pythos is doing?'

Ske Vris nodded, her smile huge. 'It welcomed us with fury, as we knew it would. We must earn our home here. We will be tested every day. This is right. This is the way of faith.'

Faith. The word haunted him. It rose everywhere Kanshell turned. Since the first night on Pythos, it had become harder for him to dismiss it as he knew he should. Tanaura had offered him its reassurance after the death of Georg Paert. He knew he should accept that he had hallucinated. That was to be expected in a region where the boundary with the immaterium was ragged. But the insistent reality of what he had seen refused to be banished. And in the presence of evil miracles, what recourse was there, Tanaura had asked him, but faith? Did he think the simple application of force, no matter how great, was the solution?

Faith. Here it was again. He looked into the radiant face of Ske Vris. He felt a desperate hunger. This woman had lost hundreds of her fellows over the course of this day, yet she was staring towards the future with something much stronger than hope: confidence. Kanshell wondered what it would take to shake this being.

Nothing, he suspected. He was looking at a woman whose faith was an impervious shield. Perhaps it was even stronger than Tanaura's. She was frightened, whereas Ske Vris was glowing from the events of the day.

'Why?' Kanshell asked. 'Why is it necessary that you be tested?'

'To be made strong. We have to be strong to complete our work.'

'What work is that?'

Ske Vris looked up to the sealed heavens. She raised her arms high in welcome. 'That revelation is yet to come.' She paused, basking in the ineffable. She lowered her arms and her eyes were somehow even more joyful than before. 'It will come here,' she said. 'Soon. So my master says.'

'Your master?'

Ske Vris pointed to one of the robed figures. He was near the landing pad, observing the debate between Atticus and the colonists' representative. Even in the falling night, he was easy to pick out. He stood at least a head taller than most of his fellows, who kept a respectful distance from him.

'What is his name?' Kanshell asked.

'I have yet to earn the right to speak it.'

Kanshell looked at Ske Vris's attire again. The woman's tunic was longer than those worn by most of the other colonists. It also had a short hood. Kanshell saw a link between it and the dark robes. 'You are a religious apprentice?' he asked.

'A novitiate. Yes.'

Kanshell hesitated before speaking. Then he realised that he must. If he did not, he would be admitting the defeat of what he knew to be the truth. 'You are wrong to stay,' he said. 'You have been led here by a delusion. There is nothing to worship. There are no gods.'

Ske Vris's smile did not falter. 'You think so? Are you sure?'

'I am.'

'How do you come by this certainty?'

'The Emperor has revealed the truth to all mankind.' *And that includes you, doesn't it?*

'What is a revealed truth except a gift from the divine?' Ske Vris asked.

'No,' Kanshell stammered. 'No, that isn't right. It... I...' he trailed off. His will to buttress his position leaked away.

'Yes?' Ske Vris prompted.

'Nothing. You're wrong, though.' Kanshell could hear how weak his argument sounded.

His distress must have been visible. Ske Vris grasped his shoulder in a gesture of solidarity. 'I think we will have more to say to one another in the days ahead, my friend.'

'You really plan to stay.'

Ske Vris laughed. 'It is not a question of planning. This is home! This is destiny!'

DARRAS WATCHED THE spectacle on the landing pad. *This is theatre*, he thought, disgusted. The humans were done up for show. They were ragged, but there was pomp and ceremony and pride in their motley. They should have been humble, but though they expressed gratitude, they radiated entitlement, as if the Iron Hands were the ones who had just arrived and were being welcomed as guests to Pythos. The answers he had received to the questions he had put to over a dozen of the refugees only reinforced that impression.

Galba joined him beside *Unbending*. 'Any luck?'

Darras gave a short bark of a laugh. 'I ask who they are, they tell me they're pilgrims. Pilgrims from where? From lies, coming to truth. From which planet? They have crossed into the realm of the truth, and so the past, like all lies, no longer exists for them. And when I ask how they got here...'

'They were transported on the wings of faith,' Galba finished.

'Exactly.' Darras snorted. 'Nonsense.'

'Nonsense that they appear to believe.'

'Well, that's all right, then. We rescued fools instead of liars. I consider the day well spent.' He waved his arm, taking in the base and the crowded slope beyond. 'These are your works, too, brother. Look upon them.'

'I didn't advocate for this.'

'No, you didn't,' he conceded. 'But are you disappointed?' He

watched Galba carefully. He was not surprised when the other sergeant shook his head. Galba was being honest with both of them,
and that was good. But it bothered Darras how much influence
the Raven Guard and the Salamanders, Khi'dem in particular, were
having on Galba. His battle-brother was drifting from the machinic
path. 'You think we did the right thing, don't you?'

'I do.'

'Where is the worth in this carnival?'

'That has yet to be seen. But the honourable choice is not necessarily a utilitarian one.'

'Nor is it necessarily the *right* one. I didn't ask if you thought we
had chosen the honourable path. We did, without question. But
there is more than one form of honour. Today, we honoured the
flesh. Is our Legion in the habit of doing so?'

'I don't need to be instructed in our tenets.'

Darras pretended he had not heard. 'The flesh is weak, brother.'
He left unspoken the fact that so little of Galba's had been pared
away. 'It makes bad choices. It is corruptible.'

'I know,' Galba said softly.

'I think you are listening to yours too much.' When Galba said
nothing, Darras continued. 'Strategy and reason are the paths that
honour the machine. When reason is abandoned, betrayal follows.'

Galba's eyes flared with anger. Good. 'Are you accusing me of
something?'

'No. Just reminding you of who we are.'

SHE KNEW WHO had entered her chamber. The insanity of the warp
filled her world to the point that she barely had any awareness of
her own body. But the presence that had arrived was powerful. Its
hard, unforgiving reality countered the blandishments of the immaterium. 'Hello, captain,' Erephren said.

'Mistress Erephren.'

'They aren't leaving, are they?'

'They are not.'

'How could they, even if they wanted to?'

'Some repairs might be possible. The planet Kylix is just capable of supporting life. It is a harsh world, but not a mad one. We could transport them to the empty ships in orbit.'

'That does not sound like a fit duty for the Iron Hands.'

The electronic grating was eloquent with the captain's disgust. 'It does not. Nor is playing nursemaid to these fools. I hope you will provide my salvation.'

'How?'

'Give me a target, mistress. Find us a mission.'

She sighed. 'I wish I could.'

'Your sight is failing you?'

'No. The problem is the warp. I have never seen such storms. We cannot travel it. No one can.'

'When did this begin?'

'Just after our return. We are trapped here until the storms subside.'

The presence was silent.

'Lord?' Erephren asked.

'I was thinking,' Atticus said, 'how much I distrust coincidences.'

'Can the enemy have the power to cause warp storms?'

'No. No. That is impossible.' There was the sound of his heavy bootsteps. 'Do what you can,' he said.

'The moment I see a path for us to take, I will let you know.'

'I can ask no more.' The presence began to withdraw, taking its reality away.

'Captain,' Erephren called.

'Yes?'

'I want to thank you,' she said. 'The confidence you place in me is a great honour.'

'It is only right,' he answered. 'We find ourselves in unique circumstances. We must rely upon each other. We are more alike than you realise, mistress.'

'I do not understand.'

'We are tools, you and I. We have been moulded. To accomplish our duties to the fullest, we have surrendered almost everything that once made us human. We have become weapons, and nothing more. We are unfit for anything else. That is our price, and that is our great honour.'

'Thank you,' she said. Renewed strength of duty flooded her system.

THE BOMBARDMENT WAS sporadic, but it did not end. The Vindicators lit the jungle with a slow, emphatic beat of fire. Galba found Khi'dem standing beside *Medusan Strength*. 'Are you pleased with yourself?' he asked.

'I am grateful to your company,' Khi'dem answered. 'I am glad the right thing was done. I am not gloating, if that's what you mean.'

'I hope you are right that this was necessary.'

'How can you doubt it?'

'The cost.'

'I mourn the losses. I do not take them lightly. Our numbers have been reduced still further as well.'

'And what has this price bought us?'

'The right to call ourselves defenders of the Imperium. Brother-sergeant, if you weigh today only by military gain, you are making a mistake.'

Galba laughed softly. 'I knew you were going to say that.'

'Then you knew the truth. You felt it.'

'Perhaps.' Galba doubted it. The refrain of *are they worth it?* still troubled him. 'And what is the new truth? What do we do with these people now that we have saved them?'

'We are responsible for them.'

'You are being vague.'

'I do not command this company.'

'Don't you?' Galba did not try to hide his bitterness. *Medusan Strength* thundered again. Galba pointed to the sudden glow of destruction in the trees. 'Look upon your works, brother.' He was conscious of echoing Darras. Was he shifting blame? Was there blame at all? He did not know. 'Every expenditure of a shell is in answer to your desire.'

'No. It is the expression of your choice. The correct one.'

'Then you are pleased.'

'I am relieved.'

Galba snorted. 'As you will. Your *relief* will no doubt be buttressed by the news I bring.'

'Which is?'

'As we are saddled with the responsibility of these mortals, we begin construction of a more permanent settlement tomorrow.'

Khi'dem was silent. After a moment, Galba noticed he was shaking. 'Is something wrong?' he asked.

Khi'dem shook his head, then burst into laughter. 'I'm sorry, brother,' he gasped out.

'Do enlighten me.'

Khi'dem mastered himself, but when he spoke, Galba could hear the laugh forcing itself to surface again. 'I have lived to see the Iron Hands build a village. This is indeed a rare day.' Then the fit was upon him again.

Galba knew he should be offended. He found he could not summon the indignation. Instead, he saw the irony, and the corner of his mouth began to twitch up. When had there last been laughter in the company? He could not remember. Laughter had been drained from the galaxy. But Khi'dem had summoned it. The noise was defiance hurled into the night, and now Galba joined in, and it felt right.

The reason was unimportant. The worth was in the act itself.

✠ ✠ ✠

TWO MORE SERFS died during the night. One ran into the jungle. His devoured remains were found as the work began. The other lay behind the armoury. He had inserted his hands between his jaws. He had found the strength to pull his own head apart.

TEN

The touch of the numinous
Not a crusade
Intelligence

THE CONSTRUCTION BEGAN with more destruction. The low plateau near the site of the column was chosen as the site of the settlement. The colonists clamoured for that spot. Atticus agreed that it was the most defensible position. It was also strategically useful. From this location, it would be possible to extend the pacified zone to the anomaly itself.

'The Salamanders may have been right about stability,' Darras said to Galba as they organised the work details.

'They know how to hold ground,' Galba admitted.

The plateau was cleared by more firebombing by *Iron Flame*. The bombardment was intense. The fires rose high enough to be visible from the base. They glowed and flickered beneath a cloud of smoke that spread beneath the clouds, turning the grey of Pythos's sky to a dirty black. The gunship circled the plateau, using cannons and missiles to gouge an encircling trench. A strip of trees was left standing between the trench and the top of the plateau. This narrow, circular forest would be the source of raw material.

When the fires died, the Iron Hands escorted a group of colonists, a few hundred strong, back the way they had come only the day before. The pilgrimage was more organised, less of a pell-mell flight. The group was limited to a size that was easily defended. Even so, there were casualties. Three more battle-brothers and fifteen colonists died on the way there. Another five mortals were taken by predators that dared to venture onto the top of the plateau.

Temporary barricades were brought down from the *Veritas Ferrum*. They were used to create a secure zone on the west end of the plateau. In that zone, the felling of the trees began. The massive trunks were cut into uniform sections, and the erection of a permanent palisade began.

The Iron Hands provided security. They blasted down the largest of the trees. The construction of the settlement itself was entirely in the hands of the colonists, but a large contingent of serfs was tasked to aid the process. The serfs had the skills needed to build a stronghold quickly. They had the recent experience.

They needed to be kept occupied.

KANSHELL WAS AMONG those sent to the plateau. He had, with Galba's permission, volunteered. He had been aboard the *Veritas* in Harmartia. He had been spared several nights on Pythos. The journey back through the warp had been a bad one, filled with nightmares. He had put that down to his fear of returning to the planet. The first night back had been tolerable, perhaps because of the overcrowding on the base. The sheer numbers were a source of reassurance.

And yet the deaths had occurred. Two people had somehow found a way to be alone and meet the terror.

Poor judgement had left them vulnerable to hallucinations, and they had killed themselves. This was clearly explained to all.

Kanshell thought of Georg Paert, and of the eyes that screamed. And he doubted.

Tanaura tried to speak with him. Kanshell brushed her off. He was clinging to the Imperial Truth with all the rational force that remained to him. He did not want her undermining that. So he asked for the work. Back-breaking labour, he hoped, would exhaust him to the point of instant, dreamless sleep come the night.

No sun broke through the clouds. There was nothing by which he could monitor the passing of the day except the gradual tempering of the light. He imagined it was failing faster than it was. He tried to will it to be slower than it was. He threw himself into the work, hauling logs, lashing them together, raising the wall. He worked as if his body would use up the energy his mind needed to worry. He could tell that he was not the only one who had taken this quest. The faces of the other serfs mirrored his determination. Their eyes were haunted. Their jaws were set, the tendons of their necks standing out with tension.

The colonists, by contrast, were celebrating. They had begun singing again as they had during the march from the base. Unlike the day before, there was more than one melody in the air. Kanshell thought the songs were matched to particular activities – for walking, for the hewing of wood, for building. The words were unintelligible, but the tone was clear enough. It was always triumphant. Kanshell suspected the songs were hymns of praise. The colonists were more joyful than was rational. They were being buoyed by the wings of superstitious belief. He disapproved.

He envied.

Along the circumference of the plateau were a number of low mounds. They had been invisible prior to the deforestation. They were set back about twenty metres from the edge and were no more than about four metres high. The tops of the mounds were level, rough circles ten metres in diameter. One was contained within the initial secure zone. The colonists not working on the wall were busy constructing a framework on the top of the mound.

The structure went up quickly. It was square, with a peaked roof.

Kanshell paused in his work of hacking a log into a spiked shaft. He watched a colonist clamber up to the top of the building's roof. In the centre, the woman fixed one of the ornate staffs of the priest caste. Ske Vris stood at the base of the mound, calling encouragement and approval as the woman finished her work. She climbed back down to her applause.

A massive figure passed in front of Kanshell and marched over to Ske Vris. It was Darras. The sergeant towered over the novitiate, who looked up at him with a smile. Kanshell watched them speak. Their words did not reach him over the noise of the construction. Ske Vris listened to the legionary, then shook her head, still smiling. She pointed to the structure, then spoke for a few moments. Her gestures were expansive. She finished with her arms spread wide enough to embrace the world. She bowed, inviting Darras to precede her to the doorway. Darras strode up the rise. He ducked to look inside the door. Then he turned and walked away, his hand gesture to Ske Vris as dismissive as a shrug. The colonist remained at a half bow before Darras's retreating back.

Kanshell leaned his axe against the log and made his way to Ske Vris. 'What did Sergeant Darras want?' he asked.

Ske Vris straightened and clapped Kanshell's shoulder in welcome. 'He was asking about the nature of what we have built.'

'It's a temple, isn't it?' He was stunned by the colonists' foolishness. The Iron Hands would never permit such a flagrant violation of the Imperial Truth.

Ske Vris chuckled. 'There are no gods in there,' she said.

'Then what is it? A shelter?'

'We will use it in that way at first, yes. But it is more than that. It is a gathering place. There is where we discuss the concerns of our community. It is where we experience and reaffirm our bonds of fellowship. It is a lodge.'

'But you don't deny that you engage in worship.'

'I will not renounce what I said to you yesterday, no. But we will not offend the great warriors who have given us aid. We take our bonds with them very seriously, too.'

Kanshell grunted. 'I doubt that they feel the same way about you.'

'In time, they will. We have a common destiny. Why else would we all find ourselves on this world in these days of war?' That eternal smile was there still. The woman's pleasure in the world was hard to dismiss.

The envy tightened Kanshell's chest.

Ske Vris touched his arm. 'Come inside, my friend. You labour and are heavily laden. We will give you rest.'

Loyalty to the rationalist creed bade him refuse. But night was coming. So he followed Ske Vris up the slight rise to the entrance. He was not committing to anything, he told himself. He was just curious. There was no harm in taking a look.

He was struck, as he neared the building, by the care that had gone into its construction. The logs that made up its walls had been cut into shape very quickly, and their dimensions were irregular. Even so, the joins looked solid enough to weather years and decades. He noticed that there was no daubing to fill the gaps where the lengths of the logs did not meet. 'What are you going to use for weatherproofing?' he asked.

'Nothing,' Ske Vris answered.

'Nothing?'

'Is the work not beautiful?'

It was. The gaps had a serendipitous pattern to them that gave the simple architecture a complexity that was invisible from afar, but dissolved into individual fragments when too close. 'This will make a poor shelter from the first wind,' Kanshell commented.

'Look inside,' Ske Vris urged.

Kanshell did. There were no windows, but there was light. The perpetual overcast of Pythos was still enough to shine through the gaps in the walls. The pattern Kanshell had seen outside was multiplied in the interior. It seemed to him that the ambient exterior light was sharpened as it passed through each slit, creating an interlocking overlap of light on light. He tried to see the pattern's precise contours, but could not. The light was too diffuse. He was not seeing beams crossing each other. Rather, he was experiencing the layering of shades and tonalities. This was a play of light that was felt instead of seen. The effect was extraordinary.

'How...' Kanshell began. His sentence trailed off, beset by too many questions. How had the colonists done this work so fast? How had they done it with such crude material? *How did they do it at all?*

Ske Vris brushed past him and walked to the centre of the space. 'Join me,' she said. 'Come and see the touch of the numinous.'

Kanshell took a step forwards. The lightweb intensified as he entered the lodge. It danced over his nerve endings. His skin broke out in electric gooseflesh. The hair on his arms stood on end. The space did not grow brighter, but he could see more clearly. He was on the verge of making out the details of the pattern. If he joined Ske Vris in the centre of the web, he would surely see it then. There would be clarity. He would understand the meaning of the pattern.

And Ske Vris promised the revelation of the divine.

No. The promise of comfort was great. It would be easy to surrender to his instincts. His mind and his heart were exhausted from the effort of clinging to rationality. But his pride would not yet admit defeat. He wanted to believe that loyalty was urging his steadfastness, but that argument rang hollow. There was no questioning Tanaura's loyalty. She would tell him to walk forwards.

'No,' he said to Ske Vris, to Tanaura, to himself. 'Thank you, but no. I have to get back to work.' He backed out of the lodge.

'Another time, then,' Ske Vris called after him. 'There is no door here. Only a doorway. Cross it when you are ready.'

☩ ☩ ☩

THE SERFS WERE returned to the base before nightfall. The colonists kept working. The labour would not cease, they said, until it was done. More of their number had been escorted to the plateau during the day. Close to half their total numbers were now at work on the settlement. The wall was spreading its reach by the hour. Between it and the barriers from the *Veritas Ferrum*, there was enough protection that only one squad of Iron Hands, under the command of Sergeant Lacertus, stood sentry that night.

'The morale of these people is high,' he told Galba and Darras as they were about to head back to the base. 'It's sickeningly high.'

The atmosphere was different at the base. There was enough room, now, to shelter the remaining colonists within its walls. The grounds were crowded with them. Most of them were asleep. Those still awake were singing softly. The melody was a low, tenor, background hum, the slow sweep of its phrases like the murmurs of wavelets of a lake at twilight.

'I think they've built a temple,' Darras said to Galba as they crossed the base's plasteel gate.

'That structure does look like one,' Galba admitted. 'You made inquiries?'

'They deny it is any such thing. "There are no gods there." That's what I was told. It is only a gathering place.'

'Were you being lied to?'

Darras hesitated. 'The curious thing is, I don't think I was. And yet...' He gestured, taking in the resting colonists and their song.

'Yes,' Galba agreed. 'Superstition has deep roots in them. It has not been eradicated.'

They found Atticus standing outside the command unit. At first, Galba thought he was surveying the colonists. But as they approached, he saw that the captain's gaze was elevated. He seemed to be watching for something. 'Well?' he asked.

Darras briefed him on the plateau and the lodge.

'Should we demolish that structure?' Galba asked.

'No,' Atticus said after a moment. 'Not unless there is a direct violation of Imperial Law. There are a number of pacified worlds whose
cultural traditions are very close to the edge of theism, but have, for
strategic reasons, been allowed a provisional measure of tolerance.
We have taken on more than enough with these wretched mortals
already. We are not engaged in a crusade. We are fighting for the life
of the Imperium. If the Salamanders wish to spend their time edu-
cating the savages, let them. For now, if these people can be of any
tactical use to us in stabilising this region, then I would have them
do so. I will not spend any more time and resources on them than
is absolutely necessary. You say the plateau is becoming secure?'

'It is,' Galba confirmed.

'Is our presence required at all?'

'Minimally, for now,' said Darras. 'They should be able to fend
for themselves, properly equipped, within a few days. Some continued losses are to be expected, but…'

'They have the numbers to sustain that. Good.'

'Has Mistress Erephren found another target?' Galba asked. He
understood his captain's frustration. Every day spent on Pythos
was another small victory handed to the traitors.

'No,' Atticus grated. 'The warp storms continue to intensify. But I
will have us ready to depart the moment action against the enemy
becomes possible. Then all this flesh,' he waved his hand in contempt, 'can learn its strength or weakness on its own.'

GALBA WAS WALKING past the serf barracks, heading for the wall,
when he saw Kanshell hovering by the door. 'Lord,' Kanshell said,
bowing low.

'Hello, Jerune. You should not be alone.'

Kanshell glanced back into the dormitorium. 'I'm not.' His voice
shook.

'Were you watching for me?'

The serf nodded. 'Forgive me for presuming…' he began.

'That's all right. What is it?'

'Those things I saw the first night–'

'The hallucinations.'

Kanshell swallowed. He began to tremble. His eyes reflected the arc lights of the base. They were shining with terror. 'I'm sorry, lord. I tried to believe that I was seeing things. Please believe me. I have tried and tried. But I know it was real.'

Galba shook his head. 'This is precisely why the warp is so dangerous. Of course it seemed real. It–'

Kanshell fell to his knees, his hands clasped in supplication. 'But it's happening again! Now! Right now! Please, oh please, in the name of the Emperor, tell me you can sense it too!'

Galba was so startled that his serf had dared to interrupt that he did not respond immediately. The hesitation was long enough for his own certainty to crumble. The memory of the taste of shadows assailed him with renewed venom, strength and conviction. And then it was more than a memory. The taste was there again. The shadows that were darker than any absence of light reached tendrils into his being. He tried to shake them off. He fought them with reason. He was not immune to the mental depredations of the warp. There was nothing real in what he was experiencing.

The shadows gripped harder, sank deeper. They insisted on their reality. They took Atticus's declarations of rationalism and shattered them, leaving Galba exposed to their black truth.

Kanshell suddenly put his hands over his ears. 'No no no no,' he whimpered. 'Can you hear? Can you hear them?'

Galba did. Though the shadows were smothering his senses, some perceptions were sharpened. They were the allies of the shadows, more claws of the warp. Barely audible beneath the quiet chanting of the colonists came the sounds from inside the serf barracks.

The people inside were murmuring in their sleep. Their words were slurred, inarticulate. The noise was the mumble of stones, the insinuation of breeze, the whisper of the night stream.

'I can hear them,' Galba said. His own words were muffled, as if he were speaking through a cloud of lead. But the act of speaking gave him some agency. He moved towards the doorway. More shadows waited there, coiling, ready to spring. 'How many?' he asked.

'All of them,' said Kanshell.

It was absurd. Every one of the hundreds of mortals asleep in the rows of bunks could not be sleep-talking. Galba stepped inside, leaving Kanshell at the door.

He saw right away that the man was wrong. Not all the serfs were whispering. A few were awake. They were weeping, curled up into balls of terror on their cots. All the others had joined the nocturnal choir. Their words were unintelligible, but Galba could tell that each person was reciting a different litany. The voices came together in a struggle of syncopation and layering. The whispers piled up on top of each other, a different hiss rising to the surface with every passing second. The murmurs ceased to be human. They were no longer the product of lips and vocal cords. They were rasping sound-shapes unto themselves. They coiled around Galba's hearing. They were serpentine fragments twining into a whole. They summoned the shadows closer. The darkness squeezed. Galba began to choke. The moaning, rattling, snickering choir became more intense, though the volume remained barely above a grave's silence. The fragments joined and moulded, joined and laughed. As before, Galba felt an unveiling loom over sanity's horizon. It was not enough that he be assailed by a truth made of butchered minds and desecrated corpses. It was not enough to feel the presence of the truth pressing against his mind like an expanding tumour. He must be shown the nature of the truth. He must hear it speak. He must know what it had to announce.

His vision began to darken. His eyes were being covered by a membrane that was insubstantial, yet it clung, veined red, like muscle. The truth slithered closer. He divined its shape. It was a name. Behind the name, an intelligence lurked. The name took shape behind his eyes, and the shape was *Madail*. Its rhythm was the beat of a reptilian heart. It forced its way up his throat. It would have him speak it. And then it would claim him as its own.

MADAIL, MADAIL, MADAIL.

Galba roared. He released his anger free of all form, of all words. It was a blast of untainted fury, and it tore through the membrane. It ripped the night in two. The whispering faltered. Galba grabbed his chainsword. He raised it high and let its snarl shred the whispering. 'Awake!' he shouted. 'In the name of the Emperor, *awake!*'

The whispering stopped. The shadows withdrew. He could breathe again. The serfs were conscious now, sitting up and staring at him. They were frightened, but not of him. They did not look confused. He saw, on their faces, the mark of a collective nightmare.

He turned on his heel and marched out of the barracks. Kanshell was still on his knees. He was limp, whether with exhaustion or relief, Galba was not sure. 'Keep everyone awake,' he told the serf. He gave the order so Kanshell would have a purpose. He did not think anyone was likely to sleep now.

The singing of the colonists had stopped. The atmosphere of the base was tense, as though a storm, instead of having passed, was about to break. Galba strode towards the command post. He was not the only one. Many of his battle-brothers were converging on the base's nerve centre. He felt eyes on him. He had expected that. He had raised an alarm.

Not all the legionaries were looking at him. Their faces, in the hard illumination of the base, were grim. They had the looks of men who knew they were at war, but did not understand the foe.

He had not been alone, Galba saw. Some part, at least, of what had attacked him had also touched them.

This was no hallucination. He braced himself for the confrontation with Atticus. The captain would not be receptive to those words. Galba himself did not want to speak them. They raised too many questions. They attacked the foundations of reality. They undermined the regime of truth under which they all lived. But they must be spoken. They must be confronted.

Atticus was outside the command post, as if he had not moved since Galba and Darras had left him there. He stood with his legs spread, his arms folded. He was as immovable as the column of stone. He was not wearing his helmet. His single human eye shone with a flame as cold as the void. He was staring into the night with a pure, machinic hatred. Galba's words died on his lips as he drew near.

There was nothing to say. Atticus knew.

The captain of 111th Clan-Company, X Legion, turned his terrible gaze on the Iron Hands. 'We have an enemy on this planet,' he said. 'It attacks from the shadows. Bring it into the light.' He uncrossed his arms, opening hands that had been designed to do nothing but destroy. 'And I will annihilate it.'

AND AT DAWN, something rose to the surface.

ELEVEN

The chosen ground
Beneath the surface
The need for comfort

THE SHADOWS CAME for Erephren during the night. The attack was sudden, and took her by surprise. All of her defences were directed towards the empyrean itself. They were the filters through which she looked at the madness. They did nothing to protect her from the power behind the shadows. It had a half-presence on the planet. Its influence was leaking through the barriers. Reality began to suffer distortions. The madness of the warp was acquiring an empirical substance on Pythos. It did not yet walk unfettered on the surface of the planet. But the madness was coming. Its advance guard was already strong.

Erephren was watching, with growing dismay, the course of the warp storms. A sea of perpetual turbulence had roused itself into a gale so monstrous, she risked everything in contemplating it. The source of the tempest was the Maelstrom. Hungry, raging with a sudden influx of power, it spread its reach to infinite horizons. Erephren saw some loyalist ships that had dared to venture into the cauldron. They foundered. Some were destroyed, and she saw every detail of their agony. Others disappeared into the heaving waves of unreality. She did not like to think what would be left of the minds of those on board, should those vessels ever reappear.

She searched in vain for the echoes of the Astronomican. There was no failure in her vision. The waves had submerged the great light.

And it was as she gazed upon the storm that the attack came. It invaded her chamber. She sensed the not-quite-presence as soon as it arrived. She was strong. She was quick. She shut her psychic senses to the warp and withdrew her consciousness from its clutches. She snapped her shield up.

Speed, strength and training did her no good. She was ready even for such horrors as bred in the zones of weak boundaries. But the dangers for which she was prepared were inchoate. They did not have volition. They were not sentient.

The shadows smashed her shield. They laughed, and the laughter was the scrape of razors over her skin. They roared, and they were the voice of a word: *damnation*. The voice smashed her into oblivion.

When she woke, it was to true blindness for the first time in her life. She gasped, fighting a smothering panic in the absolute winter of her senses. She felt the expansion of her chest, and that gave her back her body. She flexed her fingers. They scratched against a metal floor. So she had fallen from her throne. Her neck and the back of her head were sore; the brass antennae and mechadendrites that helped tune her mind to the warp had been torn from her when she fell.

Bit by bit, she acquired the knowledge of her location and condition. Her senses awoke from their paralysis. She gathered her identity and hugged it close. A terrible shame enveloped her. She had been weak. She had no idea how long she had lain unconscious, derelict in her duties.

Worse was her knowledge of what had happened. She had been attacked. There had been an *attacker*.

She pushed herself up off the floor. Her awareness of her surroundings returned to her, but imperfectly, as if they were a degraded hololith transmission. She reached for her staff. It was where it should be, resting against the throne. She clutched it, steadied her stance, then braced her mind. Cautiously, she reached out to the warp.

She grunted in pain. Warm tears of blood trickled from the corners of her eyes. Harsh, jagged, silver static disrupted her perception of the empyrean. It stabbed at her mind. It was claws and broken glass, absences in the shape of pain, distortions that were madness layered on madness. She withdrew before she collapsed again.

She wiped the blood from her cheeks. She steadied herself, found her core of strength and left her dark chamber. She had to speak to Atticus. Yesterday, she had assumed the warp storms were the inevitable result of random processes in that realm. The attack changed that. The implications were too immense for her to accept. The direction down which her thoughts were flowing had to be mistaken. But something had attacked her, and that must be reported.

There was very little sound in the command block. Erephren passed a few serfs, but she encountered no presence of the Iron Hands. As she approached the door to Atticus's quarters, a woman emerged from them. 'Mistress Erephren,' the serf said. 'I'm sorry, but Lord Atticus is not here.'

Erephren sensed the other woman's deep bow. 'Where is he?' she asked.

'He and a great many of the legionaries have gone to the settlement.'

'Why?'

There was a hesitation. 'I do not have the honour of the confidence–' the woman began.

'You have enough of the captain's confidence to be given the duty of caring for his chamber,' the astropath interrupted. 'Serfs listen, observe and talk among themselves. Now you will enlighten me. What are the rumours?'

'They say that something has been found there.'

'And that is?'

'I do not know, mistress.'

Erephren thought for a moment. The attack; the interference with her connection to the warp; this discovery, whatever it was, that had summoned away the leadership of the company: these things were linked. She had to inform Atticus about what had happened to her. 'I need a vox operator,' she told the woman.

'I will summon one,' the serf answered. But she did not leave immediately. Erephren heard an intake of breath, the sound of someone gathering courage to speak again.

'What is your name?' Erephren asked.

'Agnes Tanaura, mistress.'

'You wish to ask me something, Agnes?'

'You do not believe that what happened last night was a simple warp effect, do you?'

'I do not.'

'Do you know what it was?'

'No,' she said. She was about to add that she would not engage in speculation, but then realised that Tanaura did not expect her to have an answer. The serf had one of her own. Whether presumption or courage was pushing the woman to talk, either was impressive enough to make Erephren listen. 'Do you?' she asked.

'Not exactly,' Tanaura said. 'What I know is that it was something unholy.'

'Unholy,' Erephren repeated, bitterly disappointed. 'You are risking severe sanction, using such a benighted term.'

'Forgive me, mistress, but I must speak the truth, and it *is* the truth. You were touched by this evil in the night. I can see it.' There was a rustle as Tanaura took a step forwards. 'We are not alone in our fight, though,' she said. 'There is comfort. There is hope. There is a sacred–'

Erephren held up a hand. 'Stop,' she said. 'You are blithering, and I do not have time for nonsense.'

'The Emperor,' Tanaura hurried on. 'In His divinity, He will save us, but we must accept Him before it is too late.' Erephren felt a tug on her robe. The serf was daring to clutch at her. 'Please listen to me,' Tanaura begged. 'Please listen to what you must know, in your heart, to be true. The legionaries will listen to you. They must. Oh, they must.' She was on the verge of weeping.

Erephren pulled her robe from Tanaura's grasp. 'Must they?' The flush of contempt she felt was a relief. She was almost grateful to this woman and her forbidden superstition. She was being reminded of her true responsibilities, and jolted away from the temptations of irrationality that had loomed large since the attack. 'Why is it so important that they listen?'

'Because we must leave this place,' Tanaura said, her voice very small.

Erephren snorted. '*That* is the extent of your faith? You believe, against His explicit teachings, that the Emperor is a god, but that He is too weak to be of aid to us?'

'That… That isn't what I mean…'

'Then make yourself clear, and do so quickly.'

'We may not have chosen the battleground wisely–'

'*We?*' Erephren demanded, enraged by the woman's arrogance.

Tanaura stumbled backwards. 'I did not intend to suggest–'

'As you value your life, I hope you did not!' Erephren tightened her grip on her staff. She was not cruel. But there were limits before effrontery must be punished.

'Please understand,' Tanaura begged. 'Not all battles can be won. We already know this. Perhaps we face another Isstvan here. Perhaps the true struggle is elsewhere.'

Erephren's rage subsided as she heard the agonised hope in the serf's voice. The woman was no coward. She was acting as her conception of her duty dictated. When the astropath spoke again, she kept the threat from her tone. But she remained firm.

'You may think so. But your worship is a delusion, and it is only by an act of mercy that I do not have you silenced.' She paused for a moment, letting Tanaura realise her near escape. She went on, 'And a delusion is not a weapon. It is a weakness. I follow the Emperor's teachings, and I use the force of reason against our foe. Until such time as Captain Atticus declares otherwise, Pythos is *ours*. It is the key to the Tenth Legion's ability to strike back at the traitors, and I will not turn from it, unless our commanding officer so orders.' She leaned towards Tanaura, and the presence of the serf shrank before her. 'This is my battle. *Here*. I will not retreat. I have been attacked, and I will make the enemy, whatever it is, rue the day it crossed my path.'

As she spoke, she felt the truth of her words gather iron. The terror of the night had evaporated, leaving a precipitate of cold rage.

'Do *you* understand *me*?' she demanded of the serf.

'I do, mistress.'

'Now summon the vox operator. There is work to be done.'

ATTICUS WALKED THE edge of the pit. Galba and Darras followed. A few hundred metres away, Lacertus and his squad mounted guard over a second subsidence. 'And the colonists have done no work on this?' the captain asked.

'They say they have not,' Galba confirmed. He looked down into the deep chasm. 'I do not see how they could have.' The pit had opened up in front of the mound on which the lodge was built. It was forty metres wide and ten across. Its depth was hard to guess. It fell into darkness after about a hundred metres.

'Though they *have* been industrious,' said Darras.

It was true. During the night, the wall had been extended along half the perimeter of the plateau. The secure zone was twice what it had been when Galba and Darras had left the evening before.

'Hundreds of people working without cease,' Galba answered. 'What they accomplished with the wall is well within the possible. This pit is not. And Lacertus saw no sign of explosives being used. The ground collapsed. That is all.'

'Could the construction of their meeting places have been a factor?' Darras wondered. A second lodge was nearing completion on the mound before the second pit.

'No,' said Atticus. 'If the ground were that unstable, we would have known. I believe what caused the subsidence is a symptom of our problem, and not the cause.' He paused, cocking his head to one side as he listened to his ear bead. Then he turned to the sergeants. 'News from Mistress Erephren,' he told them. 'She had her own battle last night, and the attack continues. Her ability to read the warp is being sabotaged.' He looked into the pit. 'The subsidence is not our concern,' he emphasised. '*That* is.' He pointed at what was revealed in the pit.

Beneath the colonists' lodge was a massive stone structure. The mound was nothing more than the peak of the squat dome of the building. It appeared to be made of the same sort of stone as the structure at the epicentre of the anomaly. But that column remained an ambiguity, neither clearly natural nor artificial. There was no such ambivalence before them now. Even so, what was visible of the cyclopean structure had a disturbingly seamless quality. Galba could see no joins, no mortar, no hint that the edifice had not been carved from a single mass of black rock. It was as if an entire cliff face had flowed into this shape, and then been buried by the passage of thousands of millennia. A similar structure was visible at the site of the second subsidence.

Galba said, 'If this is what lies beneath two of the mounds...'

'Yes,' Atticus replied, turning around in a slow circle. 'Is it also true of the other mounds?'

Galba followed Atticus's example. He realised now how evenly spaced the four mounds were. Diagonal lines connecting them would meet in the centre of the plateau. 'Why,' he wondered, 'has there been no subsidence at the other two locations? It has only happened where the colonists have been building.'

'There must be a connection,' said Darras. 'We just can't see it yet.'

'If there is, we shall find it,' Atticus declared. 'What is important is that our enemy begins to show his hand, and so becomes vulnerable to counter-attack.'

Galba frowned. 'How do you mean?'

Atticus pointed to the xenos structure. 'No saurian built that. It is direct evidence of intelligent life on Pythos.' He turned his gaze on Galba. 'No ghost built this, either.'

Galba refused to be cowed. 'How long would it take for natural processes to bury something like this? What evidence do we have that the race that constructed it is still with us?'

'The fact of its return is evidence. Who else would have an interest in it? Beyond that, I care little for the nature of our enemy besides the best way to destroy it. The interference Mistress Erephren is experiencing will stymie our war effort. Our foe's psychological attacks are also proving costly.'

'What are your orders?' Darras asked.

Atticus walked to the edge of the chasm. 'We expose the truth,' he said. 'And we descend into the heart of the lie.'

THERE WAS MORE work than ever. There was urgency to it, too. Atticus had commanded that the full extent of the underground structure be revealed. All of the colonists had now been shipped to the plateau. Every serf not essential to the running of the base had been brought here, too. The command was a simple one: *dig*.

Kanshell did as was commanded. The equipment was limited. The *Veritas Ferrum* was equipped for destruction, not colonisation. Most of what was available had come with the refugee fleet, and what had been salvaged from the landings before the saurian onslaught was as worn and patchwork as the ships themselves. There were no earthmovers. There were shovels and picks, and many of those had been assembled from bits of wreckage. The task was immense. The means should have made it almost impossible. But the will and the hands were there. The colonists were eager to help. Half their number worked on the wall and held off marauding preda- tors. For the moment, the saurian incursions were an occasional event, easily repulsed. The other half joined the serfs in attacking the ground at the base of the mounds.

Kanshell no longer held the hope of sleep induced by exhaustion. He knew that the night would bring screams, and there was noth- ing he could do except hope the screams were not his own. He still welcomed the work. It gave him focus during the day. It was something he could pretend was useful. Over vox-horns broadcast- ing the entire width and breadth of the plateau, Atticus promised that war was about to be brought to the enemy's home. Kanshell wanted to believe him. But the more he dug, the more that was uncovered, the shakier his faith became.

His faith was shaken because of how quickly the work progressed. The earth seemed eager to give up its secrets. Kanshell, along with dozens of other workers, attacked the edges of the second pit. The ground fell away with every blow, tumbling down into the dark, pebbles and clods striking the face of the black structure. More of it was visible all the time, though its mystery deepened also. The scale of the building became more apparent. Kanshell wondered if it might not encircle the plateau. Atticus had directed other teams to start excavations at a point equidistant between the four mounds. So far, they had nothing but a deep hole to show for their efforts.

His faith was shaken because of the structure's mystery. As it became exposed to light, it mocked rationality. The façade was a riot of ornate sculpture. There was nothing representational about the artwork. The twisting lines and bulges of the stonework were an abstract language of ghastly majesty. When Kanshell looked at the carvings directly, he saw power frozen into stone, and stone about to explode as power. He could not stare long. The designs hurt his head. They tried to strangle his eyes. His skin crawled so much, it felt like it was sloughing off his bones. When he averted his gaze, the torment changed its nature. His peripheral vision kept picking up movement. Serpentine beckoning called to him. When he looked, of course there was no movement. But the immobility was a mockery, a lie. The terror grew that the next time he looked, the stone would squirm, and that would be the moment of his end.

The colonists sang as they worked. They were as committed to the dig as they were to the wall. They transformed their labour into an act of worship. They showed no fear. Kanshell was sick with envy. On the faces of the other serfs, he saw the reflection of his own terrors. Their eyes jumped and skittered as his did. They were pale, taut from lack of sleep. The energy of their actions was fuelled by desperation. But there were some, frightened though they were, who seemed more composed. They were drawing on a deep reserve of inner strength. Kanshell saw something different in them. They had something in common with the colonists.

They had belief.

Atticus held off the descent until the excavations were well under way. Kanshell watched him march from one work site to another, evaluating. The captain observed with the dispassion of a cogitator. He did not rush his legionaries into the gulfs. He was gathering what intelligence could be gleaned, though Kanshell could not guess what the colossus learned from the gradual exposure. After three hours, though, he prepared to lead a mission into the largest chasm, before the first of the lodges that had been built.

Kanshell paused in his digging to watch the two squads gather at the lip of the drop. They anchored rappelling cables strong enough to support the weight of a Space Marine clad in power armour. A group of the Raven Guard joined them. They were wearing jump packs.

'You are frightened,' said a voice. It was deep as a mountain chain. Kanshell turned and looked up. Khi'dem of the Salamanders stood before him. Though the legionary wore his helmet, Kanshell sensed a stern kindness in his eyes. It was something he had never found in any of the Iron Hands, except Galba.

'I am, lord,' Kanshell said.

'You should not be. You should have confidence in the Legiones Astartes. There is no xenos force that can stand before us.'

'I know.'

Khi'dem cocked his head. 'My words give you no comfort, do they?'

If any member of the Iron Tenth, even Galba, had asked that question, Kanshell would have answered honestly because, however much he might be reluctant to admit the truth of his weakness, he was more terrified of lying to his machine-like masters. Now, Kanshell felt the truth invited, rather than extracted, from him. 'No,' he admitted. 'I'm sorry, lord, but they do not.'

'Why is that?'

'I...'

Had it been night, had he been ringed by the terrors that came with the dark, he would not have hesitated. Though the respite of the day was a weak one, it was enough to hold him back from a criminal admission.

Khi'dem took pity on him, and provided the answer himself. 'It is because you think this is an enemy of a very different order.'

Kanshell gave the tiniest nod.

'This belief is becoming commonplace in the ranks of the serfs. It is a mistaken one. Place your belief in your captain. I'm sure what you have experienced is terrifying, but these are attacks. If this were all a manifestation of how thin the barrier to the immaterium is on this planet, there would be little we could do. But an enemy can be fought. It is that simple.'

'Yes, lord,' Kanshell answered. *No*, he thought. *It is not that simple.*

The son of Vulkan watched him a moment longer, then walked away.

He knows I don't believe him, Kanshell thought, his face flushing with shame.

He threw himself back into his work. He dislodged more clumps of earth that fell into the dark. The strip of ground on which he stood, between the chasm and the plateau's slope, felt like thin ice. It was distressing to realise how much beneath his feet was hollow. The dark below was a maw that waited for him.

He kept working out of duty, not belief. He looked up at one point, and saw that the squads had gone into the chasm. Their brothers stood guard over the cables. Kanshell looked away, trying to summon the confidence Khi'dem had said he should feel. He failed.

And then, sooner than he would have wished, his shift ended. Evening was closing its grip on Pythos, and the moment came to return to the base.

There was enough clear landing space at both the base and the settlement for a troop transport to be able to ferry the large numbers of serfs back and forth. When Kanshell alighted from the crowded hold, he went, for the first time in his life, looking for Tanaura.

He spotted her near the landing pad. More supplies were being brought down from the *Veritas Ferrum*, and she was among those hauling plasteel crates of ammunition to the armoury that occupied the north-east corner of the base. She was looking as grim as he felt. He almost despaired, but he had nowhere else to turn, so he followed her to the armoury, and waited outside its hangar door for her to emerge.

'Agnes,' he said.

She turned, surprised. 'Jerune? What is it?'

'I need to speak with you.'

She took a trembling breath. She was more than exhausted and scared. She seemed defeated. 'Why?' she asked.

Kanshell hesitated. Was her faith no stronger than his, then? The evening's gathering darkness rushed forward. 'I'm sorry,' he said. 'It's nothing.' He turned to go.

'Wait,' she caught his arm. She held it with the ferocity of sudden, desperate hope. 'Tell me.' Her need was at least as great as his.

'The things that have been happening,' he began. 'The things that I've seen...' This was more difficult than he had expected. 'I don't...'

Even now, with his old belief structure in ruins, his loyalty made it impossible to speak what he felt. It was too much like betrayal.

Tanaura helped him. 'The secular universe cannot explain these things.'

'That's right,' he said, grateful. The constriction around his chest lessened. The relief was minute, but it was real.

'What is it you're looking for?' she asked.

'Strength,' he answered. 'Hope.'

She was suddenly possessed by both. 'There *is* hope,' she said. 'And it will grant you strength.'

'Will it help me against... against the night?'

'It will help you face the night.'

'Is that all?'

'The Emperor calls on all of us to have courage. And doesn't it help to know that though the forces of darkness are real, so is the force of light?'

Kanshell thought about that. 'Perhaps,' he said, and that admission, that first acceptance of what Tanaura preached, opened a door in his psyche. It opened a door to the sun. *Yes*, he thought. *Yes*. He had always had faith in the Emperor, but to know Him as a god was to realise there were no barriers of distance to His power. The Emperor could see him here. The Emperor could reach him here. The warmth that came with the retreat of despair flowed through his veins.

'Yes,' he said aloud. He smiled.

'The Emperor protects,' Tanaura said.

'The Emperor protects,' Kanshell repeated.

That night, he was curled in his bunk, awaiting the horrors that stalked the night. He was terrified. The horrors arrived, walking on dreams of shadow. They made the sleepers gibber and sing. They made the waking scream. But Kanshell clutched a copy of the *Lectitio Divinitatus* to his heart, and he was comforted.

TWELVE

Down
Machine
Flood

THE IRON HANDS rappelled down the façade. The Raven Guard preceded them using their jump packs. It was the first time that Ptero's Assault squad had brought its true calling to bear. The two squads from the X Legion were led by Atticus and Galba. Darras had accepted his squad's posting as guards at the mouth of the pit with ill grace.

'I mean no disrespect, brother-captain,' he had said, 'but why?'

'Because this is a reconnaissance mission, not an invasion. And because Sergeant Galba has, of all of us, had the most intimate contact with the enemy. If the foe approaches us below, I want as much warning as possible.'

He still believes I am some sort of psyker, Galba thought. He resented the idea, but if Atticus thought he could be useful, so be it. He knew his duty.

He pushed off from the stone wall. Did it twitch beneath his boots? Did his heels sink into it for a moment, as if it were flesh? Did he see the relief work writhe, like a nest of serpents? No, none of these things happened. He could be sure, he hoped, of that. Yet he felt an atavistic disgust as acutely as if they had.

He dropped another dozen metres, pushed off again, and came down on a wide ledge where Atticus and his squad were waiting. Below, the pit fell away into dark silence. The ledge was a kind of terrace outside an opening in the wall.

'This is the work of unhealthy minds,' Atticus said, eyeing the entrance. 'We will be doing the galaxy a service by exterminating them.'

The architecture of the entrance was as disturbing as every other aspect of the façade. Galba did not know if he was facing a window or a doorway. It rose to a pointed arch, but the sides were asymmetrical, curving in and away from each other. Looked at directly, the entrance was a ragged wound in stone flesh. Seen from the corner of the eye, it was a dance. The arch was narrow, and angled slightly off the vertical. It stabbed at the eye, and it took Galba a moment to realise the full extent of its perversion.

'The sides don't meet,' he said, pointing. The arch was an asymptote. The sides closed with each other, then narrowed to a razor line, but they never joined. The arch was a lie.

'That isn't possible,' Techmarine Camnus said, offended. 'That must be a fissure.'

'No,' said Atticus. There was a barely audible whir as his bionic eye moved up the face of the building, adjusting wavelengths to adapt to the lack of light, magnifying the objects of his gaze. 'Brother Galba is correct. The division becomes part of the ornamentation. It goes all the way up.'

Camnus turned his own artificial eyes on the arch. 'The building is divided into two?' he wondered.

'Worse than that,' said Galba. He pointed to the left, then right, at other openings. Each had its own particular deformation, as if once finished, the structure had begun to melt. The arches visible in the gloom had the same infinitesimal gap. The façade, which had appeared seamless at first, upon closer inspection was a web of tiny gaps. It was a three-dimensional mosaic.

'Not possible,' Camnus said again, only now his denial was an expression of horror.

'It was built into the hillside, that is all,' Atticus said. 'It is being held up by the earth into which it is sunk.'

The ledge was at its widest in front of the centre of the opening. At its edge was a curved, tapering cylinder twice the height of a legionary. It looked like an enormous tusk, projecting into the empty air of the pit. Camnus walked the few steps over to examine it. His servo-arm shone a beam over the black stone. He lit up the same fractal division. What looked like an arabesque of cracks glowed. Nothing prevented the tusk from falling to pieces, unless it was that aesthetics had a gravity of their own.

'Brother-captain,' Camnus said, 'I can think of no plausible explanation for what we are seeing.'

'It is an effect of the warp,' Atticus replied. 'More of the leakage in this region. We should not be surprised by aberrations.'

'With respect, their existence is not what is troubling,' Galba put in. 'It is the organised form in which they appear. Something has moulded the stuff of the warp into this shape.'

'If it can affect the material world, it can be destroyed by it,' said Atticus.

The Raven Guard had continued further down, and now returned to the ledge, wounding the darkness with the glare from their jump packs.

'Well?' Atticus asked. His acceptance of the other Legions was as grudging as ever. He refused to extend more than the barest courtesy. But he was working with them. Galba was relieved that he was not being called on to play the diplomat.

No, said the unwelcome voice in his head. *You are not the diplomat anymore. You are the psyker.*

Ptero said, 'The architecture is much the same as far as this crevasse descends. Some of the structure is still buried, however. We cannot tell how much.'

'Are there any openings that appear more important than the others?'

'No. To the contrary...' Ptero hesitated. 'Each opening is different in shape from all the others. But I am struck by the impression that they are also copies.'

'Copies?'

'I do not want to say that this building was created through replication.'

'Yet you have just done so.'

'Unwillingly, as I said.'

Atticus made the electronic grunt that was his equivalent of a snort. 'These are speculations that might have interested remembrancers. They do nothing to advance our campaign.' He marched to the opening. The squads fell in behind him.

Crossing the threshold felt like penetrating a membrane. Galba expected to find himself in a narrow tunnel, expected the walls to contract, then spasm, a gag reflex to expel the intruders. Instead, the squads were in a vast chamber. From without, the interior had appeared to be in total darkness. Inside, there was faint illumination. A dull red wash, light from blood, filled the space, overwhelming the feeble glow from the exterior. The ceiling was a distant vault, supported by pillars that all leaned off the vertical. The walls were hundreds of metres away to the left and right. Fifty metres forwards was a blank impassivity. The back wall corresponded with the rise of the plateau. Behind them, the wall was broken up by rows of the twisted arch openings.

'Auspex,' said Atticus.

'Nothing,' Camnus answered.

'Energy sources?'

'None.'

'Naturally. What can you tell me, Techmarine?'

'Captain, even this space defies a coherent interpretation. The readings are contradictory and keep shifting.'

Atticus nodded. 'What was true moments ago is true now. The warp is at work here. What it has created is stable, so we shall navigate it until we find the enemy where he cowers from our advance.'

They moved off. Straight ahead, near the rear wall, a ramp descended to the next level. Its slope was steep. The sharp diagonal took the legionaries down into a chamber identical to the one above. There was a ramp here, too, taking them to another space, another twin. And then another ramp.

The pattern very quickly became dizzying. If it were not for the variations in the angles of the twisted pillars, Galba might have started to think they were descending through the same vast room over and over again. There was an eerie purposefulness to the reproduction of the chambers. There was meaning here, though he could not guess what it was. He was very conscious of the size of the rooms. They were enclosures, yet they were vast, and so they became an incarnation of the idea of space. As they repeated, they gestured towards the infinite. There was nothing functional about them. There was nothing stored in them. But they did mean something. There were voices that had shaped this stone. There was intent that had bathed it in uniform, shadowless crimson.

Atticus was not interested in the voices or what they had to say. His one purpose was to march and kill. He would bring the rational to Pythos in the form of unblinking destruction. Galba was not satisfied. He wanted to understand. If they did not know what they were fighting, how could they hope to destroy it? Perhaps, if he could hear what was being said, he would know how to cast those words into silence.

If he knew what this building meant, he might be able to anticipate its attack.

They reached the bottom level. Several floors up, the exterior openings had begun to be blocked by earth and rock. The squads were now in the still-buried depths of the structure. The glow remained unaltered. This room was the close kin to all the others through which they had passed, but it had no windows at all. Instead, the exterior wall had a single, circular opening, giving onto a stone tunnel leading towards the centre of the plateau. Its shape made Galba think more of a pipe than a passageway. It advanced only about fifteen metres before a cave-in blocked the way. There were no other paths. Their journey ended here.

'I still have no readings,' Camnus said before Atticus asked.

The captain said nothing for a moment. His helmet lenses appeared to shine with a brighter red, piercing the ambient glow with his frustration. 'This ruin was uncovered by means that were not natural. There was a force at work. Its source must be *somewhere*.'

'But perhaps not here,' Camnus suggested. 'The enemy could be operating at some distance from here.'

'Where? To what end?' Atticus did not sound as if he were expecting answers.

Galba looked at the curve of the pipe's walls. There was something about the design of the stonework that nagged at him. He examined it more closely. It was real brickwork here, not the impossible construction of the main ruins. The seams were almost invisible, the stones meeting in perfect joins without need for mortar. And each stone was carved with the image of a room like the ones in which he had just stood. There were the pillars, the rows of windows, the vast space, so reduced that they were just abstract lines.

Lines that connected.

Like a circuit.

The light dawned. 'This is a machine,' Galba said.

'A machine,' Atticus repeated, as if Galba had blasphemed.

'Look.' He pointed to the walls. 'We have been seeing so much repetition, and spaces that make no sense on their own. They are meant to work together. Like cells.'

'To do what?' Camnus asked.

'I don't know,' Galba admitted. 'But we can see the energy that is filling them.'

'I see nothing that cannot be explained by the vagaries of the warp,' said Atticus. 'If it is a machine, it is an inert one, and this knowledge is useless to me.' He strode back down the pipe, towards the chamber. 'In fact, this entire action has been useless. This structure is dead. We must seek our enemy elsewhere.'

Galba hung back for a moment. He ran a gauntlet over the rubble blocking the way. It crumbled to the touch, looser than he had imagined, though shifting it would still be a major undertaking. He noticed that the Raven Guard were also waiting. 'Something?' Ptero asked.

'No.'

'You sense nothing?' Ptero had removed his helmet, and was watching Galba closely.

'No.' The other warrior's focused stare made him uncomfortable. 'Do you?'

'I do not.' The Raven Guard's answer seemed incomplete.

Galba headed off to rejoin his squad. He took three steps, and Ptero spoke again, completing the response. 'Doesn't it seem like we should?'

'No,' Galba told him, more quickly, and with more emphasis than he intended. *No*, he repeated to himself as he picked up his pace. *No*.

As the squads climbed back up the last ramp, the denial matched the rhythm of the thuds of his boots against stone. It sounded far more hollow. He was not sure what Ptero was implying. He had his suspicions. He rejected them all. Yet he also felt that, at a level neither of them understood, the Raven Guard was correct. Galba should sense something. All of them should. Atticus was wrong. The machine was not inert. It might be dormant. Galba suspected it was poised. There was energy here beyond a sick glow. There had to be. In this he agreed with his captain: the revelation of the structure was itself evidence of great power at work. He and his battle-brothers were moving through its domain. They had not found the enemy they expected. Perhaps they were inside it.

What will you tell the captain? he asked himself. *How will you convince him that this is the enemy. Will you tell him it is a form of Titan? Is that what you believe?*

He did not know. He was not sure what he believed, but as the Iron Hands entered the first of the cells above the foundation level, he was filled with a terrible sense of urgency. There *was* a threat here. Atticus had to take it with the utmost seriousness.

He had sensed nothing when Ptero had spoken to him. But he felt it now. *It's coming,* the inner voice said. The words were as clear as if they had been spoken aloud. The voice did not sound like his own. *Warn them,* it said. It was the rasp of rusted hinges, crumbling skulls, and bitter stone. *Warn them,* it said, and a thing of thoughts and iron murder parted its lips in an anticipatory grin. Galba's denial evaporated. The sound of his breath became deafening inside his helmet. Festering teeth gnawed at his consciousness. *Warn them,* said the whisper. *It's coming,* said the whisper, and once again he could see it, hovering just behind the crimson glow. The taste of shadows filled his mouth. *Look to your right.*

He looked. He faced the blocked windows. There was nothing to see. *Warn them.*

'Captain!' he called. 'The exterior wall! We are under attack!'

The legionaries rotated as a single unit, bolters ready. There were five rows of arches, ten openings in each row. Gun barrels panned and tilted, trying to cover a huge field of attack. Nothing showed in the red wash. There was no sound.

'Brother-sergeant?' Atticus said over the combat channel. 'What have you detected?'

Galba hesitated. The urgency was still growing. Something was rushing at them like a mag-lev train. 'I...' he said, and that was all. He could be no more precise. He could not pinpoint the source of the attack.

The sound arrived. It was a scrabbling crunch of stone and scrape of earth. It was massive, a rogue wave of gravel. The chamber shook with the reverberations. Then rubble burst inward from all the arches. Behind it came the invading force. The creatures resembled maggots. They were pale, the length of a man and as thick as an armoured Space Marine. Though they had no eyes, they had heads of a kind, and above and beneath them were pairs of forcipules, short legs angled towards each other and extending just beyond the circular, saw-toothed mouths. They snapped together with the speed of a fly's beating wings. Their edges rubbed, creating a noise like thousands of sabres forever being pulled from scabbards.

The maggots were a writhing flood. They cascaded into the chamber, a torrent of hunger the colour of diseased bone. Over the rustling of bodies was the wet, gurgling hiss of the monsters as they flowed over each other. They rushed for the legionaries, who opened fire. For a full second, Iron Hands and Raven Guard poured shells into the storm surge of devouring life. Maggots exploded in showers of blood, but the chamber continued to fill. The onrush of squirming horrors was unending. The legionaries were firing into a rising tide.

'*Up!*' Atticus commanded. The squads pounded up the ramp, sending bursts behind them, fighting to delay the flood by even a few moments. Bringing up the rear, the Raven Guard tossed frag grenades. The explosions were muffled. White, torn muscle flew up in a geyser. The blasts punched craters into the flesh. The gaps

filled an instant later. One of Ptero's brothers was swallowed by
the rising tide.

As the squads neared the top of the ramp, they heard the same
slithering, crawling roar from above. The maggots were pouring
in there too. The legionaries ran straight into the suffocating mass.
Firearms were useless. Galba barely had time to swap his bolter for
his chainsword before he was engulfed. He fought blind. All light
was extinguished by the ocean of flesh. The creatures rose up over
and around him like quicksand. Coils wrapped around his legs
and torso. Warning runes lit up as the pressure tested the limits
of his armour's strength. Teeth ground against ceramite. His blade
tore through the maggots.

He could barely move his arms, but whatever touched the sword
was shredded, and that was just enough to allow him to take one
step forwards, then another. He was clutched by a fist, one whose
fingers tightened, relaxed, and tightened again. Blood coated everything. His chainsword coughed as gore threatened to clog it. The
bodies of the maggots on which he trod became slippery. Some
burst beneath his weight, and the slick made his footing even more
treacherous. If he fell, death would be swift.

There was nothing but the crushing grubs, nothing but the fist and
the teeth. Galba butchered, sawed, shredded and moved upwards
one gradual step after another. He had no sense of progress. He
fought alone. It was impossible to link up with his nearest brothers. The only signs that they still existed were his retinal displays
and the constant shouts over the vox.

And there was the presence of Atticus. The captain's voice was
there always. He commanded, he exhorted, he cursed the foe with
creative venom, and his tone never varied from the calm of implacable, endless murder. At the head of the advance, he was the first to
reach the next level. It fell to him to find the next ramp by feel alone,
and call out the directions to the warriors who followed. Galba

growled in frustration when that happened, extinguishing the faint hope that the level above was clear of maggots. He growled again, in anger, when he heard a series of sharp, splintering cracks and the identification rune of Brother Ennius pulsed red, then winked out. Three more runes went dark before the squads reached the top of the next ramp.

'Push on, brothers,' Atticus ordered. 'There will be no defeat for us here. There can be no defeat, because we battle the flesh, and the flesh is weak. Behold the flesh at its most base. This is what we have risen above forever. The machine cannot be brought low by this vile excess. Let the monsters come. Let them fill this chasm to the top. They cannot stop us, because they are that which is past, and we are on the journey to the pure strength of the mechanical.' There were no pauses in his speech. There were no grunts of effort. He spoke with a metronomic tempo. Each syllable was the punctuation of a blow. Every word was the death of another grub. Every sentence was a step closer to victory.

As he listened, even as he slipped on a twisting body and almost fell, Galba was seized by the conviction of the inevitability of victory. For how could such things of flesh possibly overwhelm the will, forged and tempered into a resilience beyond steel, of Atticus? The impossibility of such an event gave him the strength he needed to remain standing, to slice away once more at the crushing fingers of the fist, and to take another step.

Every metre the legionaries climbed was a battle. And every metre was the same. The fist would never let them go.

Until, suddenly, it did.

They reached a level that was not still buried, and that the rising tide of invertebrates had not reached. Galba ripped through another maggot that had wrapped itself around his torso, shoved the blade up through the jaws of another, and then he was out. He could see. He had the freedom of movement. He stayed long enough to help the rest of the rearguard, and then he was racing upwards with the remainder of the squads.

We are victors, he told himself. *We are not survivors. We are victors.*

Behind them came the maggots, the squirming froth of an overflowing cauldron. The Space Marines were faster. They put distance between themselves and the hungry flesh. As they ran, Galba heard Atticus vox to Darras, ordering him to send down more climb-cables. They reached the top level of the chambers, and re-emerged on the ledge. The cables were not strong enough to support the weight of more than two legionaries at a time, and now the wait began.

'We shall depart last,' Ptero said.

Atticus hesitated before answering, visibly galled by the prospect of owing any debt to the other Legion. But the Raven Guard had their jump packs. They could leave at the last second. Atticus gave a curt nod, conceding necessity. He ordered the rest of the legionaries up ahead of him. Galba stood at his side at the threshold to the chamber, also waiting to the last. He stared into the crimson. There was nothing to see yet, but he could hear the rising tide of the maggots. The sound of the obscene excess of life made him regret his own flesh. He envied his captain's near-total purity. He felt a renewed love of the machine, its order and its logic. The flesh was weakness and disorder. It was a threat, as the maggots were, only through grotesque overabundance.

He had wondered if Atticus had sacrificed too much in his journey towards the absolutely machinic. He had wondered if too much of the human had been cut away. In this moment, his doubts fled. To become the machine was to become order. It was to take a stand against the perverse. The maggots were life as it too often was. Atticus was life as it could be: uncompromising, unbending, precise, free of ambiguity. Atticus was an embodied fragment of the Emperor's dream. That dream was in danger. Galba did not know if its grand design could be saved, but portions of it could be. There it was, standing invincible in Atticus. His own duty lay before him, crystalline. He must walk the same path. He, too, must be order. He must be the dream.

There might be no other way to defeat the nightmares.

Now Camnus and the last of the Iron Hands were climbing. Another few minutes and it would be time to leave this cursed ground. The squirming hiss and rush of the maggots drew closer. The stone of the chamber began to vibrate.

'You knew,' Atticus said.

'Captain?'

'You warned us of the attack. Before there was any sign of it. You knew.'

'I didn't... That is...'

'How did you know?'

The whispers. The grin. The voice that commanded. Reveal these things, and then what?

'I'm not sure,' he said. That was true, at least.

'Then *be* sure,' Atticus told him.

The maggots arrived. They boiled up the ramp, covering the floor in a heaving mass. Standing just before them, the four remaining Raven Guard sent more frag grenades into the creatures. The explosives landed in a line, creating a barrage. Ptero and his brothers followed the blasts with a stream of fire, stemming the flow for a few seconds.

But only a few. The maggots came on, piling one on top of each other, surging forwards in a gathering wave.

'Captain Atticus,' Ptero said. 'It is time.'

Wordlessly, Atticus turned his head to Galba. The sergeant took a step back and looked up the façade. Camnus and the others were close to the top. He would be adding undue strain to the cable, but Ptero was right. They had stayed as long as possible. He slammed his gauntlets to his chest in the sign of the aquila, and began to climb. He looked down and saw Atticus stride out onto the ledge. He stood beside one of the other cables.

'You have my thanks, Raven Guard,' the captain said. 'Your duties here are at an end.' He still did not take the cable. Galba paused and watched.

The black-armoured warriors of the XIX Legion shot out of the structure. The exhaust on their jump packs flared as they rose skyward. Only then did Atticus grasp the cable and begin to climb. His feet left the ground just as the wave crashed through the arch. He did not look down, refusing to grant his foe anything but the most sovereign contempt. He climbed hand over hand, and was soon level with Galba. The two legionaries moved up the lines.

Galba did look down. The momentum of the maggots' rush was such that they plunged from the openings in an obscene cataract. But then the fall slowed bit by bit, and then the grubs began crawling up the façade. 'They are not done with us,' he said.

Atticus grunted. 'Good. Because I am not done with them.' Then, 'Sergeant Darras, have flamers ready.'

'Will we have enough promethium?' Galba asked.

'I will use my hands if necessary.'

Before they were halfway up, the strain on the lines eased as the other Iron Hands reached the top. No longer concerned with snapping the cables with sudden jerks and swings, Galba and Atticus climbed faster, gaining a few more seconds on the maggots that now covered the façade like a squirming veil. When they reached the lip of the chasm, Darras and two others were waiting with flamers.

Now Atticus did look down. He leaned over the edge, gauging the movements below. 'Stand at the edge,' he ordered. 'Close together, and remain visible. Be prey. Give them a target. That will keep them concentrated.'

The Iron Hands joined him. He was right, Galba saw. Though

they had no eyes, the maggots were somehow aware of their presence, and grouped closer together instead of spreading over the entire face of the structure. They became a rippling, pale wedge.

The twilight of Pythos was falling. The perpetual cloud cover permitted no sunset. There was only the slow death of the day, a layering of shrouds until all was black. During the final breath of light, when the torches that dotted the wall and the infant settlement were lit but did not yet have full night against which to stand out, the maggots reached the surface.

'Welcome them,' Atticus said.

The light of the flamers was searing. The stench of the burning creatures was corrosive. Galba did not mind. It was the smell of retribution, of purgation. It was evidence of the corrupted flesh being excised from a universe that demanded order. Darras and his men aimed their flamers at a steep angle, sending the wash of burning promethium over long swaths of the wedge. The maggots burned well, some of them swelling and popping as noxious gases ignited within their bodies. Writhing and hissing, they fell, and set fire to their kin as they dropped. The Iron Hands launched the lethal streams in quick bursts, setting one section of the advance alight, then another, moving the barrels back and forth along an arc, bringing death to the entire width of the undulating mass. The fires spread, moving quickly beyond the range of the flamers. The maggots came on, driven by mindless hunger. They rushed to their doom.

'A gunship could launch a Hellfury strike into the gap,' Camnus suggested.

'We will be done soon enough,' Atticus said.

In answer to his will, the flames broadened their reach, embracing the vermin. As night fell, the entire façade was a curtain of fire.

'Purged,' said Atticus, echoing Galba's own thoughts. He turned his back on the dying enemy and stepped away from the edge. 'So we have spectators,' he muttered.

Galba turned around. A large crowd of the colonists had gathered. Their eyes glittered, reflecting the flames that licked out from the chasm.

'Do you understand what you see?' Atticus asked them, his voice a harsh, electronic slash in the night. 'You are subjects of the Imperium. You are subject *to* the Emperor's will. This is the fate of anything, animal, xenos or man, that would defy that will. Work well, fight hard. Earn our protection. Or you will earn our *mercy*.'

The last word became a hiss. Galba did not blink at the contempt. As he looked at the crowd of mortals, he saw a collection of the flesh. How different were they, in their weakness, from the immolated insects? Was Khi'dem right, in the end, to see them as any real use? Unless they were able to protect this settlement on their own, they were a drain on precious resources. And here they were, watching war from the sidelines. Was that eagerness he saw on their faces? Yes, it was.

'*Do you hear me?*' Atticus demanded. His voice was an electronic whip, his body a motionless silhouette, an angry god of war backlit by the flames of the hell he had called into being.

The people recoiled. But when they cried out that they heard, they did so with more excitement, and less fear, than Galba had expected. He felt the gulf between himself and the mortal variant of humanity widen. The flesh was becoming incomprehensible to him.

But then the face of Kanshell flashed before his mind's eye. He saw the serf's undying loyalty, and his mortal terror. His contempt withered. His pity bloomed, even for the sheep before him. He vacillated between hatred of the flesh and the need to protect it, and then realised that Atticus was now looking at him.

'Are there more?' the captain asked. His voice was quiet, for Galba's ears only. His tone was cold.

'More?'

'Is there another attack imminent?'

'Brother-captain, I don't know.'

'You knew down below.'

'Yes,' he admitted. 'But not why.'

Atticus leaned in towards him. 'Listen well, brother-sergeant. You will inform me of any such information you acquire, *immediately*.'

'Of course, but I–'

'Remember this, though. No matter what the state of the Imperium, this Legion remains faithful to the Emperor's commands. I will brook no violation of the Edict of Nikaea. I will tolerate no sorcery in our midst. Do you understand?'

'I am not a psyker, captain. I am–'

'*Do you hear me?*'

'I do, my lord.' He heard the voice of the machine-warrior. He wondered what other voices he would hear again, and what they would cost him.

THIRTEEN

Taking stock
The fires of faith
The dance

'THAT WAS AN impressive speech,' Khi'dem said.

Ptero nodded. 'Perhaps a telling one, too.'

They stood beneath the palisade, watching the crowd disperse after Atticus's harangue.

'He has no love for mortals,' Khi'dem admitted. 'That is nothing new. Do you see this as evidence that his antipathy is becoming something more dangerous?'

'No,' Ptero said after a moment. 'Not yet. Do you?'

'I do not.' Khi'dem told himself that he was not being foolish in his optimism. He knew what the consequences of ignoring danger signs could be. He also knew how little the remaining Salamanders and Raven Guard would be able to do should the worst occur. There were four of his battle-brothers remaining, one more than Ptero's contingent. 'He was explicit in demanding loyalty to the Emperor,' he went on. 'I heard contempt. I witnessed a leader who is quite willing to govern his charges through fear. But he is doing nothing criminal. I disagree with his means, but I cannot find fault with the goals.' He gave Ptero a crooked smile. 'Please tell me that I am speaking from reason and not from hope.'

Ptero's laugh was dry and very brief. 'How will you know that my reassurance has a basis that is any more sound?'

'Then we are left where we have always been. We must have faith in our brother.'

'Faith,' Ptero muttered. 'The Emperor has taught us to regard that word with suspicion. Perhaps, if we had done so with greater rigour, the Imperium would not have come to this.'

'He cast down faith in false gods,' Khi'dem corrected gently. 'Not faith in each other. Or in the dream of the Imperium. He has shown faith in His children.'

'And this is how we have repaid it.' There was no cynicism in Ptero's words. Only an enormous grief.

'We will yet prove worthy of it. We must.'

'Agreed,' Ptero said, and they watched the dying of the flames in silence for a minute.

Khi'dem cleared his throat. 'I'm sorry for the loss of your brother down there.'

'Thank you. The life on this planet...' Ptero shook his head. 'Its absolute hostility should not surprise me any longer, but it does. It makes no sense at all. I still say it cannot be natural.'

'If it was engineered, that gives further credence to Atticus's belief that there is an enemy intelligence working against us.'

'Of that, I have no doubt.'

Khi'dem chose his words carefully. 'You have evidence, then, that most of us would be unable to perceive?'

Ptero smiled. 'Yes, brother, I was once of my Legion's Librarius. But I have not been acting in violation of Nikaea.'

'I never thought you were.'

'I have no wish to conceal what I am. It is, after all, no longer relevant under the Edict. But I did think it... politic... not to trumpet my nature before Atticus.'

'Mutations do not sit well with his understanding of a proper, regimented universe,' Khi'dem concurred. 'I'm sure he sees them as a great failing.'

'The flesh is unstable. Therefore it is weak.'

'Quite. I applaud your wisdom. But tell me, your battle against those insects...'

'I do not believe it was a directed attack. Simply more of this world's general malignity.'

'You don't sound entirely sure.'

Ptero grimaced. 'Not entirely, no. Our enemy, whoever it is, uses the powers of the immaterium. That much is clear from the attacks on our base. There have been such currents in the warp during the nights... Keeping my abilities in check has been painful. Today, I detected no more than a faint ripple. Not enough to direct an attack on that scale.'

'But?'

'But Sergeant Galba warned us of the assault just before it happened. Before there was the slightest sign of the insects' approach.'

'Is he...?'

'I don't think so.'

'How is this possible?'

'It should not be.' Even in the dark, Khi'dem could see how troubled Ptero's face was. 'How this came to pass does not worry me as much as *why*.'

The fire was done. There were no power generators in the settlement, and its only light now came from the torches scattered over the grounds. An oily, putrescent smoke drifted over the plateau from the chasm. It carried the stench of a rancid sea. Khi'dem thought of cancers eating at dreams, hope and brotherhood. 'All we are doing is watching and waiting,' he said. 'If we are not careful, we will watch and wait until doom is inevitable. We both know something is going very wrong here. We must take action.' Even as he spoke, he thought, *Grand words, you poor fool. Go ahead, then. Take action. Oh, and what action would that be, exactly?*

But Ptero was nodding. 'There is sorcery at work. We must counter it.'

'Careful,' Khi'dem cautioned.

'I will not disobey the Emperor's will. But there is one among us who *is* a sanctioned psyker, and who might be strong enough to do some good.'

'The astropath,' Khi'dem said.

THE NIGHT WAS a bad one. Again. So were the ones that followed. Terror had been Kanshell's shadow since the arrival on Pythos. He could not shake it. It clung to his heels. It capered at his back and stretched its darkness before him. He did catch broken shards of sleep, exhaustion plunging him into unconsciousness, where he wrestled with nightmares that mirrored the ones that slithered through the night of his waking life.

He was not alone in confronting the horrors of the dark, but this was no comfort. The people around him had the same haunted look, the same sunken features, the same taut, nervous energy. They would be running, if only there was a refuge to which they might run. There was no comfort, because when the night came, and reached for them all with its terrors, they could not reach for each other. Kanshell, like all the others, curled into a tighter and tighter ball, as if he might curl into nothingness and so avoid the gaze of the thing that walked behind the dark. There was nowhere to hide. There was no way to fight. There was nothing to do but tremble and whimper and hope that this night was not his turn. Nothing to do but pray that the following morning, he would not be the one found mad or dead.

His prayers were answered, yet each day someone else's were not. No matter what precautions Atticus ordered, no matter how many guards were posted, or how frequent the security sweeps through the camp, the deaths continued. Always one or two serfs, never more, but also without fail. It was as if the curse that haunted the camp were taunting the captain, dancing a macabre waltz to its own tune and paying no attention to the futile efforts of the Iron Hands.

There was nothing the legionaries could do to stem the slow attrition. And so the fear spread. It grew. It intensified. It was a venom of deep, complex vintage. Its vines grew from the toxic soil of Isstvan V. The fact of defeat formed a rich loam and there festered the anticipation of more terror and grief. The nights did not disappoint. They were the consummation of dark expectation, and each dawn was another forced drink from the poisoned chalice. Day after day, the chalice filled higher. When it overflowed, Kanshell knew, the likes of him would drown in the horror. There would be nothing left of the mortal psyches. The base would become an asylum. Then a sepulchre.

If the Iron Hands were helpless against the cancer, what could its victims do? All Kanshell asked was the chance to fulfil his duty. But there were no actions to take against the terrors. The visitations stalked the shadows on spider limbs. They brought the worst dreams of madness to the surface, and made them real. But the visitor itself was not real, and so could not be fought.

No, not real yet, a slithering promise whispered to the back of Kanshell's neck. *Not quite yet, but oh, how close, how very, very close. A little more effort. A little more patience.*

Sometimes, he thought he heard hissing during the day. Sometimes, during the grey noon of Pythos, a chuckle like the scrape of a spade on dry skulls would make him start. He would turn and look, and there would be nothing there.

Not yet. Not quite yet.

There was nothing to do but pray. He had abandoned his faith in the rational. It lay in blackened ruins. It could not stand up to the nights of Pythos. He could draw no strength from it. Hewing to it would be an act of mortal foolishness. He would be hanging on to a lie, rushing headlong into the jaws of the coming evil. He no longer felt any shame in his apostasy. And truly, was it not supremely rational, when confronted by the proof of the daemonic, to turn to the divine for succour?

He attended his first meeting the morning after he spent the night behind the shield of the *Lectitio Divinitatus*. Tanaura led a group prayer in a corner of the mess, snatching a few moments for communal comfort just before the serfs plunged into their allotted tasks. Kanshell approached the gathering tentatively. He was not sure if there were rituals he should observe, or if the worshippers were even aware of his presence.

He needn't have worried. 'Jerune,' Tanaura said as he came near. 'Join us.'

The circle parted, then embraced him. He looked at faces as ravaged by terror as his own. They also shone with a desperate hope, one for which they would fight and kill. Their smiles were as tentative as his, but their welcome was fervent. He understood why as he took part in the worship.

Tanaura took them through the prayer. 'Father of Mankind,' she said, 'we seek your guidance. We beseech your protection.'

'The Emperor protects,' the other worshippers responded, Kanshell among them.

'See us safely through this time of trial.'

'The Emperor protects.'

'In our despair, we say that surely the darkness shall cover us, and the light about us become night.'

'Yet even the darkness is no darkness with thee,' came the answer.

'And the night is as clear as the day,' Tanaura finished.

Now the smiles were far less tentative. Kanshell felt stronger. This was the glorious truth he had never known about these meetings. There was power in brotherhood. It gave him comfort during the day, because he was not alone. None of them were. They had each other, and they had the Emperor. That night, there was no less terror, but he had more strength. He was able to face the dying of the light with greater resolution, and though he still trembled, though he still curled into a tight, paralytic knot of fear, he had the strength to withstand the trials. There was hope. And the next morning, with more prayer – and a circle grown a little larger yet – there was the renewal of strength, the flaring of that spark of hope.

These were the only things that sustained him as the nights marched on, and the toll rose.

During the day, he continued to work at the settlement. The labour of serfs and colonists was divided between construction and excavation. The palisade was complete. Yurts were appearing now, scattered about the centre of the plateau. Actual shelter had come to the colonists. They seemed hardly to notice. The yurts were afterthoughts, thrown together only once the lodges were built. There was now one on each of the mounds that marked the buried structures.

The digging carried on at the base of the mounds. The wedges of four deep pits now bit into the plateau. The upper halves of the structures were exposed. The Iron Hands had ventured into the depths three more times. They had found nothing, and there had been no further attacks. Atticus was not satisfied. There was still an enemy present, and he declared that it would be found. Rubble blocked all the tunnels that led towards the interior of the plateau. Atticus ordered it cleared.

The colonists cheered the command. They volunteered by the hundreds. Far more stepped forward than could be put to use. Kanshell was glad. He knew that a monstrous foe stood against the Imperial forces. He did not think it would be found in a den beneath the ground. But he heard about the vast chambers, the twisted pillars and the glow of rotten blood. The ruins were the space of further nightmares. He was visited by enough. He did not need to go looking for more.

On the third day after the discovery of the ruins, he was helping raise another yurt when he heard a scream. It came from the north-west, where a gate had been built into the palisade. Half the construction team was composed of colonists, and they dropped the circular wooden framework of the yurt and went running towards the gate. Kanshell and his fellow serfs followed. The screams continued from the other side of the wall. They were interrupted by reptilian snarls. After a few moments, the shrieks became softer moans of agony, then those, too, died away. The growls became muffled.

Its mouth is full, Kanshell thought, aghast.

There were tearing sounds, and the snapping of bones. Then a brief burst of fire, the unmistakeable deep staccato of a bolter at work.

Silence fell. The group before the gate waited motionless. Kanshell spotted Ske Vris at the fore. A platform ran the length of the palisade, a metre-and-a-half below the tips of the pointed logs that made up the wall. Colonist guards had come running along it, and were now watching the scene below them. One of them signalled, and four colonists stepped forwards to pull open the heavy gate. Khi'dem, his helmet mag-locked to his thigh, passed through it. The corpse he carried was barely recognisable as human. It was a bag of butchered meat. But he handled it with dignity, and turned it over to the men who approached to claim it. Over his shoulder, he carried a lasrifle. He unslung it and passed it to Ske Vris. 'This is still usable,' he said.

'Our thanks, great lord,' Ske Vris said. She bowed.

Khi'dem snorted. 'Your people would thank me better by ceasing to engage in such follies. These risks are pointless.'

'We have traditions to uphold,' Ske Vris answered. 'We have duties that are sacred. I am sure that you do, as well.'

'Be it on your head,' the legionary answered, and strode off.

The colonists who had opened the gate now went through it themselves, disappearing down the slope of the plateau. Kanshell walked up to Ske Vris. 'What happened?' he asked. 'Why was someone out there?'

'He was hunting.'

'Hunting?' Kanshell's jaw dropped. Humans could not behave like predators on Pythos. They were only prey, and survival depended on recognising that very basic fact. There were enough supplies in the settlement. The food was rations scavenged from the landing sites. It was not enticing, but it would keep the people alive until the construction was complete and large hunting parties, who *might* bring individual animals down without suffering massive casualties, could be organised. A lone mortal venturing beyond the wall was suicidal. 'Hunting for what?' Kanshell demanded.

Ske Vris looked at him as if he were simple-minded. 'For the homes, of course.'

Kanshell looked over his shoulder at the yurts, then back at Ske Vris, horrified. Saurian hides were stretched over the wooden frameworks, creating the walls and roofs. There had been no time to tan and cure the hides. They were the flesh of the beasts, cleaned and stretched. The skin was so tough that it served the purpose, though Kanshell found the material unpleasant to handle. It made the homes far too organic, as if they were alive. He would have preferred huts constructed out of sod or logs. There was enough of that raw material lying about, despite the construction needs of the lodges and the palisade. But the colonists insisted on the necessity of this form of shelter. Kanshell had assumed that the hides came from the many saurians killed during the pacification of the plateau. He had been wrong. 'Are you mad?' he asked.

Ske Vris smiled. 'Is it mad to live, and perhaps die, for one's traditions? For one's beliefs? Are you unwilling to make such a sacrifice?'

'Of course not,' Kanshell answered, heated. 'But if those beliefs are irrational...'

'Yours are not?'

He had no answer to that. He was struck, even as he floundered, by the distance that Ske Vris appeared to mark between her traditions and those of the Imperium. Kanshell wondered again if the colonists were a lost people, one who had never received the benefits of the Imperial peace. He pushed the question away. The issue was beyond his station. If Atticus was not concerned with the heterodoxy of the colonists, then he would not be, either.

He kept watch with Ske Vris before the open gate. He was anxious, expecting a saurian to come charging through. He could hear the predators in the jungle beyond the palisade. They grew louder each day. None came, though, and after a minute, the four colonists returned, dragging chunks of the beast that Khi'dem had killed. Ske Vris clapped her hands together once as the gate was closed. 'There,' she said. 'Meat for food, hide for shelter. We have lost, and we have gained.'

'I'm sorry for the death of your kinsman,' Kanshell said.

'He will be commemorated. He will live in our memories and in our walls, and he died in the land of our dreams.' Ske Vris spread her arms wide in a joyous embrace of the world. 'What is there to regret?'

Kanshell looked at the open, shining pleasure in the woman's face. Snatches of the colonists' songs as they worked drifted to him. These people had no experience of the fear that tormented the base. 'I envy you,' he said.

'Why?'

'How can you be so happy?'

Ske Vris cocked her head. 'Why wouldn't I be?'

The answer came in the form of a hoarse shriek from above. Kanshell and the novitiate both ducked. A flying saurian came in at a sharp angle. Claws extended, it dived straight at one of the wall guards. It had a wingspan of ten metres. Its head was almost all jaw, longer than a man. Confused lasfire rose to meet it. The beast was too fast, the defenders untrained. With a second, mocking, shriek the reptile snatched a guard up in its talons. Khi'dem came charging back, but the monster had already dropped from sight before he could fire.

He lowered his bolter. Ske Vris bowed low. 'Please accept our thanks once more, lord,' she called.

Khi'dem looked at the novitiate. His disgust was clear. 'Why are you smiling? Do you take pleasure in seeing your people devoured?'

'Not at all, lord. It is simply that we walk the earth of our destiny. Every moment is one of fruition. In the end, we shall all die here, in our home. The hope of centuries has been realised. Our joy is invincible.'

'Your joy is quite insane,' Khi'dem muttered, and left.

Kanshell checked the sky for more of the winged hunters. There were none, but he felt no confidence in the men and women patrolling the wall. They handled their rifles like children. Did none of these people have combat experience? He was no soldier, but he could not spend his life on a strike cruiser and not acquire some basic knowledge of military craft. He was surrounded by naïve fools, but the lion's share of the protection of the settlement fell to them. The Salamanders were few in number. They refused to abandon the people to their fate, but they could not be everywhere at once.

The Iron Hands ignored the settlement. Atticus had his forces mounting guard in the depths of the structure, and protecting the base. The colonists had to earn their survival. Those working in the ruins were of direct use to the Iron Hands, so the legionaries watched over them. Every so often, the muffled, hollow echo of gunfire would rise from the chasms. There were sporadic attacks by maggots, but not on the scale of the initial one. The Iron Hands seemed to have decimated the population of the underground inhabitants. The creatures had swarmed over the invaders of their domain, and been defeated.

But on the surface, the wildlife of Pythos was becoming bolder. It seemed to know that the prey was more vulnerable. By ones and twos, the monsters attacked the wall more and more frequently. Kanshell was grateful no pack had launched a concerted assault, but when he listened to the chorus of snarls in the jungle beyond the palisade, he grew sure that day would not be long in coming.

Ske Vris straightened, still smiling as she watched the departing Space Marine. 'What do you think, my friend?' she asked Kanshell. 'Is our joy insane?'

'I think you might be. All of you.'

'We are all on this planet together. We rejoice in our fate. You clearly fear yours. Are you better off for being so "sane"?'

There was a frenzied roar, and the sound of heavy feet pounding the earth. A massive bulk slammed against the palisade. Three guards rushed into position and started shooting. They were laughing. There was something giddy about their joy, as if they were intoxicated by belief. Kanshell winced. Ske Vris looked down on him, her smile unwavering. The las-fire continued until the roars turned into howls, and then silence. The laughter continued.

'Well?' Ske Vris prompted.

'I don't know,' Kanshell whispered.

'You seek strength.'

Kanshell nodded.

'Strength comes from faith,' Ske Vris told him.

'Yes. So I am discovering.'

Ske Vris gripped his arm. 'That's wonderful! Perhaps the time has come for us to worship together.'

Kanshell glanced uneasily at the nearest lodge. 'I'm not sure.'

'Then be sure. We will be celebrating our fallen comrades shortly. Join us.'

'Perhaps,' he conceded.

'You will be inspired,' Ske Vris promised.

KANSHELL RETURNED TO the yurt. The rest of the day passed. The saurian attacks continued. All but one were repulsed without further casualties. As evening fell, one of the guards overbalanced and fell over the wall. His screams were mercifully short. They caused barely a ripple in the delight of the others as they brought down the beast. Kanshell wondered where the line lay between optimism and callousness. Repulsed, he decided he would not attend the service. He would, he told himself, work until the transport back to the base arrived.

He held fast to the resolution until the ritual began. The sound of chanting made him look up from the hides he was helping stitch together. Hundreds of colonists had gathered at the first lodge. They filled the space, and spilled down the mound. The song was as celebratory as any Kanshell had heard from these people. But there was power there, too. The song was triumphant.

He skirted the pit and moved towards the lodge. He listened to the chanting in a way he had not before. It spoke to him. It claimed a bond between them. Until a few days ago, he had looked down on the colonists' songs. They were the products of superstition. They were a sign of delusional thinking, a denial of the hard, insistent realities of the universe. So he had told himself. Now he thought that the denial had been his. He had refused to hear the truth in this music. He had refused to hear the praise, because he had not wanted to believe there was any being who would hear and receive the praise.

He drew closer. He repented his foolishness. The sound of

hundreds of voices lifted in song swirled around him. He was swept up by the need to worship. The melody opened up vistas of infinite possibility. It demanded he accept them. It imposed greatness. His skin tingled with the brush of undiluted sensation. His chest swelled with pride and humility. He took a deep breath, and was startled when it hitched. He raised a hand to his cheek. His fingers came away wet. Though his tears flowed, his vision was clear.

The crowd parted for him as he reached the base of the mound. He walked up the centre as if flowing down a rushing stream. The song had a fragrance: the sharp, sweet tang of apples. It became his world, shutting him off from the mundane. He could no longer feel his legs. He was floating, not walking. He was a consciousness only now, a soul freed from the corporeal vale of tears. Somewhere far below, his body was raising its arms, expecting to float upward, lifted by the strength of the song. He laughed at the body's presumption, he laughed at the exhilaration of the senses, and he laughed at being free of fear for the first time since Callinedes.

Ske Vris was standing before him. The novitiate took hold of his shoulders. 'I rejoice to see you here, brother,' she said.

The words cut through Kanshell's joyous haze, bringing the world back into focus. He was in and of his body again, though the ecstasy was just as strong. He found that he could remember how to form words. 'Thank you.'

'Come forward.'

The lodge was filled to bursting, but somehow the people made room. A path appeared before Kanshell, leading to the centre of the floor. Ske Vris gestured, inviting him to approach the priest who stood there. Kanshell guessed this was Ske Vris's master, though he had never seen the man's face. Even now, the priest was hooded. He was dancing. His steps were both sinuous and martial. He was worshipper, and he was warrior. His staff was the sign of his office, and it was the terror of his foes. His robes swirled as he danced, and the tunic beneath them was that of a soldier. Though much smaller than a Space Marine, he was a giant among these people. Other priests surrounded him, echoing his dance. They, too, were robed and hooded. They were almost as tall as the head priest, though they were much thinner. Their dance was the swirl of the melody; his was the force. And it was he who was the focus of the lightweb.

The light.

The extraordinary patterns Kanshell had seen when the lodge was empty were even more pronounced now. He stared in wonder. It was impossible. Outside was deep twilight. Though torches surrounded the lodge, they could not account for the intensity of the illumination. Light shone through the slits in the walls as if the lodge were inside Pandorax itself. As before, the closer Kanshell came to the centre, the more the web assumed definition, the more it came to be a language. It would speak to him, if he let it. It had a message, one that the priest had heard, and he danced, rejoicing. The lightweb interwove with the runes on his robe. Kanshell saw call and response, and he saw a constant exchange of roles. The priest was calling to the numinous at one moment, and answering a divine summons the next.

Now, finally, Kanshell felt he understood the colonists. He understood how they retained unwavering hope no matter how many of them fell to the jaws of Pythos. It was inconceivable that they should do otherwise.

The priest stopped dancing. The light did not move, but such was the complexity of the pattern, Kanshell's gaze did not stop the dance. It stepped nimbly from point to shaft to nexus, round and round, mesmerising, intoxicating. The priest held out his arms, palms facing Kanshell.

'You are welcome,' he said. 'Stand with me.' His voice was deep, rough, yet liquid. A glacier whisper.

Kanshell advanced. He had been reluctant before. Now he was eager. He almost stumbled in his joy. He ran towards the priest.

Three steps from the centre, the message crystallising before him, an immense truth on the cusp of revelation, he paused. He blinked, uncertain. His feet were rooted.

'What troubles you?' the priest asked.

Kanshell swallowed. His lips were dry. His throat was parched. The apple fragrance was heady, and he so wished he could slake his thirst. But he could not. He mustn't. He had to wait. 'Something...' he croaked. He tried again. 'Something is missing.'

The priest cocked his head. 'Yes?'

Kanshell tried to look away. Perhaps if he could close his eyes, he could concentrate and discover what was wrong. 'I feel...' He trailed off, helpless.

'You are not yet at home,' the priest said.

Kanshell almost sobbed with gratitude. 'Yes.' Yes, that was it. He still did not belong here, though that was what he wished, as powerfully as he dreaded the nights on the base.

'Our song and this space are still unfamiliar. You need reassurance. You need a sign that you are not betraying your own faith by sharing with us.'

'Yes,' Kanshell said. The tears were flowing again.

'And if I said that our faiths were the same?'

'I want to believe that.'

Though the priest's face was hidden, Kanshell was sure he smiled. 'Sometimes, proof is the proper support for faith. You shall have proof. Come to us again, and bring a symbol of your faith. Then you shall know the truth, and we will rejoice together.'

'Thank you,' Kanshell whispered.

He tried to back away. His knees had gone weak. If he tried to walk, he would collapse. But then Ske Vris was at his side, taking his arm over a shoulder. Kanshell leaned against her and staggered out of the lodge. As they left it behind, Kanshell noticed a few other serfs at the periphery of the crowd, watching and listening, their faces hungry with envy. The chanting still filling his ears, his heart hammering from its brush with the power of faith unleashed, Kanshell was struck by a vision of what might be. He thought about the strength he gained from the morning prayer circle. He imagined how much greater that strength would be if there were as many worshippers as there were at the lodge. To praise the Emperor as He should be praised, to do so openly, to do so by the hundreds – that would, Kanshell was sure, strike a death-blow to the fear.

And why stop there? The vision soared. He pictured thousands, millions, *billions* raising their voices to the glories of Emperor. His breath stopped. He was not a violent man. He had never fought. He had cleaned weapons, serviced them, knew their names and uses, but had never fired a single shot. He was Jerune Kanshell, menial serf, an insignificant, eminently replaceable cog in the machine of the X Legion, and nothing more. But in the service of this dream, he felt ready to kill.

The need and the glow of the vision did not leave him as he boarded the transport back to the base. When he disembarked on the landing pad, and heard the noises on the other side of the walls, he lost the glow. The need remained, and he clung to it, and to the promise of strength, even as the fear returned, boasting new claws, new teeth, new ways to murder hope.

The young night echoed with a very different chant. It was the song of the carnivore. Kanshell's ears rang with another call and response: the roar of alpha predators, and the answers of their packs. There had been a sudden gathering of saurians here. There had been nothing like this cacophony in the morning. Now he could hear countless reptilian voices growling challenges to the walls. The beasts were taunting their prey.

Kanshell walked away from the landing pad. He was in no hurry

to reach the dormitorium. He paused in the open between build-
ings, legs still shaky, the howls in the dark hurting him as if jaws
were already closing around his head.

He was still there when Tanaura found him. She looked as hag-
gard as he felt, though the iron was still there in the set of her jaw.

'How long has this been going on?' he asked.

Bolter fire from the wall. Roars turning to shrieks and then silence.
Echoes of the siege at the settlement. Monsters testing the defences.

'It started this morning,' Tanaura said. 'They've been growing more
bold all day.'

'Why?' he demanded to no one. The saurians' actions here bothered him more than the assaults on the wooden palisade. Its
vulnerability was clear. But the promontory was a strong position. The base's walls were solid. Its defenders were strong as gods.
Why would animals stalk such a target? Why such stubbornness?
'They can't hope to break through.'

'They're animals,' Tanaura said. 'They don't hope.'

'Really? Then what is keeping them here?' *These animals can hope,*
he thought. *They hope for our blood.*

The crack of snapped branches. The crash of heavy bodies against
each other. Snarls of rage and pain. Some of the monsters were
tired of waiting, and were fighting each other.

'I don't know.' Tanaura shrugged, trying to be dismissive. 'Perhaps
they hope, but they don't reason. They won't get in. The legionaries massacre them as soon as they approach the wall.'

'And when there are no more munitions?'

'It won't come to that.'

'You sound very sure.'

'The mission of the Legion will not drag on like that.' She spoke
as if the decision were hers to make. Kanshell almost remarked on
her presumption, but then he saw how her eyes burned. Determination, hope, desire, prophecy... They were all combusting in her

gaze. So was desperation. 'This is not where the war should be fought,' she told Kanshell.

'But it *is* being fought here,' he answered.

Beyond the wall, the roars grew louder. The sound was a rising tide, coming to drown them all. It would never ebb. And inside the wall, the thoughts of the deep night waited, eager to test Kanshell's faith.

FOURTEEN

The tightening noose
Shadows against shadows
Mission of the blind

GALBA SAID, 'THE planet is turning against us.'

'That is an irrational statement,' Atticus snapped.

'I did not mean to imply sentience.'

'You did not? You were not speaking from a hidden spring of knowledge?'

Galba sighed. Unlike the captain, he still had the ability to do so. 'No,' he said. 'Merely from observation.' He gestured to the jungle beyond the wall, covering the eastward slope of the promontory. The lights of the base illuminated a narrow band of foliage and trunks, bleaching the green to silver. Behind was only hulking black, shaken by the endless, growing rage of the monstrous life within.

'You do not see those animals as a realistic threat,' Atticus informed him. The statement had the finality of a direct order.

Galba turned to Darras for help. The other sergeant said nothing. He kept his gaze steady on the jungle. He had spoken little to Galba since the battle in the ruins. Atticus's suspicion shrouded Galba like a disease. The rumour was running through the ranks of the company – one of its number might be using forbidden arts, powers doubly forbidden for contravening the commands of the Emperor and for violating the spirit of the machine. Intuition was almost as suspect as sorcery. Sorcery itself was beyond the pale.

'What I see, brother-captain, is a change in a pattern of behaviour. As unthinking as this enemy is, the effect of its actions are the same as if there were a concerted campaign.'

'I am not unaware of that, sergeant. I am cognisant of everything that plagues our mission. But that,' he pointed at the jungle, 'is not our principle threat.'

'No,' Galba agreed. 'It is not.'

They fell silent. Behind them, the sounds of nocturnal terror filtered out of the serf barracks. None of the Iron Hands reacted. The howls of damnation were expected. There was nothing to be done except deal with the casualties come dawn. Even so, Galba could not bring himself to ignore the screams. He knew something of what the mortals were experiencing. He sympathised, though he recognised their suffering as a weakness of the flesh. Atticus, he suspected, heard only a reminder of futility.

Galba tried again. 'All the same, I do think the saurians *are* a threat that we should not ignore.'

'What would you have us do? Burn the jungle down?'

'No.' They could no more do that than drain the ocean. The green and its monsters were infinite. But the word *burn* stuck with him. It rattled around his mind. It suggested something. It was the seed of an idea. Its contours were unclear to him, but if he was patient, they would resolve themselves in time.

Burn, said the thought, the echoing refrain, the nascent obsession. *Burn*.

Atticus returned to the command block. Darras, maintaining his position on watch, waited for Galba to head off on a patrol.

Galba stayed where he was. At length, he said, 'I am not a psyker.'

Darras turned to face him. 'I don't think you're lying to me, brother, and *that* is the problem. You're lying to yourself.' Galba opened his mouth to answer, but Darras held up a hand, cutting him off. 'You are not following reason. You are listening to what you want to believe. That is a failing of the flesh.'

'You don't trust me.'

'No, I don't. You're denying logic. You're straying from the path Ferrus Manus showed us, and breaking from the Imperial Truth as surely as if you were deliberately exercising sorcery. So no, I can't trust you. You shouldn't trust yourself, or any decision you make.' He faced the jungle once again. Rejecting his brother was painful, but necessary. The battlefield was unforgiving in its rejection of error.

'And if I'm not wrong,' said Galba, 'what then?'

'Then the universe is filled with terrible irrationality, and there is no such thing as reason. The madness is yours, brother. Keep it away from me.'

THE ATTACKS WERE more concerted. The disruptions were worse. Erephren fought back. She was on her guard now. She would not be taken by surprise. She still felt the anger from her confrontation with the serf, Tanaura. It was not aimed at the woman herself. It was directed at the surrender her position represented. The X Legion had suffered enough humiliations. She had played a role in restoring its pride. The destruction of the *Callidora* and its escort was a real victory. She would not let the enemy they had encountered here rob them of further vengeance.

Tanaura had her faith. May it grant her a measure of comfort as the screams of the night began. A delusion could do little more. Erephren had her fury. It drew upon the empirical, insistent, bloody reality of war itself. She needed the anchor to cast her mind into the immaterium and not go mad. She used it now to defend herself against the enemy. The cutting edges of darkness sliced into her consciousness. Laughter and jaws surrounded her. Something that had the very shape of terror tried to form before her. She repulsed it. It retaliated by tearing her perception of the warp apart.

She hissed. Her hands were clumsy and numb, light years away from her mind, but she worked them just well enough to disconnect herself from her throne. She staggered away on legs that were as rigid as death one moment, weak as air the next. Her head was filled with lightning and broken glass. Voices of hell shrieked at her. She defied them. This time, she would not black out. She shut herself off from the warp, choosing blindness instead of being thrust into it. The intensity of the voices diminished, but they were not silenced. Slivers of the unreal followed her. They were gossamer-thin, fragile as a dream at the moment of waking. But they were toxic, serrated, and they clung. They left incandescent scars on her mind. Far in the distance, her lips pulled back in a rictus. Her teeth clacked together. She tried to bite off the pain. She would have torn out the throat of the enemy with her teeth if it had stood before her.

Coward, she thought, embracing rage. *I cannot see. I can barely walk. Still you hide. You are nothing. You are not worth my time.*

The whispers showed their power by ignoring her taunts. They slithered around her. They teased her perceptions with the threat of sudden reality. When she reached out her hands to find her staff, she twitched away from the brush of the imminent. But her left hand closed around the haft, and her right found her cane. 'You are not real,' she told the shadows.

Not yet, they murmured. *Coming,* they promised.

She sent a dispatch to her arm, and it banged the tip of her cane against the floor. The sound belonged to another world, but it was present. She banged again, again, tapping the beat of her march.

She felt her way forward, engulfed in the coils of the dark. They could not hold her back. When her hand touched the door, her heart swelled with triumph. She pushed it open. In the corridor, she sensed a hulking presence. It was massively real, yet cousin to shadows. As much as she had closed herself off, she still sensed warp currents affected by the being ahead of her. She took a step back and raised her cane, braced for a fight. What confronted her was huge, and the fractured, painful chaos of the warp had crippled her. She had no illusions about her ability to win, but at least she would leave the enemy with none about her willingness to fight.

The presence spoke. 'Mistress Erephren,' it said. 'Do not be alarmed.'

She lowered the cane and leaned on it, partly from relief, partly from the pain that crackled down the base of her skull and spine. The voice belonged to the Raven Guard, Ptero. She heard some of her own strain in his tones. 'You are being attacked, too,' she said.

'All of us are. Some more acutely than others.'

'The psykers.'

'Yes, we are among the special targets.'

She was startled and honoured by his open admission. It took her a moment to notice his qualification. 'Among?'

'There are others, not of our number, who are in the foe's sights. For what reason, I do not know.'

She straightened up. Ptero was of the Legiones Astartes, and she owed him every respect. But she represented, in this moment, the X Legion, and she would stand tall. The assault did not end, but it became a background siege. Her shields were strong. Her will stronger.

'You wished to speak to me?' she said.

'Yes. You would agree that our foe cannot be defeated by force of arms alone?'

Though the Raven Guard was careful in his wording, Erephren bristled at the implied criticism of Atticus. At the same time, she knew Ptero was correct. 'I do,' she said.

'I believe you have a critical role to play against this enemy.'

'I am an astropath. Nothing more.'

'You are an astropath of enormous ability. Your perception of the warp is greater than that of anyone else on this planet. This is a power.'

'I am bound by the Emperor's Will.' She won back a greater awareness of her body, and felt the embrace of the ceremonial manacle on her ankle. It was the symbol of her unbreakable fealty.

'So are we all,' Ptero reminded her. 'But you have already done more than transmit communications.'

This was true. 'What do you want of me?'

'The use of your gaze. To look is not a passive act. It is aggressive. It can destroy. The annihilation of the *Callidora* was as much the work of your hands as it was those of Captain Atticus. The enemy sees us. It knows us. It probes our defences, learns our weaknesses. This siege cannot continue. I agree with your captain's goal in descending into the ruins. We must seek the enemy out. We must find it on its home ground, and then *we* shall be the ones besieging. But we need to know where to look, and we need to know how to strike.'

'Have you spoken to Captain Atticus?'

'I do not think he would welcome my suggestions. But I know you have his ear.'

She managed a smile. 'And thus you shape war from the shadows.'

'We of the Raven Guard flatter ourselves that we do it well.'

PTERO WAS RIGHT. Atticus did listen.

It helped that she had a specific strategy to suggest. With dawn, the enemy retreated, leaving the field to the still-growing number of saurians. Her mind clear, Erephren cautiously opened her senses to the warp. The vista before her was still disordered fragments and pain. The only thing she could see with any precision was the storms. They defied her comprehension. They were so vast, they seemed to merge into a single expression of absolute chaos. The empyrean rose up in waves that dwarfed even the conception of mountains. Lurking behind the tempests was the terrible suggestion of intention. The awful idea formed that here she saw the works of an enemy of inconceivable malice and power. She looked away from the storms before the idea became a conviction. The foe on Pythos was threat enough.

She forced herself to engage with the interference. It shattered any attempt to read the details of the warp. It turned her vision into splinters, shards, jagged energy, all dividing, overlapping, colliding in a frenzy of illogic. It was a torment to consider. Her mind tried to fly apart, but she disciplined it. She stopped trying to see past the distortion. She looked at the distortion itself. *You are what I seek*, she told it. *You are the sign of the foe. You are its trace.* Even the pain it caused was evidence. She seized on her own suffering. She made it her guide. She followed it to its source.

Then she spoke to Atticus.

An hour later, she was at the settlement, standing with an escort of Iron Hands at the edge of the first of the pits.

'You're sure the interference comes from here?' Atticus asked.

'I am.'

She found the effort to speak exhausting. Being this close to the epicentre of the disruption meant weathering a constant assault. She had all but shut herself down again, but the disorder still reached her, striking through the tiny opening she left. That was its mistake. This was how *she* could reach *it*. This was how *she* could strike. The foe would pay for daring to confront her.

'We have combed the structure,' said Atticus. 'There is nothing. No one. There is a region to which we do not yet have access, but there is no way in or out of it.'

'Nevertheless.'

'You still insist on descending?'

'I do.' She felt his evaluating gaze on her. 'Captain, I am strong enough for this task. My pride will not permit me to be a burden to you or your men.'

'I have many burdens,' Atticus growled, 'but you are not among them. You found us a target before. Do so again, and I will be forever in your debt.'

'My duty to the Legion is the only reward I seek.'

'You speak for us all.' The voice was Sergeant Galba's. Though he was addressing her, the remark seemed to be for Atticus's benefit. Erephren did not like the implication of division within the ranks of the officers, but she placed the worry to one side. It was not her concern. Her mission would require all of her concentration. She could not risk the opening that a distraction or stray worry might give the enemy.

'This way, then,' Atticus said.

She followed the sounds of his footsteps. The dull thud his boots made on earth gave way to the hollow knock of wood.

'Be careful here.'

'Thank you.' She stepped onto a narrow platform. If she had still had access to the full scope of her psychic half-vision, she would not have needed Atticus's caution. She would have sensed the precise dimensions of the platform, known how many steps forwards she could take before plunging over the edge. But the world was no longer conjured by spontaneous knowledge. Now it was tactile. The *tap-tap-tap* of her cane gave her the contours of reality. She could navigate, but her surroundings were shadowed. There were large blanks of ignorance around her, making her walk more tentatively. She was used to a sovereign authority over the spaces through which she moved, on the material and immaterial planes. Being reduced to mundane human blindness was an affront she would never forgive.

The colonists had built a rough scaffolding against the face of the structure. This pit, at the base of the main lodge, where the earth had first collapsed, was where Atticus had commanded the primary excavation take place. Secondary ones continued in the other three chasms, but with no clear advantage in one location over another, the bulk of the effort was concentrated here. Volunteers made do with lines to climb up and down the façades elsewhere. Here there were steps. They were uneven, crudely hewn, zigzagging down between platforms that were just as rough. But they were sufficient to their task. With the help of her cane, Erephren was able to make her own way down. She could, she thought, indulge her pride to that degree.

The further she descended, the more the blank spaces of the world grew. The disruption intensified. She had to commit almost all her psychic resources into blocking out the damage. She was left with mere traces of energy to keep herself mobile and able to interact with the physical realm. Two things gave her the push she needed to continue: unceasing rage, and the consuming desire to punish.

She was aware of the Iron Hands speaking to each other, but their voices were reduced to impressionist bursts of mental static. There was anger in the tones. Inflections of doubt and suspicion. The thought came to her that here was another sign of the enemy's campaign: machinic impassivity was being stolen from the Iron Hands. Isstvan V had dealt a blow that was as psychological as it was military, and that trauma was being worked on, deepened, shaped into something profound, something that might outlast the stars. Rage had become the heartbeat of the company, rage sharp as a dagger, yet wide as the galaxy. Rage in response to betrayal, a betrayal so great that it revealed the treachery in all things. She understood, because she had her small, mortal share of that rage. How much more incandescent, how devastating to all around them, would be the anger of the demigods.

She found that she rejoiced at the idea. As long as the rage was not directed inwards.

The anxiety rose, a bubble forming in the cauldron of her psyche. It was without value. It was dangerous. She suppressed it with the greater force of anger, and moved forwards. Downwards. One step at a time.

Ahead of her, the sound of Atticus's heavy footfalls changed again. Now there was the hard echo of stone. 'We are about to enter the ruin,' he told her. He had turned to the right.

She thanked him. She followed his voice, felt the platform give way to the smoothness of the structure itself. Then she was passing through the threshold. It was a stark reality, cutting through the enveloping blankness. She sensed the contours of the arch as clearly as if the disruption had abruptly ceased. But when she was through, the scrambling of her perceptions increased a hundredfold.

Time vanished. The world vanished. There was only disruption. She had stepped inside the assault, and it came in from all sides, overwhelming her barriers. She was drowning in malformed energy.

Something that was not random intruded. It had a shape. It had a purpose. It had an existence in time, and its existence gave her back the succession of moments. The thing became clearer. It was a voice. It was Atticus, speaking her name. She grabbed the fragment of reality and struggled against the stream of madness. She reached a shore, and bit by bit, reclaimed the nature of sounds, of touch, of thought. She was surprised to discover that she was still standing.

Atticus asked, 'Can you continue?'

'Yes.' The word was a victory. Its truth was a greater one. 'Captain, you said this building was inert. It is not.'

'We know there is ambient warp energy at work here, but that is all,' Atticus replied. 'Auspex?' he called.

'No change.' The speaker was the Techmarine, Camnus. 'No coherent waveforms.'

'Yet the attacks are directed,' Atticus mused, 'and are growing stronger.'

'This is a machine,' said Galba.

Atticus grunted and moved on.

Down, down, deeper. Erephren was spiralling into a searing gale. The taking of a single step was a war in itself. She claimed one hard victory after another, and the greater the pain, the greater her sense that she was closing with the enemy. Time disintegrated again. She existed on the fuel of rage and expectation. When next she was aware of the world outside her struggle, she had stopped moving.

Atticus's voice penetrated the galvanic haze, a transmission from a distant star. 'We can go no further.'

Complete your mission, she thought. The effort to speak brought her to the point of collapse. Duty held her upright. 'We are very close,' she said. She reached out with her left hand. Her palm brushed against a rock barrier. 'What is this?' she asked.

'The barrier at the end of this tunnel,' Atticus told her. 'The excavations here have removed all the collapsed stone, but now this blocks our path. It is too uniform to be natural. It is part of the xenos construction of this site. Its purpose is unclear, and we can find no way around it.'

'One of the other tunnels, perhaps...' Darras began.

'No,' she said. She ran her fingers over the rock. Its presence filled her mind. 'The surface has a curve to it,' she announced. 'This is a sphere. A very large one.'

'Brother Camnus?' said Atticus.

'Our readings are nonsense, brother-captain. It is impossible to say with certainty. But it is very possible, yes. I think we should trust what Mistress Erephren detects.'

'Can you tell what is on the other side?' Atticus asked. 'If we break through, will we find our enemy?'

She pushed through the torment. She forced herself to look more

fully at the disruptions, here in this place that was more warp
than reality. She braced for the worst attack yet. She was convinced
that she was about to encounter the heart of the disruptive power.
Instead, she found nothing. The sphere was hollow. It was a vast
emptiness, a void that crackled with potential, but there was no
enemy.

'There is nothing there,' Erephren said. 'This sphere...' *A shell?* 'It
is the centre of the interference.'

'The source?'

'No. The centre.' She took her hand away. 'The entire structure is
the source.'

'A machine,' Galba repeated.

'The attacks are deliberate,' Atticus said. 'They are not just the effect
of a mechanism at work. If this is a machine, someone is using it.'

'Yes.' Erephren agreed. With nothing more for her to see, she reinforced her barriers. She retreated into the relief of blindness. She
could not close off the energy altogether. It was too strong. It leaked
in. Her head rang like a cathedral bell. She wished this conversation would wait. 'But that someone is not here.'

'Then where?'

Atticus's question was rhetorical, but the answer loomed before
Erephren. It was one she should not believe. It was also one she
could not avoid. She waited, though. She wondered if Galba had
come to the same unwanted, insane conclusion.

He had. 'Nowhere on this plane.'

'Yes,' she said.

The silence was a heavy one.

'I will not countenance absurdities,' Atticus declared, his fury
expressed in cold, mechanical syllables. 'I cannot fight myths.'

'Captain,' Erephren said. 'I will not try to convince you of something that I wish, with all my heart, to be a mistake. But this I
can tell you beyond any doubt – this structure is the cause of the

interference. If you have any faith in my abilities, believe me now.'

'Then we must end the interference.'

Galba said, 'Burn it.'

FIFTEEN

Refrain
Communion
Defiance

Burn it.

The idea was his, wasn't it?

Galba brooded over the question on the way back to the surface. He wrestled with it on the *Unbending* as it flew to the base. Atticus kept his council, perhaps giving Galba time to marshal his arguments or repent his madness. He did not change his mind. The ruins must be destroyed. That was self-evident, surely. They caused the disruption of Erephren's ability to monitor the warp. Eliminate them, and the problem ended.

That was logical.

But he had been thinking *burn it* before Erephren's diagnosis. He tried to justify his conviction. He tried to construct that rational set of observations and conclusions that had led to that idea. And to those very precise words.

Burn it.

He failed. Reasoning became rationalisations, and he discarded them in shame. He was honest with himself. The idea had come to him during the night, and nothing could be trusted in the nights of Pythos.

He found that he could not even trust his dilemma. He was even more uncertain when Atticus took him aside. They spoke in the captain's quarters, a small prefab chamber attached to the command centre. It was a windowless, almost featureless space. There was nothing on the plasteel walls. In the centre of the room was a table on which were spread star charts and a growing collection of maps of Pythos. Atticus had not given up on the idea of finding an enemy encampment, and had been sending the gunships out on reconnaissance missions, surveying more of the coastal region every time. The results consisted of contour maps of unbroken jungle. The parchments were covered in annotations, almost all of them crossed out. They were the leavings of frustration.

There was nowhere to sit in the room. There was only the table. Atticus shut the door. He removed his helmet, placing it on the table. He began a slow, measured pace around the room, and Galba knew he was seeing how the captain used the chamber. This was the space of restless thought.

Atticus said, 'So you would have me burn the ruins?'

'I feel very strongly that you should, brother-captain.' That was the purest, most honest answer he could give. He hoped the captain would pick up on his choice of words.

He did. 'You *feel* this, do you?'

'Yes.'

'And what do you *think* we should do?'

'I'm not sure.'

Atticus stopped pacing. From the other side of the table, he faced Galba. His gaze was cold, precise, anatomising. Galba felt himself being judged by an intellect as inhuman as a cogitator. Just as the left eye was the only visible echo of the flesh left on Atticus, the last emotion to live within his frame was rage. 'Explain yourself,' said the monster of war.

'My primary impulse is to burn the ruins. Destruction would be the inevitable result of this action. But my impulse is to burn. I *must* take this action, captain. It is all I can think about. But...'

'But you did not deduce that this was the way to achieve destruction.'

'That is correct.'

After a few seconds, Atticus mused, 'The strategy is a rational one. The most effective way of destroying that structure would involve one form of fire or another. Sergeant, when did this desire to burn strike you?'

'Last night.'

'I see. You did not come to the conclusion that the ruins were the source of the interference before Mistress Erephren did?'

'I did not.'

'What might be the source of your inspiration?'

'I have no idea.'

'Oh?'

There was little inflection in Atticus's bionic voice. There were levels of volume, and there was the length that he chose to give his syllables. Those variations were enough to convey a wealth of expression. Galba had no difficulty reading his scepticism in that single word. Even so, the sergeant stood his ground.

'I do not know what the source is. I *do* know what it is not. I am *not* a psyker. How would I have concealed that from you, and from all of our brothers, for so long? Captain,' he pleaded, 'have I ever given you any cause to doubt my loyalty?'

Atticus's head tilted a fraction of a degree to the right. 'You have not,' he admitted. 'But some of your behaviour on this planet has been difficult to explain.'

'I share your puzzlement.'

The electronic grunt was noncommittal. It was not hostile. Nor was it merciful. 'Understand me, sergeant. Whatever the nature of the weakness that assails you, the only aspect of it that interests me is what consequences it might have for our tactical situation. Will you hurt or harm the mission? Will you hurt or harm the company?'

'I would never–'

Atticus held up a hand, cutting him off. 'If you do not understand what is happening to you, if it is happening despite your will, your intentions are irrelevant. So, therefore, is your loyalty.'

Galba had no answer to that. The logic was unforgiving. It was also unassailable. 'What do you intend to do with me?' he asked.

'I am not sure. I do not like uncertainty, brother-sergeant. I especially despise it in myself. But this is our position. Whatever the source of your knowledge, you were able to warn us about the attack by those vermin in the ruins. That was useful, if inexplicable.' He tapped a finger against the surface of the table. 'Describe to me again exactly what happened.'

'I sensed something coming.'

'Sensed how? Was it an intuition?'

'No.' He paused. 'I heard whispers.'

'The night of the first attack, you said you smelled whispers.'

Galba nodded. 'I did.'

'My diagnosis was a warp-induced hallucination.' *Tap-tap-tap* went the finger. 'Events point to the inadequacy of that theory. Whispers, you said. Were they coherent?'

'In the ruins, they were.'

'What did they say?'

'"Warn them. It's coming. Look to your right."'

The tapping stopped. 'Very coherent. Were they in your voice?'

'No,' he said. He bit the word off with disgust. The memory of that voice – *rust, skulls, stone* – grated.

'And now? Have the whispers spoken to you again?'

'Not as they did then. But the need to burn the ruins is an articulated one. The words *"burn it"* are in my head.'

Silence. Immobility. The warrior-machine deep in thought. Then,

'The coherence of these messages is in keeping with the presence of a sentient enemy. The nature of the technology that would permit their transmission is beyond me, but I will set that aside for now. The content of the messages is what must be dealt with. And we were not harmed by those whispers in the ruins. We were aided.'

'Do you think we have allies as well as enemies here?' Galba asked. The idea felt wrong.

'I am growing weary of hearing about invisible entities,' Atticus said.

'With respect, captain, you are not half as tired as I am of hearing *from* them.'

Now the sound that emerged from the expressionless skull was an approximation of amusement. 'I should imagine,' Atticus said.

That sentence bridged the gulf that had been growing between the two legionaries. Galba felt his breathing become easier. 'What action should we take?' he asked.

Atticus was still again. Then he gave the table a decisive rap with his fist. The surface dented. 'My misgivings are legion. But the first message in the ruins was valuable. Ignoring the second might be foolish, and its urging does coincide with my own strategic evaluations.'

'We are going to destroy the structure?'

'We will burn it.'

KANSHELL THOUGHT THAT this might be his last time in the settlement. The excavation operations had been called off. Kanshell did not know what, if anything, had been found in the depths, but it seemed that the X Legion had little reason to maintain a presence here any longer. The word circulating among the serfs was that the time had come for the colonists to stand on their own. The palisade was solid. Enough lasrifles had been distributed for the people to defend themselves. Now they had to show that they were worth the effort to save.

This was the information that floated Kanshell's way on the currents of conversation during the last few hours of the last day. It
was surface chatter. Below were the important flows. The fears of
the nights on the base were now tangled with the hopes ignited by
the ceremonies held in the settlement. The serfs had been cautious,
if fascinated, spectators. Only Kanshell had set foot in one of the
lodges. Now there would be one last chance to take part. The currents roiled with unstated confusion, uncertainty, worry. Kanshell
suspected that most of the serfs, even followers of the Lectitio Div-
inatus, would hold back. The fear of so visible a violation of the
Imperial Truth's secularism was too great.

Kanshell knew what Tanaura would do if she were present. He
could hear her voice urging the courage to stand by the truth, no
matter what censure would follow. He had a spiritual debt to her.
She had never given up on him. He could not back down. And if
he truly had faith in the God-Emperor, that faith carried responsibilities. He would live up to them.

Evening came. The work details ended, but the transports had not
yet arrived. Kanshell could see no legionaries at all. Even the Salamanders had left shortly after the Iron Hands and the astropath had
emerged from the depths. The independence of the settlement had
begun. The jungle roared as if the saurians knew this and rejoiced.
The guards on the walls were more numerous, and seemed to be
getting better, if only through sheer concentration of fire, at fend-
ing off the beasts. Even so, the occasional flying reptile succeeded
in taking off with a shrieking trophy.

The colonists began their ceremonies. The rituals were the
largest, most enthusiastic to date. All four lodges were bursting
with celebrating crowds. The chants embraced in the air over
the settlement. They became a round. Kanshell headed towards
the primary lodge. His copy of the *Lectitio* was inside his work
fatigues. On this day, he would advance to the centre of the

lightweb. He would accept the welcome. He would engage in the full measure of worship.

IN THE COMMAND centre of the base, Atticus addressed his officers. The Salamanders and Raven Guard were present, too. Khi'dem was not fooled by the courtesy. He knew that this was no consultation. He was present to hear the dictates of the commander of the Iron Hands. A decision had been made. An operation of some scale was about to begin. Khi'dem could not imagine what it was. The war had stagnated. He worried that Atticus's level of frustration might be reaching the point where he would plunge into action for the sake of action.

He was uneasy, too, about leaving the settlement undefended. He understood that the colonists could not be protected indefinitely. He agreed that they must be responsible for their own survival, once they had the means to do so. And he acknowledged that perhaps they now did. What he did not see was that the tactical situation had changed at all. He would rather fight a useful struggle at the settlement than rot in a holding pattern on the base, waiting for a mission that might never come.

Atticus activated the hololith table that dominated the command centre. A projection of the settlement appeared. Highlighted was a representation of the ruins, based on the observable portions and extrapolations of those regions still inaccessible. A massive underground hemisphere in the centre of the plateau shone with the greatest brilliance. Runes appeared indicating the estimated depth from the surface of the ground to the top of the dome. Khi'dem frowned. Another dig? That did not seem worth this level of briefing. He grew uneasy.

Atticus said, 'With the help of Mistress Erephren, we have determined that the xenos structure is, in fact, a weapon. Though we have yet to pinpoint our enemy's location, we know that this is the tool he is using against us. So the time has come to remove it from the field.' He touched the table's controls, and a marker of the *Veritas Ferrum* appeared, indicating its geosynchronous position over the settlement.

Khi'dem's unease turned into shock.

THE WELCOME WAS as warm as before. Kanshell was swept up in the ecstasy of worship again. The experience was even more intense, because this time he had come with no hesitation. He had come with his own joy, his own anticipation. And he had come with the object that would mark the event and the place with proper sanctity.

Once again, Ske Vris walked with him towards the centre of the lodge. The woman's smile was beyond joyful. It seemed to Kanshell he was not the only one for whom the event was charged with greater meaning than before. Ske Vris's face shone with the triumph of immutable destiny. The chanting was supercharged. This was a night of climax. Perhaps, Kanshell thought, as he surrendered himself to the sensory overload of praise, he was completing something for these people as well as for himself. Perhaps, at some level, they realised that something was missing from their rituals. Now he was bringing the Emperor to them, and their worship would have a true centre.

The tall, hooded priest stood in the same spot. Had he danced again? Kanshell was not sure. The details of reality were slipping away from him, the material falling before the might of the spiritual. He saw the world in fragments. It had become an endlessly shifting kaleidoscope, the fragments spinning away in scintillating bursts of the sublime. He grasped enough to be able to walk – *he was walking, wasn't he? Was he floating?* – and he held coherent thoughts just long enough to know what he must do in each of the moments where he was granted some portion of awareness. He moved – *flew, walked, floated, swam* – forwards, breath by breath, beat by beat, measure by measure. He was almost at the centre, where all the vortices and lattices of light found their nexus. Here was where meaning died and was reborn, renewed.

The priest said, 'Have you brought an icon?'

Civilisations rose and fell before he found his tongue. 'Something else.' He produced the *Lectitio Divinitatus*.

Silence. The universe paused. Kanshell was suspended in a limbo filled with an infinite potential of meaning. Something immense transpired. Significance towered over Kanshell, its extent lost beyond perception. He vanished in its shadow, and the silence filled him with cold. What had he done? Had he offended? How?

A hand reached into the limbo. The world coalesced around it. Kanshell could see again. Time advanced, but the silence continued. The priest took the offered book. He handled it with reverence. He lifted it towards the ceiling of the lodge. He spoke. 'The word.'

The silence ended in eruption. It was as powerful as the cry of a volcano, but it was the fullest paroxysm of celebration. Kanshell wept that he had done so well. The effect was beyond his fiercest hope. For the first time in his life, he realised that even he, the most insignificant of menials, had a destiny, and that his role in the Emperor's plan might well be far more important than his state should permit.

The priest took a step back. He knelt, and placed the *Lectitio* in the centre of the floor. The book was battered, dog-eared, curling. It was humble. But it was transformed in the nexus. It became more than words, more than teachings, more than a symbol. Kanshell saw it as the product and source of forces beyond his comprehension. The galaxy turned on the axis of that book. What had been, what was now, and what was to come were reflected and shaped there. His sublime joy was mixed with an awe just as sublime, and so there also came terror. He was too small. The meanings were too vast. If he looked closely, if he understood all, then he would be blasted to nothing.

But would that be so terrible? Would that not be the culmination of his life? Was this not the greatest thing he could ever hope to accomplish? Was there any point in living a perpetual anticlimax?

The priest was holding out his hands again, inviting Kanshell to join the book, to know all, to receive the gift of full revelation. Kanshell embraced the moment. He gave himself as an offering to the God-Emperor. He stepped forwards.

Only he did not. His mind sent the commands. The impulses reached his legs. His body had lost the unity of self, and was slow to react. In the gulf between his thought and his act, the shadow fell. The flow of voices was disrupted by the harsh, merciless cacophony of machines. Engines roared. Heavy boots marched. A voice that held not even the echo of humanity gave commands.

The lightweb shattered, went out. The song died. The world clamped back into place around Kanshell. He gasped at the shock. He stumbled, first out of weakness, and then again as the crowd rushed from the lodge, pursued by the anger of a weapon that walked and judged.

'This superstition is at an end,' Atticus declared. 'So is my patience. So is this settlement. It is over. All of it. *Now!*'

Kanshell fell to all fours. His head rang as running legs struck it. He curled into a ball, trying to ward off the blows. They did not last long. Even the most devoted of the colonists hurried to obey the terrible giant that had come among them. Only the priest and Ske Vris were unhurried. As Kanshell raised his head, he saw the two walk past the looming Atticus. Ske Vris had her head bowed in deference, but the priest, still hooded, stood straight. Then they, too, exited into the night. Kanshell was alone in the lodge with the captain of the Iron Hands.

'My lord,' Kanshell whispered. He had done nothing wrong. At the most important level, the spiritual one, he knew this to be true. But in the realm of secular laws, and in the eyes of the coldest of legionaries, he had trespassed. He did not beg forgiveness. He would not betray the truth of his faith.

There were also beings for whom forgiveness was an alien concept.

'What do you think you're doing, serf?' Atticus said. The low electronic voice, barely audible over the rumble of transport engines outside, was terrifying.

Kanshell opened his mouth. Nothing came out. There was nothing to say. No truth, lie or plea would make a difference now. His words would be as well spent trying to stop the fall of night.

Galba entered the lodge and came up behind Atticus. 'Captain,' he said, 'they are gathered. If you want to speak to them...'

Atticus turned to the sergeant. 'I do not want to *speak* to these fools,' he said. 'But I will *tell* them where they stand.' He left. Kanshell was forgotten. He was so far beneath notice that he could not retain the legionary's attention for more than a few seconds.

Galba remained behind. He looked down. 'Get up, Jerune,' he said.

Kanshell struggled to his feet.

'What were you doing here?' Galba's question was not rhetorical menace. He was genuinely puzzled.

Kanshell had not known the true meaning of worship until he had embraced the teachings of the Lectitio Divinitatus. But he had experienced its simulacrum, and the object of that fidelity had been Galba. Of all the Iron Hands of the *Veritas Ferrum*, he was the one who stooped to see the serfs. He acknowledged the presence of the weak mortals. He was capable of kindness. He seemed, at times, to have an understanding, or at least a form of sympathy, for the pitiful beings that scurried about, fulfilling the menial tasks of the great ship. Futility had stopped Kanshell from answering Atticus. He knew Galba would not be any more receptive to Kanshell's new truth than the captain. He also knew that he must be open with his master.

'I was making an offering to the God-Emperor,' he said.

Galba closed his eyes for a moment. Kanshell was surprised to see that a Space Marine could look tired. When Galba looked at Kanshell again, he wore a pained expression. 'I should censure you. At the very least, I should explain the absurdity of what you are doing, and point out that you are acting in direct violation of the Emperor's dictates *and* His wishes.'

'Yes, sergeant.'

'But I imagine that if you are able to surmount the ridiculous paradox of worshipping as a god a being who has forbidden precisely that belief, then I would be wasting my breath to point out your smaller lunacies.'

Kanshell said nothing. He bowed his head in agreement, in humility and in defiance.

'Has this cult become widespread among the serfs?'

'It has.'

The sergeant grunted. 'The nights, I suppose,' he muttered, more to himself than to Kanshell. 'Irrational horror breeds irrational hope.' His laugh was short, soft, grim. 'Jerune, if you knew how much of the irrational there is to go around...' He turned to go. 'I have no interest in punishing you,' he said. He gestured with his right hand, taking in the space of the lodge. 'This will all be over with soon enough, anyway.'

'Sergeant?' Kanshell asked, but Galba kept walking. He started to follow, then remembered his *Lectitio*. He ran back to the centre of the lodge. The book was gone.

GUNSHIPS AND TRANSPORTS idled, ramps down. The Vindicators had arrived at the gates of the settlement. *Engine of Fury* had advanced inside the palisade, moving between and ahead of the Thunderhawks. The entire population, thousands strong, milled in the centre of the plateau, herded there by the warriors of 111th Company. Galba eyed the scene while Atticus climbed atop *Engine of*

Fury. It occurred to him that the scene looked like an invasion. At a word, the Iron Hands could annihilate the population before them. Atticus's impatience had found expression in the brutal efficiency of the operation.

Vox-horns on the vehicles sent the captain's voice out over the crowd. It was a harsh rent in the night air. He did not greet his listeners. He said, 'We have entered a new stage of the war. A drastic step is required, which makes this plateau unsafe. You will be evacuated back to our base and its vicinity, until we find you a more suitable location. That is all.' He was about to dismount from the tank, when the head priest approached. The man stopped with the barrel of the Vindicator soaring over his head, pointing towards his flock.

'This location is most suitable,' the priest said.

'Not any longer.'

'I'm sorry to irritate you, captain, but we disagree. We shall remain here.'

Atticus was motionless. Galba wondered if he might crush the man's head for his effrontery. He did not. 'The decision is not yours to make,' Atticus said. 'It has been taken. You will be moved now.'

'No.'

The silence seemed to cut through the noise of the engines.

'How, exactly, do you think you can defy us?' Atticus asked.

'Simply by doing so. We will not go.'

Atticus reached down from the tank, grabbed the front of the priest's armoured tunic and lifted him high. He held the man at arm's length. The priest did not struggle. He held his dangling legs still. Galba was impressed by his self-control, even as his revulsion for the turbulent flesh rose afresh. Atticus said, 'Do you defy me still?'

'I do.'

'Yet I can move you as I will. You are leaving.'

'We are not.' The priest's voice was strained, but its pride was untouched. 'You will have to kill us first.'

'You will be killed if you remain.'

'I think not.'

'You do not know what is coming. You are a fool.'

'I think not.'

Atticus grunted. 'No, you really don't, do you? So be it.' He dropped the priest. The man fell in a heap, but rose again with a sinuous movement. He stood as he had before, dwarfed by *Engine of Fury* and the dark colossus. 'You wish us to leave,' Atticus proclaimed. 'So we shall. You do not wish our help. So you shall not have it. You wish to stay. *So. You. Shall.*'

He pronounced the last three words with the slow beat and terrible emphasis of a tolling bell. 'You are welcome, of course, to change your minds. Should you choose to flee into the jungle, and throw yourselves upon the tender mercies of the saurians, feel free to do so. We will not stop you. We will not interfere. We will not help. We will not be here. But you will know of us. At dawn, this plateau will cease to exist. The wrath of the Iron Hands will burn it from all living memory.'

The last words of Atticus's judgement echoed across the settlement. There was no murmur from the crowd. The priest remained where he was. His stillness rivalled the captain's.

'Legionaries,' Atticus said, 'we are done here.'

The exodus began. As Galba watched the serfs climb into the transports, he caught sight of Kanshell. The man looked much worse than he had a few minutes before. Then he had been frightened, dazed, desperate. Now he looked sick, broken. His face was grey. It sagged with horror. Many of the other menials, Galba now saw, had the same look. Horror, not terror. They were not dreading the night on the base and the fearful thing that would come for some of them. They were shocked by the fate that loomed for their new friends.

Galba felt a flare of sympathy. He crushed it. He had been pushed to the outside of the company. Since he was not a psyker, how had he been vulnerable? He could guess the answer: the flesh. He had not carved away enough of it. Its weakness had opened the door to the enemy. Well, he was back in Atticus's confidence again. He would not betray that trust. He would not allow sentiment to get in the way of necessary strategy. The serfs lacked the discipline to see the world as it was. The Iron Hands should, he now realised, have been more vigilant and more ready to stamp out the magical thinking that had infected large numbers of the serfs. *He* should have been more vigilant. He should have been less lax.

Less human.

Burn it.

He looked away from the shocked humans and walked over to *Unbending* where Atticus now waited. It was true that he had not imagined Atticus would punish the recalcitrance of the colonists with such finality. He could allow himself the luxury of being surprised. But he was wrong to feel shock, too, he told himself. There was no alternative to the current action, he told himself.

And so he struggled to restrain his own mounting horror.

SIXTEEN

The Wrath

KHI'DEM DID NOT restrain his horror at all.

He stormed into the command centre just before dawn. Atticus had barred access to anyone other than his own officers until the last few minutes before the strike. By then, the *Veritas Ferrum* was in position. Helmsman Eutropius was on the vox, waiting for the command to unleash its wrath. Galba had stood by during all the preparations. He said nothing to sway Atticus from this course of action. He knew he should. He was convinced he should not.

He could not think. Inside the centre, he could not hear the screams and moans of the serfs suffering at the hands of the shadows. He very likely would not have heard them even if he had been standing in the centre of the dormitorium. His head was tolling with the endless command to *burn it, burn it, burn it, burn it*. The trochaic metre of the urge beat at his mind as if it had taken over the pulse of his hearts. He managed to remain at attention. He was even able to pierce through the battering obsession when his captain spoke to him. He was able to listen. He was able to answer. But within seconds, he could not remember what he had heard or said. There was only the command. He would have ordered the strike in that instant if it had been left to him.

The hour of Pythos's mournful, grey dawn drew close. Galba greeted it with relief. The compulsion eased, transforming into a grim eagerness. Soon, the Iron Hands would act. Soon, the ruins would be no more, and the machine would be destroyed. Soon, the storm in his skull would cease.

Soon, soon, soon.

And yet, when Khi'dem arrived, his face contorted with fury, his intentions obvious, Galba was glad. The son of Vulkan's protest was as necessary as the strike. Galba's lips curled as the contradiction rippled from his temple to his gut. Once more, he blamed his flesh for trapping him in the paradox. He cursed it. He wished it gone.

Soon.

'This is murder,' Khi'dem said.

'It is not,' Atticus replied, calm and indifferent to the other's outrage. 'We offered safety, and were refused. We have not trapped anyone in the target area. They are free to leave. They still have a few minutes to do so.' He spoke without malice. Or pity.

'You will be knowingly exterminating a civilian population, when no enemy is present. This is wrong. How can you still claim to be any better than the World Eaters or the Night Lords?'

Galba tensed at the insult. Atticus did not react. 'Ridiculous,' was all he said. He seemed to have Khi'dem's measure. An age ago, over Isstvan V, the situation had been different. Khi'dem had convinced Atticus to pick up the escaping Thunderhawks by appealing to something in the captain that went beyond the cold expediency of war. He was trying again, but his efforts were slamming into a blank wall. He was speaking to something in Atticus that was no longer there.

Atticus leaned over the hololith table. The representation of the *Veritas Ferrum* was directly above the coordinates for the settlement.

The dagger was about to plunge into the heart of the enemy's campaign. 'Brother Eutropius,' Atticus voxed.

'Your will, captain?' Eutropius's voice crackled with static, but it was clearer than surface-to-ship communications had been for days. The warp's erosion of real space around Pythos could not stop the coming blow.

'On my mark, the count is five hundred.'

'So ordered.'

'Captain Atticus,' Khi'dem pleaded, 'please think about–'

'Mark,' Atticus said.

'The count has begun,' Eutropius reported.

'Thank you, helmsman.' Atticus shut the table down. The hololiths vanished with a flicker of harsh snow.

'What have you done?' said Khi'dem.

'Do spare me the sentiment of your Legion. I find it of very little interest.' Atticus headed for the command centre's exit. 'Brothers,' he said, 'shall we?'

Galba blinked. The compulsion had left him the moment Atticus had issued the command. His head felt clear for the first time in days. Nothing spoke to him. There were no warnings or refrains. The absences were a boon. The return to clarity was a sign, he thought. The strike was the right move.

He followed Atticus outside. The sky was still dark, but when they climbed the wall and looked over the parapet towards the east, in the direction of the settlement, the contours of the jungle were beginning to distinguish themselves. A glow was slowly filtering in through the cloud cover. The navigation lights of *Unbending* were visible in the distance. Under Darras's command, it was flying within sight of the plateau.

All along the parapet, the warriors of the X Legion had gathered to witness the great fire. The Salamanders and Raven Guard were there, too. Atticus nodded to them. Galba saw Khi'dem exchange a look with Ptero. 'Do you agree with this?' Khi'dem asked.

'The structure must be destroyed.' Ptero answered.

'At this cost?'

Ptero seemed pained. 'I don't know. Is there an alternative? I can't think of one.'

'This is a crime,' Khi'dem insisted.

'What news, Sergeant Darras,' Atticus asked over the company vox.

'There is a gathering,' the answer came back.

'At their lodges?'

'No. They have formed a circle around the target site.'

'Suicidal idiots,' Atticus commented. 'Thank you, brother-sergeant.'

'What are you going to use?' Khi'dem asked, his voice dull. 'Cyclonic torpedoes?'

'Far too destructive. We must preserve the warp-anomaly. The strike must be very precise. Sergeant Galba's insight has proven vital.'

'It has?' Khi'dem gave Galba a sharp look.

'The captain gives me too much credit,' Galba said.

'You said we must burn it,' Atticus said to him, then turned back to Khi'dem. 'So we shall. A concentrated lance salvo, strong enough to punch through the earth and destroy every trace of the structure beneath. We will cauterise the landscape.'

Khi'dem rounded on Galba. 'This was your idea, then? I thought better of you.'

'Then you, also, give me too much credit,' he muttered. He watched the lights of the Thunderhawk, and waited for the great illumination of the strike. He was filled with disgust. It was directed at himself, at the colonists, at the imminent slaughter, and at all the confusing, contradictory, maddening weaknesses of the flesh. He wished the cauterisation would extend to him.

'The count approaches one hundred,' Atticus said. 'Sergeant Darras, let the mortals know. We will do them the courtesy of giving them a final warning.'

'*There is no need, captain,*' Darras responded. '*They know.*'

'What do you mean?'

'*They are looking up. All of them. They are waiting for it.*'

'Thank you, sergeant. Pull back to a safe distance.' To Khi'dem, Atticus said, 'Be at peace, Salamander. This is not murder. It is suicide.'

Khi'dem glared, but did not answer.

Atticus looked up to the sky. The cloud cover was just beginning to be discernible. 'We are not responsible for the lunacy of the weak. We are sworn and duty-bound to crush the Emperor's enemies. That is our task. All else is luxury.' Then he said, 'Time.'

The wrath pierced the clouds. The lance fire from the *Veritas Ferrum* slashed down. For several seconds, a pillar of fire linked earth and sky. The thunder of its strike reached the base a few moments after its light. The world shook with the crackle of energy and the deep bass rumble of purified destruction. This was war at one remove: the iron hand of the X Legion reaching from the heavens to smite the weapon of the enemy.

The salvo ended. The fire vanished, leaving a fading glare like a livid scar on the dawn. The thunder, however, did not stop. It built. The sound grew until it was a towering wave. Galba frowned. Was he hearing the sound of the ruins collapsing? No, the sound was too big. And the crackle of energy had not ceased. The air became supercharged with the smell of ozone.

'Darras?' Atticus's voice was clipped, urgent. 'Report?'

Static from *Unbending*. Galba could see its lights, though. It was still airborne.

The sound grew louder yet. The wave crashed down. Galba staggered. He wasn't wearing his helmet, and there was nothing to shield his senses from the overload. Then the light returned.

Burn it.

Fire erupted from the jungle, a return volley from the location of the plateau. It was all the devastating power of the lance strike concentrated, transformed and amplified into the realm of the transcendent. It was a retaliation so immense, it was as if the planet's molten core had lashed out. As focused and narrow as it was intense, the incandescent scream speared the clouds. The sky glowed ferocious orange. The clouds boiled with exultant anger.

Then, through the cover, another flash, a point of supreme brilliance, the message of a terrible explosion beyond the atmosphere. Galba knew what it was. His frame was wracked by a silent howl of denial, but he knew what he had seen. The thunder continued to crash over the base, and it was now the sound of mockery, the laughter of the burning sky.

Galba knew. He knew. He knew. But *no no no*, he thought, all the strength of his will pushing back against what had happened, against the sight that was sure to come. Something scratched at his ear, barely perceptible through the roar of the world. At the back of his mind, he registered that it was his vox-bead. There was a voice there, the voice of his captain, calling to the helmsman of the *Veritas Ferrum*, demanding an answer, demanding a reality other than the one that was upon them. Then there was another voice, Darras, somehow breaking through the static long enough to shout, *'What have you done?'* The fury there was directed at Galba, and at him alone.

The blast ended, its work done. The rage in the sky dimmed to the red of flaming blood. Then the clouds writhed as an immense shape descended through them. The presence resolved itself into several distinct masses. They carried with them the searing glow of renewed fire.

No no no, Galba still thought, but the iron truth was deaf to his entreaty. The shattered bulk of the great strike cruiser came into view. The *Veritas Ferrum* dropped like a rain of broken cathedrals. The blasted sections glowed from the heat of re-entry and the mark of the dismembering wounds. The ship had been smashed into chunks hundreds of metres in length. They were so huge, they seemed to float towards the ground. The sight was so powerful in its malevolent grandeur, it paralysed time. Galba had lived through page after page of the 111th Clan-Company's blackening history, but these moments were the darkest. They were the death of hope. They were the final fate of the company scrawled across the sky in words of metal and fire.

The fragments of the ship struck the earth. None fell on the plateau or on the base, as if tyrant destiny had decreed that all should witness the despair to come. They hit on all sides, the nearest barely a kilometre away. The impacts were the hammer blows of doom, the drumbeat of a judgement beyond the will of any human.

The ground shook, and kept shaking with each cratering strike. Galba crouched and grabbed the top of the plasteel parapet. The world tried to hurl him off his feet. Hurricane winds blew from every direction. They screamed over the base. They warred with each other. Any serf caught outside was battered to the ground. The legionaries kept their feet by tucking low and holding on. Only Atticus remained standing, defying the fury that tried to uproot the base. He was immovable. Even in the grip of cataclysm, he stood against the very idea of defeat.

The strikes, the winds, and now the fires and the dust. A cloud was hurled skyward at each impact site, and the dawn fell back into night. Waves of flame rippled out across the jungle. The promontory was an island rising above a blazing ocean. The death of the *Veritas Ferrum* thundered on in a shriek of wind and a roar of firestorm. Dust and smoke and ash choked the air, spreading across the sky, killing day forever and slamming down a sarcophagus lid over the land.

And through the raging clash of the end, through gale and rage and holocaust, reaching into Galba's head with sickle claws, came the laughter, and it was laughter in the shape of damnation, laughter in a shroud of words, laughter that was a repeating, monotonous, cackling chant.

Laughter that would be his eternal companion.

Burn it.

PART THREE

THE MIDNIGHT REVEL

SEVENTEEN

Reckoning
A miracle
The faces of truth

'WE WILL DIE here,' Atticus said.

His words, Galba knew, were not a lament. They were a statement of fact, one that stripped away all useless, comforting illusion. It was a truth that the entire company must process.

The captain stood on the landing platform, before *Unbending*, which had managed to stay aloft in the blast winds and return to base. His legionaries stood at attention in rows before him. Diminished rows. In the front rank, Galba could still feel the strength of brotherhood, sense the might of the wall of armour. But the memories of the *Veritas Ferrum*'s full complement were still vivid. He could picture the absent brothers, officers, veterans. Of the Dreadnoughts, only the Venerable Atrax remained. The Iron Father was gone. So many gone. So many hundreds. Their absence was a phantom limb. It ached.

We are still strong, he thought. They were. Then the sight of the shattered *Veritas* rose before his inner eye. *Not strong enough*, came the doubt, and he could not blame it on a malign intelligence whispering in his head. The thought was his own.

He shook it away. *For whatever needs doing here, we are strong enough.*

'We cannot leave the planet,' Atticus went on. 'We cannot communicate with any of our brothers or other Imperial forces outside the system. Even if we could, I would not countenance bringing them here. The risks are too great. The rewards are too little.

'We will die here. You are of the Legiones Astartes, and you are Iron Hands, and I know that death holds no fear for you. But defeat carries a special dread. We have experienced defeat. We have experienced loss. We would be poor warriors to pretend that we have not suffered attendant consequences. He who claims he has not been injured by the death of our ship has no place in my command. I say this to you so that we look to our destiny with clear, rational eyes.

'We will die here. Even our gene-seed is lost. Our company will vanish without trace. Our history is at an end. We shall have no legacy. But we will not die in vain. We will find the enemy. We will grind him beneath our boots. Before we are dust, the enemy will be less than a memory.' Atticus's voice rose in volume. 'We will destroy him with such violence that we will tear him from history. His past, along with his present and future, will be no more.'

Could Galba believe what was being said? His hearts swelled. Yes, he could. He had seen Atticus stand unbowed before the worst catastrophe this world could throw at them. Atticus had not mourned the *Veritas Ferrum*. He had simply become possessed by a rage of chilling rationality. He would not surrender. And now there was truly nothing left to lose. The Iron Hands would march until they had taken their foe into oblivion with them.

'You will ask how we will hurt an enemy we cannot find,' Atticus said. 'You will wonder what madness prompts me to imagine his death, when we stare at the catastrophe of our last attempt. This is my madness – if what we attempted to destroy defended itself with such violence, then its importance is critical. What we could not do from a distance, we will do at close quarters. What reflected energy weapons will succumb to other means, even if I must smash each stone of that xenos abomination with my fists.' He paused, then, lowering his voice, and asked, 'Well? Do you share my madness, brothers?'

They did. Galba did. He and his brothers roared. They slammed gauntlet against bolter in unison. Yes, they shared his madness. Yes, they would march with him.

The flesh is weak, Galba thought. *Let it be consumed in this manner. Let me give it to the forge of war, that it might be burned to nothing, and leave only the force of the unstoppable machine.*

Behind the legionaries, the serfs were massed. They were exhausted, traumatised. Galba was uneasy when he thought of their fate. They did not have the psychological conditioning of the Space Marines. They did have a fear of death, one that had been intensified greatly during the stay on Pythos. With the loss of the ship, they had nothing to look forward to but endless terror until a hideous fate. Galba could hear sobs over the crackling of the jungle fires.

'Servants of the Tenth Legion,' Atticus said to them. 'Your lot has been the most cruel. But you have sworn oaths, and you remain bound by them. I will not release you from your service. In gratitude for your loyalty, I will do something else instead. Something better. I will arm all of you. You will fight alongside us. You will strike back at that which has tormented you. You will wage war as best you can. Your losses have been immense. Your suffering worse. But you shall have honour until the end, and that is no small boon.' Another pause. 'Servants of the Tenth Legion! *What say you?*'

To the snarling metal rasp of the machine-warrior, they cried, 'We march!'

'Yes,' Atticus said, lowering his voice, filling the air with the electronic thrum of vengeance. 'We march. We march to crush.'

✠ ✠ ✠

'YOU WILL BE marching without me, I imagine,' Erephren said to Atticus. He had come to speak to her after his exhortation. She had listened to him from the doorway of the command unit, then retreated to her chamber. She stood before her throne, unable to use it, yet reluctant to abandon her post. She wondered if Strassny, at least, had believed he was being useful in the final seconds of his life.

'You march on a different path,' Atticus replied. 'What would you do with a lasrifle?'

'Nothing very useful,' she admitted.

'You are now the company's sole astropath,' he reminded her. 'The choir was lost with the ship.'

'I am no use to the Legion in that role, either. The interference is worse than ever.'

'We march for you. We will clear your path.'

To what end now? she wanted to say. She stopped herself. She had no use for self-pity in anyone, least of all herself. To cry helplessness would be to plunge into the worst indulgence. Atticus was right. She had her own march to undertake. The legionaries were heading off to fight an enemy that had yet to be defined. They could well be marching to futility. But they would not be passive in the face of the loss of the *Veritas Ferrum*. Nor would she. The 111th Clan-Company could not leave Pythos, but she was an astropath. It was her gift and her duty to bridge the void, to make distance meaningless.

'Thank you, captain,' she said. 'March well. I will wage my own campaign.'

'I know it.' His respect was clear.

HALF THE SERFS and a third of the legionaries, under Darras's command, remained to guard the base. The rest moved down towards the settlement. Vindicators at the front, Thunderhawks overhead, it was as large-scale an operation as the taking of the plateau. It was bigger, with the armed serfs following in the wake of the Iron Hands. It was also more vague, its objectives more uncertain. And it was full of desperate rage.

The lasrifle was turning slick in Kanshell's hands. He had broken into a jogging run to keep up with the pace of the Space Marines, but his sweat was a cold one. He glanced at Tanaura. He was just able to match her pace. He was breathing hard. She, much older, looked as if she could keep up her unwavering gait for the rest of the day. 'I don't know if I can use this,' he said to her.

'You know very well how to do so. We've all been trained.'

'I've never been in combat. Have you?'

She nodded once.

'I'm afraid I'll miss.'

'Take the time to aim before you fire. Anyway, you can't miss. Not anything on Pythos. Look around.'

He did. The world had been transformed by the fall of the *Veritas Ferrum*. The holocaust had incinerated the jungle. For kilometres on either side, the landscape had become a vista of scorched earth and smoking stumps. Gone was the oppressive night of green. In its place was a brown-grey day of ash and smoke. The rumbling growls of the saurians were more distant than they had been. The monsters had fled the conflagration. They were slow to emerge from cover and venture onto the blighted terrain. Some of the larger predators, in ones and twos, were testing the ground. They were in the middle distance, moving parallel with the company. They issued the occasional roar of challenge, but did not approach any closer. There was no war here yet. And Tanaura was right. There was no way of missing a beast that was close enough to attack.

The flames had washed up against the plateau, scorching the exterior of the palisade. Beyond the blackening of the wood, the wall was intact. The settlement seemed to be untouched. Kanshell could not see any guards at the top. He wondered if all the colonists were dead. He could not imagine anything in proximity to that blast having survived. He was surprised to see the palisade still standing. And as the Vindicators rolled up the low slope of the plateau, the gate opened.

The company marched into the settlement. As he passed through the gate, Kanshell's eyes widened. There was no damage. The colonists stood as he had seen the night before, as if they had not moved. There were only two signs of the event. One was the acrid sting of the air. The other was what waited at the centre of the plateau.

At first, Kanshell thought it was a crater. From the gate, all he saw was the circular depression. He drew closer as the company spread out around the hole, and saw that he was wrong. It was a shaft. It was a perfect circle, and its walls were vertical. Even as he processed the shape, he still imagined that it had been created by the lance fire.

That was wrong, too.

Tanaura was praying under her breath. Kanshell discovered that he was, too.

The shaft was artificial. It had not been dug. It had been revealed. There were engravings on the walls. They were huge, abstract designs. Looked at directly, they were loops and jagged lines. They suggested runes, but never quite became them. But in the corners of his eyes, Kanshell kept picking up on movement. Things coiled as serpents and squirmed as insects. Shadows flowed up the shaft, whispering knowledge of the terrible nights. Kanshell squeezed his eyes shut. The engravings reached in through his lids, becoming silver lightning in the dark. They began to laugh. He opened his eyes again. The world beyond the shaft was enough to dim the laughter.

It did not extinguish it.

A ramp spiralled down into the depths of the shaft. It stuck out from the walls, a ribbon of stone wide enough for two Space

Marines to walk abreast. The slope of the ramp was steep. Kan-shell thought that if he set foot on it, he would hurtle along its path until his legs outran his balance and he pitched over the edge into the gloom. The ramp looked smooth as marble.

Kanshell backed away from the edge. He looked at the colonists, trying to decide how he should understand the miracle of their sur-vival. He saw that a large group had begun to gather once again at the primary lodge. He nudged Tanaura and pointed. 'They're going to worship again,' he said.

'Why now?' she asked. 'It isn't even midday. You said their ser-vices are always held in the evening.'

'Because we're here?' he suggested. 'Perhaps they are praying for us.' He glanced at the shaft. 'Because of where we're about to go.'

Tanaura was still looking towards the lodge. 'That is where you took your *Lectitio Divinitatus*?'

'Yes.'

'I wonder why it was taken.'

'I never said it was. Just that it was gone.'

'What else could have happened?' Her face was grim. 'I would very much like to know what they want with it.'

'I wish you had seen the ceremony.'

'So do I.' She did not sound wistful.

'You don't understand,' Kanshell said. 'I was in touch with some-thing divine in there. I was closer to the Emperor.'

Tanaura grunted, sceptical.

'Why do you doubt me?' he asked.

'I don't doubt you, or that you experienced what you said you did. I worry that you misinterpreted what happened.'

'Why?'

'Did any of these people actually speak of worshipping the Emperor?'

'No,' he admitted. 'But they should all be dead, and they were spared. Isn't that a sign of the Emperor's hand at work?'

Tanaura turned away from the lodge and gave him a significant look. 'Is it?' Then her attention was taken by something over his shoulder. She lowered her head in respect. Kanshell spun around. Galba and Atticus had come up behind him. 'My lords,' Kanshell said, bowing.

'You have friends among these people,' said Atticus.

Kanshell thought of Ske Vris. 'I believe so.'

'In the religious caste?'

'Yes, captain.'

To Galba, Atticus said, 'I trust your judgement, brother-sergeant. Do as you proposed. Remain in constant communication.'

'Yes, brother-captain. And thank you.'

Atticus gave his officer a curt nod and moved off towards the top of the spiral ramp. Galba remained. Just behind him were the members of his squad.

'There is something we would like you to do, Jerune,' Galba said.

THE THUNDERHAWKS OVERFLEW the plateau in tight, circular patterns. As *Unbending* passed beyond the palisade, the Salamanders' *Hammerblow* entered the airspace above the settlement. The Vindicator *Engine of Fury* guarded the gate. *Medusan Strength* was positioned by the barrier on the other side of the plateau. Atticus did not trust the wooden wall to withstand a truly concerted rush by the saurians. Anything that managed to break through would be blasted to flecks of blood and charred bone.

The Demolisher cannons were facing outwards, but it would be a simple matter to re-orient them, and unleash their monstrous rage on the settlement. Atticus had not left orders covering this contingency. It was understood. None of the Iron Hands trusted the miracle that had preserved the colonists.

Mistrust was useful, but it did not provide intelligence. Standing at the lip of the shaft, Galba had said to Atticus, 'I don't think we should leave these people unobserved while we descend.'

The captain had agreed. A day earlier, the idea of a rearguard being necessary would have been laughable. The colonists were mortals, badly armed, and barely competent with the weapons they did have. They could not offer a threat. But a day earlier, the *Veritas Ferrum* had still been in orbit around Pythos.

Atticus led the bulk of 111th Company down the xenos ramp. The Raven Guard descended too, using their jump packs to drop quickly from level to level of the spiral. Galba stayed at the surface. He had the tanks, the gunships, his squad, the serfs and suspicion.

And Khi'dem. While the rest of his brothers flew overwatch in the *Hammerblow*, he had chosen to bear witness on the ground. 'Keep watch on the people you have fought to preserve,' Atticus had said to him. 'See to it that they were worthy of your efforts.'

Galba ordered the serfs to arrange themselves along the perimeter of the settlement. Facing inwards. The colonists had split into two groups. One was at the lodge. It was a big crowd, but unlike the last few evenings, all of its members had found room inside the building. The other group, by far the largest, clustered towards the gate. The mortals kept a respectful distance back from the *Engine of Fury*. They were quiet as they milled about. They were, Galba thought, expectant, as if waiting for their purpose to arrive.

He and his squad headed towards the lodge, an anxious Kanshell walking before them. Khi'dem said, 'The confidence these people showed in their survival was well founded.'

'Yes,' Galba returned. 'They seem to be the only ones on this planet who are never surprised.'

'True.'

'Are you pleased with our good works?' Galba spat. He still writhed at the thought of how he had been manipulated. He was relieved that Atticus did not appear to have lost all faith in him, perhaps because the enemy had contrived to make the terrible mistake appear the logical course of action. Still, he needed redemption. And Atticus had agreed so quickly to his suggested course of action that he wondered if the captain saw this as a test.

Or perhaps, he thought, *he is sending the tainted to deal with the tainted.*

He needed to lash out. He cursed the flesh that had withstood the impossible, and so whose very existence was suspect. He cursed his earlier mercy for that flesh, a mercy that Khi'dem and the other Salamanders embodied. He needed an enemy he could kill. They all did.

If the enemy turned out to be these luck-blessed savages, then so be it.

'I don't know that I am pleased,' Khi'dem answered. 'I remain satisfied that we did the right thing.'

'Even if we were tricked?'

'We acted in accordance with what we knew. If we had abandoned these people, we would have demeaned ourselves. We would have acted without honour. There is more at stake in this war than simple military victory.'

Galba snorted. 'Ridiculous.'

'Really? Will you do anything to defeat the traitors?'

'I will.'

'No matter how debasing? No matter how much it distorts who we are? You saw the same things I saw on the *Callidora*. Are you willing to become the same sort of abomination as the Emperor's Children?'

Galba said nothing. They had almost reached the lodge. He had no answer for Khi'dem. No, the Iron Hands would never follow the path of the Emperor's Children. And yet no, there should be no obstacle to prosecuting the war against the enemy by any means necessary.

Khi'dem was not done. 'This war is about our very identities. If we give them up, even if we win the battles, what will remain of the Emperor's dream? Will we recognise what we will have made of the Imperium?'

Galba paused at the base of the rise. Now he had an answer. There was a way out of the impasse of needs. 'We will embrace the machine,' he said. He had to raise his voice. The chanting coming from the lodge was deafening in its enthusiasm.

'I don't understand.'

'The Emperor's Children are slaves to desire. We will expunge desire from our beings. Our decisions will be dispassionate. We will fuse absolute rationalism with absolute war.'

Khi'dem looked mournful rather than horrified. 'You are justifying my worst surmises. When we met, you did not reject your humanity to the degree that your captain does.'

'I have learned the error of my ways,' Galba replied. He put his helmet on. Neural connectors plugged into his cortex, removing him further from the flesh, gifting him with the enhanced vision and senses of the mechanical realm. He looked up at the lodge entrance, and the ritual going on beyond the door. *The divine?* he thought. *If you could see as I do, you might know something about the divine.* It occurred to him that the adepts on Mars were connected to something far more sublime than whatever delusion was the object of the colonists' veneration.

Delusion? Something rattled like bones in a distant wind. It pried at his thoughts. He shook it away and turned to Kanshell. The serf was jittery.

'You are worried, Jerune,' Galba said. 'Don't be. You have done nothing wrong, and you will be protected.' Kanshell opened his mouth as if he were about to correct Galba on a point, but he said nothing. 'They want you to celebrate with them,' Galba went on. 'They will give you different answers than they would give us. Go and talk to them. We will hear, and act as necessary.'

Kanshell swallowed. 'Yes, sergeant.' He walked up to the entrance.

'Is it possible that these people are innocent of anything more than false belief?' Khi'dem wondered. 'And they had nothing to do with what happened?'

'They knew,' Galba replied. That was enough to condemn them.

Kanshell disappeared inside the lodge. It was as if a current pushed him deep into the crowd. Galba waited, his Lyman's Ear picking out the serf's voice from the uproar of song. He was trying to speak to someone. His questions kept being cut off. He was moving, closer, Galba guessed, to the centre of the lodge.

The chanting stopped. In the silence, Kanshell whispered, 'What is happening?'

'Why, the truth is happening,' a woman's voice answered. 'Revelation.'

'That's my book,' Kanshell said. 'Why did you take it?'

'For the truth,' came the reply, with the cadence of a refrain.

'*Truth,*' the congregation echoed with a massed whisper.

'That's what you want, isn't it?' asked the first voice.

'I already know the truth,' Kanshell protested.

'You know it without knowing it.' The new speaker had deeper, harsher tones. Galba recognised the head priest. 'You swim at the surface. Now you will plunge. All of us will.'

'All,' said the woman, and the choir whispered, '*All*.'

'Bid them come,' the priest commanded. 'The truth is theirs, too. And then you will truly worship with us.'

'I can't bid them,' Kanshell protested.

'Oh, I think you can,' said the priest.

The silence was broken by the sounds of a struggle.

In three strides, Galba had reached the entrance to the lodge. Followed by his squad, he marched inside. He shouldered through the colonists, sending them flying. He stopped a few steps before

THE DAMNATION OF PYTHOS 289

the centre. The priest stood there, hooded, facing him. Beside him, the assistant, Ske Vris, had Kanshell's arms pinned behind his back. Galba blinked rapidly, trying to clear his vision. The light patterns in the structure were toxic fragments, weakening the bedrock of reality. On the floor, at the nexus of the web, sat a worn book.

'Release him,' Galba said. He was almost disappointed that the perfidy of the colonists was revealing itself so easily, and in such a mundane fashion.

'Of course,' the priest answered. Ske Vris let go of Kanshell, who stumbled to the side.

Galba frowned. The priest held what looked like a ceremonial dagger, but it was pointing to the floor. No weapon had been held on Kanshell. He had been restrained, nothing more.

'You have come at last,' the priest said.

'Not to worship,' Galba snarled.

The priest cocked his head. Galba sensed a smile within the shadows of the hood. 'Perhaps not. But to witness, certainly.'

Ske Vris moved to one side, leaving the priest alone. The man was a single step away from the centre of the room. The novitiate went beside Kanshell, and draped an arm around his shoulder, as if reassuring him that all was well. These people had not planned to harm the serf, Galba realised. They wanted his conversion. And they had wanted the presence of the Space Marines.

Galba raised his bolter. Behind him came the *chunk-clack* of his brothers making ready with their weapons. He scanned the lodge. The priest was the only one armed, and he presented no threat. Even so, Galba felt the tension of imminent combat. There *was* a threat here, though he could not see it. He kept the muzzle of his gun trained on the priest. 'Cover all sides,' Galba spoke over the vox battle channel.

'*I have the exit,*' Khi'dem reported.

'Anything?'

'*Quiet here. The larger crowd is still concentrated near the gate.*'

To the priest, Galba said, 'And what are we here to witness?'

'We have already said it. Truth. Revelation.' He raised his hands to his hood and pulled it back. Scattered around the congregation, other members of the priest class did the same. The man before him had the face of brutal, feral corruption. His black hair was a leonine mane. Ritualistic scars and tattoos ringed his hairline. A lower canine had been fashioned into a fang that protruded over his upper lip. His eyes were a liquid crimson, devoid of pupil. His acolytes were just as debased. Some had faces that lives of violence had turned into masses of scar tissue. Others had been marked in more precise fashion, with sinuous runes running across forehead and eyelids. All bore some kind of injury like a badge of office. Galba saw missing ears, cheeks cut in half, scalps peeled back to the skull. And in every face was a sick, cancerous joy.

With the religious caste unmasked, the appearance of the rest of the people seemed to change. The new context altered Galba's perception of the other colonists. Their glow of faith now had an ugly hue. Their rough appearance was the product of a cultural choice. They had embraced something dark, and now they waited for a culminating event.

The cultists stared back at Galba with a gloating triumph.

'My name, legionary, is Tsi Rekh,' said the priest. 'I am proud to be a priest of Davin. I am proud that the Gods of Chaos opened the warp to me and my fellow pilgrims, transporting our humble craft to this place made sacred in their honour. I am proud to walk a world shaped by other worshippers, shaped to find its true purpose on this very day. And I am proud to have reached the moment of my destiny.'

Galba's finger tensed on the trigger, but Tsi Rekh did not attack. The cultists raised their voices again. The song had no words. It was a sustained cry, rising and falling, twisting through overlapping chords. It was moan and sigh, howl and magnificat. Tsi Rekh did not join it. He took the last step to the centre of the lodge.

He stood over the book. The lightweb reacted. Galba's perception changed again. The light beams did not move, but the presence of the priest completed a portrait painted by jagged slashes in reality. Where there had been a pattern of painful madness that tortured by hinting at meaning, now that meaning was made manifest. Tsi Rekh was standing in the midst of an altar of light, a light made of wounds.

Tsi Rekh raised the knife.

Galba fired.

Reality trembled.

EIGHTEEN

The priest
The offertory
The feast of all souls

THE BOLTER SHELLS struck Tsi Rekh. Some tore right through muscle and flesh and flew on to kill the Davinites in the rows to the rear of the lodge. One struck the dagger, smashing it to iron slivers. The other projectiles punched into the priest's body and exploded. Fountains of blood burst from the wounds. Flecks that had been bone shot through the air. The wounds were terrible. They were craters. Tsi Rekh's form was hammered to crimson meat. His silhouette disintegrated.

Yet he stood.

The rest of Galba's squad fired less than an eye-blink after the sergeant. The Iron Hands raked the ranks of the cultists with shells. They were methodical. Their commanding officer had responded to a manifest threat, and they were acting in kind. There was no doubt that the cultists were the enemy. It did not matter that they carried no weapons. An attack was under way. Galba knew this to be true, even if the nature of the assault was still hidden from him.

The squad turned the lodge into a slaughterhouse. The air became

moist with blood. The bass rattle of the guns competed against
the wet *thchunk-thchunk-thchunk* of bodies being rendered by the
devastating firepower. The flesh was weak, and it flew into pieces
before the unbending warriors. The cultists were decimated, and
more died with every fraction of a second.

Yet still they sang.

The choir redoubled its celebration. There was no pause in the
hymn. The awful joy rose higher. Blood washed over the floor of
the lodge. It covered Kanshell, who lay flat, cowering. The vitae
of Tsi Rekh's congregation mixed at his feet with his own. His life
cascaded down his legs, coating the book. He was barely a form
anymore.

Yet still he stood. And still he smiled.

Galba stopped firing. Tsi Rekh's armoured tunic hung in tatters.
There were holes in his torso wide enough for Galba to see right
through his body. The priest could not be alive. Galba did not know
what force was holding him up. He did not question it. He knew
only that he must bring the foul thing down. He mag-locked his
bolter to his belt and brandished his chainsword. He would cut
the remains of Tsi Rekh into pieces if that is what it took, but this
thing would no longer mock him.

He stepped forward, revved his blade, and raised it over his head.
Around him, the killing was almost done. Most of the Davinites
lay dead. A few, among them Ske Vris, had dropped to the ground,
sheltering behind ruined corpses. They were no longer singing. That
did not matter. The song continued. It was carried by the lodge
itself, echoing from timbers drenched in gore, thrumming in vibra-
tions from beams that Galba now realised only appeared to be light.

Tsi Rekh's nose was gone. Black clots and grey matter oozed from
the void in the middle of his face. But his eyes were alive. Their
redness burned. They stared at Galba with sickening triumph. As
the chainsword paused, roaring, before descending on its killing

arc, Tsi Rekh opened his mouth wide. His jaw was half shot away. His teeth were missing or reduced to jagged stumps. His chest was a broken, pulped mess. There was nothing left of his lungs. Yet a coughing hiss emerged from his ruined mouth. Galba heard it over his chainsword, over the guns of his brothers, over the dreadful song. The priest was laughing.

Galba brought the blade down onto Tsi Rekh's skull. The whirring teeth ground through bone. They turned brain into paste, and then to mist. Galba bisected the priest's head. His strike was fast, violent. The Davinite's body offered no resistance to the weapon or to Galba's strength. The killing blow took no time at all.

But time itself was taken. It was stretched. Galba moved against a thick current, and the single act became a gallery of frozen hololiths. The chainsword took an eternity to come down. Each step of the mutilation became a sculpture in metal and flesh. As the skull parted to each side, the eyes did not die. They blazed with victory. They held Galba's gaze. The moment stretched on and on and on. It waited for Galba to realise everything.

He saw, then, the full canvas of desolation. He had been lured into the lodge. He and his squad had been manipulated into butchering the cultists. He knew, with an awful certainty, that the blow he was now striking would have consequences as terrible as the lance fire from the *Veritas Ferrum*.

Blood everywhere. A luxuriousness of blood. A stinking, dripping, celebration of blood. An exaltation in a temple. Before an altar. Drenching an icon created by the first among traitors.

An offering.

In this moment of the death of illusions, Galba also saw the death of the real. The eyes flared, and time resumed its lethal march. The crimson light embraced the death by chainsword. It burst from the eyes. It engulfed the skull, and then, as the corpse laughed one final time, it swallowed the rest of the body. It was an old light, rotten as a dying star, but also burning with stellar force. Galba yanked his blade free and staggered backwards. The light unfurled from within the priest, yet it was not truly light. It was what had been seeping through the pattern of the web. It was energy, and non-matter, and madness. It was the rage of the warp.

The storm burst over the space of the temple. Galba heard the shattering cracks of wood. The lodge was flying apart, but he could not see the destruction. He could see nothing but the insane howl of blood. It was blinding, but his helmet did not recognise the glare as light and did not shield his senses from the rage. The song became even louder, deafening. Galba heard scratching coming over the vox, but could not make out any words. He stumbled, buffeted by the fury of the monstrous event.

He was standing metres away from a tear in the fabric of the universe. The wound in reality opened wider and Galba crouched, refusing to fall, unable to do anything but keep his footing. The tempest buffeted him, clawing at his eyes and ears and mind. The world teetered on the edge of dissolution.

Instead, something else materialised. It grew from within the storm. It stole the stability of the physical plane, twisting the raw stuff of reality to its own purposes. It gathered in the eye of the gale, using the still-standing remnants of Tsi Rekh as a core around and upon which it constructed something huge. Darkness twisted, gathered definition, became a silhouette. The shadow became a form, taking on mass. The shape stopped changing, though the suggestion of writhing remained in the form of vicious coils and curved spines breaking up its outline.

The non-light faded, sucked into the being that had taken the offering and stepped out of nightmare and into the world. Galba could see again. He saw the enemy the Iron Hands had been seeking.

'*Daemon!*' someone was screaming. It was Kanshell. He was curled in a ball, his lasrifle forgotten, his arms hiding his face. 'Daemon!'

The being cocked its head Kanshell's way for a moment. It made a sound that Galba knew was laughter, though it filled his head with the shrieks of diseased infants. Then it strode towards him, the last of the warp-light trailing from it like candle flame.

Daemon. Galba could not reject the word. The truths he had known lay in ruins before him. He knew something about the superstitions of the past. He knew about the monsters conjured by the darkness of human ignorance. One of those monsters now stood before him, and the myths were but pale whispers next to the reality of the thing.

It was immense. It towered over Galba. Its head would have broken through the roof of the lodge, had the building still been standing. It was bipedal, a distortion of the human form that stopped just short of being unrecognisable. Its limbs were grotesquely long, but rippled with taut muscle. Its pelvis was skeletal, and just above it nestled the cleft skull of Tsi Rekh. Its chest was a broad carapace covered in slit-pupilled eyes. They looked exactly like those on the armour of the thrice-cursed traitor Horus, but these were alive. They blinked, twitched and stared at Galba.

The daemon's head was all fanged maw surrounded by a halo of giant, twisted, asymmetrical horns. They pointed forwards and back, sprouting from the forehead and the base of the skull. Two massive ones curled downward like tusks, almost as far as the creature's chest. Its forked tongue, long as a snake, whipped and coiled as if seeking prey, the movements strangely echoing those of the abomination's jointed tail. Beneath a heavy brow, the eyes were as blank and featureless as Tsi Rekh's. They had the glow of a firestorm. Galba thought they were blind with rage, because the head always turned in the direction the chest-eyes were looking.

In its right hand, the daemon clutched a staff that ended in a vicious collection of blades. It looked like nestled tridents, but there was also something ceremonial about the configuration. There was artistry in the angles of this metal forged in a delusion's furnace. There was meaning. The daemon held the staff in a way that reminded Galba of how Tsi Rekh carried his. The weapon was a mark of office. The implications of that idea were as horrific as the being's presence.

It spread its arms, welcoming the world to its toxic embrace. It opened its jaws wide. It sighed, releasing an *aaaahhhhhhhh* of unspeakable appetites. It tilted its head back, turning the blank eyes to the void above. It was midday, but darkness rose like vapour from the daemon, forming a canopy of empty black that stretched over more and more of the settlement with every passing second. It was like ink spreading through the air, yet it was something more ominous than that. It was an acid that devoured reality, leaving nothing in its place.

The surviving cultists whispered. The daemon cocked its head. Its tongue licked at the sound, and found it good. The monster spoke, and its voice was the one that had been Galba's torment since the first night on Pythos. The sound was the mockery of every principle and every hope. It was huge and deep and sibilant. It was a slithering of mountains, a thunder of serpents.

'*Speak my name*,' the daemon said, and it laughed its delight in its voice. It laughed, and nightmares echoed.

'Madail, Madail, Madail,' the Davinites whispered. The crowd by the gates picked up the chant, and made it vast.

'*Madail*,' the daemon repeated. It savoured the syllables, dragging them out: *Madaaaaaaaail*. The second half of the name became an ecstatic exhalation. It was the shape of the synaesthetic shadows Galba had tasted. He had been assaulted by premonitory echoes, and now, at last, here was the sound, coming in judgement and night. *Madail*.

The daemon gazed down upon the Space Marines. '*I am the*

shepherd of the flock,' it announced, turning the words into obscenity. *'And I am here to bring my charges to new pastures.'* Madail leaned forwards, its eyes rolling in eagerness. *'Throw wide the gates,'* it commanded.

'Now!' Ske Vris yelled.

Explosions erupted at the base of the palisade. The gate disappeared in a pillar of flame. An entire section of the wall, a hundred metres long, collapsed, opening the settlement to the teeth of the predators beyond. The Legion serfs recoiled from the blasts. Some were crushed under burning trunks. But they held their ranks, and they began firing at the cultists. The Davinites, unarmed, did not retaliate.

'The offertory,' said Madail.

The Davinites moved as if possessed by a single mind. Those nearest the serfs ran into the streaks of lasfire, laughing as they were cut down. The rest of the crowd rushed through the fallen gate.

Madail sighed again in anticipation. *'And later,'* it said, *'the communion.'*

The Iron Hands and Salamanders unleashed the full fury of their bolters on Madail. Dark ichor erupted from the impacts. For a moment, the daemon revelled in the sensation of being struck. Then it brought the haft of its weapon down, striking through the bloody floor of the lodge, down to the earth itself. A wave rippled out from the point of the hit, the ground suddenly as volatile as a lake in a storm. It threw the Space Marines into the air. Galba landed heavily but rose to his feet, firing again. Madail gestured, its free hand clawing at the air, gathering reality into a cluster of folds. The shells fell into the folds and vanished.

Galba found it difficult now to look at the daemon. Madail was advancing behind a shield of damaged materium. The daemon appeared as through a crack-riddled mirror. Its image broke into overlapping segments, and the fractured lines brought tears to

Galba's eyes. The tears ran down his face. When he tasted them, he realised they were blood.

'Brother-captain,' he voxed. He could see each move of the coming seconds, and what the endgame would be. If he could warn Atticus, perhaps those seconds would not be futile. But there was only static on the vox network. He could barely make out the transmissions of his own squad members.

'Brother Galba,' Khi'dem said. *'Forgive me. I was wrong.'*

'We all were,' Galba snarled. But if this was his end, he thought, he would meet it as was worthy of the X Legion. He switched to his chainsword and charged the daemon. The blade roared at his side. He prepared a two-handed swing. At the periphery of his tunnel vision, he was aware of his brothers storming forwards with him. He could hear the growls of the manoeuvring Vindicators. From somewhere above came the rage of the Thunderhawks. The Iron Hands were closing on the monster, and the machine would hurl this absurdity from the rational world. This was Galba's vow.

It was not his hope. He did not hope for anything, not any longer.

The daemon was two steps away. Galba was the point of the attack. The distortion would not stop him. The cracks in the real were too small. He was a juggernaut. He was sheer mass propelled by righteous vengeance. He was not flesh. He was force itself.

Madail struck first. The daemon shot its trident forward, its full, monstrous reach concealed by the collapse of vision. The weapon glowed darkly and plunged through Galba's armour. It shattered his black carapace and reinforced ribcage. It punctured his hearts. The sudden pain and shock were eclipsed by something worse: a terminal letting go. His body loosened itself from his will. His extremities went numb. His useless fingers dropped his chainsword. Madail laughed and hoisted him into the air. Galba's helmet readout flashed a cascade of critical red runes, then went dark.

The dark stretched out from the wound, wrapping its fist around his body. It was cold. It was strong. Stronger than he.

He was flesh after all.

KANSHELL SAW MADAIL raise the skewered Galba high. He saw the Space Marine's struggles diminish, then stop. The daemon did not pause. It moved with speed and grace. It was a dancer at last performing its great work upon the stage. Its spear arm took out the sergeant, and its left hand made a sweeping gesture. Its claws opened ragged tears in the fabric of the world. It made a fist, drawing the real into a tight knot. The rest of the Iron Hands squad closed with the daemon, and they seemed to rush faster as Madail drew its fingers together. They rained blows upon it, and the monster staggered. Its arms shook with strain. But its blind head laughed, and its many eyes looked down upon the legionaries with a cold, knowing indifference. The movements of the Iron Hands were odd. They jerked, and rushed, as if moments of time were missing, or they were moving through a compacted, folded universe.

Madail opened its fist, releasing the real.

The materium snapped back. A shock wave of brutalised physics travelled a dozen metres from the epicentre of the daemon. The Space Marines were caught on the folds, and as the world righted, they were suddenly in several places at once. They flew into pieces, severed by impossibility as if by wire. There was a fog of blood. The legionaries fell, sectioned like logs.

Kanshell wanted to close his eyes. He wanted to shut out the sight of the demigods being cut down. The stalker of the Pythos nights had arrived, and its reality was worse than all of its dark promises. Nothing lay ahead but the fulfilment of a terrible dream.

He did not close his eyes. He saw the Space Marines fall, and he knew that if he surrendered, he dishonoured the Legion to which he was devoted. He saw his fellow serfs engage the cultists, and knew what he must do. Though he and every other mortal would be destroyed the instant Madail's attention fell their way, that did not absolve him of his duty.

And he had his faith. It was with him more than ever. He had before him the proof of divine powers. If the dark ones walked in forms of flesh and bone, then how could he have ever doubted the divinity of the Emperor and His light? Kanshell's *Lectitio Divinitatus* was lost. He did not need it. He had sworn his oath. He had a duty twice over. He had been shown an example, and he would follow it.

He would die in a manner worthy of the X Legion, and fighting for the Emperor.

He stood, his feet squelching in blood. His hands were slick, his hair matted, and his eyes gummed half-shut. He found his lasrifle beside the eviscerated body of a cultist. He clutched it, fired off a shot to see that it still worked, and then ran towards the other serfs.

His path took him behind Madail's back. The daemon was whispering something to the surviving Space Marines as they crawled along the ground. Kanshell did not listen. Even the sound of the creature's voice ate away at his sanity. He saw the Vindicators rolling forwards. The gunships were overhead, but hidden behind Madail's shield of darkness. They would have nothing on which to train their weapons. No matter. *Engine of Fury* and *Medusan Strength* had clear lines of sight, and only the presence of critically injured but still-living Space Marines delayed their barrage. In another instant, this section of the plateau would be obliterated by high explosives.

The serfs were giving chase to the cultists. There was nothing to be gained by confronting Madail. But the Davinites had a mission, and they were mortal. Kanshell had plenty of evidence of that. A twisted miracle had spared their lives once, but there were no such miracles today. They could and did die. *Find Ske Vris*, Kanshell thought. The simplicity and need of the mission kept him focused on it, and not on the terrors around him. *Find Ske Vris. Stop her.*

His duty would be his revenge. For a brief second, he allowed himself to think that he knew something more now of the heart of the X Legion. Then he pushed all thought away and did nothing but run, racing to stay ahead of his terror and catch up with his anger.

He joined the rear ranks of the serfs as they went out beyond the walls, and emerged from the shield of darkness into a feral day. The cultists were racing over the blasted land towards the base. They were still chanting. The song was a riot of victory and abandon. It was also a summons to the predators. The saurians were closing in from both sides. They no longer feared the open ground. Perhaps they knew that the rival predators in ceramite were no longer present. Perhaps their numbers had reached the point that no threat could hold them back. The ground shook as the monsters stampeded towards the promise of easy kills. The horde was immense. But there were thousands of Davinites.

A banquet of plenty.

The serfs paused in their pursuit. Kanshell shared in the mass uncertainty. The cultists were running towards extinction. Any pound of flesh that the serfs exacted would be taken many times over moments later by the saurians. If they went forwards, they would become prey themselves.

But at their back was a worse monstrosity.

Death ahead. Damnation behind. Duty was reduced to a choice of dooms.

Kanshell kept moving forwards on sheer momentum. He advanced to the front ranks. Further ahead, he saw Tanaura hold her rifle above her head. She shouted something. Her words were lost in the chaos of roars and the thunder of the Thunderhawks and Vindicators beginning their barrage. But her defiance and call to purpose were clear. Her eyes blazing with desperate rage, she pointed. Kanshell looked, and saw that the Davinites were not just throwing their lives away. There was an order to their sacrifice. They were forming lines facing the saurians. The people in those barriers linked arms and stood fast, still chanting, bracing themselves for the impact. Between the lines, the rush towards the base continued. The cultists were selling their lives so their fellow worshippers could reach the Iron Hands' stronghold.

At the centre of the worshippers, Kanshell saw Ske Vris. She had claimed Tsi Rekh's staff, and was leading the flock forward. Kanshell saw the mirror of Tanaura's zeal. He vowed to smash the reflection. He ran forwards. Tanaura was right. If the Davinites still had a mission, so did the servants of the Iron Hands. If they could stop the cultists, their own deaths would have meaning.

The saurians arrived as the serfs caught up to the first of the Davinite lines. Kanshell saw a multitude of spines and horns, shapes squat and elongated, bipeds and quadrupeds, necks like massive serpents, forelimbs with claws as long as his arm, and always the jaws: massive, savage, hungry. He was running a gauntlet of muscle and teeth.

The saurians struck. The cultists laughed. They threw themselves into the jaws. The slaughter was enormous. The monsters ripped into the Davinites. They buried muzzles into ribcages and dragged out viscera. They gutted with claws. The largest beast Kanshell had yet seen, a quadruped ten metres high at the withers, lowered a huge boxy head almost the size of a Dreadnought. It bit the head off a cultist. It swallowed the skull whole, then, with a sudden downward lunge, snapped up the torso before the body hit the ground.

There was blood everywhere. It streamed over the ground. It fell in showers from the victims that were hauled, wriggling, into the air. Kanshell had fled the site of a lake of blood only to find an ocean. And still the chanting did not stop. The victims screamed as they were devoured, but the shrieks had the ring of triumph. Kanshell was back in the lodge, witnessing another dark consecration.

The saurians were performing the same ritualistic duty as the Iron Hands. The hand that butchered was unimportant. The spilling of blood was what mattered. The ceremony that had begun in the lodge was not complete. It had moved to a larger canvas. Kanshell could feel the weaving of something immense, and knew just how insignificant he and his efforts were, and how futile. Killing cultists would only feed the creation of the coming horror.

But they would die anyway, and honour demanded some form of judgement.

Kanshell focused on the sight of Tanaura running just ahead of him. Her face was taut with unwavering determination. She was firing from the hip. She could not miss, and she was felling cultists, searing them with lasfire. Ske Vris, deep in the centre of the crush, was as yet beyond reach.

Stop her, Kanshell thought. *Stop her. Stop it all.* Perhaps the last of the priest caste was important. Perhaps that death, that bit of vengeance, might mean something. He chose to follow that flutter of hope. For the first time in his life, he pulled a trigger with the intent to kill. He found that Tanaura had been right. When the time came, it was not difficult. And he did not miss, either.

The serfs burned away the rear ranks of the Davinites. They rushed up the avenue created by the willing sacrifices. But the barrier did not hold long, and the saurians pounced on the new influx of prey. The road to the base turned into a feeding frenzy.

THE LAST COMMUNICATION Darras had received from the settlement was over half an hour old. The sounds of battle were echoing in the distance, now half-obscured by the howling of the saurians. The lines of sight from the top of the wall were good. With the jungle gone, the plateau was just visible through the low-lying smoke and haze. The Iron Hands could see the madness of the running crowd and the feasting of the reptiles.

All this was presented for Darras to witness. It was a tapestry of disaster.

'Secure the base,' he ordered. 'Nothing gets in.' He eyed the tide of animal rage heading up the slope. There were limits to what the walls could resist. 'Saurian or colonist, kill anything that leads a charge our way.'

He tried raising Atticus on the vox again, then Crevther in the *Unbending*. Nothing, but at least he could see that the Thunderhawks were still in the air. He switched channels. Within the base, the vox network functioned, though not well, not since the explosions had begun at the settlement. He could barely make out the reports from the wall on the opposite side of the base. At least he could reach Erephren in the command centre clearly enough. He did so now, and told her what he could see. 'Have you detected any changes?' he asked.

'*Yes.*' The word was spoken by a warrior in the midst of heavy combat. '*The interference has lessened. The enemy is no longer attacking from the warp.*'

A billow of fire in the distance. Darras cursed under his breath. 'The enemy is using more direct means,' he said.

'*There is more,*' Erephren told him. '*The anomaly is becoming much more powerful.*'

'Meaning?'

'*I'm not sure, sergeant. A dark energy is flowing into it and being stored.*'

'You have tried reading the anomaly?'

'*I have...*' She trailed off, sounding awed and drained.

'And?'

She whispered. '*I had to pull away. I was about to see* everything.'

The mistress of the astropathic choir did not stoop to exaggeration. Darras took her at her word. 'Your evaluation?'

'*I have little to offer, sergeant. But I can think of only one reason to store energy.*'

'To then release it,' Darras said.

'I have observed something else,' Erephren said. *'The energy level is building very quickly. It has been accelerating over the last few minutes.'* Her delivery was matter of fact, belying exhaustion and battle.

'I see. Thank you, mistress.' Darras looked out at the massacre. It was drawing closer. The saurians and colonists would be within bolter range shortly. Darras was reluctant to pour precious rounds into targets that were about to die. There would no longer be any resupply. If he let matters take their course, the mortals would be obliterated within a very short time span. Without prey, the saurians would disperse.

But Erephren's words made him uneasy. Something was powering up the anomaly.

'Brother-sergeant,' Catigernus said, 'they are singing.'

Darras listened, finding the voices of the colonists between the roars of the saurians. The other legionary was correct. And the cries that grew louder with every moment were celebratory. Darras's reason rejected a link between the spilling of blood and the anomaly. His instinct said otherwise.

His options vanished. By tooth, by claw or by bolter, the colonists would die, as they intended. No other outcome was possible. He knew again the acidic taste of defeat, grown too familiar. 'Hold your fire,' he ordered, fury turning every syllable into a curse. 'We must conserve our ammunition. There is worse to come.'

So there was. With every beat of his hearts, worse came. The landscape filled with the rampage of death. The saurian numbers climbed beyond all logic. There were more of the monsters now than there were humans, and still they arrived, pounding across the tortured earth. Darras saw the reptiles now as part of some gigantic mechanism, a clockwork that was being wound turn by turn until it was ready, at last, to perform its great work.

He knew that the final turns of the key had arrived.

✠ ✠ ✠

KANSHELL HAD ADOPTED tunnel vision. It was the only way he could stay sane long enough to do what he must. He was surrounded by howling monsters. The Davinite's lines had collapsed. Their rush up the promontory had disintegrated into a pell-mell dash. Strategy had vanished. Not a single cultist would make it to the gates of the base, but perhaps, Kanshell thought, that had never been the goal. The wall was only a hundred metres away. The predators were everywhere. The cultists' mission had been achieved.

Tunnel vision. If he allowed himself to take in the full carnivorous maelstrom, the fear would take him again, and he would do nothing but cower and die. So he followed Tanaura, and he watched Ske Vris. He treated the massive legs that thrashed on all sides like a forest in storm. They were obstacles, and he looked at them only long enough to avoid them. The blood that fell on his face from victims lifted and ripped apart overhead was just rain, warm and salty. If death came for him, he would not know it. Tanaura was faith, Ske Vris was duty, and nothing else was useful to him.

He weaved in and out of crushing masses in pursuit. The afternoon light was dimmed by the press of giant bodies. The feeding frenzy was escalating, the predators turning on each other when they ran out of human meat. The ground was a mire of blood and muck. Kanshell slipped and fell. He slithered as he tried to rise. A three-toed foot, almost as long as he was, came down within centimetres of his face. He rolled away, choking on gore-drenched earth, and then was up and running again. He still held his lasrifle. He could still see Tanaura. And he could still see Ske Vris.

He was catching up.

He pulled the trigger again. His power pack was close to drained, but there were still half a dozen shots remaining.

'*Stop,*' Tanaura shouted, too late.

Kanshell could not aim and run, and his shots went wild. Still, he could not miss, and he struck a beast ahead of him. The wounds were enough to make it stagger. Its defences were down for a moment, and it was set upon by two others. Tails thrashed. One ended in a knob of bone the size of a power fist. It struck Tanaura a glancing blow, and she went down. Kanshell stumbled back, and the tail mace blew by his chest. If it had hit, it would have caved in his ribs. Tanaura, stunned, tried to raise herself. Kanshell paused to help her up.

'Go,' Tanaura hissed. Ske Vris was putting more distance between them.

Kanshell ran on through the meat grinder. Ske Vris moved as if engaged in a dance, dodging around the monsters with ritualistic grace. Kanshell gradually caught up, and realised that Ske Vris *was* dancing. There was a purpose to each movement. She was forming a sentence, one that no tongue could speak, but that every soul would hear.

And then, somehow, there was a clearing, an eye in the reptile storm. Ske Vris stopped. She faced Kanshell. She was covered in the blood of her kin, and her smile shone all the brighter. She extended her left hand to Kanshell.

'Join in the worship, Jerune,' she said. 'You see the only real Truth. Sing the praise of Chaos.'

Kanshell did not answer. He brought the lasrifle up instead. Before he could pull the trigger, Ske Vris lashed out with the staff. A beam shot out from the ornate bladed tip. It was a dark energy, the deep, rotting violet of pain. It knocked the rifle from Kanshell's hands and threw him onto his back. It spread over his limbs, a crackling slick. For a moment, his arms forgot what they were. They wanted to change, to become strange. Then the energy dissipated. Ske Vris stood over him. Around them, the war of predators spun. Blood fell in sheets.

'Are you convinced?' the Davinite asked. 'Can you see?'

Kanshell tried to rise. His arms and legs were weak. The ground sucked at him. He saw the moment of his death, and the death of all sanity, of all hope, on Pythos. But he saw nothing to worship. He spat bloody phlegm.

Ske Vris shrugged. 'A shame. No matter. You were adequate to your purpose.' She raised the staff.

A las-shot sheared through the cultist's shoulder. It sent her spinning. Ske Vris grunted, stumbling. Fist still closed around the staff, her arm fell to the ground. The stump smoked. Blood trickled down her flank, but she did not fall. She backed away on clumsy legs.

Tanaura entered the clearing. She had been clawed. Three huge diagonal slashes ran from her neck to left hip. She bore the injury with contempt. Her face was set with the righteous fury of the faithful confronting the heretic.

Ske Vris sagged, but still she smiled. 'Yes,' she gasped. 'Yes, you understand. You will appreciate…'

She paused. The world paused. The saurian war stilled on the lip of a great precipice. Ske Vris looked down at her blood striking the ground. 'Can it be so?' she whispered, full of wonder. 'Am I so blessed?' She dropped to her knees. She turned to Tanaura. 'Yes,' she said, beatific. 'The offertory is complete. The communion begins.'

There was a huge boom, as if the planet were an anvil struck by a hammer. Then more beats, smaller, but ominous because they did not stop, and they were coming closer.

The day fell into darkness.

NINETEEN

The shaft
Unbending
Now

THE FIRST SOUNDS of battle did not reach Atticus until the Iron Hands arrived at their target. But he saw the handiwork of a foe long before that. As the company spiralled deeper into the earth, he looked at the xenos architecture in a new light. His perspective was due to more than the revelation of a new region of the structure. This creation had destroyed his ship. Galba had been right: it was a machine, and it had attacked.

The shaft was more clearly a weapon than the rest of the ruins had been. He felt as though he were moving down a rifled gun barrel. The ramp was part of the scoring of the weapon, but so were the runes. They were also part of the power source. He accepted the fact as self-evident. He was conscious of their effect. Even when he closed his human eye and looked at the world solely through the filter of bionics, they still squirmed at the periphery of his vision, still whispered subaural obscenities. He could hear them now, hear them as a shifting fog of nightmare images before his mind's eye.

He knew something now of what Galba had faced. He still rejected the idea that the powers at work could not be fought by the strategic application of physical force. Whatever used weapons could also be destroyed by them. If the runes were a source of energy, then he would scour them from the shaft walls. But he also acknowledged there were other types of force. Rhydia Erephren used one, with perhaps even more aggression than she would admit to herself. Galba was not a psyker, Atticus accepted that, but the sergeant was more attuned to these energies than he was, more open to oblique thinking. That was why he wanted Galba dealing with the colonists and their worship. He could not imagine how they had played a role in the death of the *Veritas Ferrum*. But they had. Galba had a better chance of piercing that veil.

The thought crossed Atticus's mind that he could have explained to Galba why he was entrusting the legionary with this aspect of the mission. He processed the consideration, acknowledged its truth, then filed it away.

Halfway down, he asked Camnus, 'Any thoughts, Techmarine?'

'Captain?'

'This must be more than a fixed cannon.'

'I agree. I cannot guess at its intended function.' His servo-arm waved at the serpentine runes. 'The glow troubles me,' he said.

'We have seen it before.'

'The intensity is greater. It is clearly concentrated in the runes.'

'What do you conclude?'

'Nothing definite.'

'Extrapolate, then.'

'That our ill-fated barrage was not just reflected...'

'I saw that for myself,' Atticus snapped.

'I mean to say that it seems to have been absorbed, too.'

'Madness,' Atticus objected. The beam that had downed the ship had been far more concentrated than the lance fire.

'Agreed,' said Camnus. 'Nonetheless, I believe it to be true. We should prepare ourselves for worse.'

Atticus cursed the warp, cursed the race that had found the means of harnessing its powers in the physical realm, cursed this manifestation of architecture and machine.

Down, down, into the twisting of stone. The dirty light of Pythos's day did not reach far. It was replaced by the slow throbbing light from the runes. What lay at the bottom of the shaft came into view. A rheumy eye opened. Beneath the shaft was a circular shape of the same diameter. It was marked by a single rune, the largest and most complex of the entire system. The beat of the light was the pulse from this sigil. Atticus returned its glare. 'That,' he announced to the company, 'is what we have come to destroy.'

The Raven Guard had plunged on ahead. They waited on what appeared to be the last spur of the ramp. *'Captain Atticus,'* Ptero voxed, *'Do you wish us to begin placing charges?'*

How very politic, Atticus thought. Still, he accepted the gesture of respect. 'At once, legionary,' he said. 'My thanks.'

Then, bouncing down the shaft came the echoes of weapons fire. Atticus tried to raise Galba. He found nothing but white noise. 'We complete the mission,' he told his warriors. 'Our brothers know what they are about.' And he led the way down.

The giant sigil did not mark the end of the descent. The shaft opened up in a vast hemispherical cavern, almost completely filled by a rock dome. This construct was what the tunnels led to, its curved surface their dead ends. The spiral ramp divided as it left the shaft. It became a shelf that ran around the entire circumference of the cavern, hugging the concave wall. Steep staircases zigzagged off from it at regular intervals. The stairs stopped every three metres at a landing. A glance told Atticus the nature of the stairs' function: they were what had permitted the xenos architects to carve the runes into the cavern wall. The dome itself appeared featureless apart from its one great rune at its peak. The rest of it was smooth black stone. It had no seams that Atticus could detect. It was as if an immense bubble of magma had cooled into a formation as black as obsidian and smoother than ice.

'We were unable to damage the base of this thing,' Camnus pointed out.

'Then we will attempt its roof,' Atticus replied. *Everything has a weakness*, he thought. *I will wager it is your eye.*

Legionaries leapt from the ramp, landing with dull thuds on the roof of the dome. They began to place linked charges. The work had barely begun when the sounds of the war from above changed. There was a lull. Then a greater fury, one that grew in waves, echoes building on echoes.

Then light. Coming closer.

KHI'DEM'S LEFT ARM vanished below the elbow. The shock of elastic reality returning to stable form disrupted every electrical impulse of his armour and every synapse of his nervous system. For several seconds, his lungs forgot how to breathe, and his hearts stilled. His mind stuttered, his very identity ripped from him. Breath, pulse and thought returned together. He blinked, trying to make sense of the runes that blinked crimson before his eyes as his armour restarted the systems that still worked. The Larraman cells of his blood were forming scar tissue over his stump before he had full knowledge of his mutilation.

In these first moments of reality's return, he knew only one impulse: *move*. He did. He rolled out of the path of the striding daemon. He tucked his knees under his chest, shoved against the ground with his right arm, and made it to his feet. He was surrounded by the dismembered pieces of legionaries. He saw Apothecary Vektus, reduced to a writhing head and torso, grunting his final curses before his fall into silence. Then Khi'dem heard the coming of a storm beyond the patch of night that floated above Madail. He managed to put some distance between himself and the daemon before the Hellfury missiles struck. The force of the blasts knocked him sideways. He staggered, but kept his feet.

Madail stood in the centre of the explosions, bathed in fire. The eyes of its chest were closed. Its head was facing up, its maw wide open in chilling ecstasy. It jabbed its staff upwards. The fire-ball reversed, shrank with a thunderclap of displaced air, and was absorbed into the blades of the staff. Then the flame returned in a stream of concentrated energy. It shot through the shield of darkness. Khi'dem heard the shriek of tearing metal, then a new explosion. *Unbending* fell through the dark. Streaming smoke, one wing gone, its engines aflame, it streaked in like a comet. It passed over Khi'dem. It touched earth once, rose as if denying its fate, and then slammed down, digging a massive furrow, disintegrating yurts, and roaring towards the centre of the plateau.

'No,' Khi'dem whispered as he realised what loomed. Behind him, the daemon laughed. The Demolisher cannons of the Vindicators boomed, and the daemon laughed.

Unbending's nose was crushed by the impact. The gunship's speed bled away. Its momentum lasted longer, and it began a slow, ago-nised somersault. The fire embraced the rest of the hull as secondary explosions touched off. It had turned into a towering torch when it toppled into the great shaft.

FIRE AND METAL roared towards the Iron Hands. Atticus looked up from where he was standing overlooking the sigil. He saw the burn-ing gunship, and knew it as the herald of catastrophe. No orders were needed, and he gave none. The Space Marines scrambled for cover. Atticus glared at what hurtled his way, taking a full second to blast the fates with his hate, and then he too moved. He threw himself to the right, pounding along the perimeter shelf behind his troops. The legionaries on the dome were leaping for the lower shelves. The company moved fast.

The blow came faster. *Unbending* struck the top of the dome with the force of doom. Its frame compacted like a god's fist. The ship's propulsion system was breached. The explosion filled the cavern with killing light. Behind the flash came the flames. They washed over the dome. They raced around the cavern. There was no shelter. There was only distance from the immediate blast. There was the fortitude of metal and the strength of armour. And there was luck.

Precious little of it.

The wreckage of the ship crushed legionaries. The anger of the explosion reduced others to cinders. Atticus's auto-senses shut down, blocking the flash. In the moment of blindness, he stopped running. He crouched, grounding himself on the ledge, leaning against the wall. The flames and the wind slammed into him. His armour's temperature shot up to critical levels. A giant's hand sought to pry him from his perch and hurl him to the storm. He held fast, and after the first moment of the assault, he had the firestorm's measure. He rose in defiance.

'*We will not fall!*' he shouted. He was surrounded by a cyclone of fire. The howl of the winds was such that he could barely hear his voice inside his helmet. The vox was caught in its own storm, and he did not know if any of his brothers received his words. None of this mattered. He stood, and as long as even one of the Iron Hands still lived to fight, the Legion did too.

He turned around, rejecting the heat that reached through to the traces of the human that still remained and reminded him of the reality of pain. He lifted a foot, challenging the wind to do its worst, and took a heavy step forwards, into the gale of fire. The readouts on his lenses were blinking, erratic. He had no sure knowledge that he was not the sole survivor. No matter. Battle was engaged. He was at war, and there would be no further retreats for the X Legion. Not one more step. And so he walked into the fire.

A body stumbled past him, propelled towards the edge of the shelf. Atticus snapped out an arm and caught the legionary by the wrist as he started to plummet. Atticus dropped to a knee and held fast. The other warrior dangled, then managed to grab on to the ledge with his other hand and haul himself up.

'My thanks, brother-captain,' he said. He was Achaicus, from the Assault squad commanded by Lacertus.

Atticus heard him clearly over the vox. The storm was abating. 'Give me your thanks in force of arms, brother,' Atticus said. Over the company channel, he voxed, 'Report, Iron Hands, and regroup. Retaliation calls to us.'

The fire burned itself out. Nothing remained of *Unbending* except smoking, twisted fragments. Looking down from the shelf, Atticus saw them scattered around the base of the dome. They did not resemble the bones of a gunship. They were shrivelled detritus. They were another shame, another humiliation that Atticus would carve from the enemy's hide.

The company shook off the effects of the blast. The Iron Hands acknowledged Atticus's orders. There were gaps in the roll. Fourteen more battle-brothers had died in the destruction. Atticus could hear the rumbling beat of combat coming from the surface. Big guns firing. The Vindicators. He cursed his luck. He ran back to the shaft and looked up. The Thunderhawk's fall had smashed entire sections of the ramp. The Raven Guard and the Iron Hands' Assault squad could make it back up. Not so the rest of the company. Atticus growled. He looked at the dome. It was untouched. The impact and explosion had not even scratched the sigil. His fists tightened.

He called Lacertus and the Raven Guard to him. They looked up the shaft, and he did not have to explain. 'Go back to the surface,' he told them. 'Provide support.'

'What about the rest of the company?' Lacertus asked.

'We will find a way.'

'How?'

'We will punch handholds into the sides of the shaft if we have to. All I ask is that you leave some of the enemy for us to kill.'

Arms crossed and gauntlets slammed against chestplates as the squads made the sign of the aquila. Atticus turned away as they rode the fire of their jump packs back up the shaft.

'*Captain?*' It was Camnus.

'I order you to give me good news, brother.'

'*I may have found a way forward.*'

'Where are you?'

'*On the floor of the cavern.*'

Atticus ordered a rally at Camnus's position, then made his way down, leaping from landing to landing of the nearest staircase. He reached the base of the dome in less than a minute. A number of his legionaries had arrived first, some clearly thrown down by the explosion. He saw damaged armour. He also saw a few fatalities.

Running from the base of the dome and back towards the main body of the ruins, precisely spaced along the cardinal points of a compass, were rocky tubes about four metres in height. Camnus had taken up a position beside the nearest one. 'These are the tunnels,' he said.

Atticus nodded. 'And?'

'They are not made of the same rock as the dome.'

He was right, Atticus saw. The tube's brickwork used the natural rock of the plateau. It was not the deep, glistening black of the hemisphere. 'You think we can break through,' he said.

'Yes. Then make our way back up through the ruins.'

Atticus nodded. 'Do it.'

'So ordered.'

Then, as the Techmarine began to direct the placing of charges, the great blow came. It had no source, but the entire chamber rang.

Something all-important *changed*. For a moment he thought the world had shifted under his feet. Then he realised he had felt the beginning of a rip.

And then, the light. Light from the worst of darkness.

ENGINE OF FURY and *Medusan Strength* fired in unison. The colossal shells landed with lethal precision at Madail's feet. The ground erupted. Boulders and dust were thrown dozens of metres into the air. They rained back down as the next salvo arrived. For almost a minute, Khi'dem could see nothing of the daemon. He saw only the plateau transformed into a volcano.

Madail reappeared. Chest-eyes still closed, head still tilted back in rapture, the daemon strode out from the geysers of earth. After two steps, it opened its eyes and ran to Khi'dem's left, heading for *Medusan Strength*. The Vindicator surged forwards to meet it. The Demolisher cannon roared again. The daemon seemed to wince in anticipation at the moment of the barrel flash. The shell struck the abomination in the chest. Huge as Madail was, no mass even its size could survive such a blow. Any mass that belonged to the materium would have disintegrated.

The daemon laughed. There was the huge flash of the blast. There was the great thunderclap. And there was the laugh. Khi'dem blinked. The explosion was strangely sanitised, as there was no debris. The blow knocked Madail back several paces. The daemon laughed again as it spun once, recapturing its momentum with the grace of a dancer. Its delight in the experience was clear. It charged *Medusan Strength* again. Behind it, *Engine of Fury* closed in. It approached in an arc, staying out of the way of the other Vindicator's fire, and keeping its own cannon silent for fear of striking its brother. Its engine howling, it rushed in to smear the monster over the landscape with its siege shield.

Medusan Strength fired once more. As it did, Madail leapt. The

daemon sailed high over the shot and came down on top of the
tank. It landed hard enough to drive the Vindicator's treads into
the ground. *Medusan Strength* reared up like an enraged animal. The
legionary riding in the hatch fired upward with his combi-bolter.
Madail plunged the tip of its weapon down, spearing the Space
Marine. The daemon pushed down harder, and the blades stabbed
all the way through the chassis and embedded themselves in the
ground. For a surreal moment, Khi'dem saw the tank pinned like
an insect to a board.

Madail hissed with pleasured anticipation, and the staff glowed
an incandescent red. The heat was savage. Khi'dem saw the armour
near the staff turn molten. Ruptured fuel lines and ammunition
ignited. The tank shook with a chain reaction of internal explosions. Then it blew apart. Madail exulted in the centre of light and
tortured metal.

Above, the darkness was spreading, as if the longer the daemon
walked the earth, the further the stain of its existence spread.

Engine of Fury reached Madail. The massive siege shield struck the
back of the daemon. Madail did not move. The Vindicator came
to a sudden halt. The towering figure vaulted over the tank as the
cannon fired. Madail leaned down and stretched out its immense
arms. It embraced the rear of the vehicle. It laughed as the treads
turned the ground into mud, fighting in vain to break free of its grip.

The daemon waited. Khi'dem heard the snarl of the other Thunderhawk close in. He could not see it through the darkness.

Madail could.

A steady barrage from *Hammerblow's* battle cannon chewed up
the surface of the plateau, carving deep trenches towards the daemon. As the shots struck it, and Khi'dem stared in horrified wonder,
Madail hurled *Engine of Fury* into the air. The tank flew up like a
missile. It passed through the darkness, and Khi'dem heard the sickening, crunching bangs of massive bodies in collision. *Hammerblow*

hurtled into view, locked in a fatal embrace with the Vindicator. The two machines slammed into the ground, shaking the plateau.

There was a moment of relative calm. The sounds of crackling flame and secondary explosions were the echoes of battle, the fading uproar of a war lost. Khi'dem looked around. He was the only legionary standing. But the Thunderhawk and tank had not gone up. Perhaps there were survivors. Khi'dem stumbled towards the wreckage. He was halfway there when the explosions came, knocking him down, robbing him of the last of his brothers.

Madail bestrode the battlefield, basking in the glory of its good works. *'A fine dance,'* it called out. In its mockery, its voice became musical, but it was the music of ragged dreams, the chords of strangled hope. *'Is there no one else?'* it asked.

Rising once more, Khi'dem could not imagine that the daemon was speaking to him. He was, in this moment, beneath notice. But he wondered that the daemon spoke in Gothic. There was something directed, personal about the doom that was unfolding, as if these awful moments, this tragedy of the warriors of the *Veritas Ferrum*, had been waiting since the dawn of the galaxy.

'Ahhhhh,' said Madail, slicking the air with hungry delight. *'Welcome.'*

Khi'dem saw jump-packed legionaries rise from the central shaft. They began firing at the daemon. It ignored their shots.

'Welcome,' Madail said again. *'Witnesses. Witnesses to the great communion.'* It advanced to the edge of the shaft. It looked out beyond the plateau. It pointed with its staff. *'Servants of the toy god,'* it called out, *'look what you have brought me. Behold what you have wrought.'*

Khi'dem looked. The need to face the worst allowed him no other option. He knew that the Iron Hands and Raven Guard were looking too.

To the east, with the immense, rumbling crack of an earthquake, something was rising. It glowed with a malevolent light, the crimson-streaked deep orange of burning blood. Coils of energy, like solar prominences, flared and danced around the object. The impossibility of the vision confused Khi'dem at first. He did not know what he was seeing. Then he realised it was the stone pillar, the anomaly that had been the nexus of all the struggles on Pythos.

The monolith climbed towards the sky, and its true nature was revealed. The pillar was merely the tip of a cyclopean structure that was not a column at all. Other, lower columns now appeared, rising in parallel. Then the bases of the columns, curving inward towards each other, joining together. To his horror, Khi'dem saw a gargantuan replica of Madail's staff. It was a symbol and a weapon. It was an aeons-old monument that had been created not as a commemoration, but in anticipation of this moment. Apotheosis had arrived. The bladed stone rose now to claw the sky. It climbed and climbed, a hundred metres, two hundred, three hundred, and still more. It was a tower so laden with significance that it threatened to shatter all meaning. It rose until it loomed over the Pythos landscape. No tree or hill for hundreds of kilometres in all directions was its equal.

The multifoliate tower reached higher yet, and now there came a new sound. To the grating of stone was added a great, rhythmic pounding. Behind the glare of the monument's infernal energy, Khi'dem saw shifting, hulking shadows. Hills, his eyes tried to tell him. Hills that rose and fell to a massive beat.

Waves, his mind realised. Waves a hundred metres high. The ocean had joined in the dark celebration, paying tribute to the terminal event. It heaved itself up again and again, rising and falling to the beat of sanity's funeral, a massive darkness beneath the grey sky, its surface reflecting the apocalypse fire of the monument. Khi'dem thought he saw things disporting themselves in the waves. Monsters of the deep, forced up by instinct to celebrate as the planet fulfilled its destiny.

The sounds became ever more deafening, a symphony of deep madness, the endless grinding of stone punctuated by the *boom*, rasp, *boom*, rasp of the ocean. And underneath, another theme was preparing itself. It was coming closer, beat by beat, moment by moment, doom by doom. When it arrived, it would be the only sound. It would swallow everything. It would crush everything.

It would be everything.

Madail moved to the lip of the shaft. It raised its arms, holding the staff up towards its gargantuan model. The light from the monument was so intense it dimmed the day. It pulsed even brighter as Khi'dem watched. The energy was being fed by something. Strands like ectoplasmic vitae flowed to it through the air, the echoes of distant violence coming to add their deaths to the growing toll.

The moment approached. The tower rose to its full height. The energy reaching the critical point. Madail stood in ecstasy before the sights, a priest with the powers of a god.

'*Now*,' the daemon cried out, in command and prayer.

Now.

TWENTY

The end of day
Horn of plenty
Drumbeats

IN ANSWER TO the daemon, the sound that had been rising beneath the earth and sea arrived. It was a single beat, so profound that it tore reality asunder. The beat came from the monument. The sound was a ripple that raced from that centre to embrace the world. At the same moment, the energy burst free. It took the form of directed, cancerous light. It shot from the points of the black stone blades, the individual beams joining into one that descended into the shaft.

The great beat shook the world so hard that it knocked the Iron Hands and Raven Guard out of the air. They had only just risen from the hole when the beam struck. Ptero hit the ground. He rolled up and was on his feet in an instant. His brother, Judex, and one of the Iron Hands were less fortunate. They were clipped by the beam. That was enough. Where they were touched, their armour and body ceased to exist in the material sense. An explosion of unreal being overtook them. Madness given form ballooned and crawled from their wounds. Eyes and fangs and clawed limbs multiplied. The two legionaries were dead before they landed with sickening wet thuds. Their corpses devoured themselves until they were nothing but a squirming, senseless mass of snapping entrails and moaning, whistling bone fragments.

The energy from the monument poured itself into the shaft, and Ptero felt that awful rip widen. The tear was, he realised, more than a shift in the nature of all things. It had a specific location. There was a plague about to be unleashed, and it had a source, a point in reality that had been so corrupted that it was now going to burst and spew forth abomination.

Already, the disease was propagating. The stain of night that hovered over the daemon now established its dominion. Tendrils that looked like vapour but moved with the slash of lightning rose to the cloud cover. They altered the clouds. The black spread like oil over water. The day of Pythos, never more than a sour insult, died in agony.

Something worse than night stole over the firmament. The black was absolute, and it was deep. It was not a veil that blocked the light, beyond which the galaxy remained sane. It was a theft. The sky was gone. The stars were gone. Over Pythos now was nothing, a void made terrible by the absence of all that should be, and even more terrible by the sense of ghastly possibility, of imminence. Something would fill the void. Something that should not be.

And from the bottom of the shaft came a noise, an uproar, the rising cacophony of a great horror unleashed.

THE LIGHT STRUCK the sigil of the dome. Standing at the base, Atticus could not see the rune react to the contact, but he could hear the result. He could *feel* it. He heard a huge door opening, a door that was stone and iron and flesh. He felt the dome fill with the rotten energy. The black stone pulsed with an abyssal light. The tearing continued, and now Atticus knew that this worst thing was occurring inside the dome.

'Get us into this tunnel,' he ordered Camnus. 'Do it *now*.'

'We are ready, brother-captain,' the Techmarine replied.

The company drew back. Camnus set off the charges. The explosion sounded muffled, drowned by the thrumming of the energy beam. But the power of the blast was more than enough. It punched through the wall of the stone tube, creating a breach the width of three legionaries. The Techmarine's demolition was skilful: the charges were strong enough to pulverise the wall, so there was little debris inside the tunnel, but not so indiscriminate that they weakened the ceiling and brought it down. The way in was clear.

Atticus entered first. His warriors had a clean run open to them back to the surface, where he knew war awaited. But he paused. He was sure that what was happening in the interior of the unbreachable dome was critical. He looked again at the dead end. What, he wondered, was the point of these tunnels if all they did was run into a wall? The xenos creation – whether architecture, mechanism, or both – was perverse, its functions opaque. But he was learning that there was nothing futile about any of its elements. The tunnels had a purpose. If they existed, it was to bring something to the dome, or to release something from it. As the company gathered in the tunnel, Atticus examined the dome wall once more.

'Something is changing,' he said. The pulsing was much faster here than over the rest of the hemisphere. It was painful to observe. It was a blackness that strobed, an energy detached from any known configuration of the eletromagnetic spectrum. It was light's diseased twin. The intensity of the disturbance rose even as Atticus spoke, and as it did, it crossed a threshold.

Atticus blinked. Each of his eyes was receiving radically different data, and the split was disruptive, assaulting his mind with a fusion of migraine and digital feedback. He shut one eye, then the other. The human eye saw the pulse as a perverse impossibility. His bionic one registered something far more profound. It saw a flicker. The wall was phasing in and out of existence at the speed of insect wings. Atticus picked up a piece of rubble and tossed it against the wall. The stone was atomised.

Camnus joined him. 'That,' the Techmarine said, 'is a gate.'

Atticus nodded. 'And it is opening.'

The pace of the flicker increased. A vibratory thrum filled the tunnel, shaking dust loose from its roof. The black became so intense, it was almost blinding.

'Iron Hands,' Atticus called. 'Weapons ready.' An eager certainty took hold of him. 'We are about to find our enemy.'

The thrum built to a piercing whine. The nature of the flicker changed once again. The gate's moments in the material realm became fewer, then shorter, then irregular. Winning the war were the time fractions when the barrier was only an illusion, a memory of a wall.

The memory faded. With a sharp crack of dissipating energy, the gate vanished. The way into the dome was open.

As was the way out.

Atticus did not wait for the enemy to declare itself. He had been forced into fighting a reactive war ever since the return from the Hamartia raid. No more. He entered the dome with his finger already depressing the trigger of his bolter.

The space was suffused with a dirty glow. It was the diluted form of the ray that had struck the sigil. The floor was level and featureless, except for what looked like a dais, fifty metres in diameter, in the centre. The interior walls were festooned with runes, larger and more complex than the ones on the wall of the outer chamber. They were the source of the light, but they faded as the thing in the centre of the dome manifested itself. It began as a thin line in the air, stretching from the apex of the vault to the dais. The line twitched and jerked like captured lightning. With each movement, it left a copy of itself behind. Within a few seconds, a black, jerking web occupied the central ground. It spread farther, shorter segments multiplying, connecting, the formation becoming more and more jagged.

Atticus scanned quickly, saw that there was no shelter. The Iron Hands' armour would have to suffice. 'Form an arc,' he commanded. 'Keep the gate at the centre. It is ours. Let nothing pass. Prepare to concentrate fire on what stands before us.'

The pattern froze. When it did, Atticus realised he was not looking at a web, but at a pane of cracked, shattered reality. There was the blast of a horn, long and deep at first, then rising in pitch from mournful horror to shrieking delight. The broken pane fell in pieces, the edged fragments cutting more chunks out of the materium as they dropped. Behind the fragile layer of reality lay the great depths of madness.

And from those depths an army came.

Bellowing, braying, laughing, snarling, singing, cursing, gibbering, the hordes poured into the dome. They were a cascade of monstrosity, a flood of the perverse: flesh, horns, hooves, jaws, claws, wings, tails, pincers. Arms that were blades, blades that had eyes, weapons and armour and life made indistinguishable. Hide the crimson of anger, the pink of hideous infants, the green of disease, the white of corruption. The frothing, squirming swarm of the maggots was as nothing to this onslaught. The maggots had been a mere sketch, the planet rehearsing an idea now terrible in its blossoming.

Atticus had his enemies, and they were daemons. Perhaps, at a level he did not acknowledge as existing, he had always known this would be his fight. Or perhaps he simply rejoiced at having something to kill. He did not know what the truth was, and he did not care. He adjusted to the reality of the impossible without a pause, and that was all that mattered.

'Kill everything,' he said. He raised his voice over the howling mob that raced towards the company. He became the machine. 'Spare no flesh!' he snarled as the rounds raked into the front lines of the monsters. 'This is nothing but the endless spew of weakness. We have abandoned the flesh, and will not be dragged down into its swamp. Exterminate it! Scour the planet of inferior life!'

The explosive shells ripped their targets apart. Some of the daemons fell, killed as easily as any other form of sentience. Others absorbed the damage without slowing. Still others underwent a transformation, writhing and screaming, muscles and skin and bone ripping and cracking until there were two monsters where there had been just one. From the smashed hole in the real, the monsters continued to arrive. The abyss of the warp was full of distorted, ravening life, and the numbers were beyond counting.

Legions were descending on the single company.

The leading edge of the daemon plague was almost upon the Iron Hands. Monsters *were* going down, pulped and torn beyond repair by the lethal hail. When they died, they lost their form, flesh revealing its essential flaw as it dissolved. The floor of the dome was slick with deliquescing bodies. The advance did not slow. At its centre, giving it shape, was an ordered force of blood-red, horned, sinewy beasts armed with blades almost as long as a man. They were surrounded by a plague of monsters like an explosion of foam on the crest of a great wave. There were so many daemons that they were climbing over each other to reach the Space Marines. The shapes were as varied as madness. Some had just enough of the human about them to make the distortion of the form all the more perverse. Others were vaguely canine, but horned, armoured, massive. And still more were of no recognisable derivation at all. They were chaos made flesh, a cancer of grasping jaws and tentacles.

Atticus could see the truth: the army of damnation was infinite.

So much the better.

'*Take them!*' he roared.

So ordered, the Iron Hands did not meet the wave on the defensive.

The offence was all they had left, and so they took it. They attacked. A metal battering ram surged forwards to crash into the daemonic multitude. Bolters were mag-locked. The weapons were chainblades, power fists and flame.

Atticus swung his chainaxe into the twisted visages before him. He felt the impact of his blow up the haft of the axe, a satisfying jar to his arms. Perhaps the flesh he destroyed was a lie, but it tore and died as well as any truth. Ichor sprayed over him. A daemon raised its sword over its head, two-handed, and brought it down at Atticus's face. He grabbed the blade with one gauntleted fist and snapped it in half. With his other hand, he swung the axe in and decapitated the daemon for its effrontery. The head snarled at him as it arced away to be trampled by the melee. The body flailed at Atticus for several more seconds before it collapsed. It was smashed to pulp before it even had a chance to begin dissolving back to the formlessness of the warp.

The Iron Hands were relentless. Atticus was surrounded by a brotherhood of destruction. He and his legionaries were confronted with the naked truth of the flesh. It was a taint upon the galaxy, upon reality itself, and now it was the time for the Iron Hands to smash it, shred it, burn it. Annihilate it.

The flesh grappled with Atticus. A thing reared up over him. It was like a monstrous slug, an excrescence of muscle and teeth. Its skin rippled. Pustules oozed and dripped. It was rot, it was disease, and it would consume him. As it dropped over him, he lifted the axe. It plunged into the centre of the creature's mass. Rubbery filth parted. Atticus forced the weapon higher, bisecting the daemon. It howled idiot pain. Its blood, if blood this was, gushed forth in a torrent that was thick, viscous, translucent and streaked with green. It was illness in liquid form. Atticus felt it tug at his boots. His armour was slick with the effluence of rendered monsters. It was a badge of honour. He raised his axe all the way. When it pulled free, the daemon stopped screaming and fell away on two sides.

Over its twitching corpse came more horrors, always more, floods upon floods of the enemy. Atticus swung and punched, swung and kicked. He killed and smashed. With every move, with every step, he sent another daemon out of the physical realm. He commanded but a splinter of what had been the X Legion, but even one warrior of the Legiones Astartes could destroy armies. The Iron Hands pushed hard against the wave of daemons. They halted its advance. The enemy would not pass. It would not reach the surface by going through the Space Marines.

It was a meaningless victory. His forces were only blocking one exit. There were three others, and the gates were all open. Through a momentary gap in the wall of monstrosities, Atticus saw the streams of the mob stampeding through the other openings with raging abandon. In the ceiling of the dome, where the sigil had been, was a huge aperture, and the creatures with wings were flapping up through it and to the shaft.

'*Captain*,' Camnus's voice came over the vox. Atticus was surrounded again by the clawing, slashing horde, and he could not see the Techmarine. He could not see any of his brothers.

'Yes, brother.'

A grunt of effort on the vox, then a large, wet crack to Atticus's right. Camnus was nearby, slaying well.

'*What is our goal?*'

And there, with the question before him, Atticus had no answer at first. He had been so focused on locating the enemy that he had not thought through the implications now that he had found it. There was no victory to be had here. The company could fight until the inevitable, and that would be nothing more than another kind of futility.

What is our goal?

To stop this warp-fuelled machine. And if that were not possible, to somehow use its power against itself. *We read the warp through it before,* he thought. *It is vulnerable to us. We will find a weakness.* And for that, Rhydia Erephren was key.

'We make for the surface,' Atticus told the company. He whirled with the axe, slicing through a massive tentacle that had wrapped around him like a python. 'We make for the base.'

They would not be retreating. And he vowed that he would yet tear a victory from the throat of this monstrous planet.

DOOM MARCHED IN on a heavy, echoing beat, the shout of volcanoes forced into a regular metre. It was as much a spectacle as dark music. Darras watched the rise of the monument. Even at this distance, it was clearly higher than the promontory, and it changed the shade of the day. That was the first beat. And then the great *boom*, the greatest beat, as the light struck downwards, and Darras knew that something fatal had been destroyed.

He knew this because he now saw death take the day. The black beyond night, the black of ending, spread out from the direction of the settlement. It swarmed up into the clouds and swallowed them. It rippled outwards, eating the sky and leaving the great and endless nothing behind.

But then, as the black overhead was complete, something appeared in the empty vault. Pure void pulled back to reveal a sun. It sat in the sky directly above the monument. It was in the position that the Pandorax star would have held, had it ever been visible through the cloud cover. There was no doubt that it was a sun.

But it was stone.

Darras felt the foundations of all certainty crumble away beneath him. The celestial body seemed close enough to touch, the details of its rough, cracked surface as clear as if it were a planetoid no more than few hundred kilometres in diameter. Yet it was a star. It filled a third of the sky. It radiated a cold, grey light. It hung over Pythos, a mass heavy with infernal judgement. It was without sense, without logic. It had no meaning, and for that very reason was dreadful in its significance. It was madness given immense, implacable form. It was a stone against which any semblance of reality and sanity would shatter.

Still the beats came. Still the *doom, doom, doom* march of catastrophe. These newest beats were softer. They were not globe-ringing strikes as the unleashing of the monument's energy had been. They were less metaphysical. They were concrete, a true sound. Something in the distance was striking the ground again and again with slow, relentless regularity.

Coming closer.

The sounds came from the north and south. Darras knew the promontory was caught in a pincer movement before he saw what approached. Then, bathed in the frozen, corpse-light of the stone sun, the threats appeared over the horizon.

Darras heard the serfs on the wall whimper in terror. He had no patience for their weakness, but he would have been surprised if they responded otherwise. Mortals were weak. They had brittle limits to their courage. What had been summoned broke those limits. The thing in the sky was a terror, but it was also distant. It was not an immediate threat.

The animals that lumbered towards the base were.

Pythos had held back the worst of its horrors until now. Perhaps, Darras thought, these monsters would not appear until there was a sufficient concentration of prey. They would need unimaginable quantities of meat to live. He remembered Ptero's refusal to accept as natural the carnivorous ecology of the planet.

'You are vindicated, Raven Guard,' Darras muttered. There was nothing natural on this planet. The Iron Hands, of all Legions, should have recognised technology when they encountered it. Everything, from vegetation to animal life to monstrous artefacts, had been created for a purpose, and that purpose was at last being fulfilled.

The creatures now approaching were immense. They were the size of Battle Titans. They were at least fifty metres tall, perhaps more. Their heads were long, crocodilian, with forward-pointing tusks at the hinge of the jaws. Conical spikes the height of missiles lined their spines and clustered at the end of their tails, forming flails that would smash a tank flat. They walked on their hind legs, but their forelimbs were huge, reaching down almost to the ground from shoulders as wide as weapons platforms. Now and then, they would lean forwards and use their arms to propel themselves a bit faster through the jungle. Trees splintered and fell before their advance. Then they were crossing the burned land, rumbling over it, as big as hills, terrible as myths.

Catigernus said, 'They'll knock the wall down.'

'They won't have to,' Darras told him. 'They'll step over it. I doubt they'll even notice it.'

The great beasts descended on the feast. Their smaller brethren were still devouring the colonists. There were enough mortals left to keep the air filled with shrieks and song. The giants reached down with their colossal claws and scooped up handfuls of struggling prey. Their jaws clamped down on humans and saurians alike. The air filled with the sound of cracking bones. The monsters advanced to a beat of earthquakes. They were only a few strides from the base. They towered into the empty night, the light of stone washing over their scales, transforming them into gargoyles larger than cathedrals. They devoured all life from the land, and soon would turn their hunger on the Legion emplacement.

'Here is why we conserved our ammunition,' Darras voxed to the base's forces. 'Open fire.'

A storm burst from the walls. It was a hurricane wind of mass-reactive destruction, the lightning of las-fire and the thunder of

rocket launches. The storm smashed into the nearest giant. Its flank
was lit by flame and tiny geysers of blood. It turned slowly, as if
barely aware of the attack, to face the base head-on. It growled in
building anger. The night shook with the rumble of its threat.

'Eyes!' Darras commanded.

The beast ducked its head forwards, jaw opening to swallow its
attackers whole. *How very cooperative*, Darras thought. His shells
found the monster's left eye. The saurian shrieked as a jellied explosion erupted over its face. The other eye burst a moment later. The
monster thrashed, arms sweeping in huge arcs.

'Throat!' Darras shouted.

Aiming was difficult. The target was big enough, but the animal was
convulsed in pain and rage. Its movements had gone from majestic to
frenzied. But a missile struck it in the throat. The blast ripped through
the flesh and unleashed a torrent of blood. The howls became rak-
ing, choking gurgles. The beast tried to retreat. It turned its back on
the wall, but fell to its knees. As it pitched forwards, its tail swept
over the parapet. Plasteel crunched and folded and shattered. Serfs
were reduced to bloody smears. Three of Darras's battle-brothers
died, their ribcages crushed, hearts punctured, as they were struck by
a spiked battering ram the size of a Land Raider. Darras threw himself flat. The flail smashed down on the parapet a few metres from
him, punching a huge gap in the wall, then bounced up, flying just
over him to come down again an arm's length further on. Catigernus had to leap to the ground to avoid being pulped. Darras stood
again as the beast collapsed. The earth shook with its death.

The others looked at their fallen kin. Two of them began to feast
on its body. The others advanced upon the source of the threat.

'*Sergeant Darras,*' Erephren voxed.

'Is this urgent?' Darras asked as he started firing again. Perhaps
they might bring one more beast down before the rest of them
marched over the base. Perhaps.

'*I believe I can use the anomaly,*' Erephren said.

'Then do so now,' Darras told her. 'Our time is brief.' His sight of
the lifeless sun was blotted out by the approaching monsters. The
Iron Hands' fire was unabating, but the targets were on their guard
and attacking in unison. He was shooting at a mountain chain.

Arms greater than trees rose and struck at the wall. Jaws gaped
like hangar doors. There was nothing weak about this flesh. The
mountains slouched forward, and the defences of the base collapsed like eggshells. A leg clipped Darras and sent him flying. He
landed a dozen metres from where the wall had been. There was
nothing left but ruin and savagery now. Very few of the serfs were
still alive, but they fought on, loyalty to duty and Legion winning
out over the instinct for futile flight.

The Iron Hands had been scattered by the blows. They fought
back, the unalterable discipline of the machine coordinating their
fire even now. But the monsters had broken the formation, and it
was no longer possible to concentrate all the shots at a single target.
A clawed foot came down and crushed the serf barracks. Venerable
Atrax poured the full anger of his twin-linked heavy bolters into the
monstrous ankle. He blew away bone and muscle, and the saurian
fell. The immense frame collapsed across the camp, levelling still
more structures. The avalanche narrowly missed the command unit.
Atrax had foreseen the trajectory of the fall, and had a clear shot
of the skull. Before the animal could lash out, the Dreadnought
hammered it with a stream of fist-sized, armour-piercing shells.
He smashed the creature's brain. The body twitched and writhed,
spreading more ruin, then stilled.

Two dead. The end delayed by a few more seconds. Perhaps Erephren would have time to do whatever she had in mind.

In between the deafening roars, through the unceasing pounding
of bolter fire, Darras realised the astropath was speaking to him.
'*Sergeant,*' she said. '*I have tried. I cannot act here.*'

'What?' He changed a clip and resumed shooting with barely a break in rhythm. He kept moving. Claws almost as large as he was raked furrows in the ground where he had been a moment before.

'The connection must be total.' There was a calm in her tone that spoke of a terrible decision. Even through the fracas of devastation, her voice was chilling. *'I must be in physical contact with the source of the anomaly.'*

Darras grunted, staggering backwards as a colossus reached for him, his death glaring from its eyes. He blasted a finger off the hand, forcing a moment of recoil. 'Do you understand our situation? And what the anomaly has become?' He wondered if her blindness was shielding her from the full scope of their fate.

'Better even than you, sergeant,' she answered. There was no hope in her words. Only the determination of war.

'Then wait for me,' Darras said. The run was impossible. It was also imperative.

'I will meet you at the ship,' she answered.

'What?' Disbelieving, but then he saw her. She was already halfway from the command centre to the landing pad. She moved with the same determined assurance as ever, but more quickly than he had ever seen. She held her staff as though she were a banner bearer. Her cane barely touched the ground. She did not run, but she avoided the gigantic, trampling steps of the monsters with ease, changing direction in anticipation of every movement. The Salamanders' second ship, *Cindara*, had been crushed, but the *Iron Flame* was still intact. Erephren was making for it in as direct a line as the dance of destruction would permit.

Darras raced after her. 'To all within reach,' he voxed. 'With me at *Iron Flame*. Brother Catigernus, we need a pilot.'

'At your heels, brother-sergeant.'

'Brother Atrax...' Darras began.

'Understood,' the Dreadnought answered. *'I will give you the time you need.'*

Darras rolled beneath the swing of a tail. It smashed through the wall of the command centre. 'Thank you, venerable brother. You will be remembered.'

A noise came over the vox, a laugh almost as divorced from the human as Atticus's. *'None of us shall be remembered. But swear to punish the enemy.'*

'I swear it.'

Atrax lumbered towards the centre of the base. He fired his bolters in a circular pattern, striking the three saurians in the base, and one still feasting on victims beyond the wall. They turned on the small creature that had the temerity to injure them. The Iron Hands who were too far from *Iron Flame* converged on Atrax and added to his fire. A dark order coalesced out of the vortex of the base. Legionaries reduced to the size of ants beside the sky-high beasts ceased evasive manoeuvres. The carnivore gods zeroed in on them and ignored the few who boarded the Thunderhawk. The monsters did not look as the engines ignited with a roar.

In the cockpit, Darras stood behind the seated Catigernus and watched the final curtain fall on the base. The saurians pounced. It was obscene that monstrosities so gargantuan could move with such vicious speed, yet they did. The battle was over in seconds, and even that length was a testament to the force of the Iron Hands' assault. Greater glory yet came when another of the creatures fell. It crashed on top of the armoury, the impact of its tonnes setting off enough ammunition to trigger a chain reaction. The beast's torso was consumed in a fireball that spread over half the base.

One creature looked up as the flames washed partway up its back. The others paid no attention, consumed with destroying the Iron Hands. They crushed the legionaries beneath their feet, picked them up and tore them in half. As *Iron Flame* rose from the landing pad, one of the saurians twisted and smashed Atrax with its tail. The blow crushed the Dreadnought. Inside the chassis, the atomantic arc-reactor went critical. Catastrophic failure ensued. For a moment, everything vanished from Darras's sight in a searing flash. When the light faded, Atrax had disintegrated, and the explosion of the reactor had blown apart the lower half of the saurian. The monster lived a moment more, even as its viscera plunged to the ground. It raged mindlessly, still trying to devour its prey. Then it collapsed.

It was a victory, of a kind. But then the remaining saurian was joined by its brother from beyond the wall, and there were still more on the promontory slope. For the Iron Hands on the base, the stolen seconds ran out. The battle ended. Hope disappeared beneath claws and between teeth.

Catigernus took the gunship up in a steep climb. He pushed the engines hard. He fired all forward-facing weapons at the same time. Twin-linked heavy bolters on the fuselage, lascannons on the wings and the massive dorsal cannon opened up. The monster that rushed at them, eager to embrace the new prey, vanished in a tremendous eruption of fire and blood. *Iron Flame* rose through the thick cloud of vitae. Then it was clear, rising higher, flying faster.

Not high enough. Not fast enough.

A colossus reached up with both arms and struck home.

TWENTY-ONE

The message
The revel
Juggernaut

When the day fell into a tomb and the stone sun came to drench the land in the chill of dead marble, Kanshell looked to Tanaura. She did not respond, as transfixed as he was. But then the footsteps of the great saurians drew closer, and the island of calm vanished. The frenzy resumed. Tanaura hesitated, looking first towards the wall, then down the slope. Kanshell felt the panic of indecision. There was no clear path, and no clear duty, and in moments they would be trampled or devoured.

The new monsters arrived, creatures so huge that Kanshell felt the touch of the sublime once again, and he wept that it could take on forms so dreadful.

'Back,' Tanaura decided, and ran down the slope, making for a brief gap between beasts. Luck, or the lingering aura of the final step of the ritual, was with them. They had not come to any of the reptiles' notice. The beasts were consumed with savaging each other and the diminishing crowd of voluntary sacrifices.

'Why?' Kanshell shouted as he rushed to keep up.

'The battle here is over. It may not be at the settlement.'

There was no further speech, then. As before, there was the jerking, stop-start-sprint-hide race through legs and past snapping jaws. There was a difference, though. Earlier, anger had coursed through Kanshell's blood. There had been the need to strike back at Ske Vris. He had had a target upon which to focus and block out the horrors around him. There was no such goal now. There was only horror, and the need to escape its teeth for one more heartbeat. He followed Tanaura, but to sustain him, he had but one thing: his faith in the Emperor.

It was enough.

He did not despair. He knew that every step he took in the service of fighting the unholy foe of the Emperor was an act of righteousness. If he died in the next second, he would die as one of the faithful. Perhaps even as a martyr, though he did not imagine anyone would ever hear of what had transpired on Pythos. Behind them came the sound of destruction and war as the god-beasts attacked the base.

They were well down the slope when they heard the familiar engine howl of a Thunderhawk. Kanshell's heart soared. The rout was not complete. The company still had the means to strike hard. He heard the full-throated rage of *Iron Flame*'s guns. He hoped punishment would pound down the length of the hill, putting an end to the terrible life that surrounded him. He would not mind dying in such a conflagration. He hoped for the dignity of death by weapon over the rending by teeth.

There was the sound of a great impact, and the voice of the engines became a stuttering shriek. The guns fell silent. The craft passed overhead. It was streaming fire, dropping lower. Kanshell caught only a glimpse of it as he and Tanaura fled the reptilian murder on all sides. Then, ahead, a boom and a grinding crash. The night was lit by the brighter, warmer glow of another disaster. Tanaura angled her run in that direction. Kanshell did the same. He was no longer following her. They were both racing towards a new goal. The fall of *Iron Flame* was the site of their battlefield. Duty summoned them.

There was a change in the current of the savagery. Some of the beasts were moving in the same direction. They, too, were being summoned, but by the call of large and helpless prey.

DARRAS KICKED AT the buckled door to the troop compartment until it gave way. Beside him, Catigernus was struggling to free himself from the mangled controls. The legionary's right arm hung uselessly at his side. *Iron Flame* had hit the ground nose first, hard enough to crumple the forward fuselage, and it had crushed his armour on one side.

Darras paused at the bulkhead. 'Do you need help, brother?' he asked.

'I can manage. See to the others.'

See to the astropath, was what he meant. Their battle-brothers could withstand worse crashes than this. Even with the flight controls reduced to a farce, Catigernus had managed to bring the Thunderhawk in at a relatively shallow angle. The bulk of the ship was still in a single piece.

But Darras smelled smoke.

He entered the troop compartment. The Iron Hands had removed themselves from the grav-harnesses and were taking up positions at the side door. It looked as though it might still open without a struggle. Erephren was seated. She was not moving. Darras went to her, cursing.

She startled him by speaking. 'I am well, sergeant.' Her lips barely moved, but her forehead was lined with effort. Darras saw that she was locked in some unseen mental combat. 'How close are we?' she asked.

'Perhaps halfway there. Your connection is stronger?'

She nodded, the gesture slight and tense. But when she spoke, it seemed that the effort to interact with immediate reality helped anchor her. 'It wants me to become lost in the contemplation of the warp's vistas. Its pull is strong.'

'I don't see how increasing proximity even further will help, then.'

'I have a strength of my own.' She was silent for a moment, a swimmer wrestling with a sudden riptide. Then she continued, 'As astropaths, our training is limited to the permissible uses of our abilities. I believe I can do something more. But I cannot act over a distance. If I can touch the object, I can engage with it on my terms.'

She was speaking of matters that did not sound in keeping with the role of an obedient and sanctioned psyker. Darras found he did not care. The puritanism he had embraced until now, that had driven a wedge between Galba and himself, no longer had a useful part to play in this war. To throw away any possible weapon against the forces that could steal the sky would be to embrace defeat.

Then Catigernus was at his side. The other legionary was moving well and quickly, shrugging off the loss of the use of his arm. 'Where is this smoke coming from?' Darras asked him.

'A number of small fires. We have the ones we can reach under control.' Catigernus looked up and nodded towards the dark smoke emerging from a vent. 'A lot of smouldering going on with the internal systems. Nothing we can do about that.'

'The engines?'

'Offline, but I don't think the damage is critical.'

Darras gestured to the flames visible outside the viewing blocks. 'What am I seeing there?'

'I jettisoned the missiles and auxiliary fuel tanks before we hit.'

Darras went to the door and opened it. A huge trail of flame, the result of the explosive destruction of ordnance and gunship fuel, led back up the slope. Saurians were loping down the hill, but were being held back by the fire. In the distance, the great monsters were

just beginning to focus their attention on the crash site. 'We don't
have much time,' he said.

'Can we proceed on foot?' Erephren asked.

'Too far,' Darras told her. The reptiles would be upon them before
they had gone fifty metres. At a squad's strength, the Iron Hands
could hold the beasts at bay for some time, but there were thousands of the saurians abroad. The chance of Erephren being killed
by a lucky attack was too great. His mission now was seeing that
she survived long enough to complete hers.

'We cannot stay here,' she protested.

'We can hold out longer,' he said. They would have, he thought,
until the god-beasts reached them.

'And then?'

He turned to her. 'We need reinforcements if we are to reach the
anomaly. We need to contact Captain Atticus. He needs to know
what you hope to do. And the vox still can't break through the
interference.' He paused, letting the implications sink in. Outside,
the flames were already beginning to die. The death of the *Veritas
Ferrum* had consumed everything on the ground that could burn.
The growls of the saurians were drawing closer. 'We both know
what is causing the interference,' he said.

'You think I can break through?'

'I know you are the only person who has even a chance of doing
so. You are an astropath. Sending messages through the warp is
your vocation.'

'The captain has no one with him who could hear me.'

'Perhaps not. But if the interference is reduced, I can use the vox.
I understand that you cannot defeat the anomaly, mistress. But
fight it. Fight it just enough.'

She nodded once, and threw herself into the struggle. She grew so
still, she did not appear to be breathing. The creases on her forehead deepened. Her skin paled until it was the same pallor as the

stone sun. Narrow trails of dark, rich blood trickled again from the corners of her eyes.

Outside, the slow drumbeat of approaching annihilation began once more. It was joined by a new sound, coming from the direction of the settlement. Darras's eyes widened.

He could hear laughter.

REACHING THE SURFACE was like rising up from an ocean. An ocean of blood. An ocean of monstrous flesh and horn. Atticus was no longer even thinking in terms of destinations. Twice now he had fought his way up from the depths. Both times, the foe had come in a swarm, and combat had indeed meant swimming, a grinding exercise of brawn and chainaxe.

There was no room to move. The only way up was through warp-flesh. But the maggots had been mindless. The new foe was sentient, eager, armed. Too eager, too numerous, for the daemons could not unleash their worst either in the frenzied crush. They were too hungry for the blood of the Iron Hands. That was their mistake, and they shed their own instead, pouring their perversion of vitae over the warriors that advanced through them, one step at a time, never retreating, one gutted body after another, always forwards, always upwards.

Always killing.

And then the surface. Atticus allowed himself a single moment of satisfaction at having reached the first goal. He could think ahead again. He took stock of the new battlefield.

He saw the monument, the glowing mockery of reason hundreds of metres high.

He saw the stone presence in the infinite void.

He saw the air filled with flying daemons. Some of them were in combat with Lacertus's squad and the Raven Guard. The battle had the rhythm of a sea in storm as the warriors on either side rose from the ground, dropped, then rose again. Most of the winged monsters were flying away from the settlement, cavorting and shrieking in glee as they made for some triumph he could not imagine.

He saw the mutilated dead. The Iron Hands had emerged from the chasm that opened at the base of the mound where the primary lodge had stood. The bodies of colonists and Space Marines were everywhere. And there was a special insult. In the centre of what had been the floor of the lodge, metal torn from the wreckage of the Vindicators had been planted. Its configuration imitated that of the tower. A legionary's body was draped and impaled over the framework, like a torn, bloody scarecrow. It was Galba. Atticus confronted the severed head of his sergeant. He felt anger at the desecration of the warrior's body. He added the atrocity to the tally of the enemy's crimes.

In the lower depths of his identity, something stirred. It was something he had starved into atrophy. He had managed to cut most of it away. It was a human response, an impulse born of generosity and empathy. As it fought to spring back to life, its form became more defined. It was guilt. It was regret.

It was unprofitable. It was a luxury impermissible in combat. And it was weak. Atticus snuffed it out.

Then he turned to behold his true enemy, the shadow he had been hunting since Hamartia. He saw it stride across the plateau, through the flames and smoking ruins of yurts and vehicles. He heard its name chanted by a thousand twisted throats.

MADAIL! MADAIL! MADAIL!

Madail held its staff high, laughing with delight as it conducted the infernal symphony. With every sweep of its arms, a huge current of daemons rushed forwards along the arc of the gestures. Madail was leading its ground troops in the same direction as the aerial daemons. It paused, its flock streaming past its legs. It turned. From its position near the gate, the eyes on its chest stared at Atticus. The

daemon's mouth opened wide. It let out a sigh of hideous pleasure. *'Ahhhhhhhhhhtticus. At last. You are welcome to the revel. Will
you join us? The feast will not be complete unless you witness it.'*

The daemon gestured with a hand, and scores of its lesser kin
broke off from the main flow and launched themselves at the Iron
Hands.

'Fight hard,' Madail admonished. *'Fight well. Earn the reward
of my art.'* It turned away and resumed the procession from the
settlement.

Then it stopped again, cocking its head in puzzlement. The light
from the monument flickered, a slight but distinct cut interrupting its radiation of disease. And through that fissure in the chaos
came Darras's voice over the vox. The sergeant's message was quick,
clear and confirmation of Atticus's earlier determination. Rhydia
Erephren *was* key. She *had* the key. The conduct of the war became
simple. Atticus doubted he heard the voice of hope. He knew that
had been silenced long since, and would be heard no more by
the 111th Clan-Company. But he had something more tangible: a
mission.

'Forward, legionaries!' he called. 'Cut through the foe! The means
to punish him is within our grasp, and the grip of the Iron Hands
is unbreakable!'

They charged. They had lost many of their number on the long
climb to the surface. They were all battered, their armour scored
by blade and acid, slicked with filthy gore. There were only a few
dozen warriors left of a company that had stood a thousand strong.
They bore all these wounds, and yet attacked with a ferocity even
greater than they had inside the dome. They were a machine that
had been given a precise goal, and that made them a juggernaut.

The daemons that rushed forwards to meet them were serpentine and insectoid, human and bovine. Their bodies were long and
slender to the point that they seemed to be nothing but a tail with

head, limbs and stinger. Their legs were long, jointed like an insect's, elegant like a human's. Their movements had a hideous grace. In the days before madness, when the Iron Hands ventured aboard the vessels of the Emperor's Children as brothers, Atticus had, out of courtesy, sat through some of the remembrancer performances so beloved of the III Legion. He saw an echo now of those ballets. The daemons danced, and through their very art, they flew over the ground with the speed of rapiers. And they sang to each other, weaving a siren song of melody and dissonance, beauty and corruption. It was a complexity that sliced the real. It summoned the mind to the dance, and distorted the body. Atticus felt the song try to reach into his form. It wanted his bones to be water. It wanted his flesh to be glass.

His flesh.

That was the daemons' mistake. They were singing for beings much closer to the human than the weapons that charged towards them. Atticus had never known the sublime in art, and as he had travelled further and further down the machinic path, his perception of music had become the cold eye of an anatomist. He rejected the song and all its works. His body gave it no purchase.

He slammed into the daemons, swinging his chainaxe in a wide, horizontal arc. In a single gesture, he severed four limbs, to either side and before him. He ruined the dance. He killed the song with the outraged shrieks of his targets. The rest of the company followed on, an engine of annihilation that savaged the daemons. None of Atticus's battle-brothers were as transformed as he was, but if they had been injured by the song, they showed no sign. The advance did not slow. They cut the monsters down, trampling the obscenities under their boots. Atticus heard the howling of the daemons cease. It gave way to the crunching of bone.

Do you see? he wanted to shout at Madail. *Do you see what happens? This is the fate that awaits your kind. If not on this planet, on some other, at the hands of our brothers. You will not win.*

As he fought, he saw shapes drop on torn wings. Lacertus, Ptero and the other assault legionaries were carrying the day against the flying daemons. Other shapes flew away to rejoin the main swarm.

The Iron Hands stormed to the edge of the plateau. Madail sent no other contingents against them. The daemons continued to pour in an unending flow from the chasms before the ruins of the lodges. The streams skirted the Iron Hands, rushing to the promise being enacted on the Pythos landscape. For the moment, the daemons had lost interest in the legionaries.

Atticus paused. Spread out before him was a vista of mad carnival and absurd warfare. The daemons and the saurians met. They were two waves of monstrosity, colliding in a storm of perfect destruction. The reptiles roared their challenge to the new enemy. Their jaws parted in anticipation of new, unlimited prey. The daemons laughed. They fought the saurians, and they danced with them. Atticus saw the clash of monstrous flesh, of reptile and warp-born, of savage instinct and perverse refinement. The land itself was almost invisible. A new forest had appeared to cover it. It was a writhing forest, the slashing, bleeding, eviscerating forest of monsters vying for supremacy.

More saurians were arriving from all sides of the plateau. More daemons raced from the depths to meet them. And in the distance, from the direction of the base, Atticus saw the giants come. The flying daemons were already swooping around the colossi. The monsters swatted at them as if they were insects. Other, larger, more hulking daemons were moving up to grapple with the giants. They were still smaller, but there were many of them.

'And these are our works,' said a voice beside Atticus.

The captain turned, and found Khi'dem standing beside him. The son of Vulkan had lost an arm, but seemed no less steady, no less derived of the bedrock itself, than Atticus had ever seen him. 'What do you mean?' he asked.

Khi'dem nodded at the spectacle. 'We have been manipulated every step of the way, Captain Atticus. All of us. But we all acted in accordance with our beliefs. I don't know if we could have done anything differently. This result was inevitable, given who we are. And though we were tricked, we have done this. We opened the way.'

'Then we must atone,' Atticus told him.

Khi'dem nodded again.

Atticus pointed to the guttering trail of fire about a kilometre distant. 'We are awaited there,' he told the company. He looked at Khi'dem. He no longer felt any animosity toward the Salamander, though he felt no kinship, either. There was nothing left in his world except the battle ahead, and the hatred for everything he would kill. He asked, 'You will fight beside us?'

'Until the end.'

'I don't think you will need to wait long,' Atticus told him.

The Iron Hands descended the slope of the plateau, picking up speed as they plunged into the rampaging hell.

WHEN KANSHELL SAW that the Thunderhawk was still largely intact, he was surprised. He was also surprised that he and Tanaura had survived their journey this far. His surprise gave way to a sick awe when he saw why the saurians had ignored the insects running at their feet.

A tide of daemons was heading their way. Leaping, striding, hopping, flying, the abominations came on with a chorus of murderous joy. The stone sun looked down upon the army of its children, and the light was the blessing of death. Every fragment of hell that had haunted Kanshell during the nights of torment had become a full, monstrous manifestation. The screaming end to hope and life was here. All that the divine reality of the Emperor stood against had been unleashed. He quailed, and clutched the thread of his faith with all his strength. His instinct was to close his eyes and wait in terrified prayer for his doom. But Tanaura was still on the move, running to the side door of the gunship. He joined her. They reached up and pounded against it.

Darras threw the door back. He looked down at them for a moment, and then, to Kanshell's shock, he laughed. 'If you two are the answer to my call,' the sergeant said, 'then the Iron Hands have come to a sorry end, indeed.' He turned sombre. 'Get in,' he said, as saurian and daemon came together.

Kanshell and Tanaura scrambled aboard. Darras slammed the door closed. Tanaura turned to the viewing port and looked out at the war of madness. The earth was shaking with the blows of monsters, and there was still the deeper, slower booms of the approaching giants. 'Do we fight?' she asked. She sounded eager. Her wounds were bleeding freely, but her eyes shone with the mission of her faith. Inaction was heresy.

'We will,' Darras told her, 'if we must. And we will strike when we have a purpose. Until then, I will willingly let our enemies fight each other. I have no respect for suicide disguised as bravery.'

Tanaura looked at him, her face flushed with indignation, but she had the sense to bite down on her retort. Kanshell felt a rush of sympathetic anger. Darras did not understand the nature of faith. The struggle they were engaged in went far beyond the material world. Kanshell did not want to die, but if the right thing to do was charge back out and claw at the monsters with his bare hands, then he vowed that he would do just that. To die with the praise of the Emperor on his lips was not suicide. It was martyrdom.

Darras moved to Erephren. The astropath looked ghastly. Blood flowed in a constant stream from the empty-looking orbits of her eyes. Her skin had thinned and tightened over her skull. Her breath rattled like stones. She was a funerary sculpture that had been given a dry, whispering life. But the will that animated the frame was so fierce, it burned. Kanshell kept thinking he saw an aura in his peripheral vision, a spiky black crown of crackling determination.

'Any chance of clearing the way again?' Darras asked.

A tiny, sharp shake of the head. 'I have the strength for one last battle with the anomaly, sergeant,' Erephren said. 'I cannot squander it.'

'So be it.'

Kanshell cleared his throat. When Darras's helmet turned his way, he dared to ask, 'You have spoken with Captain Atticus?'

'I have. He brings the rest of our forces. And then,' he nodded at Tanaura, 'you will be part of a great charge.' He paused. The compartment filled with the sounds of the revel. He spoke again, and he was addressing his fellow legionaries. 'This action will be worthy of song, though those songs shall never be written. But brothers, *we* will know the full measure of our worth. And could we ask for a better reward in our final moments? I think not.'

In unison, the other Iron Hands clapped arms to breastplates, an accord in action that was more eloquent than any oath.

And in the next instant, the ship was rocked by a gigantic blow. It knocked Kanshell off his feet. The blow came again. Something huge was slamming against the gunship. Darras checked out the viewing port. The amourglass had been knocked out of the frame, and the foetid air of Pythos was coming in, filling the compartment with the stench of too much life.

'Brace!' Darras yelled, and the ship heaved again. A horn almost as tall as Kanshell punched through the fuselage. It withdrew, then hit again, tearing the side of the gunship open. One more hit, and there was a hole large enough for the monster to stick its head inside the compartment.

The thing looked like a saurian, but it was covered in crimson metal plates. Kanshell could not tell if it wore armour, or if the metal was the daemon's hide. Its hinged jaw opened wide and from it issued a roar like the grinding of immense gears. It shook its head back and forth, widening the hole still further, the thick shielding of *Iron Flame* giving way before the daemon's eagerness to reach its victims. On its back rode one of the horned, sword-wielding horrors. The smaller daemon laughed and urged its mount on to greater violence.

Darras and the other Iron Hands retaliated, but the daemon shrugged off their rounds. Kanshell backed away as far as he could from the daemon. He fired his lasrifle, knowing the act was futile, grasping for a shred of meaning in the fact of the gesture alone. He tried to hit the juggernaut's eye. It was not a small target, but he was too unskilled, and the daemon's movements were too violent. It shoved its head further. It was trying to force its bulk into the ship. Its jaws snapped in Erephren's direction. The monster had come to neutralise a threat.

Catigernus lunged forwards, a krak grenade in hand. When the daemon's jaws opened, he threw the grenade down the monster's throat. Instead of recoiling, it snapped at him, and severed his arm at the elbow. As he fell, the grenade went off inside the daemon. There was a muffled detonation, and the daemon's throat blew out. Somehow the daemon still had a voice, and its shriek went so high, it climbed beyond hearing. Then it cut off as noxious ichor, a stew of blood and oil and venom, poured to the deck.

The daemon convulsed so violently that its rider fell off. When it rose, trying to squeeze into the hole past its agonised mount, Darras blew its head apart with bolter shells. The juggernaut refused to die. Its pain and its fury were silent, but the violence of its actions was eloquent. It shook its head back and forth, horn tearing the ship asunder. Its jaw swung like a broken flap and one of its eyes had burst outward, but it had been slowed only for a moment, and shouldered its way in, ignoring the weapons fire. Its remaining eye fixed on the astropathic wraith. She returned its stare with a blind gaze that was almost as inhuman.

A krak missile streaked past *Iron Flame* and slammed into the side of the daemon. Its rear legs buckled, and it slid from the Thunderhawk. It turned to face its new attackers. It was struck by a second rocket that reduced the armoured flesh on its right shoulder to slag. The murderous stream from an assault cannon hit its chest and head. For a moment, the daemon leaned into the salvo. Then its form disintegrated into jagged wet shrapnel.

Kanshell blinked at the gap where the daemon had been. Some distance from the gunship, the warp spawn and the saurians struggled. But nothing else was attacking the ship in this moment. Then massive silhouettes appeared. They were the Imperium's way of war given form. Atticus had arrived.

The captain stepped up into the ship. He clasped forearms with Darras in greeting. Atticus was even more fearsome than when Kanshell had seen him last. He was drenched in ichor. His armour was scarred and gouged. Kanshell could hear its servo-motors whirring at a louder volume than was healthy, and now and then there was a stuttering grind. The damage was not slowing Atticus, but it stripped away still more of his vestigial humanity. He was an autonomous weapon, pausing from killing only to find a new target.

He stood before Erephren. The being of metal and the being of vision. Neither of them had any use for the sad limitations of the flesh. Kanshell shivered, feeling his puny condition reduced to pathetic insignificance in a universe where only the likes of Atticus and Erephren mattered. He clung to the Emperor's divinity. That was a truth beyond any other, and it mattered even more than the majestic and terrifying inhumanity before him.

The Space Marine spoke to the astropath. 'We have a great work ahead of us.'

'Then we must begin,' Erephren replied.

Outside, the sound of frenzied battle and massive footsteps drew closer. The time of last things had come.

TWENTY-TWO

Resurrection
To the tower
Witness

ATTICUS WAS SURPRISED to see any of the Legion's serfs still alive. He would not have thought any mortal could survive more than a few seconds of the new face of Pythos. He nodded at Tanaura as the forward elements of the company formed up with Erephren at their centre. 'You have done well,' he told his serf.

'The Emperor protects,' she answered.

Atticus said nothing. Her blatant flouting of the Imperial Truth did not so much anger as disappoint him. He looked at Kanshell and saw the fervour in his eyes. Superstition was giving both of them the strength to fight on. He turned away, disgusted by their weakness, and disgusted that their crutch was serving them well.

Atticus took the head of the formation. The wreckage of *Iron Flame* was still surrounded by a diminishing oasis of calm. The daemons and the saurians had not finished their dance, though the respite was almost over. The giants were a handful of strides away, slowed by their conflicts with the largest daemons. Atticus's impressions of those warp monsters were fragmentary. They had emerged from

the shaft while the Iron Hands were still fighting their way through
the ruins, and they had remained huge shadows in the distance.
There was something different about this variant of monstrosity,
something more than their great size. Their movements suggested
the mechanical along with the perversity of warp unlife. Atticus
felt the hint of a kinship that he rejected even as he recognised it.

He chose not to look more closely at those shapes. There was no
useful knowledge that awaited him there. All that mattered was the
destruction of anything that stood in the path of this final advance.

'We march!' he shouted.

The Iron Hands moved forwards. They left *Iron Flame* behind.
They headed back in the direction of the plateau, in a straight
line towards a tangle of warring monsters. Though the pace was
slower than the bloody rush to the gunship, Erephren was finding
the strength in some hidden reserve to walk. She strode like the
whisper of death over the blasted earth, her steps precise. Blind,
she was unmoved by the phantasmagoria on all sides. Sighted in
a more awful sense, her face was set against visions Atticus could
not imagine.

The two serfs ran parallel to the formation. They had no protection from the warriors of their Legion, nor did they expect it. But
Khi'dem walked with them, the last of the Salamanders 139th Company staying true to his Legion's misguided concern for preserving
that which was not strong enough to preserve itself.

As they crossed the last dozen metres of open ground, a light to
the north caught Atticus's eye. It was a bruised glow, deep shades
of violet and blue and red mixing and staining. It was the light of
putrefaction. It was growing brighter. Where it shone, the daemons
had ended their celebratory war with the saurians. They were building something. It was huge. It was being constructed of countless
fragments.

No, Atticus realised, it was not being constructed. It was being *summoned* into existence by the combined powers of thousands of fiends. He saw jagged chunks of metal flying into place, pieces of a gargantuan puzzle. They were rising from the ground for kilometres in every direction. The fragments were just one of the elements of the assemblage. There were also the bones and ragged flesh of saurian and human. And the daemons themselves. They threw themselves into the creation, becoming a hideous, squirming mortar that cemented the fragments, made them a whole, and gave the form definition.

The form was the greatest horror. Atticus's vision swam with a rage that threatened to devour his reason, leaving nothing behind but a howling engine of destruction. He knew this shape. He was witnessing a resurrection. The *Veritas Ferrum* was coming into being once more. But the proud, soaring lines of the strike cruiser were now distorted, bubbling, carrion things. Forming over its prow was a figurehead hundreds of metres long. It was a thing of horns and a gaping maw filled with needle teeth, and it moved. It lived. It had eyes that shone the white of lunacy, and it laughed. The ship was corpse, and it was scavenger, as ready to feast on itself as on any uncorrupted thing that crossed its path.

It would have a path, Atticus knew. The ship would traverse the void once more. It was the means by which the daemonic legions would leave Pythos and spread their curse through the galaxy. Sickened, he saw how utterly the Iron Hands had danced to Madail's tune. Their every act since arriving in the Pandorax System had been in the service of this moment. Even their coming had been no bit of happenstance. They had been lured, and then they had been made to cavort for the amusement of the daemonic puppet-master.

As if in answer to his despairing fury, the monster arrived. Madail travelled on a high mound of bones that moved over the landscape like a wave. The remains were bleached clean of all flesh, but shone with traces of blood and the clear slick of agony. The daemon's course stopped a dozen metres from the Iron Hands. Madail made an expansive gesture towards the reforming ship. *'Behold the art,'* the monster said.

From behind the company came the *boom* of the giant saurians taking another stride closer. Atticus kept moving. The Iron Hands did not pause. Madail's hill of bodies moved in parallel with them.

Madail's chest-eyes were wide with eager hunger. *'The machine and the spirit,'* it said. *'That is your goal, though I think you would turn from the words. Yes, yes, I think you would.'* The tongue whipped its length through the air, tasting the daemon's own speech. *'Come, then. Rejoin your ship. Be the full expression of your being. Become the undivided vessels of Chaos.'*

'No,' Atticus said. He spoke quietly, to himself more than to Madail. He was done with the dance. His reason cut through the fog of rage, and he saw the doom the daemon was tempting him to embrace. The seduction of Madail's words was a lie. The fiend did not believe the Iron Hands could be corrupted so quickly. It did not expect their surrender. It expected their fury. It expected their futile attack. If the company charged, it would face not just the might of Madail, but that of a thousands-strong daemon army and the already sentient obscenity of the *Veritas Ferrum*. Annihilation would be certain.

No, then. *No.*

And if Madail desired that attack so much, perhaps it feared the alternative to the same degree.

'Confound the enemy!' Atticus shouted. *'Onward to our victory!'* He tasted his own eagerness to exploit the daemon's mistake as he increased the speed of the march. He glanced back, saw that Erephren was keeping up. She was striding as if possessed by the energy of death itself. She had an appointment with her fate, and it was not in this place.

Atticus led the way forwards, on the original course, making for the plateau and, beyond it, for the tower whose power would be wrested from his foe.

'You will stop,' Madail announced.

Atticus ignored him. A wall of daemons waited just ahead, but it was a thinner wall. So many of the abominations were still fighting the saurians or being consumed by the resurrection of the *Veritas*.

The wall was too thin. The Iron Hands struck, sending bolter fire on ahead of their advance, then smashing into the enemy. They were a battering ram, unstoppable, and this was their true identity. This was what they were, not the submission of the purity of the machine to the corruption of the warp. With chainblade and fist, they smashed the daemons down. Even the serfs fought without fear. Their weapons were weak, but the accumulation of blows took its toll, and they moved with surprising agility, desperation keeping them out of the grasp of claws, and off the point of blades.

'Stop!' Madail shouted, and for the first time, Atticus heard something like tension in the daemon's voice.

The legionaries punched through the line and marched faster. The route ahead was clear.

'Stop them!' Madail roared. Waves of daemons broke off from the summoning of the ship. The counter-attack raced forwards on the winds of madness.

'Brothers,' Khi'dem said, 'You sacrificed much for the remnants of my Legion. You have my thanks.' He left his position from the side of the serfs and ran back down the length of the column.

'What are you doing?' Atticus demanded.

'Finding time.' Khi'dem stopped beside Ecdurus and took the legionary's rocket launcher. He angled away from the company, heading straight for Madail, whose raised staff was shining with a building, trembling glow.

Madness, Atticus thought, but the leading daemons were upon them. The crimson, blade-wielding horrors fought to the front of the line against graceful grotesqueries that married the illusion of human femininity with savage claws and talons.

DAVID ANNANDALE

'Into the fires of battle,' Khi'dem intoned as he reached the base of the moving hill. He wrestled the rocket launcher onto his shoulder with one hand. He fired. The missile streaked past the daemon. Madail laughed, ignoring the single Space Marine, unleashing the built-up energy of its staff. As the rear of the Iron Hands' column was consumed by a violet fire that melted the warriors to slag, the rocket exploded against its target.

Khi'dem had not missed. He had struck a colossus in the corner of the eye. 'Unto the anvil of war,' he whispered over the vox.

The saurian snarled, and it turned to find its attacker. In its line of sight was the giant daemon. With a heave, the reptile hurled its opponents aside and brought its immense anger down upon Madail. A foot larger than a tank smashed the hill to shards. It obliterated Khi'dem, and drove Madail down under hundreds of tonnes of mass.

The daemons howled, hurling themselves at the monster that had committed sacrilege. A tide of obscene shapes swarmed up the legs of the saurian. Its brothers came roaring to its aid. The assault on the Iron Hands faltered.

Atticus had his time. He used it. The march ate up more ground. The Iron Hands reached the plateau before more waves of daemons caught up. The company repulsed them. The daemons attacked again and again, their forces beyond counting. Their leader had not returned, was perhaps destroyed, and the daemons' tactics fell victim to their own chaos. Their anger made them reckless. They fought each other for supremacy. And they failed to stop the advance.

But their numbers made the result inevitable. They eroded the formation. Discipline preserved the Iron Hands' cohesion, but the unit became smaller with every metre of ground. Then the winged daemons arrived. Ptero and Lacertus's squads had hurt them, but they, too, had infinite forces to spare. They swooped down on the company with screams so piercing, Atticus saw wounds open on the faces of the serfs. The daemons flew as swimming through the air, and indeed they resembled creatures of the sea. One executed an elegant dive and decapitated Tanaura. Her body ran on for a few steps as though supported by a faith that persisted beyond death. It collapsed in front of Kanshell.

'The Emperor...' Kanshell gasped. 'The Emperor protects.' He fired upwards, scorching the belly of the demon with las-fire. It squealed and flew to the side, into a stream of bolter shells from Darras. Then it fell to the ground, twitching.

'The Emperor...' Kanshell kept repeating. His eyes were wide, unblinking. 'The Emperor... The Emperor...'

Atticus realised he was hearing a prayer, the only one Kanshell had either the breath or the mental capacity left to utter. The little man's religion was what kept him in the fight. The reason disgusted Atticus. Was this the shape of mortal fidelity to the Emperor? A superstitious worship that made a mockery of the truth for which the Emperor and the Legiones Astartes had sacrificed so much? If so, what point did anything have?

There was duty. There was war. There was the fact of being true to what it meant to be a legionary of the Iron Hands. If there was nothing else, that was still enough.

Over the plateau, past the shaft, through the ruins of the settlement, the advance continued. Then the company was moving down the final slope. The monument waited for Atticus. It was serene, towering so high that it was above any petty concern on the ground. It did not care. It pulsed with the glow of Chaos's great revel.

Another light, a huge flash from behind, as if a true sunrise had come to Pythos for the first time in its history, a sunrise that contained no life, but only the promise of crematoria. Atticus looked back. The light came from one of the giant saurians. It bisected the monster, then blew it apart. Streaking from the centre of the blast, riding a dark comet, came Madail.

The remnants of the Assault squads and the Raven Guard rose to meet the daemon. Madail struck with indifferent impatience. A beam from the staff caught Lacertus. His ashes drifted to the ground while the daemon picked off the rest of his command.

Ptero alone reached the prophet of the warp. He landed on Madail's neck and drove his lightning claws into the creature's right eye, but the chest-eyes never lost their focus on the targets on the ground. The daemon's only reaction was to reach up with its right hand. It mimicked Ptero's attack and drove its huge claws through his chestplate. The Raven Guard shuddered, but stabbed again at the punctured orb. Madail's hand tightened into a fist. It yanked the Space Marine's hearts free and squeezed them to pulp. Ptero fell. A split second after his body hit the ground, Madail landed, crushing and burning all within a five metre radius. Camnus existed as a mechanical silhouette for a moment, and then he, too, was gone.

The daemon spread death, but missed its target. Erephren ran, sprinted, in the last moment before the impact. *She can see you coming*, Atticus thought. *You cannot surprise her.*

And now the final reckoning. They had reached the monument. Erephren ran past Atticus. 'Time,' she murmured. Her movements were strange, savage jerks, and Atticus thought again of puppetry. Erephren's body, he saw, had become the puppet of her will.

The daemons fell upon the last fragments of the 111th Clan-Company.

Erephren touched the tower.

THE FORCE SWALLOWED her with a hunger that said *got you*. Erephren let it. She fell into the infinite depths. The vistas of absolute insanity surrounded her. But she was not a mere bit of psychic flotsam to be absorbed. Her physicality, however small, was as real as the tower's. She used her materiality as an anchor. She shaped her identity into an adamantium kernel. She weathered the attacks. From the consuming deluge of revelation, she seized on a fragment of knowledge: the hulks of dead ships around the Mandeville point of Hamartia. The mines had done good work. She made a weapon of that small triumph. She used it to forge her war song.

We have hurt you. We will hurt you. I will hurt you. She became a single purpose.

She became a voice. She was a message. She was a cry of warning.

The warp was infinity. It was also zero. There was no space between Pythos and Terra.

She gathered her will, drawing on the final sparks of her life. She used the perfect, mad clarity of the anomaly. She prepared to send her shout across the zero.

THE PULSE OF the cyclopean structure stuttered. Madail howled curses whose shape snapped the bones of the air. It lunged for Erephren. Atticus launched himself upwards from daemon to daemon. He was climbing an avalanche of warp-flesh. Darras was with him, and they both rose before the great daemon. Darras swung his blade at Madail's chest. The eyes blinked shut. The blade shattered. Madail snarled and impaled Darras with the staff. The weapon went all the way through the body of the Space Marine and struck the writhing daemons below. Madail struggled to pull it free. Atticus made a final leap, hurling himself, chainaxe raised, at the monstrous head.

The head snapped forwards and sideways. The jaws caught Atticus around the torso. They squeezed, crushing. The damage alarms flashed before his vision. He ignored them. He felt no pain.

He had so little flesh remaining.

And he had seen the daemon's defensive reflexes. What it protected was what he must strike.

He made as if to swing the axe one last time at the daemon's blank left eye. The chest-eyes looked up at him in amusement. Atticus seized his moment. He reversed the chainaxe and brought it down with terrible speed at the daemon's true vision. His surprise was total. The axe ground deeply into the eyes. Acidic jelly poured down Madail's torso.

The daemon screamed, releasing Atticus. He fell on a carpet of struggling abominations. He tried to rise. His armour did not respond. It was a coffin enclosing the inert metal of his body. Deep inside his shell, there was an awful, swimming movement where none should be.

But Madail was staggering too, for a few more precious seconds. And then the glow stopped its flicker. It became a single, steady, magnificent beam that shot up and, for a moment, pierced through the nothing, opening a window to the stars.

Only for a moment. Then the light resumed its malignant pulse, and the absence consolidated its grip around the planet. Atticus managed to turn his head. He saw Erephren release the tower and collapse. She lay on her side, her face towards his. Her eyes were the terrible, clear absence they had always been, but he felt her true gaze on him. She nodded once, and then was still.

Atticus looked back at Madail. The daemon had mastered itself. Its uninjured eyes regarded him with a perfect rage. 'You have not won,' Atticus ground out.

Madail advanced.

Feeling all that was left of him puncture and bleed out, Atticus uprooted the last of his humanity from his awareness. The machine rose to his feet for one last time. He closed with the daemon. *'The flesh is weak!'* he roared, and met the darkness.

KANSHELL SAW IT all. He saw his nightmare injured. He saw the light from the tower. And he saw the nightmare kill his captain.

The daemons ignored him. They let him live. They flowed around him, an ocean of madness, as they feasted on the bodies of the Iron Hands.

They let him see. They let him see that the stone sun did not set. They let him see the slow rise of the reborn, daemoniacal *Veritas Ferrum*. They let him see the moment of the next dark exodus approach.

He clutched the single moment of hope to his heart. *The warning was sent*, he thought. *The Emperor will know. The Emperor protects. The Emperor protects.*

His refrain faltered only when Madail loomed over him and a vile, pustule-ridden hulk with a horn where its eyes should be seized his arm.

'Little creature of faith,' Madail said, *'will you show the strength of your belief? Will you bear witness?'*

Kanshell's long screams began as he was carried towards the unholy ship.

EPILOGUE

ASTROPATH EMIL JEDDAH stiffened in shock. His mouth gaped wide, his face contorted. Mehya Vogt, his scribe, saw that look countless times every day, and she always winced in sympathetic pain. How could she not, when she knew the damage he was suffering with every message he received? This one, it seemed, had pierced his cortex like a stiletto of ice. It spread through his nervous system, hijacking his entire being for the length of its reception. His blind eyes rolled back in his head. His jaw worked, and he began to sing. Vogt grabbed her stylus and tried to start the transcription. The sound coming from Jeddah's throat was plaintive, urgent, agonised, an atonal chant filled with the smoke of distant war.

It was also largely unintelligible.

The song ended. Vogt looked down at what she had written on her tablet.

Jeddah used a cloth to wipe away the blood from his nose. 'What...' he began, then stopped. He rubbed at his temple. He tried again. 'What is the message?'

Vogt hesitated. 'It is priority extremis,' she said.

'I'm aware of its urgency.' He ran a hand over his scalp, wiping away the sweat of pain. 'I felt it.' What he meant, Vogt knew, was that he had *suffered* it. He measured urgency by the severity of the

psychic wound the message caused. 'But what is the content?' When
Vogt did not answer right away, Jeddah continued, 'I couldn't tell
for myself. There was too much distortion.'

'I… I find the message disturbing,' Vogt said at last. 'There was
only one word I could pick out, but it makes no sense, and…'

'Read it to me.'

She did. The word was wrong. It had no place in the Imperium.
When she shaped them, the syllables were not just foreign in her
mouth. They felt unclean.

Jeddah sat very still. His skin, white as marble, took on a grey tinge.
When he stood, he did so gingerly, as if reality had turned to thin
ice. 'Take me to Master Galeen,' he said. 'Bring the transcription.'

Vogt took Jeddah's arm and led him from his cell. They walked
the hallways whose dim lighting was barely strong enough to illu-
minate the way for the scribes. Mosaics covered the walls on either
side, but their designs were lost in the gloom. Though she had the
use of her eyes, Vogt felt that she, not Jeddah, was the one who
was blind in this twilight world. She transcribed messages that she
struggled to understand, and moved through endless shadow on
missions whose import she was never told. She did not understand
the nature of this one, either.

But she sensed Jeddah's worry.

THEY REACHED THE processing chamber, deep within the City of
Sight. It was a vast space, better lit, but the glow-globes were so high
above in the domed ceiling that their rays felt weak and thin by the
time they reached the ground. Dominating the centre of the chamber was the message repository. Tens of thousands of missives were
amassed here in hundreds of stacks five and ten and twenty metres
tall. Balconied galleries circled the hall, and from each extended
multiple retractable platforms. Scribes, administrators and servitors
used them to have access to the repository. Sometimes, a message

was removed from the stacks, but at any given moment, dozens more were added. Sheets of vellum dropped from the upper levels of the chamber, falling like snowflakes.

Straight ahead, at the base of the repository, Helmar Galeen, hunchbacked, face pinched narrow with permanent disapproval, sat at his massive desk, examining one message after another, passing some to servitors to add to the stacks, tossing others down a chute that led to an incinerator.

'What is it, Jeddah?' he asked without looking up.

'A message from the Pandorax System. I thought you should see it.'

Galeen sighed, put down his stylus, and held out a hand. Vogt gave him the transcription. The administrator read it, then turned his cold gaze first on Vogt, then on Jeddah. 'What am I supposed to do with this?' he asked.

'I thought–' Jeddah began.

'To annoy me with an archaic word?' Galeen interrupted.

'It might be more… relevant than that.'

'So I should announce the collapse of the rational tenets of the Imperial Truth because of this single message?'

Vogt was about to retort, but Jeddah must have felt the tension through her arm – he placed a warning hand upon her shoulder. Galeen did not tolerate scribes who did not cower before him. 'That transmission is priority extremis,' Jeddah said, his voice calm.

Galeen gave a short bark of laughter. 'Of course it is. We are at war. Every message is *priority extremis.*' He waved a weary hand at the stacks before him. 'Most of these contain actual communications, or at least complete imagery. Not one talks about myths.'

A servitor approached, and Galeen handed it the message. 'Take this to the stacks,' he said.

He turned back to Jeddah. 'The priority rating is the only reason I'm not dropping that nonsense into the flames. Now return to your duties.'

Jeddah bowed. They withdrew.

Vogt paused and looked back as they reached the exit from the chamber. She wondered why she cared, why her heart had constricted in her chest as if she had lost something or someone vital. The message was only a single word. What difference could it make?

'Can you still see it?' Jeddah whispered.

'No.'

But before they walked on, she looked back one more time. She tried to spot the servitor. She tried to follow the message as it fell into the stacks. She failed. It was just another snowflake, another snowflake falling, fallen, buried. It had come out of the night, and now was returned there, smothered in the continuous *shhh-shhh-shhh* of messages covering each other in the oblivion of white noise.

ACKNOWLEDGEMENTS

IF THE ACT of writing is a solitary one, the result is nonetheless a collaboration, and I owe a great deal of thanks to my editors at Black Library: Christian Dunn, Laurie Goulding, Nick Kyme, Graeme Lyon and Lindsey Priestley. This book also owes a great debt to *Fulgrim*, so thank you to Graham McNeill for having written that marvellous tome. And for Margaux, for her love, belief and support, I have more thanks than the words to express them.

ABOUT THE AUTHOR

David Annandale is the author of the Yarrick series, consisting of the novella *Chains of Golgotha* and the novel *Imperial Creed*, as well as the Horus Heresy novel *The Damnation of Pythos*. For the Space Marine Battles series he has written *The Death of Antagonis* and *Overfiend*. He is a prolific writer of short fiction, including the novella *Mephiston: Lord of Death* and numerous short stories set in the Horus Heresy and Warhammer 40,000 universes. David lectures at a Canadian university, on subjects ranging from English literature to horror films and video games.

More Space Marines action from David Annandale
as the White Scars, Salamanders and Raven Guard battle
the mighty ork Overfiend of Octarius.

Exclusive to

GAMES WORKSHOP

and blacklibrary.com

An extract from Overfiend
by David Annandale

The sky was shifting from black to grey. In the growing light, Caeligus realised just how blasted the land here was. The orks had been on Lepidus longer than anyone had thought. Long enough to have built this hangar. Caeligus thought, at first, that this was the point to which the greenskins had been teleporting their battle-wagons from the moon. Then he realised that in that case, there would have been no reason for them to attack Reclamation from the west. This was something else, perhaps originally intended to provide reinforcements, thereby trapping the city in a pincer assault.

'The orks are looking outward,' he said. 'We will use that distraction.' He pointed. 'We land before the doors. We will destroy what the greenskins wish to protect.'

They made the jump. They came down hard, bolters already firing. The orks nearest the hangar doors died without knowing what was striking them. The next ones spun in confusion. Half of Squad Caeligus tore into them, spreading an arc of death outward from the building. The orks' fire lost all coherence as they tried to respond to eldar and Space Marines at the same time. While Havran and his brothers waded into the enemy, Caeligus and the others provided cover for Vaanis as he set demolition charges on the doors. On the other side of the iron wall, the rumble and whine of the enormous engine intensified. The sound felt loud enough to shatter bone.

The details of the cacophony were hard to sort. Even so, Caeligus realised something had changed. The sounds of construction had ceased. They were replaced by a rhythm. It was slow at first, the heartbeat of a huge machine. Within seconds, it accelerated.

It was easily recognisable. It was also impossible. It was too big.

Vaanis turned his head to look back at Caeligus. 'Brother-sergeant...' he began. He knew. They all did.

'Move!' Caeligus roared.

The locomotive smashed though the hangar doors. The iron barrier disintegrated. Metal shards flew like sleet. Vaanis was smashed against the front. It bore the shape of immense clamped jaws, and the machine leapt forward with such speed that the impact held the Raven Guard's body against the lower fangs for a few seconds before he fell. Treads ten metres long crushed him, hundreds of tonnes of mass smashing ceramite like an eggshell, smearing his genhanced flesh across the ground.

Caeligus used an emergency burst from his jump pack to hurl himself up, back, and to the side. So did the rest of the squad. Reflexes and speed were not enough. Three others were knocked down by the juggernaut's charge. Brother Cyok rose above the height of the cab, only to come into the line of fire of the enormous gun mounted on the rear car. It fired. Cyok vanished. The shell lit up the dawn with a streak of flame. When it reached the ground, kilometres ahead, it struck with the force of a meteor.

The side of the engine clipped Caeligus. It knocked his flight out of true, and he slammed into the ground at a steep angle. He launched himself back into the air immediately, shaking off the stun in mid-flight. He landed fifty metres away, then turned to fight the new enemy.

The land train was a colossus. The locomotive alone was several times larger than the battlewagons. It pulled four cars that were almost as huge. The lower half of each appeared to be troop compartments. The top half held turrets and rocket pods. Engine and cars bristled with so many guns, they looked like clusters of spines on a living animal. Running on treads constructed of metal so thick that it seemed the cars were solid all the way through, the train should have advanced at a tectonic crawl. But its engine was so overpowered that the monster tore up the earth with the eagerness of a hunting saurian. The orks on the ground shouted their joy as their great machine was unleashed. Many of them did not move from its path in time. They were pulped in their turn. The celebration only grew more frenzied.

The train's sudden emergence placed it in the path of two of the eldar jetbikes. Their drivers tried to evade. They veered hard to the left and the right. They might as well have tried to avoid a moving mountain chain. The Saim-Hann worship of speed turned them into burnt offerings. The skimmers became fireballs as they collided with the monster.

On top of the locomotive, towards the front, was the clear blister of a canopy. In it, a single ork surveyed its works, and exulted.

'Raven Guard!' Caeligus called over the vox. 'Strike the engineer!' As he began his descent, he opened the company channel. 'The orks have a land train,' he warned. 'North-north-east of Reclamation.' He fired a long burst of shells at the canopy. 'The eldar...' he began, but trailed off when he saw the look on the ork's face. The brute was a big specimen, bent over by a giant, flashing collection of coils on its back. It looked up at the Raven Guard assault squad coming at it from all angles. Still twenty metres out, Caeligus could see the monster grinning.

Laughing.

The bolter shells left the canopy untouched. One second too

late, Caeligus realised that they weren't even hitting it. There was a strange shimmer about the train. The shells were striking a force field. Then every gun on the train fired simultaneously. A curtain of projectiles cut through the squad. The bullet streams were unending. They defeated ceramite, battered and bled the Space Marines into bloody meat. The cannon fired again. All the cannons did. The train was surrounded by a storm of blasts.

The fire faded. So did Caeligus's retinal display. Havran was the last of his brothers to die. Caeligus saw him topple from the roof of the locomotive, both arms and his left leg shot away. Caeligus clung to the lower fangs of the engine's battering ram. There were large holes in his power armour. His jump pack was leaking promethium. If he tried to use it, he would immolate himself. Though he had lost his display, he knew he was suffering from massive internal bleeding.

He would rip the laughter from that ork's throat.

Strength fading, he tightened his grip on the iron fang and hauled himself upwards. He grabbed the upper teeth, found a foothold on the lower ones. Above that, there was a smooth expanse of metal. He paused, looking for any means to climb higher.

The jaws parted.

He lost his grip and fell forward. His chest hit the mouth of a stubby cannon almost as wide as the one on the rear car. He threw himself backwards as the gun roared.

The shell did not hit him directly. So he lived long enough to know what was happening to him. The damage was so great that it was beyond pain. His body was enveloped by a cold nothing. He flew in a broken cartwheel and landed a short distance ahead of the locomotive. He tried to rise. His body did not respond. He couldn't even blink. He lay on his back, his head twisted to the side. In the burning dawn, he watched the train rush towards him. Its shadow passed over him, returning him to night. Then came the treads.

And then, at the very end, there was room for more pain.

✠ ✠ ✠

Behrasi heard Caeligus's final vox transmission. Then, as if summoned by the dawn, the rest of the ork army appeared over the north horizon. A few moments before, there had been silence. The cacophony of engines and war cries did not approach: it erupted.

'How did we not hear them before?' Brother Rhamm asked.

Squad Behrasi was on one of the few roads of Lepidus. It circled the hill of Reclamation in a wide ellipse, about five kilometres from its base to the north and south, twice that east and west. On the east side, it embraced most of the colony's cultivated land. The Raven Guard were midway between the point where the road turned south, and the branch that led to the city's east side. The terrain consisted of gentle hills. Further to the east was a web of deep gullies. The road was the easiest, most likely route for the orks to take. The surprise had been in the enemy's absence until now.

'They were waiting for the signal,' Behrasi said. The strategy was simple, it was effective, and it was another lesson in the danger of underestimating the orks. 'The army and the land train will reach Reclamation at the same time.'

Krevaan's voice came over the vox. He was speaking to the entire company, demanding news of Caeligus. Behrasi said, 'We've lost all contact. I have eyes on the ork army.'

'All forces converge on Squad Behrasi's location,' Krevaan ordered. After a moment, he added, 'I will send you word about the eldar disposition shortly.'

'Will they be joining us?'

'It would be in their best interests to do so.' The comment could be taken a number of ways. Behrasi assumed that Krevaan meant them all.

He watched the rising clouds of dust and smoke that marked the ork approach. 'The greenskins will be here before reinforcements arrive,' he said.

'Slow them down,' Krevaan said. 'We must keep the two forces apart. Together, they will raze everything. We have a chance of defeating the separated foes.'

'Well,' Behrasi said to his battle-brothers when the Shadow Captain had signed off, 'shall we demonstrate how a single squad can stop an army in its tracks?'

A few hundred metres further on, the road passed between two rises. It was as close to a choke point as they would find.

'This is where we stop them,' Behrasi said.

'Will we?' Rhamm asked.

'I didn't say permanently. But long enough.'

Half the squad began laying mines. Behrasi took the other half forward. The single ambush would not be enough. Every impediment they could throw in the orks' way would make a difference. Each moment that the orks had to struggle to advance was a moment that brought the rest of Eighth Company closer to the engagement and interfered with the timing of the orks' assault.

The Raven Guard advanced on foot, at a run. They eschewed the use of the jump packs. They needed invisibility more than speed. Behrasi and Rhamm pounded along the west side of the road while the other three took the east. They would have time, Behrasi estimated, to cover perhaps a kilometre before they met the leading elements of the orks. That would be enough.

Going north, the hills became even lower. They were gradual swells giving way to prairie. There were no trees. The grass was less than calf-height. Day had come, and the sky was overcast. If Behrasi looked away from the approaching horde, if he blocked out the sound of savagery and war, he saw a mirage of peace. Other than Reclamation and its immediate surroundings, Lepidus was untouched. The roads, like the bridge, pre-existed human colonisation. They were almost completely unused by the colonists. The millennia had eroded them, just as they had toppled the city that had once stood in Reclamation's place. Though the edges were ragged with creeping growth, and there were cleavages where the ground had shifted in important ways, for the most part the pavement ran straight and smooth. Behrasi did not recognise the materials of the road's construction, though he now had a very good guess as to their origin. Other than the roads and the city, the planet was a blank slate, a garden that tended to itself, waiting to be of use.

Lepidus was, he knew, beautiful. He did not feel it to be beautiful. He experienced it as an arena of war. The peace of the landscape would vanish, ground to muck by the machines of slaughter. And this bucolic gentleness was an irritant in its lack of cover.

An irritant, not an enemy. The land was open, and the light was bright. There were still shadows. Wherever the foe was not omniscient, the wraith-slip was possible. And the orks were far from omniscient.

Now the enemy was less than a kilometre away. The Raven Guard kept moving forward, but at a diagonal away from the road. The orks were in full flight. They were charging straight ahead, hungry for their appointment with battle. They were not interested in what was happening on the sides, in movements that were visible only in the corners of their eyes.

One by one, the warriors of Squad Behrasi went to ground. At staggered intervals, the Space Marines lay prone, shadows in the grass, bolter sights set on the road. Behrasi was the closest to the enemy. He took up his position with barely a hundred metres to go before the greenskins arrived.

The warbikes came first. Their drivers leaned forward in their seats, jaws wide as they drank in the exhilaration of speed. They snarled at each other as they raced to be the first to arrive at the celebration of violence. They were within arm's reach of each other. Behrasi opened fire.

He blew the head off the leading ork. Its bike turned into the path of others as it tumbled down the road, spreading metal and flame. The next ork in line turned too hard and lost control. The bike flipped, catapulting the driver with such force that the brute left a metres-long spread of skin and blood when it hit the pavement. As at the gorge, a chain reaction built up. Laughter at the misfortune of rivals turned into screams as the bikes piled into each other. A burning mass of jagged metal screeched along the pavement and stopped.

Behind it, drivers of other warbikes managed to slow down enough to veer off the road. There was no cliff to finish them off here. Some rode past the flames and then were back on the road, roaring back to full speed. But others hit the wrong bit of unevenness of terrain. At those speeds, that was enough to send more bikes to the ground, their drivers catapulted into the air. Some of the orks survived their falls.

The army's advance began to stumble.

No orks had survived the massacre at the gorge. The rest of the army had not known there was a lesson to learn. With grim amusement, Behrasi watched history repeat itself for the first minute of the ambush. But the terrain was wider here, the orks had room to manoeuvre, and the force was so much larger. It was too big to be stopped.

The rest of the bikes found their way around the obstacle. So did the buggies. The battlewagons came up the middle and drove straight through the wreckage, scattering it to either side. The infantry followed.

To the south, more bikes went down. And then Rhamm took out the driver of one of the buggies. It slewed violently. Instead of trying to regain control, its gunner opened fire. Bullets raked across more of its kin than the landscape. A tank disciplined the gunner by putting a shell into the buggy before the vehicle could crash. More drivers died, more vehicles collided with each other, and the tangle grew worse.

Less than a minute had elapsed.